PAPER GODS

ALSO BY GOLDIE TAYLOR

In My Father's House

The January Girl

PAPER GODS

A Novel of Money, Race,

and Politics

GOLDIE TAYLOR

ALL
POINTS
BOOKS

NEW YORK

PAPER GODS. Copyright © 2018 by Goldie Taylor. All rights reserved. Printed in the United States of America. For information, address St. Martin's Press, 175 Fifth Avenue, New York, N.Y. 10010.

www.allpointsbooks.com

LIBRARY OF CONGRESS CATALOGING-IN-PUBLICATION DATA

Names: Taylor, Goldie, author.
Title: Paper gods : a novel of money, race, and politics in Atlanta / Goldie Taylor.
Description: First edition. | New York : All Points Books, 2018.
Identifiers: LCCN 2018026727| ISBN 9781250194442 (hardcover : alk. paper) | ISBN 9781250194459 (ebook)
Subjects: | GSAFD: Mystery fiction. | Suspense fiction.
Classification: LCC PS3620.A944 P37 2018 | DDC 813/.6—dc23
LC record available at https://lccn.loc.gov/2018026727

Our books may be purchased in bulk for promotional, educational, or business use. Please contact your local bookseller or the Macmillan Corporate and Premium Sales Department at 1-800-221-7945, extension 5442, or by email at MacmillanSpecialMarkets@macmillan.com.

First Edition: October 2018

10 9 8 7 6 5 4 3 2 1

This book is dedicated to my grandchildren,

Taylor-Marie, Brandon, and Nasir

For Mary Alice

God: *one Supreme Being, the creator and ruler of the universe*

god: *one of several deities, persons, or objects, presiding over some portion of worldly affairs*

A ship rotting at anchor meets with no resistance, but when she sets sail on the sea, she has to buffet opposing billows.

—Frederick Douglass

AUTHOR'S NOTE

Paper Gods is a work of fiction. While surnames, personalities, places, and circumstances may ring familiar, this story is a creature of my imagination.

PAPER GODS

PROLOGUE

March 2013

Hampton Bridges almost slipped away that night. Were it not for the steady, decisive hands of a trauma surgeon or the boundless grace of a God he had not known, folks might've said it was a shame he died so young. A multidisciplinary team was already assembled and scrubbed for surgery by the time paramedics wheeled his mangled body through the doors of the Northeast Georgia Regional Medical Center emergency room. The Reverend Gilbert Cárdenas, one of only two Catholic priests in all of Barrow County, was summoned from his rectory at Saint Matthew Catholic Church to issue a final viaticum.

There had been an explosion, one so devastating that it shook the pastor's house some three miles away. And then came the call. According to the charge nurse, the patient was clinging to life and intubated to stabilize his breathing.

"The Lord is with thee," Cárdenas prayed over the open phone line.

Hampton had dragged himself over the brush, toward the lights coming from the top of the ivy-walled ravine, until the pain got to be too much. His clothes were soaked in blood and muck, and his head was foggy with cheap liquor, a marriage gone bad, and visions of his mama claiming his corpse from a county morgue.

Splayed out in knee-high kudzu, sucking his wind, Hampton struggled to remember the moments before the crash. The locked steering column. The way the car seemed to accelerate through the leftward curve, even as he frantically jammed both feet against the strangely loose brake pedal until it hit the floorboard. The terrified screams of the beautiful girl in the passenger seat and the blinding high beams of an oncoming vehicle. Maybe a pickup or an SUV, he couldn't say with any certainty. Suddenly the brakes grabbed and he felt his car skidding, its full fuselage veering right, then left again.

Boom!

The carriage soared, nose-up, across the highway and sailed over the guardrail.

Hampton awoke, ten yards or so from the wreckage, his left leg wedged under a felled loblolly pine. He was alive, then, though not sufficiently liquored to stave off the agonizing pain. He wept like a hound in the darkness until the sweet scent of gasoline wafted beneath his nostrils. Hampton struggled, yanking his leg until it felt as if it would come off. He gave up and furled himself into a ball mere moments before the chicane yellow 370Z burst into flames. Trembling, he felt the searing heat against his back. The roar of his own cries filled his skull. He called out for Shoshana. Again and again, until he started choking and coughing up blood.

There was no answer.

He was fading in and out of consciousness now. At some point, through the thickening haze, he thought he heard the wail of sirens and then heavy voices shouting over the embankment.

It's too late.

He surrendered himself to whatever fate had stored up and blacked out.

Earlier that night, Hampton had tooled northeasterly along Highway 78, crossing over McNutt Creek and into Athens-Clarke County. He floated through a blinking traffic light and onto the University of Georgia campus. Hampton checked his smartphone for messages, for the fifth time that hour, and let the disappointment well up in his chest.

How many lawyers does it take to change a lightbulb?

Hampton weaved through the expansive grounds until he found an empty visitor's space on the far end of the packed lot behind the Administration Building, three full country blocks from the Main Library. By the time he entered the Ilah Dunlap Little Memorial Library, it was around 10 P.M., four full hours before closing time. He strode into the massive redbrick structure, fronted by grand Greco-Romanesque columns, and surveyed the vastness before him. He dutifully checked in at the curved reception desk, staffed by a couple of bleary-eyed work-study students, and glimpsed the rows upon rows of books set upon metal shelving. Dedicated on November 19, 1953, and now holding more than seven hundred thousand volumes, the Little Library was anything but small.

Hampton was growing nervous when the phone finally chimed and a flood of emails streamed in.

It's about gawd-damn time.

He stuffed the phone into his backpack and pulled out a day pass.

"Any study rooms open?"

"Sorry, full," a sleep-deprived underclassman told him, half examining the guest permit. "Midterms. But there's still some space upstairs in Special Collections if you don't mind ghosts."

Legend had it Mrs. Little, a bridge-playing, twice-married, twice-widowed socialite whose only reported occupation was "capitalist," felt so strongly about her half-million-dollar posthumous bequest to the university that she never left its halls. The benefactor, over the years and long after her recorded death in July 1939 at a hotel situated in the present-day Czech Republic, had been reportedly spotted in the archives thumbing through the biography of Button Gwinnett, the state's British-born second governor.

Hampton chuckled and said, "I hope she doesn't mind such pedestrian company."

He jotted down the wireless password and shuffled up the stairs. A motion detector tripped as he stepped inside, and the room lit up. He slid his laptop onto a table near a round-top window, opened his email account, and clicked a message marked APPROVED FOR PUBLICATION.

A mischievously satisfied grin crept across his face. He'd more than expected a rigorous vetting. After all, the story was as complicated as it was controversial. The proverbial dams would break. Hit dogs would surely holler and a passel of fish would fry. Fact-checkers had rung his phone a half dozen times or more in the last twenty-four hours alone. Corporate minions in the legal department, concerned more about protecting profits than journalism, dispatched drafts filled with the obligatory red flags. It took three full weeks to obtain final editorial clearance.

His reporting was meticulous, Hampton knew. The four-part investigative series, detailing the exploits of an indicted drug kingpin and his ties to the mayor's office, took more than a year to compile. He dug into decades-old court documents and nearly drowned himself in newspaper archives, campaign finance disclosures, and reams of government emails to chase down a pay-for-play scheme.

Predictably, precious few sources were willing to talk on the record, which complicated matters, but thanks to court transcripts and several well-placed requests citing the Georgia Open Records Act, Hampton was able to stitch together a blockbuster corruption story that would surely draw the mayor's rebuke.

Victoria Dobbs was a masterful politician, with equal parts grace and guile, Hampton was forced to admit. She was beloved and feared, and Hampton knew the mayor's meteoric rise relied on both. She knew when to push and when to pull, giving exclusive interviews to her favorite reporters and doling out political favors like a busted piñata, and, as a result, her campaign war chest was among the largest held by a sitting mayor anywhere in the country. But the way she sashayed in and out of infrequent media avails, without answering a single question on any matter of substance, was legend among the Atlanta press corps. Her squadron of aides kept all but the most dogged among them at bay.

Hampton was tossed out of City Hall thrice in as many weeks, a badge of honor he wore with glee. Written questions about city contracting were often answered with a two-line statement pledging the mayor's devotion to transparency and public accountability. If he was lucky, some gibberish about financial stewardship got tossed in for good measure. Hampton got a rare taste of her volcanic temper when he'd ambushed her after a public speech.

The incident was six weeks gone, and now, with the stroke of a few keys, the first story—one that threatened to bring her entire administration to its knees—would make the morning edition. Subscribership was dwindling, but print copies would grace the racks at every Starbucks coffeehouse in the city. Hampton planned to have the entire series framed and hung in his office. There was even talk of national journalism awards, and Hampton was already rehearsing his acceptance speech.

He read through the final story copy once and again. The headline, as proposed by the metro desk copy editor, was as deliciously tantalizing as he'd hoped. DEN OF THIEVES: HOW DID A SUSPECTED DRUG KINGPIN GET THE KEYS TO ATLANTA'S CITY HALL?

Despite his best efforts, in the end he had not been able to tie Richard "Dickey" Lester directly to Mayor Dobbs. The paper trail between them was as thin as unsweetened tea. On the other hand, evidence of her younger brother's relationship with the Givenchy-clad gang leader was clear. Prentiss "Chip" Dobbs, who managed his sister's campaigns for statehouse and mayor, was now the chief deputy in the city's contract procurement office and controlling billions in public spending. That wouldn't hold for long, Hampton figured. At least not after his secret investments in Lester's string of strip clubs and his role in greasing the skids on the liquor licenses were revealed. There was also the issue of Chip's new car—a $90,000 Porsche bought for cash right off the showroom floor—his son's tuition at an exclusive Buckhead preschool and courtside season tickets to witness the Atlanta Hawks get skinned by one visiting team or another. Chip had also developed a fondness for Givenchy tracksuits, a fact not lost on Hampton.

Chip was living a big life thanks to Lester, who was now awaiting trial on tax evasion and wire-fraud charges, as well as his alleged participation in a multistate drug-running enterprise that flooded the streets with fentanyl-laced heroin, prescription opioids, and cocaine. Eighteen months her junior, the mayor's brother was an all-too-willing sycophant—a petty crook who, last-season couture aside, wore the family's good name like an ill-fitting

bargain-basement suit. But Chip's days of lording over billions in city contracts were numbered now. The mayor would no doubt dump her own brother
in the nearest river, if need be. It was only a matter of time, Hampton believed,
before he could make the case that the Great Torie Dobbs was as mendacious
as her crooked brother. His editor shut down the initial story pitch without so
much as a full hearing.

"The decision is above my pay grade," he remembered Tucker Stovall
saying.

"This is the work," Hampton responded. "This is why we come into this
newsroom."

"So, bring me a stronger story or quit and start a blog."

That night, in a university library, as he scanned the mayor's most recent
campaign finance disclosure report, he became even more convinced that she,
too, had a price and that somebody was more than willing to pay it. That
brewing story, if it ever saw the light of day, threatened to destroy the city's
most powerful political machine, and the mayor would be but a runt among
the pigs in the poke. He might've stayed there all night, perusing potentially
illicit campaign contributions. But it was a quarter past midnight, and he was
now late for a decidedly more pleasurable appointment.

Hampton shut down his laptop and rushed out of the building. Minutes
later, he pulled up to the curb in front of the Standard, an off-campus student
housing complex, and waited in the darkness. It wasn't long before his date
for the evening, a long-legged coed with waist-length ebony hair and crystal
blue eyes, exited the lobby doors, walked up to his car, and tapped on the
driver's-side window. Shoshana Weintraub was all of twenty-one, a senior in
the renowned Grady School of Journalism who'd interned on the *Atlanta Times-
Register* metro news desk the previous summer. It took some cajoling, but before long, Hampton and Shoshana were sneaking off for midday trysts at a
roadside motel up off of I-85. When the internship was over, Hampton decided
he hadn't had enough. He was now making frequent road trips up to Athens.

He popped the lock and Shoshana climbed into the passenger seat.

"You're late," she said with a smile that lit up the night sky.

"Sorry. A bit of work to do."

"When aren't you working?"

"You wanna be a reporter? Expect long nights and short paychecks," Hampton replied. "My story goes live tomorrow morning."

"Can you tell me what it's about now or do I have to wait?"

"You know better than that."

"Ask me no questions and I'll tell you no lies," she said, reciting his mantra. "I bet you told Claire."

"There's a lot my wife doesn't know," Hampton said. "Let's keep it that way."

Shoshana reached for the door handle. "I should go."

"It's alright if you do, but I sure wish you wouldn't," he said. "At least have one last drink with me, then you can tell me good-bye."

Hampton reached behind her seat and pulled a gym bag from the rear floorboard. He snapped open a bottle of make-do rum and a Diet Coke, tossed some ice cubes into two red Solo cups, and mixed the cocktails.

She shook her head and said, "I've got class in the morning."

"C'mon, I came all this way to see you."

"And you can come again at a decent hour."

"Oh, I promise to come again," Hampton joked. "And it won't be decent."

Shoshana unwrapped her ponytail and let her bounty of hair fall over her bare shoulders.

"Atta-girl," he said.

An hour, six rum and Cokes between them, and several turns around campus later, Hampton got onto Highway 138 heading south and kicked it into high gear. Ninety minutes later, his body was rolled into an operating room where a surgeon worked to save his life.

ONE

A small commotion kicked up when Ezra Hawkins entered the sanctuary. Church folks laughed, hugging deep and glad-handing as they greeted him with effusive good mornings. The happy sounds from happy people washed over the gentleman from Georgia like the ripples of the bent creek he played in as a boy. He took his usual seat on the end of the center-front pew and laid his Bible on his lap.

Surrounded by floor-to-ceiling windows, polished hardwoods, and various and sundry dignitaries, he knew his mama, the late Julie Esther Hawkins, would be proud to see her son on the cover of the July issue of *Ebony* magazine. Be it not for her husband's sister, Miss Julie's boy would've been slinging roasted duck sandwiches out at the Lake Club over in Greensboro. He was now, by the grace of God, an esteemed member of the U.S. House of Representatives, a living legend and civil rights icon known the world over. But here in Ebenezer Baptist Church, the place he called home, he was simply known as Brother Hawkins.

He was overcome with a sudden rush of joy when he saw her coming his way. At just over five feet eight, her slender yet curvaceous frame filled out a tan linen dress to perfection as she strutted across the altar. Perfect, too, was her shock of coral brown hair, swooped up and pinned into an elegant bun just above the nape of her neck.

"Good morning, Congressman," Victoria said with a bright, expectant smile. He leapt up and wrapped his arms around her.

"I am so happy you could come," he whispered in her ear. "I didn't think you would make it this morning."

She kissed his meaty cheek and said, "There is no place I'd rather be."

An usher made room on the already crowded bench. A pianist opened with a selection, as the mayor smoothed the back of her dress and took her seat.

Hawkins, still beaming, leaned over and said, "And where is the good doctor?"

"'Good' is being generous. He's probably walking the fifth hole over at East Lake by now," she said with a shrug.

It was the kind of indifference that came with a decade of marriage, two children, and the rigors of running the city, Hawkins figured. A trivial remark, yes, but one he did not miss.

"Indeed," he said with a slight grimace.

"We're fine. I promise," the mayor assured him. "If they outlawed golf clubs, my husband would gladly do twenty years in the federal penitentiary."

After the call to worship, two selections from the Mass Choir, and a reading of the morning announcements, the Reverend Dr. Benjamin P. Melham took to the pulpit. The air-conditioning unit was on the fritz, Melham explained, and a repairman was working on it. The pastor apologized for the heat as a team of ushers dutifully handed out cardboard fans emblazoned with the face of a decidedly black Jesus.

Hawkins had been on the search committee when the bookish-looking preacher from Osceola, Arkansas, turned up at the annual Southern Christian Leadership Conference meeting a few years back and put his name in the running. The son of a junkman and part-time preacher, Hawkins found the young minister mesmerizing at the time, and the trial sermon a few weeks later drew two dozen new members.

Melham opened his sermon this morning with a prayer and a piece of

Scripture. Dressed in a flowing black cassock with royal purple and silk piping, as usual he took his time getting to the point.

While the preacher rambled on, Hawkins stared down at his Italian leather wing tips. The gone years weighed on him like a wool suit in a high sun. There was the summer of '64 in Mississippi, and that Bloody Sunday on the Edmund Pettus Bridge the following year. Then came Memphis and the sanitation strike. He had been with Dr. King in the pulpit at Mason Temple that fateful night in '68.

But knowing that you are going to die, if not the particular moment, is like being inside the mind of God, Hawkins thought. Brother Martin, rest his soul, likely found some consolation in that, but it was the kind of comfort that eluded Hawkins now. A season of grieving would be upon them again, he knew. Whether it would be hours or days, he treasured these last moments all the more.

He had loved only two women in his life, Victoria, his protégée, and another she couldn't get him to talk about. He'd been married to his work, he'd often explain. When her father, his closest friend and confidant, passed on to Glory twenty-odd years back, Hawkins readily fulfilled his promise to stand in his stead. He'd given her away on her wedding day and sat in the front row as she was twice sworn in as mayor of Atlanta.

Time was drawing short, he thought to himself, but Pastor Melham was hitting all the right notes now. Sister Epatha Flowers, her fatty girth spilling off the pew, was filled with the Holy Ghost.

"What a friend we have in Jesus!" she exclaimed. "Make it plain, Pastor! Yessuh! Yessuh! Tell it, son!"

As the sermon came to a close and Sister Flowers had finished falling out, Hawkins bowed his head. He prayed the same simple prayer before every speech, the one his mama used to say would cover everything.

I am yours, Father God. I receive the fullness of your grace.

Despite the broken air-conditioning unit, praise filled the dense air. There was little relief to be had from the large standing fans humming from the corners of the sanctuary, and Hawkins was sweating profusely by the time Melham was halfway through his lengthy introduction.

"I bring to you my brother, our leader, and our friend, Congressman Ezra J. Hawkins," Melham said with outstretched arms.

Hawkins rose to thunderous applause, adjusted his necktie, tucked the Bible under his arm, and ambled toward the pulpit. Pastor Melham met him at the edge of the stage. They embraced like brothers, gripping hands and heartily patting one another on the back. The organist unleashed a barrage of flourishes, his fingers dancing up the keys. Hawkins took to the lectern. He steadied himself, stared at his notes, and wiped his face with a freshly pressed, crisp white handkerchief.

On an ordinary day, he would simply read from his prepared remarks. He would wax poetically about his years as a movement man, the howling dogs and the water hoses, the countless days in various jail cells across the South.

Hawkins heard a popping noise coming from overhead and flinched. He quickly realized it was the air-conditioning system clicking and wheezing. Hawkins wasn't the kind to scare easily, but he measured his life in moments now.

According to the itinerary prepared by his congressional office staff, Hawkins was scheduled to fly up to D.C. that same afternoon. Delta flights ran every hour on the hour, and if he made good time, he could get a taste of Sister Lucille Ballard's buttermilk fried okra at the repast and still make the 1:50 P.M. departure. And then, the little colored boy from tiny Veazey, Georgia, the child who'd never had a pair of shoes that didn't belong to somebody else first until he was fourteen years old, would stand in the White House East Room and receive the Presidential Medal of Freedom the following morning.

If the Good Lord kept him long enough, he would get a seat next to Rep. Thad Pickett in the first-class cabin and bend his ear about how to revive that omnibus transportation bill the region so desperately needed. Hawkins had personally drafted a new amendment and was confident it would be sufficient to get the legislation to the president's desk.

But there had been a transient ischemic attack just the day before yesterday, the second in as many weeks. His physician warned that a major stroke could soon follow. Medication was prescribed to deal with his increasingly erratic heart rhythm, and Hawkins was advised to give up his beloved pulled pork sandwiches and anything deep-fried in Crisco. The blackouts were coming closer together now, though thankfully never in a committee meeting or on the floor of the House.

Hawkins opened his remarks with a glorious salutation, calling several of the congregants by name as he proclaimed his gratitude for their presence. There was little time, he knew. His chest was tightening again, so he decided, right then and there, to forget the four-by-six index cards and get right down to the crux of the matter.

He removed his suit jacket and draped it over an arm of the majestic center chair. He began to preach then, shouting and dancing, whooping and hollering, bending his knees and then swooping upward as if to take full hold of the heavens. His baritone voice climbed three octaves, shook, and broke.

"I said, glory!" he sang out in a high tenor, clutching his chest. "Oh, glory!"

He bombarded the congregation with an onslaught of soul-shaking declarations without concern for the physical toll on his body. Hawkins was preaching in rapid bursts now, sweating out the pits of his dress shirt.

"Joy!" he bellowed. "I said joy!"

"Joy!" the congregation answered in unison.

"Comes in the morning!" he exclaimed, waving the Bible above his head.

By then, the repairman had been on the roof for the better part of an hour. An embroidered patch on his work shirt read SMITTY if anyone had cared to look when he'd entered the grounds with a toolbox. The white cargo van parked in the side lot said he was from Atlanta's Best Heating and Cooling. Deacon Deray Garvin had been kind enough to escort Smitty up the rear stairs and unlatch the metal-hinged roof hatch. Perched high above the main hall, he lay prone with his belly pressed against the sloping gabled roof, attached to a harness, and went about his work.

He had never done a single religious thing in his entire life, so killing a man in church was just another job.

Smitty carefully applied the suction cup on the glass skylight and positioned the carbide tip. When he was satisfied with the cleanliness of the incision, he slipped his customized AR-15 sniper rifle and its sock suppressor from its foam-lined encasement. He quickly snapped its two major components into place, twisted the silencer around the muzzle, and clicked the preloaded 5.56 mm magazine into its slot. He could let off five rounds in 1.6 seconds, if on the off chance it became necessary, the floating mechanism minimizing any impact on his aim.

One shot, one kill.

He gripped the small black suction cup, twisting it slightly, and carefully removed the impeccably cut, four-inch glass disk. As if winding up for a pitch, he situated the butt stock high and firm in the pocket of his shoulder, right up against his jutting collarbone, and stabilized his elbow on the flat gabling. The handguard fell lightly into his slender non-firing hand. Resting his cheek on the stock of the rifle, he wrapped his firing hand around the grip. His callused forefinger now on the trigger, he peered through the ocular lens and waited.

TWO

Three miles away, in a split-level bungalow along the northwesterly edge of Candler Park, Hampton woke up with a dull pain in his neck. He fumbled around in the nightstand for a bottle of generic aspirin, but quickly decided going for water wasn't worth the trouble. Somewhere in the darkness, his cell phone was humming, and a stream of sirens swept by outside. Hampton let out a groan.

These days, getting out of bed before noon was an accomplishment. Hampton was satisfied if he could start a day with clean underwear, which at the moment seemed unlikely. The laundry was piling up and he was content to remain bare-ass in bed anyway. At least it was Sunday, he thought with some small bit of relief, and that was enough to allay the slight pang of shame tapping at the walls of his belly. Hampton exhaled, and gently rubbed the crick in his neck, his pale bony fingers pressing against the tender knot at the top his spine.

His open laptop glowed from a corner table across the room. The thought of another half-finished and overdue feature story stung like warm whiskey tumbling down his throat. He still had a paying job at the *Atlanta Times-Register*.

Though, at the moment, even that was like a drunken sea dog that had the nerve to burp and beg for more. He used to tell himself that Atlanta was going to be a stopover on his way to the big leagues. A man like him, at least with his academic credentials, belonged in D.C. or New York. That wild-eyed dream was now wasting away in a bucket of hopes he had yet to live.

He was thirty-nine and, while he was stuck covering the Dogwood Festival in Piedmont Park, younger and lesser reporters had Pentagon press badges and tossed back their copious goblets of wine on live TV at the annual White House Correspondents' Dinner. Others posted thousand-word columns on much-ballyhooed political blogs and watched their pedantic ramblings go viral. He hated watching them spew their vagaries under the klieg lights from cable news studios, while he was marooned in Atlanta "covering Dixie like the dew."

Just as he'd settled in and learned to love, or at least tolerate, the Atlanta Braves, everything fell apart. Getting reassigned to the weekly Sunday Living & Arts section was due punishment for his many foibles, he reckoned, but the bills were springing out of the cracks like kudzu. Debt collectors representing various doctors, medical facilities, and credit card companies chasing maxed-out balances still called sunup to sundown, six days a week. He'd been sued twice that he knew of, but had never answered the summons. The rent was current and the electricity was still on, and for now that had to be enough.

Such were the spoils of war, the dregs of a costly divorce. The three-paged, double-spaced final decree had left him penniless. He'd tried in vain to convince himself that the two-bedroom house with its outdated kitchen, complete with matching gold harvest appliances and water-stained linoleum tiling, was a temporary setback. But right now, Hampton wondered if he might not be better off banking a union-backed pension like his father, who did thirty-three years on the assembly line at the Chevy plant back in Michigan.

His father shook his fist in the air and called him all kinds of no-good sons-a-bitches the day Hampton told him he wanted to be a journalist. Hampton was more than happy to get out of Flint and even happier to escape his father's whiskey-fueled tirades.

He buried his head under a pillow when his work-issued smartphone buzzed again. He muttered something indiscernible and fought off the impulse to answer it. Whoever it was and whatever they wanted could wait.

It's Sunday, damn it. We're closed.

A few months back, his managing editor, Tucker Stovall, unceremoniously dumped him from the statehouse beat, suspended him indefinitely from his weekly political column, and took him off the editorial board. Hampton thought it was the beginning of the end. The drinking had been too much, the girls too young and pretty. One more false move, Hampton calculated, and he'd be lining up for Styrofoam plates of pork and beans down at the Union Mission. Then came the car accident that nearly took his life.

"Think of this as some paid time off," Tucker said. "When you're ready, we'll get you back into the thick of things."

"You want to fire me?" Hampton shouted, gripping the cushioned armrests of his wheelchair. "Be a gawd-damn man, why don't you, and fire me!"

"It doesn't have to come to that," his editor said evenly. "You were, after all, sleeping with an intern."

Tucker calmly shut the glass door and closed the blinds.

"You don't need me to tell you how good you are," Tucker said. "Don't let your career end here. Take the assignment and do what I know you can do with it."

Lying in bed, unsure of the time, still ignoring his cell phone and cooking up yet another excuse for yet another blown deadline, Hampton could hear Tucker admonishing him in his head:

Take the assignment and do what I know you can do with it.

Hampton was sitting up now. Only his mother called on Sundays, and he wasn't in the mood for that. She'd been asking about his physical therapy sessions, and he didn't have the heart to tell her that he hadn't kept an appointment in a good long while. Inman, his golden retriever, tugged at the bedcovers.

"C'mon now. Cut me some slack."

Hampton eyed the empty wheelchair stationed at the foot of his bed.

Inman sat on his haunches and whined. Hampton gave in. He slipped on a house robe, maneuvered himself into the wheelchair, and rolled himself to the kitchen. Inman followed him. The morning feeding used to be Claire's job. The marriage had been short and the split hasty, but his ex-wife had been kind enough to leave the pooch with him.

Hampton poured a mound of dry food into one dish and filled a second with cool tap water. Inman watched intently now, his tail wagging with delight. The dog's marvelously light brown eyes, the way he loved him better than anyone else, made Hampton feel as if there was at least some good left in the world.

"There you go, you greedy mongrel," he said, laughing.

Inman buried his snout in the plastic bowl. Fifteen minutes later, Hampton was sipping coffee and thumbing through *The New York Times Book Review*, still blissfully naked under the terry cloth robe, when his phone chimed again. He grumbled and finally answered.

"Where've you been?" Tucker's voice thundered. "I've been calling you since noon."

"Long night. Look, Tuck, I know I promised to turn in that piece by Friday press time, but something came up," Hampton started to explain.

"Congressman Hawkins is dead."

"Come again?"

"He was murdered, Hamp."

THREE

Mayor Victoria Dobbs lingered in the rear seat of a blacked-out Chevy Suburban, clutching the congressman's Bible. The horrific scene—the shots and splattered blood, the agonizing screams and moans—played itself over and over again in her head.

She shifted in the seat to alleviate the searing heat radiating from her left hip. The raining glass and plaster had clipped her arms and ripped a patch of skin from her forehead, but she had survived. It was difficult to see the blessing in that now, given the carnage inside the church, and nearly impossible to hold back the tide of anger flooding her bones. This was her city and her church, and they were hers to protect. That someone had come to this place, with such malice and destruction, required a reckoning that she had only begun to measure.

Every street and alleyway had been shut off two blocks to the north and south of Auburn Avenue, from Peachtree Street to the west and Boulevard Avenue to the east. Residents of Wheat Street Towers, a nearby senior citizens' high-rise, and customers at the Silver Star Barbershop next door were told to shelter in place until every inch of every surrounding building was cleared. Riot gear–clad strike forces lined the intersections, tightening the perimeter.

Victoria surveyed the chaos unfolding outside the back passenger window now, the blaring sirens muddling her thoughts. Not more than twenty yards away, under the stately clock tower, first responders were treating victims with non-life-threatening injuries. Tourists visiting the King Center were evacuated and loaded into waiting buses. She watched solemnly as a large family, dressed in matching T-shirts, was led away. The building was then chained shut.

Over her police chief's objections, the mayor refused to leave the scene, refused a change of clothes or even to be examined by a paramedic. Victoria needed to see this through to the end, she told Chief Otis Walraven, no matter how long that took and whatever that might come to mean.

The driver's-side front door clicked open. Lieutenant S. A. Pelosi, her body man and driver, slid behind the steering wheel and peered at her in the rearview mirror.

Locking eyes with her, he cranked the engine and turned on the air-conditioning.

"Sal, is he still inside?"

"Yes, ma'am, he is."

"I need to see him," she said, almost inaudibly. She steadied her voice, brushed away a rush of tears, and said, "Please, take me to see him."

Pelosi studied her face and cut the ignition. "Are you sure you want to do this?" he said.

"Yes, I am sure."

A wave of tremors swept over and through her as she stepped out of the vehicle. She lost her footing on the side step railing and stumbled. Pelosi caught her by the elbow. The open gash that snaked up her forearm was bleeding more profusely now.

"Let me help you," he said, examining her blood on his hand. "Let me call a medic over here."

"I'm fine, Sal," she responded, planting her feet firmly on the sidewalk. "It's just a little blood."

Her legs tensed, and for a moment, she froze in place. Standing in front of the old Ebenezer, where Dr. Martin Luther King was baptized and preached, mere steps from the fountain where he was laid to rest in an aboveground tomb, the gone years washed over her. Dr. King's mother, Alberta Williams King, was gunned down six years after her son had been assassinated, while sitting behind the organ in June of '74. And fifteen years ago, the mayor's own father had been eulogized on the altar of the tiny redbrick church.

There was no safe harbor here, and there never had been. The history she knew all too well rolled through her head. She felt Pelosi's light touch, his comforting strong hand securing the small of her back, as she scanned the crevices between the bricks and calculated the gravity of the loss. She felt faint, but dared not yield to that weakness now.

The mayor looked at the chain of APD patrol cars clogging the avenue and noted the scrum of somber-faced reporters sequestered between barricades in front of the King Center. To her right, oversized live-shot trucks were jammed, bumper to bumper. She had personally ordered the media pen put in place, a lesson well learned after a day trader executed his family and shot up a Buckhead office complex back in '99. She was still in law school back then, toiling in the bowels of City Hall as a summer intern, awaiting her ascent, when the mayor tapped her to support the crisis teams. In the wake of the shooting spree, Victoria was sent to work in the communications unit out of an empty office suite in Piedmont Center, the epicenter of the massacre. It was the first of many trials by fire.

A small contingent of uniformed APD officers flanked her sides and back as she crossed the street and navigated the short concrete walkway leading up to the main doors of Historic Ebenezer, the newer, larger church built in the late 1990s. A horde of reporters and photographers packing zoom lenses, still stationed behind A-frame police barricades, captured her every step. News choppers hovered above.

Even in her grief, Victoria held on to her bearings. She clasped her hands behind her as she strode past the clock tower and stepped inside the vestibule. An agent from the Georgia Bureau of Investigation met her at the framed glass double doors.

"Mayor Dobbs, I'm Agent Jason Clearwater, GBI," he announced, extending his hand.

She gave him a firm, brief handshake and nodded.

"We don't have much to go on," he advised her. "We've got techs combing the rooftop, but it's clean as far as we can tell. The van was reported stolen three days ago from an E-Z Rental lot up in Dahlonega and—"

"It's my understanding that Congressman Hawkins is still in the sanctuary," she said, cutting him off.

"Yes, ma'am. There are four bodies. If I can ask you to have a seat here, my agent-in-charge is on the third floor, in the pastor's study," he said, waving his open hand over a foldout chair. "I will let him know that you're here."

"I need to see them," the mayor said abruptly and still standing. "I need to see the bodies."

"Ma'am, I'm afraid we cannot allow that. I'm sorry, but I have to remind you that the GBI has jurisdiction now. This is our crime scene at least until the feds arrive. Homeland Security—"

"I don't really care who has jurisdiction," she said, clenching her teeth. "Not today, not tomorrow, not the day after that."

Pelosi placed his hand on her shoulder. She immediately cooled. There was a better way, Victoria admitted to herself.

"Give us a moment," she said, waving Pelosi away. "What was your name again? Clearwater, right?"

"Yes, ma'am. Agent Jason Clearwater," he responded formally. "I work out of the field office in Conyers."

Victoria studied his buzz-shaven ginger-red hair and emerald-green eyes. She silently noted the absence of a telling accent. Wherever the bookish-looking agent was from, it certainly wasn't Georgia or anywhere in the South, for that matter, and given his stone-faced demeanor, he likely had not been around long enough to appreciate how the political winds blew inside of I-285.

"Agent Clearwater, I mean no disrespect, but the congressman was like a father to me," the mayor said, looking up again, her caramel-brown eyes baking with sincerity. "I was sitting next to him this morning."

"Ma'am, I am truly sorry for your loss," Clearwater said, eyeing her bloodied dress and the open cut on her arm. "My section commander would have my head. I'd be fired before sundown."

She stepped in closer, leaning in toward his ear. "I employ two thousand sworn officers and investigators," she said, glancing back at Pelosi. "I can guarantee you that you'll always have a paycheck. If this costs you your job, you'll always have one with me."

Clearwater radioed his section chief, and the sanctuary was ordered cleared. A crime scene technician dutifully covered her Prada sling-back flats with mesh booties and helped her snap on a pair of latex gloves. The mayor was then escorted inside.

Stepping over debris, flakes of broken glass and bits of broken plaster, Victoria fixed her eyes on the wooden cross that was suspended above the regal altar.

"We don't think he expected a firefight," Agent Clearwater said over her shoulder. "Although it really wasn't much of one."

"He? One shooter did all of this?"

"Yes, ma'am, we believe so. A deacon described a man, olive complexion, average height with a slender build. He was disguised as a repairman. The first shot came from that center-front skylight," Clearwater said, pointing toward the ceiling.

"The shooter was packing enough firepower to pin down an entire Army squadron. I can't say for sure, and you didn't hear it from me, but every indication says this was a professional hit. This was an assassination, ma'am. We found a safety harness dangling from the rear of the building. Otherwise, he made a clean getaway."

The mayor nodded her head and said, "Indeed."

A hired security guard and an off-duty Fulton County deputy returned fire, Clearwater went on explaining. Both men were a part of the pastor's security detail. The deputy was cut down almost immediately, according to preliminary witness statements. His 9 mm SIG Sauer pistol was now tagged and bagged. Metal shell casings littered the powder-blue carpeting. The shooter used military-grade armor-piercing rounds with a hardened steel core, Clearwater said. By the time the first SWAT unit arrived, the damage was done and the suspect was long gone.

"How is that possible? He disappeared in broad daylight?"

"Yes, ma'am. Three more parishioners and two church staffers, including Deacon Garvin, were triaged and sent by ambulance to Grady Memorial and Atlanta Medical Center," Clearwater went on. "We believe Mr. Garvin may have led the shooter to the roof and unwittingly unlocked the door. We've got agents stationed outside his hospital room in case he pulls through."

"Deacon Garvin never met a stranger in his life. In his mind, everybody he meets is a child of God."

"There was nothing godly about what happened here, ma'am. Mr. Garvin may be the only person who can make a positive identification."

"Are you a praying man, Agent Clearwater?"

"Yes, ma'am."

"Then pray that Deacon Garvin sees another tomorrow," Victoria said, looking down at the heap of plastic on the floor.

"His name is Claude Robinson," the agent said.

Victoria stepped to the dark plastic covering, stooped down, and pulled back the sheath. She took in his lifeless face, pushing down the overwhelming sadness bubbling up in her chest.

Without looking up, the mayor said, "Mr. Robinson was a dear friend of my parents. I've known him my entire life."

Her eyes sketched his freshly trimmed, salt-and-pepper mustache, his clean-shaven, hard-squared jaw, and the deep cleft in his chin.

"He was a phone bank volunteer on my campaign," she said, growing tearful. "Retired Marine. Pulled three tours in Vietnam. He never had a lot of money, but he put everything he had into every one of my campaigns. If I could thank him a thousand times a day for a thousand years, it would never be enough."

"Yes, ma'am."

"Promise me something?" she said. "Promise me that you won't stop until you find the man who did this."

"We won't stop."

The air inside the main hall was thick and smelled of warm blood and metal. The standing fans had been shut off to preserve the crime scene, and Victoria began sweating as she moved closer to the pulpit. The deputy was laid out on the right side of the altar. A darkened pool of blood collected around the top end of the plastic sheath.

"I'm afraid there isn't a lot left to see. Deputy Finlaysen took a direct hit."

Clem Finlaysen? God, no.

Her legs locked up again, but she kept moving, one footfall at a time, until she was standing under the wooden cross dangling from the ceiling. She now had a clear view of the black sheeting in the center of the pulpit.

Hawkins had been her political godfather. Through the years, they joked that the only way he would give up his congressional seat was faceup in a pine box. He had earned his place in the sun, she assured him while staving off her own ambitions. Certainly other members had served in the House longer, and with less distinction in her mind, although Hawkins was getting up in age, and health issues had begun to mount. She'd rushed out to Saint Joseph's Hospital twice in the last month alone to see about him, only to find him giggling with the nurses while he dined on Jell-O Pudding Pops.

Victoria was in no hurry to join the partisan catfight going on inside the Beltway, and she was already spending too many Sundays on national news talk shows. Her press secretary regularly fielded calls from producers with *Meet the Press, Fox News Sunday,* and *State of the Union.* She was a national figure, to be sure, with a direct line to the White House and the Democratic National Committee. But getting the Atlanta City Council to vote for their own pay raise or renaming streets in honor of political patrons was about all they could muster. She and Hawkins used to muse about the legislative "nod squads" that her predecessors enjoyed during their terms. But the sitting council president was eyeing the mayor's office and couldn't be counted on to vote her way.

Hawkins was supposed to die peacefully in his sleep, she'd decided long ago, maybe from years of eating open-faced, fried-catfish sandwiches, mini tubs of mustard potato salad, and fistfuls of collard greens over at Paschal's, where he had a regular table. Victoria managed a slight grin at the thought of how he always ate belly-to-the-table, his elbows planted on the Formica countertop, while listening to Aretha Franklin wail on the jukebox.

Clearwater pulled back the covering, just enough so that she could see his face.

The mayor paused for a moment and said, "Please, I need to see all of him."

"Ma'am..."

"Please," she whispered.

His blood-soaked dress shirt had been cut open by a church medic in a pointless attempt to revive him. She was transfixed by the gaping hole in the left-center of his chest.

"Can I touch him?"

Clearwater gave her the go-ahead. Victoria leaned in, stroking his meaty scalp. His chocolate smooth-as-cake-batter skin now looked ashen. Another wave of tears fell. She felt her body quaking. She took hold of the Bible lying at his side.

"Ma'am, please don't touch that. It's evidence."

"It's mine," she lied.

"Even so."

"Please, it's our family Bible," she said, spilling another lie.

The coming days would bring lengthy elegies and memorials in his honor, she knew. Victoria would stand in this very pulpit to deliver her own public eulogy to thousands of mourners. Human rights leaders and heads of state from around the world would sit shoulder to shoulder alongside no-name grassroots activists and local elected officials in freshly polished pews. She wondered if she'd be able to do justice to his life, everything that he'd meant to her. The Bible was all she had left of him now.

"You said there were four."

Clearwater looked down and away, unable to stifle his own tears.

"You said there were four," she said again, gently pressing for an answer.

The agent pointed to the left aisle, just beyond where she had been sitting during the morning worship service. Victoria panicked when she saw the small brown leather shoe lying beside a plastic tarp.

She remembered the whipping sound then, and how Hawkins's eyes had widened and locked as he fell. She'd scrambled beneath the pew, instinctively clasping her hands around her head. The horrifying screams filled her ears. Victoria balled herself up and whimpered as glass rained down over the sanctuary.

And then it was over. The sanctuary was suddenly and eerily still. The moans seemed to come from all around her. She'd spotted a small, coffee-brown face under a pew across the aisle and called out to him.

"Are you okay, sweetheart?"

He shook his head slowly, from left to right and back again. The boy was maybe seven or eight, no older than her daughters, and lying on his side. There was an unmistakable look of terror in his wide, nickel-sized dark eyes. Victoria saw the smooth tide of blood oozing beneath his shoulder.

She crawled toward him, on her hands and knees, carefully taking him into her arms, cradling his body as they lay together on the floor. She pressed her hands tightly against his clavicle, his shoulder blade pinched to her breast, in hopes of stanching the flow of blood.

"What's your name?" Victoria asked, struggling to calm the child.

He parted his lips, but did not answer.

"Come on, stay with me," she whispered gently. "You're going to be okay. Stay with me."

"Keenan," he said softly. "My name is Keenan Bouleware."

"Okay, Keenan. Stay awake."

He nodded his head yes. Victoria rocked him in her arms and started to sing the first song that came to mind.

> *This little light of mine, I'm gonna let it shine.*
> *This little light of mine, I'm gonna let it shine....*

She could hear the sirens that shrieked over the distance. "Help is coming," she said. "They'll be here soon. Stay with me, son."

Then finally, the sound of boots rumbling. She was relieved to hear the heavy voices and see the beams of white light as the SWAT unit flooded into the building and entered the sanctuary.

Thank you, Jesus.

A female officer, wearing a helmet and face shield, peered beneath the bench. "Mayor Dobbs?"

"I think he's been shot," Victoria said. "I don't know…"

The last thing she remembered was someone sweeping the boy from her arms, maybe a medic, maybe an officer. Keenan's eyes were closed, his mouth slightly open.

Staring at the shoe, Victoria realized what had become of him. She wept aloud now. Her wails echoed through the grand hall.

FOUR

Just after 3 P.M., the sky opened up and an unexpected rain began to fall. Despite the warm showers, the hastily called press briefing drew two dozen reporters to the church lawn. Her dampened mess of hair, now curling into ringlets, fell over her shoulders. She took a deep breath, another, and then another.

Pull yourself together, baby.

She clutched the Bible with both hands. Victoria squeezed the Bible, bound in cowhide, and noted its tattered gold-trimmed pages. A man in a dark suit and a black felt fedora took off his jacket and placed it about her shoulders. Maybe a church member, Victoria could not say for sure, as she'd never seen him before. She gave the stranger a pleasant nod and a pained grin.

"We're here for you, my sister, whatever storms may blow," he said kindly. "This is family."

"Thank you," the mayor said. "And, yes, this is family."

There were no prepared remarks and no platoon of aides standing beside her. Pelosi and Clearwater positioned themselves a few paces away and watched intently as the mayor cleared her throat and stepped closer to the microphone.

Camera operators jockeyed for position and reporters scribbled furiously as she spoke. At one point Victoria paused midsentence and gathered herself.

"Forgive me," she whispered, stroking wisps of hair from her face.

Never had she felt so naked, so vulnerable. Her Sunday-go-to-meeting dress was splattered with hours-old blood. A small reddish-brown streak snaked along her jawline. Her elbow was still stinging and oozing through a bandage as she counted the casualties.

Four dead, five critically wounded.

"There can be no peace without love," she said. "We will come together, even in our falling apart."

She felt her chest tighten again, and again she drew a long sigh.

"I am certain that you have questions," she said, more resolutely now. "As you might imagine, the investigation will be aggressive and thorough, but we cannot provide any further information at this time. My office will release the names of the victims once we have formally contacted their families."

Tipping her head specifically in one reporter's direction, she said, "I trust that all of you understand."

Victoria noted his arched brow as she started to step away from the scrum, and caught the smirk he seemingly could not contain. Whatever Hampton Bridges thought of her, she thought even less of him. He had to know that he was at the bottom of her list, even on this day, and had been since he penned a four-part exposé on her brother's rather extensive, albeit alleged, financial ties to a local drug dealer who was up on federal kingpin charges.

The front-page story broke on the morning of the mayor's inaugural gala last January and quickly picked up steam. Her communications staff spent weeks dealing with the fallout. There had been no indictment, let alone a conviction. Nevertheless, she had been forced to fire her own brother from his cushy job as a special assistant running the city's contract procurement office. Doling out millions in sole source contracts to political patrons, Chip Dobbs was a prince in a pawn's perch. To Victoria's dismay, her brother spent his every waking moment trying to cash in on his name.

She ordered him fired. His office was boxed up and bolted shut.

A man chasing a penny will never see a dollar.

Bridges was a smaller man now, down at least thirty pounds since the accident, she guessed. His once neatly cropped, silver-gray hair was now long and stringy, tied back in a loose ponytail, and he emitted a sickly stench that even she couldn't ignore. Valerie Norbreck-Haynes, the *New York Times* Southeast bureau chief, seemed genuinely embarrassed to be standing next to him.

"Will you run for Congress?" he yelled over the crowd.

The scrum went silent. Victoria addressed him, straight on.

"I am the mayor of Atlanta today, seven months into my second term, and I will be that tomorrow, Mr. Bridges," she said soberly.

Victoria turned her attention back to the crowd.

"I should tell you that when my father, Dr. Park Dobbs, passed away, it was Ezra Hawkins who stood in the altar and held my hand in that little redbrick church behind you," she added. "He convinced me to keep on loving this city, to love this state, even when it did not always love us back. He fought the good fight until the very end of his days. He loved this church like no other. We are all the more blessed because he came."

"Mayor Dobbs, will you run for his seat?" Bridges asked again.

Before he could utter another syllable, Victoria lowered her head and raised her palm. She closed her eyes for a moment, then looked up at Bridges.

"You forget yourself, Mr. Bridges," she said. "Our focus and yours should be on the lives lost in that sanctuary. Our thoughts must remain with those who are still fighting for their lives. Whatever the political questions of the day, they can and will wait. We are all here, including you, by God's mercy.

"Representative Hawkins is at rest, but if he were here now, he would tell you that the Fifteenth District never belonged to him but to the people of Georgia," she said. "Atlanta has lost another of her sons. An angel in our midst, Congressman Hawkins belongs to the ages now, but my thoughts and prayers are with all of the families. Need I remind you that four people were murdered here today in the halls of Dr. King's church? As mayor of this great city, I can tell you that no effort or expense will be spared to track down the perpetrator of these vile acts. What happened here will not go unanswered."

The mayor then paused and said, "There will be justice."

FIVE

orty-five minutes later, Hampton wheeled himself into the dimly lit newsroom and through the bank of empty cubicles until he got to the last row. He parked himself at his desk and was busy transcribing his notes when Tucker Stovall poked his head over the partition.

"Kathy Franco is on her way in. She'll take the shooting and you take the politics. I expect you to handle this delicately."

"Too late for that."

"Meaning what?"

"Meaning I already asked the mayor if she planned to run in the special election," Hampton said. "She still loves me, you know?"

"Who're you kidding? Dobbs would sooner see you run through a wood chipper, ass first. Tell me you didn't ask the mayor about her political ambitions."

"Of course, I did." Hampton shrugged. "You should've seen her making eyes at me, Tuck. It was just like old times."

"Last I recall, and correct me if I misstate the facts, she was threatening to burn this whole damn paper to the ground with an eight-fucking-figure lawsuit. It took us six weeks to get a beat reporter back inside City Hall. Dammit, I knew I shouldn't have sent you out there."

Hampton couldn't hold back a laugh. Tucker wasn't amused.

"Sorry, chief. But Her Majesty was at least generous enough to write tomorrow's headline for us."

"Which is?"

"'There will be justice,'" Hampton said, singing the words and waving his hands dramatically as if conducting a symphony orchestra.

"Well, that is beautiful," Tucker deadpanned. "Now, get me a story to go with it."

"She's running for Congress. Her name will be on that ballot. Mark my words."

"Tell me she didn't say that. The body isn't cold."

"Not exactly, but she swung the door wide open. I'd bet my last five dollars on it."

"You don't have five dollars," Tucker quipped. "Hell, you don't even have cable TV."

Hampton was forced to concede the point.

"Well, if I did," he said with a half grin, wheeling himself around. "Your mayor spat out some crap about how close she and the congressman were, and that's true enough. They were thick as thieves, emphasis on 'thieves.'"

"Now she's my mayor?"

"She isn't mine," Hampton said. "Let's get this straight. Your mayor, I mean, our mayor will not miss an open jump shot."

"You never let your crazy get in the way, do you?"

"It would be insane to think she isn't running. Hell, she was out of the gate with a press conference before any other elected official could get to the scene. She didn't even let the police chief speak."

"Just write me an obituary, Hamp. Do it right and it'll be front-page, above-the-fold. We'll run it with a big photo spread. Site traffic is already bumping off the news, so we have to go with angles the national press will miss."

"Yeah, okay."

"And get me a sidebar on Mayor Dobbs. Not a single syllable about any political intentions she may or may not have. Save it until after they get the body in the ground. If it checks out, I'll run it."

"You know we call you Fucker, right? Get it? Fucker Stovall. Rhymes with Tucker."

The editor frowned.

"Come on, now, you know it's funny."

"Kiss my black ass, Hampton."

"You haven't been black since 1975," Hampton said under his breath, muffling his voice with his hand.

"What did you just say?"

Hampton threw up a weak salute. "I said, sir, yes, sir."

"Whatever. Take a shower," Tucker said, walking away. "You smell like a bag of dead frogs."

Tucker was right. The mayor despised the very air that he breathed. He'd stalked the mayor for a comment and caught her coming out of an Atlanta Press Club luncheon. Dobbs responded by threatening to upend his career.

"Never attempt to fuck up someone else's life with a lie, when yours can be destroyed with the truth," she'd said.

Just as the mayor had predicted, Hampton's life began to unravel one thread at a time. The fight was still smoldering nearly two months later, when Hampton got into a near-fatal accident coming out of Athens, Georgia. He was rushed to a hospital. He woke up the next morning, handcuffed to the bed railing. A county sheriff's deputy read him his Miranda rights.

In court, Hampton claimed the steering column jammed and the brakes went out without warning. The accelerator stuck to the floorboard, he tried to explain. The judge was more concerned about his blood alcohol level, which tipped over twice the legal limit. Barrow County prosecutors concluded he was drunk and no further investigation was warranted. Hampton was convinced that someone had tried to kill him. He had written dozens of stinging stories over the years, and had plenty of sworn enemies to boot, though none greater than the mayor herself.

An anonymous blogger with DrivingGeorgiaRight.com had pointed the finger at the mayor's office and the suspected team of henchmen that she supposedly kept on the APD payroll. The comment section quickly filled with fanciful conspiracy theories. Although no one could definitively name any of the suspected squad members, Salvatore "Sal" Pelosi was said to be the lead man. He was officially a lieutenant, but it was no secret that Pelosi, the mayor's body man and driver, ran the department. A former Defense Intelligence officer, Pelosi had also worked for Congressman Hawkins.

Days after the accident, a string of career-killing stories was leaked while Hampton was still wired up from head to toe, and foggy from the constant flow of industrial-strength pain medication. Rumors of a potentially deadly political payback were quickly dismissed and overshadowed by revelations of Hampton's predilection for pretty young coeds and bargain-basement booze.

His female companion had, thankfully, walked away with only minor injuries. Before Shoshana, there had been Lena, another intern at the paper, who had especially talented fingers. And before that, there was Natalie, who at thirty-two was the oldest of the bevy, and a string of other nameless beauties.

A man is only as faithful as his options.

Hampton emailed his first draft to a waiting copy editor just before sundown. The obituary was a damn fine job and read like a novel, he had to admit to himself. All twenty-two hundred words of resplendent glory were written mostly from memory. He had followed the congressman's comings and goings for years on end. Surely, nobody in the newsroom knew Hawkins better than he did. The sidebar was clean, as Tucker had ordered, and contained nothing Hampton thought would set the mayor off or get him fired.

Hampton reared back in his chair and let the front wheels ride up. He admired the songlike tribute he'd composed and how he had carefully woven in a few perfunctory lines that alluded to the congressman's previously covered misdeeds. He couldn't resist the urge to mention the time Hawkins nearly got himself clipped on a misdemeanor solicitation charge at a run-down motel on Spring Street back in '85. Although the incident happened some thirty-odd years back, Hampton was sure he'd be stirring that pot again before long.

SIX

Just before midnight, near on thirty-six hours after the massacre, the mayor's three-car motorcade turned off Peachtree Street and onto Andrews Drive. The SUV inched its way up the cobblestone driveway, guided by a string of glowing ground lights. A pair of black sedans with silent blue strobe lights crawled to a stop along the sloped curb and waited on the street.

Victoria longed for a night's sleep in her own bed, the small pleasure of sipping chamomile tea laced with honey in the morning. She examined the Bible again. It didn't belong in an evidence locker, she'd decided. There was a strange placeholder marking in Proverbs. A single verse was highlighted. It was the sort of thing Victoria might have written off to chance. But Hawkins had led an orderly life and did almost nothing without clear purpose.

Her husband was outside, barefoot and dressed in faded blue medical scrubs. Marsh traded a few hushed words with Sal, and then opened the rear door.

He took his wife by the hand, leading her through a side door, across the mudroom, and into the kitchen. It was a stunning room, not unlike the others, appointed with premium KitchenAid appliances that Victoria was never home long enough to put to good use. A rack of rarely used copper pots hung over the center island. She dropped her purse and the Bible on the custom-cut Calacatta marble countertop and melted into her husband's arms.

There was something reassuring about his rough stubble brushing against her cheek, the firmness of his broad chest, the way his strong fingertips gripped her waist. She'd missed his touch. The love that had brought them together was alive again, at least in that moment. Their nine-year-old girls had been asleep for hours, he assured her.

"Do they know?"

"They saw a breaking news report," Marsh said. "They've been asking about you."

Looking away, Victoria said, "I should've called, I know. I didn't want them to hear me cry."

"I know, baby girl. I know...."

She felt herself quaking in his arms. He squeezed her tighter.

"His name was Keenan. I went to see his mother over in Cabbagetown this morning. He was supposed to be in children's church, but she said that he loved watching her sing. She was in the choir stand when the shooting started. He was her only child."

Victoria's face was dry, though her eyes were still puffy and red as if there were no more tears left to cry.

Together, they climbed the grand stairwell, went to their daughters' room, and kissed them as they slept. That night, with City of Hills in an uneasy slumber, Victoria slipped off her shoes, slid between her husband's legs, and rested her face against his chest as they lay on a tufted leather chaise in the upper den. In the dim gauzy light, they lay together, saying nothing until Marsh drifted off.

Victoria let her eyes trace over the family photos that lined the credenza. Her daughters, Maya and Mahalia, with their bright expectant smiles, a framed news clipping of her father walking a picket line somewhere in '60s-era, segregated Alabama, and a photo of her—his eldest child—pausing to shake the dean's hand as she received her law degree from Harvard. A silver-framed, black-and-white wedding photograph of her and Marsh taken under a gazebo in Piedmont Park stood on the edge of her desk. Her dress was a flowing, jewel-busted Vera Wang purchased by Hawkins as a wedding gift. The gown was magical, just as her marriage had once been.

The winds picked up outside. The gridded, lead glass windows shook in their hardwood frames. Victoria rose quietly and tiptoed downstairs. She retrieved the Bible and her handbag, a limited-edition Hermès Birkin bag that Marsh had given to her last Christmas, from the kitchen counter and returned to the den. There was nothing in this life that she could not have, including three Birkins, a cache of Louis Vuitton handbags, and custom-built cedar closets, and she had learned to stop apologizing for that.

Marsh was Dr. Marshall Langston Overstreet, a celebrated heart surgeon, sitting president of the National Medical Association, and grand sire archon of the prestigious Sigma Pi Phi fraternity, commonly known as the Boulé. She was a Dobbs—Victoria Angélique Dobbs Overstreet—known as "Torie" to her closest friends and family. Even without the Ivy League pedigree, without her tenure in the statehouse or second term as mayor, without the various seats on charity boards, frequent appearances on NBC's *Meet the Press*, and unimpeded access to the White House, in Atlanta that was more than enough.

The bookmark was curious, if not oddly unnerving. It was a skillfully folded bird of some kind, with a long, sharp, and open beak that made it appear as if it were swooping down on its prey. She read the verse that had been outlined in yellow highlighter. It was Proverbs 21:15. The scripture read like a message from the grave.

When justice is done, it is a joy to the righteous, but terror to evildoers.

She was anxious about the whipping gales outside, and about this menacingly beautiful birdlike creature as she fingered its smooth edges. Hawkins, with advanced arthritis, could not have mastered such a thing. She knew he had received mailbags loaded with cards and letters from his constituents almost daily, usually from people who wanted help unsticking a Social Security claim or information about his stance on some obscure piece of legislation. Death threats, she knew, were not uncommon. Most of the intimidating messages came from anonymous email and Twitter accounts these days, although a few angry and invariably misspelled missives trickled in via snail mail.

A woman from upstate Washington called the congressman a dozen or more times a day to lodge her complaints against the "treasonous Marxist" until she received a visit from the FBI field office in Seattle. Gloria Cozza was cooling her heels in a maximum-security mental unit now. Before her detention, Cozza had become well known to various national news anchors. She proudly admitted to taking a one-way, cross-country Megabus to wait outside Anderson Cooper's Lower Manhattan loft. The doorman said Cozza circled the block twenty or more times before he lost count and called the police. Then there was the envelope laced with talcum powder sent from a black farmer in Mississippi.

But there was something about this bird, the painstaking detail with which it had been constructed. Victoria noted the craftsmanship, the precision of its folds. Its layered wingspan, tightly woven tail, and strong and curved beak reminded her of a vulture.

When justice is done, it is a joy to the righteous, but terror to evildoers.

Hawkins was among the righteous, she lamented. He'd used his bully pulpit in an attempt to block the new gun-carry rights that sailed through the Georgia state legislature. The irony that he had been shot down in a church was not lost on her. The governor had recently signed an open-carry law that included college campuses, houses of worship, and nightclubs.

She laid her head down on the desk and fell asleep. Her cell phone buzzed just before 5 A.M.

"Mayor Dobbs, I need to make you aware of a situation," Chief Walraven said through the speakerphone.

A SWAT team had a house surrounded on Washington Street, two blocks south of Turner Field. The suspect, a thirtysomething man, was hunkered down inside with a woman and two children, he explained.

"Ex-Army, three tours in Iraq, one in Afghanistan," Walraven said. "Thirty days in the mental unit at Walter Reed. Administrative discharge. He was a scout sniper."

"Was Deacon Garvin able to identify him?"

"I'm sorry to give you the news. Mr. Garvin passed away a few hours ago in surgery."

Victoria abruptly stood up and paced the room. "You've got eyes on him?"

"Yes. We're doing our best to take him into custody. Our negotiator made contact ten minutes ago. Said he wants to talk to the president."

"I bet he does," Victoria said blithely. "Put him down."

"Excuse me?"

"You heard me," she said, her voice growing cold and bold. "I said shoot him."

The mayor ended the call, tossed the phone onto her desk.

"Did you just say 'shoot him'?" Marsh said, rising from the chaise.

She bowed her head, drew a cross over her heart, then turned on the flat-screen TV.

"What if it isn't him? You ordered an execution."

"And what if I had taken a bullet? What if it were one of our girls instead of a little boy you've never met?"

"We don't know who killed Hawk," Marsh said, reaching for her. "It could've been any-damn-body."

"Who the fuck is 'we'?" she said, pushing past him. "That bastard shot ten people in the middle of Ebenezer with a goddamn assault rifle. Fucking Ebenezer, Marsh! He slaughtered a child! Have you forgotten about that?"

"What in the hell is wrong with you? Who do you think you are?"

"This is my city!" she screamed. "And if I have to blow that motherfucking house up myself, this ends tonight!"

"What man shoots a sitting congressman, then goes home to biscuits with his wife and children? Torie, you know better than that. This doesn't make sense. Baby, think about it."

"If he has a heart attack, I'll be sure to inform you, Dr. Overstreet. Right now, I'm the only mayor this city has. They elected me."

"So that's it?" he said. "This is what you've become? You order a man slaughtered by a SWAT team to keep your poll numbers up? What's next? Are you running for Congress? Or are you going to challenge Governor Martinez?"

Victoria smirked. She had already run the calculus on a congressional bid. Her brother's side deals had been a real problem, politically. But she'd decided that if she actually filed for the special election, she wouldn't let anybody, not even her own brother, stand in her way. He had betrayed her. These days, she talked about Chip as if he were dead.

"Damn, Torie, go on and run for president of the whole damn country. I know you've thought about it. Tell me you haven't."

"If and when I do, your bed-wetting liberal ass had better be standing right next to me, smiling in the finest Dolce and Gabbana suit you can drag out of your closet. Hampton Bridges had the nerve to ask me if I was running for Congress, and you sound just like him."

The familiar breaking news music sounded. The words SUSPECTED AT-LANTA SNIPER DEAD IN SWAT TEAM RAID crawled across the bottom on the high-definition display. A local newscaster gave the play-by-play while chopper-fed video of the scene streamed live.

"Read it, Torie! It says 'suspected'!" he shouted. "You're not a jury!"

"I am tonight."

"So, you don't have an ounce of doubt? What would your father say about this?"

"My father was a graceful man, far too hesitant to seize the mantle all but handed to him by Dr. King. Hawk won that congressional seat only because my daddy refused to run."

"You could use some of his grace."

"I am not my brother's keeper, nor am I my father's child," she said. "It's over and we got him. That bastard—" she said before she caught herself and looked up.

Dressed in matching Lilly Pulitzer nightgowns, their twins hovered in the doorway.

"Mommy, what's happening?" Maya said.

"Why are you yelling?" Mahalia chimed in.

"It's over," their mother said, taking both girls into her arms. "A very bad man killed Uncle Ezra and we caught him."

"Well, that's good, right?" Maya said.

"Yes, Maya, that's a good thing," she said, giving Marsh the side-eye. "I want you to go back to bed now. You've got tennis camp in a few hours."

"But we don't want to go to camp," Mahalia said, wiping her sleepy eyes. "We want to stay with you and Daddy."

Victoria knelt down and cupped her daughter's chin with her fingers. "Hallie, everything is okay now. I promise you."

"You promise?" Mahalia said.

"Mommy doesn't break her promises. And I promise you that I will always protect you."

Marsh left the room. Minutes later, Victoria heard the garage door go up and Marsh's Porsche Panamera Turbo rumble down the drive.

"Where's Daddy going?" Maya asked.

"Your father has a patient at the hospital," she said, spilling out the first white lie that came to mind.

"Okay," Maya said. "Can I have your dragon?"

"What dragon?"

"The red one on your desk. Can I have it? It's Japanese origami. Mrs. Connor taught us about them in school. She and Mr. Connor went to Asia last year. She had lots of pictures. I can show you on her Facebook page, if you want. They're called paper gods. She taught us how to make them, but mine didn't turn out right. Hallie's was way better than mine," Maya said.

"I'm sure it was perfect," Victoria said, giving her an assuring kiss. "You can tell me all about it tomorrow."

She shook her head in amazement. Enrolling her girls in an ultraexclusive school like Pace Academy had its political costs, especially in Southside majority-black precincts, but moments like these more than validated that decision. It was also Marsh's alma mater.

He had been a stabilizing force, the one who wasn't fazed by the trappings of marrying a Dobbs. He was his own man with his own family fortune, Victoria reminded herself. She regretted talking to Chief Walraven that way too. But the deed was done, her personal loss too great.

Victoria picked up the origami again. She had no idea what the red dragon meant, or who might have sent it or why, but it made her uncomfortable. She shooed her daughters down the darkened hallway and into their bedroom. Back in her den, she called Chief Walraven again.

A fully loaded AR-15 sniper rifle, the same type of weapon that likely killed Hawkins, was found cased in a storage room in the basement of the house, he explained in a halting voice.

"We're shipping it to the FBI ballistics lab in Virginia. We're sure it's our gun," the chief said.

"What about the woman? The kids?" she asked, examining the silky-red dragon.

A paper god?

"She's in federal custody," the chief said. "She's not saying much, but she did say that her husband was at home all day."

"What about the kids?"

"They're with Child Protective Services," the police chief went on explaining. "The feds will debrief them in the morning."

He stopped and said, "By the way, Mayor Dobbs, just so you know, we didn't shoot him. He killed himself, single gunshot to the temple. He was already dead when we got inside the house. We recovered a nine-millimeter handgun."

"That coward saved us a trial," she said with a shrug.

SEVEN

Hampton tapped the top of the fancy, single-serve coffeemaker and watched as hot, foamy milk dripped into the waiting cup. Back in the day, before the *Times-Register* relocated to a suburban office tower, the Deadline Diner used to sell real food. These days, the overworked Keurig machine and a rack of prepackaged snacks in the breakroom were among the few indulgences left at the *Times-Register.* He had his daily pick of flavors, and the very thought of sipping on this hazelnut-vanilla latte made his soul sing. And, of course, it came compliments of the house!

It was the least management could do, seeing as the editorial staff had been cut in half over the last two years, on top of the system-wide early-retirement packages that gutted the newsroom. Website traffic was up, but the print edition was thinning and failing. There were now more coupons than stories in the Sunday edition. Travel budgets were slashed, and the reporters were forced to get by on shoe leather, outdated laptops, and age-old cell phones. Every open records request had to be approved, and payment to government entities was known to take several months. Hampton slipped a couple of seemingly innocuous requests through the system without drawing the ire of the accounting department.

He was stuffing four small packs of mini-pretzels into his side pocket, when Hampton received an urgent text message from his editor. Infrequent but terse missives from Tucker always sent shock waves down his spine, and Hampton had no idea what he might have done to deserve this one.

Call me.

A second text immediately followed.

MEET ME IN MY OFFICE. NOW.

Forgetting the cup of java in the breakroom, minutes later Hampton was waiting outside the managing editor's office when Tucker's secretary strolled by. Joyce Renfro was notoriously short on words, though her demeanor always gave her away. Miss Joyce, who was aging like a bottle of buttermilk left in a high sun, glanced at him and glowered as if he'd personally strangled a litter of newborn kittens.

He was in some sort of trouble, but of what sort or severity he could not venture to guess. The look on Miss Joyce's face made him want to make a beeline for the elevators. It was just like Tucker to leave him sweating out in front of the entire newsroom.

The office door suddenly jerked open.

"Get your ass on in here, Hamp," Tucker boomed.

Hampton wheeled himself through the threshold. The editor slammed the door behind him. Before he could part his lips to say "How goes it," Tucker tossed a stack of binders onto his lap. "I thought I told you to let this go."

"Let what go?"

"This so-called investigation of yours," Tucker said. "You're going to get us both strung up."

Hampton was dumbstruck. "What investigation?"

"Don't play me, Hampton Bridges. This isn't the time. The executive publisher called me about this herself."

Hampton looked around nervously. "Reclaim Atlanta?"

"Keep it up, and you'll be claiming an unemployment check."

"What I do on company time is your business. What I do on mine is mine," Hampton shot back. "Honest to God, I will tell her that myself."

"I seriously doubt Wilma Delacourte wants to hear from you."

Hampton looked down at the heap of folders. A copy of some financial disclosure reports he'd ordered from the secretary of state's database and a time-stamped Freedom of Information Act letter he had filed with the City of Atlanta sat on top.

"How did you get this, anyway?" Hampton said without looking up.

"Don't ask me things you don't really want to know."

"You've got people spying on me? You sent those IT goons into my email account?"

"I'm just the messenger. Learn not to use company servers or your press credentials," Tucker said. "And company stationery is strictly reserved for authorized company business."

"Okay, so what?" Hampton said. "I was doing a little digging. That's what reporters do, right?"

"You're digging your own grave here," Tucker said. "I shouldn't have to tell you that this is a suicide mission. The entire executive team wants you fired."

"Then do it, Tuck," Hampton challenged. "I don't have a problem suing anybody for wrongful termination, least of all the suits upstairs."

"I would if I didn't think there was something to this."

Hampton blew out an audible sigh. "Then let me follow it, wherever it leads," Hampton said. "Let's toss some chips in the air and see where they fall."

"I'm more worried about who they might fall on."

Hampton grumbled.

"Why would you use your company laptop, anyway? And you know good and damn well that open records requests are discoverable."

"It's the only one I have. I had to pawn my MacBook to pay the damn light bill, thanks to the dock in salary."

"The mayor is one thing. But you cannot go accusing the Delacourte family of campaign finance fraud and expect to keep your job."

"I haven't accused anybody of anything," Hampton said, arching his brow. "Yet."

"So that's really what this is? You're going to haul the wealthiest family in the Southeast into federal court?"

"I'm not a prosecutor and I can't say."

"Can't or won't?"

"Does it matter?"

"Then find another way to get there. I cannot get another call from upstairs. I've put my neck on the chopping block for you a few too many times, and I won't do it again."

"So, you're telling me to keep going?"

"No."

"Then what are you saying, exactly?"

"Mr. Stovall, your editor, is ordering you to stop. Tucker, your friend, is saying where there's smoke, there is fire. The less I know, the better. You're on borrowed time."

Hampton was relieved. The wave of fear was almost gone, but he was now rummaging through his head to figure out who had snitched. He wanted to know who ordered his IT accounts scanned and why. Somebody was poking through his email and somehow knew about his latest FOIA request. He'd sent it only days ago.

Hampton hated putting Tucker in a tight spot and told him so. For that, he apologized.

"This conversation stays between you and me," Tucker said finally. "Deal?"

"Deal."

EIGHT

Victoria woke to the pleasant sounds of rustling pots. The smell of maple bacon floated down the hallway to the master bedroom. Being a self-professed albeit backsliding vegetarian, she'd denied herself the pleasures of the hog, but surely there was a pan of Mother's legendary apple-cheddar drop biscuits too! Rosetta knew how to roust her children from bed without uttering a word.

Her brother, Chip, had phoned earlier, eager to kick off the campaign. She resisted the urge to hang up on him.

"I haven't decided," she told him.

"I know you loved him, Sis. They don't make them like that anymore. But Hawk would want you to do this. You know Daddy would too," he said. "I'm ready when you are. Say the word, and we'll get to work."

"Work? You can't work for me, and don't bring Daddy into this."

"That man loved you," Chip whispered almost inaudibly. "Like you were his own."

"What did you say?"

"Nothing."

"I didn't stutter. Say it again!"

"You don't want to hear what I've got to say. I know you better than you know yourself, and that's real."

"Fuck you, Chip," Victoria said. "There is no campaign. If and when there is, you don't have a job."

"I'm still your brother," he said. "I'm still your blood and the best campaign manager you'll ever have."

"Had," she said. "Ever had. You'll be lucky if they don't put your ass in jail."

"Plenty of room in the penitentiary for two."

"Meaning what?"

"Meaning you need to think hard about these choices you're making."

"Is that a threat?"

"You know me better than that."

"Fuck you." She hung up, tossed the phone into the nightstand drawer, and slammed it shut.

Victoria gathered herself and tried to forget about Chip. She allowed herself to wallow for a time between the Egyptian satin sheets, basking in the sounds of her daughters giggling between chords as they tapped the keys of the grand piano in the formal living room. Besides, her own keys needed tapping. She ran her hand up her leg and tickled her clitoris until she felt the creaminess spill out over her fingers. She let out a gentle moan as she continued massaging herself under the comforter.

Marsh had not come home again. But Victoria could not bring herself to be concerned about his frail ego or where he was at that moment. It took several days of quiet diplomacy, but the funeral arrangements were finally complete. With the public memorial service only days away, she was certain that Marsh would show himself at some point. He would not falter on that obligation, she knew. Until then, she was happy to see after her own needs.

It was 8 A.M. or so by the time Victoria laced up her running shoes and pushed her way over, around, and down the bends of Habersham Drive. She jetted over the short stretch along Peachtree Battle Avenue and then up Peachtree Street, passing Bennington Towers, Park Place Condominiums, and the Cathedral of Saint Philip. Saturday morning traffic was in full stride. Cars spilled onto the roadway from various private drives and condominium parking decks. A spate of joggers littered the sidewalks as mothers and nannies pushed fair-faced babies in tricked-out strollers and walked their beautifully groomed dogs.

Her hip was still grumbling, over the objections of a mild pain reliever. Still, Victoria managed a two-mile run in the low summer sun. Holy Row, the strip of Peachtree Street lined with grand cathedrals, synagogues, and churches, was especially grueling, but visions of golden biscuits laden with peach preserves danced in her head. Though she did not want it, Sal Pelosi ordered an additional security detail and tightened the perimeter around the mayor and her family.

"The shooter is dead," she told him. "Do we really need this?"

"Precautionary," he explained. "A show of force is necessary to ward off copycats."

With two plainclothes officers in tow, Victoria picked up the pace as she passed Second-Ponce de Leon Baptist, a near-century-old, painted-white brick church, before finally hooking the left onto Andrews Drive. She sprinted the last fifty yards back to her cobblestone driveway and disappeared beyond the eight-foot privacy wall.

Victoria hadn't wanted this house. When Marsh ordered the eleven-thousand-square-foot, sprawling Tudor-style mansion built smack-dab in the heart of "Whitelanta" for their fifth wedding anniversary in 2010, she was initially cold to the idea of selling their home in Guilford Forest, an all-black enclave in southwest Atlanta. Her mother had warned that moving so far away from her childhood home would be both a political and personal misstep. No matter how much money they had, she should be living among the people, her people, Rosetta scolded at the time.

"That man of yours is always looking for a bigger mountain, my dear," her mother said. "Don't let all that money make you lose sight of the valley or the people in it."

"It isn't where you lay your head, it's where you lay your heart," Marsh had argued.

Victoria wanted to believe him. But even as they'd unpacked the moving boxes, she couldn't stop thinking about the rash of radio talk-show callers who had no qualms about calling her a "house Negro" on WAOK, the only black news and talk station in the city. Then there was the never-empty email inbox that overflowed with messages questioning her political loyalties from people who could not name their state representative if their very lives depended on it. Marsh kept kissing her, up and down her neck, over her shoulders and between her breasts, until Victoria agreed to put the state-issued smartphone away.

"Are you going to listen to them or me?" he cooed, leading her to the king-sized bed that hadn't been loaded into its frame. He tipped the mattress onto the floor and slipped himself between her legs. Rosetta, coughing over the intercom system, interrupted their midafternoon frolicking.

Atlanta was two cities in one: one black, one white. One sat north of I-20; another lay to the south. One of them controlled the ballot box. And the other held its purse strings. Winning in a citywide election always meant cutting a grand bargain.

Victoria knew the rules all too well. Her father, Park Dobbs, along with Ezra Hawkins and others, had rewritten the playbook decades ago, when Maynard Jackson beat Sam Massell in his first bid for mayor. It was 1973. Hawkins took his seat on the Atlanta City Council that same year. John Lewis followed in 1981.

Victoria thought about Hawkins now, his sparkling coffee-brown eyes, the way his jowls shook like saddlebags when he laughed, the way he made you feel as if you were the only person in the world when he spoke to you. She missed his soft warm hands, the lumbering gait of his stride, and his proclivity for pressed white napkins when he took afternoon tea with a spot of cream.

The funeral was set for Wednesday at noon, enough time for the glitterati to descend upon Atlanta and, she imagined, enough for Marsh to come to his senses. The memorial service would be as elegant as the man. The president, First Lady, and House Speaker were all expected. Graça Machel, wife of the late Nelson Mandela, was due in on a chartered flight from South Africa along with Archbishop Makgoba, head of the Anglican Church, that afternoon. Victoria could hear Hawkins's joyful baritone voice singing in her head.

Oh Freedom, Oh Freedom,
Oh Freedom,
Freedom is coming, oh yes I know!

It was decided, at her insistence, that the Medal of Freedom would be bestowed posthumously and placed on permanent display in the National Center for Civil and Human Rights in Centennial Park. Hawkins had been a founding board member and one of its largest benefactors. He'd circled the globe to shore up funding for the massive project.

The federal investigators were likely right, Victoria thought. To kill Hawkins in such a public place, with more than twenty-five hundred people present, rather than in the driveway of his house or some random place, was a demonstration. Finding him would've been easy enough. His address on Somerset Trail was public record, after all, and he kept to a regular daily schedule. Hawkins had been a man of convention, coming and going at the same time, an imprudence that a man in his position might've avoided. He had no standing security team, and despite her pleading, these days he often drove himself whenever he was at home in Atlanta.

The shooter, a man now identified as Caleb Vasquez, had no discernible ties to antigovernment groups, and he had no social media presence. Whether someone sent him or he committed the vile act of his own volition was yet unknown.

"Domestic terrorism," she said out loud to no one.

Victoria uttered those words as she kneeled to unlace her running shoes.

It had been nearly a week, and she had heard nothing from the governor's office. Save for a three-line perfunctory public statement expressing sympathies for all of the dead that did not even mention Hawkins by name, Governor Elena Martinez could not be bothered with the pretense of ordering state flags lowered to half-staff until a scathing *Times-Register* editorial had been published. Even so, Victoria assumed the governor would not step foot into Ebenezer for the memorial service, and there was no way in hell Martinez would greet the president and First Lady on the tarmac at Hartsfield-Jackson Airport.

Ironically born to migrant workers and growing up deep in the lower Chattahoochee River valley in the far southwest corner of the state, Elena Reyes-Martinez had once been the not-so-gentlewoman from Muscogee County, an ultraconservative ball of fire who was first sent to the Georgia statehouse in a special election.

"When all else fails, vote from the rooftops!" she was caught on tape telling a pro-gun rally during the heated primary. Governor Martinez wrapped herself in the Bill of Rights, no amendment more tightly than the Second, and railed against illegal immigration.

The governor's disdain for "race baiters" and "hustlers" like Hawkins was not subject to dispute. Martinez was cooling her jets in the governor's mansion these days, a half mile up the road in Tuxedo Park, and rumor had it that she had her eyes set on a U.S. Senate bid.

Back when she was a member of the state legislature herself, Victoria had tested the waters for a run for governor. Virgil Loudermilk, a political kingmaker who controlled much of the money flowing out of Buckhead, personally urged her to run. He was a Republican, though for Virgil there was no partisan aisle wide enough not to cross if the stakes were high enough.

Kitchen cabinet meetings were convened and conference calls with heavy-hitters representing big-name donors were held. However, the notion that a black Democrat from Atlanta could win a statewide election in Georgia was far-fetched. Hawkins had been courted too, but turned the offer down flat. While it was true that she now controlled the legendary Jackson Machine, that wasn't worth a pinch of salt in Georgia's 158 other counties. Then, too, there had been talk of a presidential appointment. Without a doubt, a bevy of white-shoe law firms would be eager to recruit her into their fold, if she ever decided to leave public life.

Victoria stripped off her clothes, stepped into the master bath, and turned on a cool shower. She craned her neck and let the water rain down on her décolletage, massaging her breasts in the soothing wetness. Reflexively, her fingers swept past her abdomen, down to the top edge of her pubic bone and over her waxed-smooth labia. She stopped there, forgoing the impulse to surrender to another moment of indulgence.

In a few weeks' time, she could be taking a chair on the floor of the House, and the Speaker would see to it that she got plum committee appointments. That congressional seat was hers, just as Hampton Bridges had been so disrespectful as to suggest, if Victoria wanted it. It took nothing short of unmitigated gall for him to show up at the press briefing, and Victoria knew Bridges had plenty of it. And she expected he would be back, beating the bushes, at some point. She'd wished him dead a thousand times in her head. She'd been noticeably indifferent about his car accident, but blithely ordered her staff to send a floral arrangement.

Bridges had written a rather nice story about her in last Monday's paper, but an aide reported that he was snooping around in her campaign finance disclosures again. When it came down to it, Bridges had to know that she had both the money and the votes, she thought as she rinsed the suds away. It was widely known that she had every big-name campaign strategist from the Chattahoochee to the Anacostia River on speed dial. Her campaign operation could be fully staffed and running in a matter of hours. One call could set it in motion. Hiring Chip was another matter. Her mother wouldn't like it, but she needed to keep some space between herself and her brother—at least publicly.

The plans were swirling in her head when Marsh came into the bathroom. His silence said he was still stewing over their argument. He didn't offer so much as a good morning. She'd missed him in their bed for the few fleeting hours that she actually slept last night, and she let herself admit that she needed him now, just as she always had. If only he would join her in the shower and finish the work that she'd left undone.

"Marsh, honey, I'm sorry," she said finally. "I was angry and hurt. I'm sorry."

There was no response. No "I love you." No "Baby, we'll get through this." There was nothing. She heard the toilet flush and the sink water turn on and off.

"You didn't have to go to a hotel," she said softly.

"I didn't."

"Then, where—" she started to ask.

The door slammed shut.

"—were you?" she whispered to herself.

Gentle, knowing tears streamed down her face.

NINE

Hampton parked his minivan outside Lenox Mall near the food court entrance. It had been two full weeks since the carnage at Ebenezer, and Congressman Ezra Hawkins was now resting in his grave in some dusty small town Hampton had never heard of.

For now, at least, Victoria Dobbs was still mayor. There was no doubt in his mind that she would file qualifying papers for the special election.

Asking Dobbs about her political intentions—before the medical examiner even had the chance to inventory the crime scene, process the bodies, and pluck the bullets from their wounds—seemed rash now. Hampton wondered how much his indelicate, hasty approach would cost him. Surely, the mayor's office had turned over that Georgia Open Records Act request to his publisher and triggered the fishing expedition into his work IT account. But pressing the question of her political fortunes out in the open gained him nothing but scorn from his colleagues and a predictable upbraiding from his mother, who stayed glued to Fox News. She'd seen the live press conference and watched her baby son make an ass of himself on national television.

"You're doing everything under the sun to prove your father right,"

Florence Bridges said, reprimanding her grown son. "That husband of mine cannot wait to throw some fresh crow on the grill in honor of your downfall. Make him eat it by himself, gosh darn you!"

No one walking the planet could dish out an expletive-free tongue-lashing like his mother. Florence, being a good Catholic and all, would never take the Lord's name in vain, but she'd make you want to beg to see Jesus by the time she was finished with you. How she'd stomached his father all these years remained a mystery to Hampton.

Hampton readily admitted that there was nothing he held sacred when it came down to chasing a story. Being a journalist, for him at least, still meant pounding the weeds until the truth ran out naked and screaming. He made no apologies for that. Though a wiser man might have eased back onto the beat and figured out a way to get at the story without having drawn the mayor's wrath so quickly. Whether immediately or eventually, he figured, there would be a price to pay for his insolence.

"I've always said you had more mouth than grace," his mother often chided.

The few friends he had left in the Atlanta press corps said little or nothing on the matter, not that he expected any of them to call or write. These days, he was less than interested in carousing at the weekly cocktail hour at Manuel's Tavern, where local politicos and reporters chin-wagged over craft beers and stuffed their faces with loaded "dogzillas."

Hampton preferred to lick his wounded paws alone, and anyway, tripping over to Manny's place was anything but a good idea. He'd been dry for months, and wheeling into the bar for a night of shoptalk over a virgin Arnold Palmer, with so much good liquor within arm's reach, was a depressing thought.

Thanks to Tucker Stovall, Hampton was back in the saddle now, on the political beat, working a story he couldn't let go. Congressman Hawkins had been caught with a prostitute back in '85, and Hampton knew exactly where to find her.

Chanel Burris was now in her mid to late forties, he estimated, and living in a make-do apartment on the far Westside in the shadow of the Atlanta University Center. She was holding down a job in the men's shoe department at Bloomingdale's. Hampton decided to ring her up and pay a visit.

He found an empty handicap spot, entered the lower level from the rear entrance, and situated himself next to Auntie Anne's pretzel shop. Chanel would be going on break in a few minutes, leaving him a small stretch to look over his notes and scarf down a pretzel smothered in mustard. The first bite was thrilling. The second was interrupted by a hubbub on the escalator.

"Hey, watch it!" a woman shouted.

A fresh-faced brownish boy, no more than fourteen or so, broke through a string of startled shoppers on the descending step risers and flung his long, lanky body over the balustrade. He jumped a clean fifteen feet and hit the checkered marble flooring with a thud. Splayed out on the tiling, he quickly yanked up his slouching jeans, hoisted a North Face backpack onto his shoulder, and took off running again. He didn't get far. A flank of security guards whizzed by.

Moments later, the rent-a-cops had the kid's face glued against the Game-Stop store display window. His caper spoiled, the knot below his eye already swelling and red as an apple, the boy was cuffed by a plainclothes store detective and led away. He didn't go quietly.

"Ayo! Somebody get this on camera!" he howled. "Anybody got that Periscope? Ayo! Tweet this shit! I got my receipts! Hit me at Babyboy404! Black lives matter! Believe that!"

"Another one bites the dust," a woman's voice said from over Hampton's shoulder. "They oughta know better than to come out here stealing from these white folk. I know he ain't think he was gone hit that MARTA train before they got hold of his narrow behind."

She adjusted her pocketbook on her shoulder, a gently used Gucci bag that matched her peep-toe shoes.

"Hey, Miss Burris. It's good to see you."

"What do you want?"

"Thanks for agreeing to see me."

"Yeah, well, I ain't got but a minute. Unless you're gonna make my sales quota, you gotta make this quick."

It had been several years since he last saw her in person, but Chanel hadn't aged any that Hampton could see.

"Well, you look great."

"Honey, you know black don't crack. But I'm here to tell you that it shole do move around. These Spanx are so tight, they got my ass sweating and itching."

She'd put on a few pounds, in all the right places, as far as Hampton could see. He did wonder how she made it through double shifts wearing four-inch stilettos. The canary-yellow toenail polish, fake eyelashes, and curly blond-streaked weave were odd choices for a woman her age. He had half a mind to ask about the clownish getup, but for once, he resisted the impulse, and he just admired her rock-hard, smooth calf muscles and the way her spaghetti straps fell across her collarbones.

Under the thick layers of makeup was a beautiful woman, the kind who would make you go searching in the daytime with a flashlight. Chanel was tall, just short of six feet, even without the come-fuck-me pumps. Hampton figured he wasn't, never had been, and never would be man enough to play in her sandbox.

Their meetings and phone calls over the years, eight of them in all, were a closely guarded secret between him, Chanel, and his dog, Inman. Even Tucker never knew that he'd kept tabs on her, and there was no need for him or anybody else to find out now. Tucker would blow his stack, and Hampton would be back plucking dandelions before he could whistle the first stanza of "The Night They Drove Old Dixie Down."

He'd have a hard time explaining all of this to his probation officer.

Hampton couldn't begin to describe it, but something about Chanel's story never sat right with him. Maybe it was the way she told the story to him one snippet at time. He listened to the recorded calls, wrestled with the details a dozen times or more, looking for the hole that had yet to expose itself.

Something isn't right, Hampton told himself as he followed her to an elevator and into the food court a floor below.

They sipped on a pair of lemonades from Chick-fil-A. He lobbed a few gentle questions. She hadn't asked him about the wheelchair or what might have caused his present predicament. She was hesitant, as always, and he couldn't blame her for that. Being an inextricable footnote in somebody else's life couldn't feel good, especially when that somebody was now a martyred congressman—the target of a domestic terrorist attack, no less—and a world-renowned champion of human rights. He'd turned up an ugly Wikipedia page and a smattering of anonymous blog posts festooned with unflattering images of Chanel. Hawkins was an American hero, and from the looks of things, Chanel's exquisite ass had proven disposable in his rise to power.

It was 1985 when the firestorm erupted. Chanel was busted half-naked in a low-flung motel room on Spring Street with one Ezra Hawkins, who was then a sitting member of the Atlanta City Council. For weeks on end, reporters circled the run-down duplex off Sylvan Road where she lived with her mother. The local ABC affiliate filed daily live reports from the scene. Bill Wilfong was the only reporter to get Dorothy "Dot" Burris on camera. Searching the archives for the tape proved easy pickings since the station and the *Atlanta Times-Register* sat under the same corporate umbrella.

"Get on outta here!" Dot Burris yelled as the camera zoomed in on her.

She wagged her finger at Wilfong and said, "The Good Lord ain't never gone bless this evil y'all doing outchear. Ya'oughta be down there on Trinity Avenue in them city council meetings. That's where all the real crime happens. My child ain't never done nothing to hurt nobody."

Chanel served a stint in jail on a misdemeanor possession charge, followed by another year of supervised probation. Curiously, Hampton could find no mention of a "Chanel Burris" in city or county detention records. He rechecked the court docket and repeatedly inspected the transcripts for clues. It was as if Chanel had disappeared the minute she stepped onto the prisoner transfer van.

"Like I said, I don't have anything to say on that. I was just a kid back then. I've got a nice life now."

"No one will ever know we spoke," Hampton said. "He's gone now. You can talk to me."

Chanel eyed him suspiciously and said, "You know they set me up, right? Didn't have no warrant or nothing. The next thing I know, they had me on the floor with guns cocked at my head like I was some kind of kingpin."

She shook the ice in her Styrofoam cup of lemonade and said, "I got pinched for a soggy bag of weed and a dry-ass crack pipe while the Honorable

Mr. Hawkins went right on with his life, got himself elected to Congress, and left me sitting down there on Rice Street with a bond my mama couldn't make. I sat in jail for damn near four months until the judge got around to giving me a public defender. He ain't send no lawyer for me or nothing. He couldn't even call me by my name."

"You still sound angry about that."

"Not really. My mama used to say I've been pissed off since the day I was born."

"Are you sure it was the Fulton County lockup? Rice Street?"

"You ain't ever been to jail, have you, Mr. Bridges?"

Hampton didn't answer. There was no sense in getting into it, he figured. The last thing he wanted was to relive those hours, handcuffed to a hospital bed.

"Well, if you did, you'd remember er'thang from the time they said 'all rise' to 'somebody made your bail.' You'd damn sure never forget where they took you, even if it was thirty years ago. I was on lockdown for two hundred thirty-eight days, fifteen hours, and forty-seven minutes."

The official story was that then-nineteen-year-old Chanel was a low-dollar prostitute known as "Che-Che" in the streets and was caught trying to flush a ziplock bag of marijuana down the motel toilet. Hampton suspected that it ran deeper than that. Expecting a sitting city councilman to spring her from jail, even one who claimed to have been trying to rescue her from the streets, confirmed it for him.

"Sometimes love doesn't love us back," he said, angling for something more.

"Look here, I got bills to pay. So unless you paying."

"Why didn't you just leave Atlanta?"

"And go where and be what?"

"Miss Burris, I couldn't find any record of your detention."

"I have to go. It was a nice going-home service. They laid him out pretty. I watched it on TV. Wish I could've been there."

"Can we talk again?"

"I really wish you ain't come up on my job like this, Mr. Bridges. I hope he didn't suffer none, for real, but like I told you, I don't have nothing else to say.

You don't know what kinna people you messing with. If they got him, please believe they can get at you and me."

"What people, Miss Burris?"

She rose up suddenly and straightened her skirt. She abruptly spun around like a beauty queen, doubled back, leaned in, and said, "You need to keep your good eye on Miss Vicki."

"Vicki?"

"Mayor Dobbs. We called her 'Vicki' in grade school."

TEN

Anybody who knows anything about Virgil Loudermilk knows that round about noon on any given Monday, he can be found in a back corner booth at the Buckhead Diner. Located a stone's throw from a row of luxury car dealerships, the upscale restaurant is a place to be seen. The well-appointed room is usually filled with a who's who of local celebrities, politicos, and housewives out on a midday shopping break.

Virgil orders his usual culinary fare and then unfurls the Sunday edition of the *Atlanta Times-Register.* He thumbs through the pages and scans the headlines until he locates the crossword puzzle. He gets through most of it with a ballpoint pen, without a single mistake, before the small plate of honey-drizzled, truffle deviled eggs with crisp fried chicken skins gets to him.

By the time the entrée hits the table, he has moved on to Sudoku, which he likens to throwing his brain on a treadmill. He saves the *New York Times* games section for dessert, having discovered the wonderment of KenKen, the reigning king of all Japanese math puzzles.

A specimen of southern heritage, he enjoys feasting on delicious foods of nearly every known variety, so long as it comes from something with two eyes, four legs, and a tail. He likes his plates piled wide and deep. Why, Virgil would eat a whole passel of field-dressed possums if it were seasoned right, soaked in buttermilk, dusted with flour, and flash-fried. He likes to hear the heart beating in his food.

Alas, he settled for a more pedestrian delicacy today. Virgil was polishing off a mile-high, hand-shaved pastrami sandwich stuffed with red cabbage slaw on marbled rye when he spotted his favorite plainclothes police lieutenant chatting up Aleixo, the host and grandson of the owner-chef, Pasha Kastansa.

Virgil watched as the men traded a few serious words, though he couldn't make out what was being said. Aleixo smiled and clapped his hands, signaling the hostess to clear and reset a four top with crisp white linens. The presence of Lieutenant Salvatore Pelosi meant one thing: Mayor Dobbs was somewhere in their midst.

As sure as day turns to night, Her Highness strutted in, tailed closely by a female assistant that he did not recognize. Victoria was dressed in a flawless Oscar de la Renta sleeveless, fold-neck sheath, neatly cinched at the waist. He dabbed the Thousand Island dressing from his lips, sat upright in the booth, and watched her gorgeous peep-toe heels click across the black-and-white marble-inlayed parquet floors. The mayor was so damn good-looking, she could make a blind man see rainbows on a cloudy day, Virgil thought to his own amusement.

He might otherwise have been delighted, but this was anything but a social call. The mayor was not prone to surprise visits. Though given his silence in the days after the funeral, Virgil knew it was only a matter of time before she graced him with her presence. Virgil imagined he would have to suffer through some small talk until Victoria got around to the point of the ambush.

Mayor Dobbs could be downright ugly when she wanted to be, a fact that was not lost on him in that moment. There was a delicate way to handle these matters, and surely she wouldn't put up a stink out in the middle of the restaurant. Or would she? He'd been at the Commerce Club when the entire hullabaloo with Hampton Bridges went down, so he braced himself.

Aleixo personally escorted Pelosi and the nameless minion to a table on the other side of the room. Without a word, the mayor slid into the booth across from Virgil.

"Well, if it ain't the Great Torie Dobbs! Isn't this a nice surprise? I must be living right!" he said in a deep Georgia mountain drawl. He flagged down a server. "Let me buy you a cup of coffee. Some dessert?"

"Thank you, but that won't be necessary," she said flatly. "I have a full calendar, so I won't take much of your time."

He sighed and said, "Well, then, let's get to it. You've got something on your mind, so let old Virgil have it, darling."

She smiled gingerly, ignored his condescending tone, and said, "I'm running—"

"Running what?" he said, cutting her off midsentence. He leaned back and let out a chuckle. "Publix Georgia Marathon ain't for another few months."

"I am running in the special election for the Fifteenth Congressional District. I will announce my candidacy next week."

"You're not going to ask me what we decided?"

"I didn't come to ask you anything. Consider this a courtesy call."

"Is that right?" Virgil leaned back farther and propped his arms over the top ledge of the booth. "Is that how this thing works now?"

"Did you expect me to sit this one out? You seem surprised."

"I'd be lying if I said I was. I was sure you'd turn up at some point, but the funeral was just yesterday week. You put on a beautiful spread. We sent a donation and flowers."

"I sent my thanks to Whit. It certainly was generous of him. But Congressman Hawkins would want me to run."

"I'm truly sorry for your loss, and I'm sure enough glad y'all got ahold of that shooter. Goddamn shame Hawkins had to die like that. But you and I both know it has never been about what Ezra Hawkins, rest his soul, would or would not want."

"What are you saying?"

"I am saying you're not our choice this go-round. Listen, gal, I'm sorry you wasted your time and that dress sure is a wonder to behold, but we decided to go another way. Let me buy you that cup of coffee, and let's you and I work this thing out."

"Again, I am not here to ask for your support and I don't need your money."

"You won't win without it," Virgil said. "You can bet your precious skivvy drawers on that."

"Who are you running? Did you go and buy yourself another preacher? I hear Reverend Goodwin is testing the waters, and heaven knows he's for sale. Hell, if you rummage deep enough in the clearance bin, you can get Boney Jeffries for pennies on the dollar."

"We took a vote, and the plain truth is you had a lot of support from our board, but I call the shots. You're playing with my deck of cards, sweetness. All I can tell you is that we're going another way."

"There is no other way, and you know it, Virgil. I've got every card I need."

"You should recheck that deck of yours, precious."

"In case your memory fails, the Jackson Machine has won every citywide election since 1974—a political operation, I don't mind telling you, that I still run. I can put five hundred feet on the street before sundown tonight, if need be, and my campaign war chest, thanks in no small part to you, is more than enough to work the next eight weeks before the special election."

"Dr. Goodwin has fifteen thousand tithing Christian soldiers in his congregation, and I like the fire in his belly. Reminds me of my mother's preacher, only he was white, of course."

"Screw you, your dead mama, and Goodwin too," Victoria said, sneering.

"Watch yourself, darling. You always did have more mouth than grace," Virgil shot back. "Is that any way to talk to the man who bought you the keys to City Hall?"

"Go to hell, Virgil, and take Reverend Cash Flow with you."

"You should run on now, pick up what's left of your dignity, and act like we never had this conversation."

The mayor dug in. "All of this because I wouldn't let you run roughshod over the FCC? I thought you were a bigger man than that. Seems petty for a man of your stature. It would be a shame if somebody knocked you off of that gilded perch."

"Oh, there's nothing small-time about the shenanigans you pulled. You cost me millions. You and I both know this is much bigger than that. My name ain't Hampton Bridges. What are you going to do, jimmy-rig my car and run me off the road too?"

"Say it louder. Give me the chance to sue your fat, greasy, possum-eating ass. Nothing would please me more than to nail your carcass to the court-house steps."

"Listen here, Honey Bun. You've more than proved that you can't be trusted. Besides, you've run out of things I want. Your president is a lame duck with a Congress full of Republicans."

"You'll need to come better than that. If Congressman Hawkins were here, he would have your—"

Virgil cut her off again. He leaned into her face and said, "Yes, yes. Let's talk about the Honorable Ezra J. Hawkins. I've got great respect for the man. He did a lot for our fine city. But let's not forget what he really was, doll baby."

"Ezra was a saint."

"That may be, but it sure would be a shame if the world knew he was a flaming homosexual."

An angry wave flashed across Victoria's face as she nervously looked both ways, scanning the room for eavesdroppers.

"Oh, you didn't know he liked to chase hard-legs? Or maybe you did. He had a whole harem of them at his beck and call back in the day. Why don't you ask Pelosi over there how he used to drive the streets, hunting for Hawkins in every underground gay club north of I-20, when he should've been in Wash-ington for a vote. Sneaking in and out of the back room at Swinging Richards out on Northside Drive. Hawkins was a queen, darling."

Virgil watched her jaws lock up, her eyes lit like torches.

"You cannot prove of word of that," Victoria said, clenching her teeth. "And even if it's true, Hawkins was a staunch supporter of gay rights. He was ahead of me and everybody else on that issue. Because of him, I came to see it as the human rights issue that it is. Times are changing, and it might serve you to change along with them."

"They really haven't changed all that much, as far as I can see. We're still in Georgia, still deep in the heart of Dixie. What will good people say?"

"Good people will say that he was a great man and that those well-regulated clubs quietly keep the convention and tourism dollars flowing. Hell, I personally extended the liquor license for the Gilded Kitty last Monday. But like I said, you cannot prove it."

"I damned sure can," he said. "And that isn't all of it, Sugarplum. There's more where that came from. Now, be a good girl and let's work something out. Think on it and let me know what you want. Despite your foul mouth and junkyard manners, I'm feeling charitable. Maybe I can get you a partnership at one of these highfalutin law firms around here. You've certainly got the pedigree for it, though you could use a bit more charm."

"I plan to run a clean race."

"'Clean' is a relative term. The facts are what they are, and as far as I see, there are no clean hands here," Virgil said. "Listen, I have it on good authority that a chief counsel spot might open up at Georgia Electric, if you play your cards right. It's a decent living, not that you need the work, seeing as how you married good money."

"And what if I don't?"

"Who can say? There are so many secrets in the garden. I wouldn't even venture to guess where this thing might go. But it'll start with your sweetbootied godfather. Or should I call him 'Easy'? He liked to get it on in public bathrooms, you know."

"Kiss my ass, Virgil."

"Well, I guess that settles it," Virgil said.

It was just like Victoria to take a high horse on a low road, and he didn't mind leading that filly out of the barn. Virgil reached into his billfold, slipped a hundred-dollar bill under his glass, pushed himself back from the table, and said, "See you after 'while."

ELEVEN

"Now, that was a crying shame," Virgil said to himself as he retrieved his black-on-black Mercedes S 600 waiting in the valet lane and eased out of the parking lot.

He didn't necessarily like hitting Victoria below the belt like that, but she had to know what she was getting into.

Virgil drove the short distance to his office at One Buckhead Plaza. He hadn't planned to spill all of the sweet tea about the dearly departed Ezra Hawkins, but the mayor needed to know that he meant business, lest she get any grand ideas about who was truly running things.

Grinning like a mule with a belly full of briars, he took the elevator to the fourteenth floor, which opened up to his private suite. Virgil unbolted the door to his office and stepped inside. The smell of lavender and chamomile hit him in the face like a cast-iron skillet. Last week, his secretary, Delores, put plug-in deodorizers in various light sockets to cover up the smell of his cheap cigarillos. He had a thing for peach-flavored Swisher Sweets, which Whit Delacourte tried to tell him didn't qualify as genuine cigars and weren't fit for smoking by a man of any means.

"If you're going to do it, do it right," Whit told him last Christmas Eve.

He'd shown up over at the house, toting an expensive box of Cuban cigars with a red bow stuck on top.

"Those are hand-rolled, fresh off the boat," Whit said with a schoolboy's glee. "Merry Christmas!"

"Aren't those illegal?" Virgil asked.

"Since when has some international embargo kept you or me from doing anything?"

Virgil conceded the point, took one look at the row of cigars adorned in gold foil wrappers, and decided even the packaging was too fancy for his tastes.

"Are these for smoking or decorating the Christmas tree?" Virgil said playfully.

Virgil and Whit were first cousins and had been best friends every day of their lives. After his father took off for Franklin, Tennessee, with another woman back in '58, Big Whit stepped in and raised young Virgil like he was his own. From that day on, the boys told everybody that they were brothers.

They were named after their fathers, but took after their mothers in every way, right down to the slue feet and the bullheaded nature that kept them hemmed up in trouble. Whit would give up both eyeteeth if he thought that would buy him some peace. True to his mother, the ever-prudent Emma Louise, he craved discipline and order.

Virgil, on the other hand, was born with a hankering for chaos. If things were humming along too smoothly, Virgil would shove the peach cart right over a cliff, further proof that he was indeed Ginny-Beth's boy. Whit had grown out of that sort of mischief, mostly, Virgil would say. Virgil blamed that on the birth of Whit's firstborn and only son Coleman in '82. His own appetite for adventure never gave up the ghost.

Virgil was thinking about how proud Big Whit would be of his boys as he sat down behind his carved oak desk and clicked on the Emeralite desk lamp. Whit was lording over the family's ever-growing media conglomerate, W. W. Delacourte Enterprises, while Virgil managed its legal affairs and saw after governmental relations. Whit's younger sister, Wilma, was the executive publisher of the newspaper division and chaired the family foundation. Together, with holdings that now topped $28 billion in stated personal assets, they were by far the wealthiest family in the state.

Virgil whipped a cigarillo out of his breast pocket and lit it. He leaned back in his chair, blowing smoke rings, thinking about all the devilment he and Whit had gotten themselves into over the years. He let out a chuckle here and there, until he remembered he had some pressing business to attend to.

Virgil knew the mayor was capable of almost anything. Cussing him like a mangy yard dog was the least of it. He'd personally spent three years working out the details of a deal to rework Federal Communications Commission regulations with the current White House, a move that would have all but stripped away provisions that increased minority ownership of media properties, only to have his efforts thwarted by a special congressional subcommittee that was handpicked by the one and only Victoria Dobbs.

That kind of power was unusual, even for a big-city mayor. Her access to the president, not to mention her frequent appearances on national cable news shows, was something he hadn't accounted for. He'd fed that monster and now he was paying for it. Then there was that omnibus transportation bill. Between Dobbs and Hawkins, Virgil wasn't sure which one of them he trusted less.

No permanent friends, no permanent enemies. Ain't nothing permanent but interests.

He picked up the phone and dialed over to Lucky Mitchell's house.

Without so much as a "how's it going," Virgil said, "Meet me over to my office."

"Can it wait? Gabriella and I were just about to leave out for Alabama. I'd like to get over to the casino before sundown."

"I'm afraid you won't make it. Dobbs says she's running for Congress and kicking off the whole shebang next week."

TWELVE

B oth the moon and the sun hung in the sky as Hampton drove east over Ponce de Leon Avenue, past City Hall East and Green's liquor store, and hooked a right onto Moreland Avenue. He worked the portable hand controls with relative ease now, and getting in and out of the wheelchair transfer took him less time these days. He never got used to crawling on his elbows to get to the bathroom lest he suffer the humiliation of pissing himself again.

Little Five Points, just east of Candler Park, was already alive with wannabe hipsters cramming into various taverns and eateries. He'd toyed with stopping into Sacred Heart, an all-night tattoo parlor, but couldn't think of anything he wanted with such permanence.

Hampton eyed the foot traffic along Moreland and Euclid Avenues, imagining himself among them. He'd gotten to the point where he could stand of his own volition for at least a few minutes at a time, though no more than that without the aid of fitted forearm crutches, which he loathed. The speed at which he would recover, if he would ever walk on his own again, depended on the work he put in, his physical therapist advised. Progress, when there was some, came slowly. Hampton couldn't afford the twice-weekly sessions anyway.

There was no way to prove it, but he was sure that the mayor and her goon squad were behind the car accident. While she hadn't exactly tied him up and pumped liquor down his throat, he'd felt that steering wheel lock up in his hands. No matter how hard he jammed the loose brake pedal to the floorboard, the almost-new Nissan 370Z kept careening down Highway 138, revving through the gears and picking up speed until he ran straight through a curve and hit the bad side of a good tree. The Special Operations Corps, the mayor's team of henchmen, was nothing more than an urban legend, according to her press secretary. The police chief publicly denied such a unit existed, and Hampton couldn't find anything out of order in the city payroll records.

Inman was barking when he turned the dead bolt on the front door. Staring up at the weather-beaten awning, Hampton couldn't shake Chanel's words.

You don't know what kinna people you messing with. If they got him, please believe they can get at you and me.

He let Inman out into the backyard and rolled himself to the second bedroom. He holed up for hours on end, reassessing a story he had been forced to let go after his car split that tree.

He wondered now what, if anything, Chanel knew about the League. It was no secret that a small band of largely white business leaders had been injecting money into Friends of Ezra Hawkins since his first reelection to city council back in the '70s.

They were captains of industry, mostly real estate developers and bankers, but wealthy one and all. Some were dead now, others aging and retired to one gated Florida house or another. A few young, big-moneyed faces joined the mix. Thirty-eight-year-old Cordie Russell, founder of a chicken-and-waffle franchise and failed candidate for Congress, was the only African American member of the League.

Hampton believed Cordie was almost as shrewd as he was lucky and rich. According to a press clipping that Hampton turned up in the *Athens Banner-Herald*, young Cordie, who was then president of the College Republicans at the University of Georgia, hosted Virgil Loudermilk for the annual Presidents'

Day Dinner in '98. It was the start of a relationship that would prove profitable for the budding businessman, as Loudermilk would later fund the first of many restaurants that Cordie opened up.

Every man has a price.

Cordie later signed up to be the Republican foil in the Fourth District race against Lorraine Macklemore in 2002. Nobody in his or her right mind believed that Cordie could win, no matter how much of a lunatic Macklemore proved to be. That was never the point, as Macklemore and her bag of loose screws didn't make it out of the Democratic primary. Cordie turned out enough Republicans in DeKalb and Rockdale Counties to put a U.S. Senate candidate over the top.

Hampton was startled by a scraping noise that seemed to come from the front of the house, but decided it was nothing. He'd grown used to the shifting foundation and squeaking pipes in the old bungalow. Inman was barking again. He'd left the pooch outside, though from the sound of things, the dog was back in the house. Hampton went back to work.

He'd kept a running tally on the League, a band of political donors who made their presence known in almost every big race around the state. There was a complex trail of money and a few endorsements, which Hampton tallied on a growing spreadsheet. Stacks of campaign finance disclosure forms, court transcripts, and news clippings were strewn across the floor. Hampton examined the "mug shots" of the suspected players he'd pasted on a far wall. Loudermilk, the unofficial chairman of the League, was tacked in the middle of the photo array next to a cheese grit–grinning Cordie.

The story, if Hampton could ever put it all together and convince his editor to publish it, was his ticket out of Atlanta.

Ah yes! Atlanta hasn't seen a fire this big since General William Tecumseh Sherman burned down the West End!

Cordie and Hawkins weren't the only beneficiaries. Hampton did the math and figured out that the League put its extraordinary wealth and political firepower to work for a slate of mostly black candidates. Back in '93, they picked a mayor, four city council members, a county commission chair, and a whole school board to do their bidding. Thanks to an independent expenditure campaign, created under state and federal election law, none of the actual donors was ever disclosed and the largess could not be directly traced back to the League. The outfit, aptly and ironically named Reclaim Atlanta, put its considerable weight behind a city councilman from Inman Park. He was elected mayor in a landslide.

Hampton twisted his bottom lip between his fingers. The League had no standing committees that he could discern. Their work was done in private during ad hoc meetings over plates of fried lobster, thick-cut filets, and roasted asparagus in the back dining room at Chops Lobster Bar. He felt his stomach rumbling. Hampton hadn't had a steak—tough or tender—in ages.

According to the few public records available, Reclaim Atlanta was being run out of a post office box on Pharr Road. Whether jointly or severally, the men of the League rarely made a public political endorsement and mostly stayed silent on city and state issues. And they were all men, twelve of them, by Hampton's best count.

Their boldfaced names frequently graced the front page of the *Atlanta Business Weekly*, the city's pay-per-play business paper. One could spot them on the dais at various high-dollar galas, supporting one worthy cause or another. Their wives emptied the racks at Phipps Plaza and noshed on make-do sushi and sugar-free Belvedere lemon drop martinis out on the patio at Twist. Their children attended private schools like Pace Academy, Westminster, and the Lovett School, and populated summer tennis league rosters at the Cherokee Town and Country Club in the bucolic, mansion-lined section of Buckhead's Tuxedo Park. More than a zip code, 30327 was a station in life. The way the League conducted their political business was as secretive as the gated driveways leading up to their multimillion-dollar homes.

At least for a time, among the League's chosen were Ezra Hawkins and his protégée, Victoria Dobbs-Overstreet. That much Hampton knew for certain. Hampton discovered that during the 2009 mayoral campaign, when Dobbs faced stiff competition from the sitting city council president, she received over a half million in on-the-record contributions from family members and employees directly tied to the League. The campaign disclosure reports were clean and there was no accounting of what came under the table and Hampton had never been able to pin down what they got in return for their generosity. But it was clear, at least to Hampton, that they were buying themselves a new mayor. He'd taken the story to Tucker, who killed it on the spot without discussion when he saw the list of suspected players.

Hampton was nervous now, just as he had been when Tucker ordered him out of his office. Somewhere in those records lay the key to the biggest political scandal since the assassination of Huey Long in 1935 touched off a wave of public corruption that implicated hundreds of Louisiana government officials and business leaders. He struggled through the minutiae, believing the answer was buried somewhere deep in the spreadsheets. Chanel's words danced in his head.

You don't know what kinna people you messing with.

He heard the scraping again, and then a banging sound came from the living room. Hampton was confused at first, and then fear tore through him like a straw hut blazing in a low wind. Living in-town had its drawbacks. A rash of home invasions had hit Candler Park, Kirkwood, and a few adjoining neighborhoods in East Atlanta, and sometimes he felt like a sitting duck.

Instinctively, Hampton reached for the aluminum baseball bat he kept propped against his desk, grabbed his cell phone, and rolled himself into the dimly lit hallway.

"Inman, Inman!"

The hound scampered toward him. Hampton was relieved to see his snout covered in red sauce and spaghetti noodles. He'd forgotten to take out yesterday's trash, leaving Inman with a feast that no self-respecting mutt could resist.

"How the heck did you get in here? Let's get you cleaned up, boy."

He rested the bat on his lap and wheeled toward the kitchen. Inman disappeared around the corner of the hallway. Hampton found the garbage can flipped onto its side. He managed to set it upright again. Inman was back now, yapping and spinning in circles.

Bang!

Hampton whipped himself around, gripping the bat with both hands. Somebody was in the house. Judging by the shuffling sounds coming from various directions, there was more than one somebody. Hampton tensed up.

Bang!

Through the small, square cutout over the kitchen sink, he glimpsed a shadow flickering across the living room and swallowed the bulge in his throat.

"Hey! Hey!" he shouted, deepening his voice.

Another shadow zipped by. Maybe white, maybe black, Hampton couldn't say for sure. One in tan cargo shorts, the other in slouching jeans. White dime-store T-shirts, one tall enough to bump his head on the light fixture hanging from the living room ceiling. Hampton tried to remember everything about them.

Maybe six foot four or five, long and lanky like a light pole.

The second guy was definitely black, a head-length shorter than the other, Hampton could see now. He was wearing a ball cap, flipped to the back, though he couldn't make out the emblem.

A third figure, a boy who was no older than fifteen or sixteen, emerged out of nowhere and snatched the bat from his hands. Suddenly Hampton was staring up into the barrel of a pistol.

"Hey, whoa!"

"You know what this is," the man-child's voice said.

There was an air of certitude to his words. Hampton took note of the shoulder-length dreadlocks, his bony shoulders, the width of his bowlegged stance, the small silver cross that pierced his left earlobe, and his narrow, jet-black eyes. Hampton froze as the men ransacked the house.

"Please, I don't have any money," he begged. "I swear. Brother, I'm broke like you."

"Y'ont know what I got, and I ain't your brother, bitch."

"I didn't mean—"

"Shut'cho gawt-damn mouth."

Hampton blinked uncontrollably. Even if he had thought to swing it, the bat would've been no match for the bullet to his skull that would surely follow.

Suddenly Inman leapt at the gunman.

"No! No!"

Pop! Pop!

Hampton slumped forward in his wheelchair, soundless and trembling.

"Nigga, we whatn't supposed to kill no fuck-ass dog," he heard one of them say.

"Mu'fuckah almost bit me in the nuts," the baby-faced gunman said with a shrug.

The nine-millimeter was on Hampton again. He felt the hot tip pressed against the center of his forehead. He slowly raised his hands in the air, squeezed his eyes closed, and started praying out loud.

"Hail Mary, full of grace..."

Click.

"God help me."

"You ain't shit your pants, did you?" the gunman said, tucking the pistol into his waistband.

The man-child smirked as he turned and trotted out of the house, leaving the front door wide open. The screen door banged against the frame. Hampton watched helplessly as the trio got into a green Camaro they'd left running in the gravel driveway, backed out, and peeled off down the street. Inman lay on the threadbare carpet, his jaws open, his eyes fixed forward.

Hampton started to dialed 911, but hung up.

The house was busted up, but the best he could expect was a crime scene tech dusting the place for fingerprints and leaving him with a file number. He didn't have renter's insurance anyway, so a police report was worthless. He wasn't even sure what, if anything, had been taken. Then an alarm bell went off in his head. He checked his laptop. The monitor was cracked, but otherwise in good order.

Hampton sat in his open doorway and let the soft summer breeze sweep over him through the broken screen. A neighbor had been robbed and shot in his front yard weeks back, while unloading grocery bags. The entire ordeal had Hampton pining for a nice one-bedroom apartment out in the suburbs. Maybe Sandy Springs or Dunwoody, he couldn't decide. But for the traffic, Alpharetta seemed nice.

That night, Hampton took a shovel, lay on the ground, and dug a hole in the backyard. He struggled to hoist Inman's lifeless body into the shallow grave and began covering him in scoops of red clay. Under the bright gray-tinged moon, he said a final prayer before he pitched the last bale of loose dirt over the body and packed it down with the back of the metal spade.

To Hampton, lying there on his back, on the flat, dry ground, alone and staring into the starless sky, the moon was as far away as it had ever been.

You don't know what kinna people you messing with. If they got him, please believe they can get at you and me.

If some low-dollar punks could get into his house, anybody could, Hampton thought as he scooted into his bedroom. He decided the wrought-iron burglar bars that his landlord offered weren't such a bad idea after all. For once, he was glad Claire had left him.

Nigga, we whatn't supposed to kill no fuck-ass dog.

THIRTEEN

Once featured on dueling covers of *The Atlantan* and *Southern Living*, the house at 439 Blackland Road, with its nineteen rooms, indoor-outdoor pool, majestic waterfalls, and dreamlike gardens, was a sight to behold. The massive French Revival home contained what one centerfold headline called THE MOST BEAUTIFUL ROOM IN ALL OF ATLANTA.

It was there, beyond a fifteen-foot arched doorway, beneath a sun-drenched atrium, that Libby Gail Loudermilk took her tea.

The week had been insanely busy, thus Libby Gail was pleased to finally have the space to herself. Their son Quinn and the daughter-in-law, whose name Libby Gail refused to utter aloud, were off on a new adventure a world away. The house staff was busy resetting the mansion for another round of expected guests. A favorite cousin from Arkansas, another from Virginia, a stepsister and her husband—a newly elected governor—coming down from South Carolina. There were accommodations to be made and dietary concerns to be addressed. Though the social season had come and gone, Libby Gail would throw a grand reception in their honor. She'd placed a special order for a beautiful white truffle to be flown in from Tuscany for the splendid cauliflower risotto she planned for the occasion.

Virgil had promised to be back within the hour, and like clockwork he appeared, dressed in a natty suit. This was unusual, as her husband was generally given to a more uninspired style of dress. A pair of pressed tan slacks, a starched button-down shirt, and a pair of well-broken-in leather loafers with which he refused to part were often the best he could muster from day to day.

Virgil couldn't find it in himself to get worked up about a houseful of their relatives. He was no fan of his brother-in-law, the "yellow dog" who Virgil said was a Republican in name only. At his wife's behest, he'd ordered a hefty campaign donation sent for their political action committee.

Virgil loosened his necktie and took a seat in a tufted armchair. "Did young Master Quinn and his bride get off well?" he asked.

"You missed them by a few minutes," Libby Gail replied, stroking the cat in her lap. "Quinn said he would call from San Francisco, between stops. Where, dare I ask, have you been off to, wearing such finery?"

"Here and there. How long are they supposed to be in Singapore anyway?"

"A few months, maybe more. He'll miss his dear mama before long."

"Of that, I am sure."

"How did your meeting with Mayor Dobbs go? You never said a word about it edgewise."

"Never said I had one."

"You know this is the biggest small town on earth. Gracious, Virgil, did you honestly think that I would not hear?"

Virgil flashed a pained smile.

"What devilment are you up to now?" Libby Gail pressed.

"A bit of company business," Virgil responded warily. "She had some things to get off her chest."

"Such as?"

"Nothing of any note, really."

"That's what you said the last go-round."

"How 'bout them Braves," he said, looking for a more manageable topic.

"Season's off to a good start, don't you think? Shelby Miller almost put in a no-hitter the other night."

Libby Gail took a long drag on her silver-plated vape, sat the cat down on the marble tiling, and tipped her nose up.

"When are you gonna learn to knock?" Virgil said.

There stood one Leland "Lucky" Mitchell in a getup that could only be described as eccentric. He was wearing a pair of red velvet loafers that Virgil hadn't seen before. He'd heard the rumors about those shoes, though he'd written them off as back-fence talk among the women. But there they were, plain as day, proof positive that Lucky had too much money for his own good. They even had a gold metallic stitching on the top just like his sister, Wilma, said they did.

"Harold let me in," Lucky said.

"Good heavens, Leland. What on earth have you got on?" Libby Gail said with measured amusement, calling him by his given name.

Lucky was having trouble catching his breath and was making sounds that vaguely resembled words. Virgil hadn't seen him like that since the time he hit the Mega Millions numbers one day and the multistate Powerball game the next. He drove around town in a spanking-brand-new Ford F-250, with spinners in the wheels. His dog, Biloxi, a mutt Lucky found wandering in the parking lot of a casino over in Mississippi, was always in the passenger seat, resting his head on his big paws.

Lucky had lost the Mitchell family fortune three times over, once in an ugly divorce to his second ex-wife-turned-politician, Sarah, but he'd more than made it back at high-stakes, underground poker tables around the world—the very reason everyone came to call him Lucky in the first place. That, and the point that he was bedding a beautiful Latina thirty-two years his junior, sealed it for Virgil.

"I need a word with you," Lucky said, still huffing and puffing like he'd run a country mile. "Alone," he said, rolling his eyes at Libby Gail.

Libby Gail quietly rose from the settee, gathered her accoutrements, and disappeared through the archway.

"Hell, Luck, you sound like you ran all the way down West Paces Ferry. What's this all about? Did you meet up with that detective?"

"Sure did."

"And?"

"This ain't right, Virgil."

"You ain't going weak-kneed on me too, are you, Luck? Where's your spine?" Virgil said. "Between you and Whit, I'd be doing better with a yard full of buckeye chickens."

"Here, look at this," Lucky said, finally laying out an array of documents and photographs on the coffee table.

Virgil took a deep breath, thumbed through the neatly laid piles, and then started purring like Libby Gail's cat.

"Well, I'll be damned," he said gleefully. "Look at here, look at here, look at here! So many secrets in the garden, and some of them even more delicious than others." He smacked his fatty palms together and said, "You know what we've got to do now."

Virgil was sure Whit would be upset, though he'd warned his softhearted brother about the storm brewing. Whit was a compassionate man who was slow to anger, and Virgil knew he could take matters only so far. Even so, he knew Whit could raise the devil out of hell if it came to it.

Loudermilk & Associates had two clients: William Whitney Delacourte, Jr., and the company his and Virgil's father started with nothing but a stick loan from a pawnshop in 1957. Whit Sr. had bought out the whole shop and the strip mall it was in with the proceeds from a big stock bet, and began investing in telephone wire. Newspapers, radio, and television stations would soon follow. They bought up everything in sight, including the *Atlanta Times-Register,* a local television station, and two radio outfits. Then came cable television and broadband expansions. One thing led to another, and suddenly Delacourte Enterprises was the largest privately held media conglomerate in the country. They went public in 1989, and the company stock never saw a bad day.

For a lot of years, working for his brother meant nothing more than Virgil's cashing quarterly retainer checks and sitting on the board of the family company. Whit had been the kind of client every lawyer dreams about. He paid his bill on time, had few requests and even fewer complaints. Virgil grew rich without so much as lifting a finger.

When he wasn't serving as executive vice president and chief legal counsel of W. W. Delacourte Enterprises and its many business units, a job with few real responsibilities, Virgil kept himself busy teaching corporate law at Emory University, volunteering at Peachtree Road United Methodist Church, playing checkers and puzzle games with Lucky, and chewing a steady diet of pan-fried catfish. At least twice a year, he and Libby Gail would head down to the Sea Island, off the Georgia coast, where they had a house on the beach, and pretend they were newlyweds for weeks at a time.

It went on like that for years until the day Whit showed up at Virgil's office, unannounced, twenty-odd years back. When Whit told him what he wanted, Virgil got up from his desk, locked the door, and pulled the blinds. They didn't come out until after the sun went down. For four days, they met at eight in the morning and closed shop at eight in the evening.

On the evening of the first night, when their wives asked where they'd been, Whit mumbled something about how they'd been fishing for bluegills and bigmouth bass out on Lake Rabun. Never mind that their trucks had been seen parked in front of Virgil's office all day, their clothes were bone dry, and neither one of them had any fish to show for it. Whit never could tell a good lie. Patsy Delacourte wanted to throw a fit, but the look in Whit's eye told her not to question him. Libby Gail took her husband's silence on the matter as the only answer she needed.

"Virgil, at least call your brother first. Are you sure you want to do this?"

"Politics ain't a bean bag, my friend."

"You ever been hit in the eye with a bean bag?"

"Whit knows what's coming. Besides, she cursed me right to my damn face. She'll pay for that. You can bet your fancy slippers on it."

FOURTEEN

She grilled two sockeye salmon fillets and roasted ears of summer corn, wrapped in foil and still in their husks, over charcoal on the back deck. There would be fist-sized dollops of egg salad, laced with sweet pickle relish and sprigs of rosemary, and homemade barbecue sauce lathered on the fish, he knew. Claire was a distinctively southern woman in all of her ways, down to the neatly placed silverware. Hampton delighted in her cooking, almost as much as her milky, peach-dipped skin and golden-brown hair that flowed like a cape over her smooth shoulders.

They took polite sips from two heavy glasses, one filled with white wine, the other with the lemonade she'd squeezed, laced with honey and spiked with cayenne pepper, as they traded small talk. How life had been, how it was now, but nothing about tomorrow. No hopes, wishes. No dreams. No well-laid plans. Being here with her, the warmth of the fire, the light in her eyes were enough for Hampton. He would not ask if she was seeing someone new. If there was somebody, and surely there was, that somebody was not him.

He'd kept up with her on Facebook. The status updates, infrequent as they were, told him that she was doing just fine. He needed to know that. He never once gave in to the impulse to comment on the happy photos she posted. Her life now was her own, and he'd done his best to move on.

The night air was pleasurable. The mosquitoes were tamed by a row of flickering citronella candles. Her shimmering sheer lip gloss and the way the straps of her sundress fell over her shoulders mesmerized him.

Hampton knew Claire would want to know what happened to Inman, a rescue dog they'd adopted from a no-kill shelter off Howell Mill Road. There had been no children, and Inman was the only thing left that tied them together. Hampton knew she would be shaken by the news. Though, he didn't expect a return text message so immediately or the invitation that followed.

Can you come for dinner?

It took a full hour to get up the nerve to respond. There was a lot he wanted to say, though he thought better of it.

Sure. Say when.
Tomorrow, if you are free. Casual. 6:30 okay?

Hampton left the office at noon the next day, went home, and tossed in a load of laundry. He took a longer-than-usual shower, scrubbing away the collected filth, before slipping on a polo shirt and a pair of cargo shorts, fresh out of the dryer, and a pair of lace-up dock shoes. He decided to leave his wheelchair at home and stopped off at Clip Appeal for a long-overdue haircut. He wanted to look good for Claire. He wanted his ex-wife to see a freshly shaven man, standing on his own two feet. For good measure, he even spritzed himself with a dash of cologne.

He was on the road by four that afternoon. A normally thirty-minute drive up GA-400 to Alpharetta would take at least ninety even if rush-hour traffic was good and his minivan didn't break down.

The Abbotts Landing subdivision was as nice as he had imagined. Middle-class people living in neat homes, with two-car garages and manicured lawns, backing up to a golf course. He found the address at the end of a cul-de-sac, a two-story traditional brick-front adorned with white columns. There were no barking pit bulls tied up in a yard behind a chain-link fence, as in his neighborhood. There was no loud music thumping out of passing cars and no sign of Beaver, the homeless guy who frequented his block. Compared to Hampton's place in Candler Park, Claire lived in paradise.

The mailbox at the edge of the driveway read TOLSEN. She'd resumed using her maiden name after the divorce, but seeing it now, spelled out in gold letters in front of such a lovely home, with its well-tended lawn and pristine walkway, reminded him of what he had not been able to give her.

Hampton pressed the doorbell, waited, and then knocked on the front door. He leaned on his crutches as he waited for an answer, until he realized it had been left unlocked.

"Ruby Claire?"

"In here!" he heard her call from the kitchen. "You're early!"

She was stirring up a pitcher of lemonade.

"It's virgin," she said. "No Jack Daniel's."

"Fair enough."

Hampton hoisted himself onto a bar chair and watched her intently as she moved briskly around the kitchen.

"Can I help?"

"Don't you move a muscle," she said.

"Well, I'm not sure how many of my muscles actually move, so . . ."

"You know you're the only person on the planet, other than my grandmother, who still calls me by my whole name, right?"

"Sorry, I can't help it. How've you been?"

"Good, good."

She smiled, cautiously, Hampton thought. He knew her expressions. There was nothing, even now, that she could hide from him. He knew she was nervous too, this being the first time they'd spent any time together since their last court date. In all honesty, he had not expected to see or hear from her again.

"Hey, you walked in here," she said. "That's progress."

"If you can call it that. These things leave bruises," he said, raising one metal support off the floor. "Nice place."

"Yeah, I was lucky to find it. Close to work, no traffic jams. It's a rental. I'm hoping my bonus check will be enough to top off a good down payment on a mortgage."

"Ms. Tolsen, I'd give you the rest of my 401(k) money if I still had it to give."

It was the first sour word Hampton uttered. He hadn't called her by her maiden name since he presented her with an engagement ring and asked for her hand in marriage. Claire let it pass.

"Let's go outside. No need in wasting perfectly good weather," she said. "We can eat out on the deck."

He followed her through the sliding glass door, hobbling over the threshold. Claire was right, it was a nice evening and even nicer that he could spend it with her. He plopped down onto a patio lounger and leaned his crutches against the deck railing. They traded more small talk, about this, that, and the other. It went on like that until he finally worked up the stomach to talk about the break-in and the goon squad that killed his beloved dog. Glassy-eyed and stammering, he told her what had become of Inman. She worked the fire as he retold the story, avoiding flourishes. He had not been brave. Hampton wanted her to know that.

"There were three of them. Two black, one white, I think. One of them pointed a gun right in my face. I couldn't keep Inman off of him. And then he killed him, right in front of me."

"I am so sorry...."

"It was bad, Claire."

"What did the police say? Do they have any leads?"

"I buried Inman in the backyard...."

"What did the police say?"

"I didn't call them. You know how it is downtown. These things happen. I'm glad you weren't there."

"I don't understand. Gunshots, call the police. That's how it works. They killed Inman, for heaven's sake!"

"Maybe out here—"

"Did you at least go to a precinct and file a report?"

"They didn't steal anything, not that I own anything worth taking. My pride, maybe."

"At least you can get that back. What did they look like?"

"Like I said, two black, one white. I thought I recognized one of them. He couldn't have been more than sixteen. I can't say for sure, but he's the one that shot Inman."

"A damn kid?"

"Yeah, a kid." He paused and said finally, "I've missed you. I miss us."

Claire's eyes started welling up. "I know it sounds funny, but Inman was like the baby I never had. I needed to hear how it all happened. It hurts so much and I guess you're the only one I can share that with. I'm sorry to bring you all the way out here. I didn't want to go through this alone."

There was a long silence, several loaded sighs, and stolen glances.

"I didn't want to leave him," she said. "I figured he was all you had left, and I couldn't take him from you."

"I was wrong. I need you to know that."

Claire gracefully ignored his entreaty, checked the fish, found the center deep pink, and decided it was well enough. The corn was done too. Hampton was intoxicated by the scent of brown sugar and butter that floated from the foil wrappers.

"Are you ready to eat? I'm sure you're hungry."

"Starving, really," he said ashamedly.

"It's been a really long time," Claire said finally. "It isn't every day that your husband gets into an accident with another woman in the passenger seat of the car you bought him."

"It was a really nice car," Hampton said, trying to break up the mood.

"What happened to her?"

"Shoshana?"

Claire nodded.

"She's fine. Moved out of state." Hampton took a deep breath and said, "I'm sorry, Ruby Claire. I'm sorry that I did that to you, to us. Sorry that this is probably the first time I ever said so."

"It is."

"What do you want from me?"

"I'm not sure what I want."

"I've always wanted you," Hampton said.

There was more silence, more sighs. For the fourth and fifth time, Hampton noticed a chilly distance open up between them. His fish and corn were getting cold now too. He took a bite of potato salad, found it heavenly, and gobbled down some more. She was rambling on about an architectural presentation of some sort, something about a newly proposed high-rise at Atlantic Station.

"It's the largest brownfield-redevelopment project in the country," Claire said. "I'm not the lead designer, of course, but my team is heading up the exterior renderings. It will be a fully green building, state of the art."

Hampton offered up obligatory congratulations as he picked over the salmon.

"How is work for you?" she asked.

"Same old shit, really."

"Still chasing that big corruption story?"

"Feels more like it's chasing me," he said, looking up. "And, yeah, I'm still working it. Writing something that Tucker will publish is a real problem, though. I suppose he's just keeping his nose clean. I can't say that I blame him. He's got a wife and kids."

"So, finish it and take it somewhere else. If it goes as deep as you say, surely the *New York Times* will want it or maybe even *Vanity Fair.*"

"Maybe. Right now it's just a bunch of dark money flowing through campaigns."

"What's dark money?"

"Basically, it's using campaign disclosure laws to buy an election with unreported money. They set up shop, and then take in as much money as they want from corporations and individuals, without fear of disclosure. Pick a candidate, back them with a shitload of cash, and then wait for the favors to come rolling in later. A bunch of groups ponied up three hundred million during the 2012 presidential cycle."

"Sounds like influence peddling. That's a federal crime. I know that much."

"I would have to find evidence of active collusion between a political action committee and a candidate, and so far, I've got nothing."

"How much money are we talking about?"

"I can't say for sure. Maybe forty or fifty million, maybe more, just in Georgia and dating back to the early seventies. And that's not adjusting for inflation."

"Fifty friggin' million dollars! Who'd they buy, the Queen of England?"

"You could say that."

Hampton was careful not to reveal too many details, even to Claire, and he was determined not to think any more than he had to about Mayor Dobbs tonight. With her congressional campaign set to launch in a few days, he found himself poring over newspaper archives, looking for something, anything that he might have missed. Things were at least quiet between them right now, their full-scale war simmering like a stewing pot of water on the back eye of the stove—still hot, but no present danger.

He found the idea that Chanel Burris and Mayor Dobbs had gone to the same high school intriguing. He'd gone down to Benjamin E. Mays High School, named for the legendary civil rights pioneer and president of Morehouse College, and checked six full years' worth of yearbooks, but didn't find a single class-year photograph of a "Chanel Burris."

Dobbs, unsurprisingly, was both homecoming queen and senior class president. He'd written about Richard "Dickey" Lester last January. He was in the same graduating class and voted Most Likely to Succeed. His nickname was Phoenix, earned for the many track records he broke in high school. There was a nice picture of the two of them—Victoria Dobbs and Richard Lester—leading the homecoming court. Hampton found that ironic, given his current circumstances as an indicted kingpin under house arrest and hers as mayor.

"She is quite the politician, I must say," Claire said at last.

"Who?"

"Victoria Dobbs, of course. I mean, you are investigating her, yes? Queen of England? I wish I had her clothes. Her shoe closet must be divine."

"You deserve a rich husband who can give you all of those things, Claire."

"No, I deserved you."

FIFTEEN

The bulky manila envelope was addressed to MRS. VICTORIA DOBBS-OVERSTREET and marked: PERSONAL AND CONFIDENTIAL. It arrived by courier. No uniform, no company logo on the delivery car, no return address.

Victoria hesitantly peeled open the package. Staring down at the pages and an array of full-color photographs, she wiped her tears on her shirtsleeve. Her daughters were, thankfully, sleeping the night with Rosetta. Unable to sit still for more than a few minutes at a time, she paced the house, then went to the garage. Finally, she dragged out a pressure washer, attached the hose, plugged in the charger, and listened to it hum in the darkness. Nearly an hour later, well beyond midnight, Victoria watched her husband's moon-silver Maserati turn into the driveway. She met him at the foot of the garage, aiming the extended wand of the pressure washer at him like a double-gauge shotgun.

"What's going on?" he said with confusion. "Honey, what're you doing outside at this hour?"

"Bitches!" she shrieked. She pulled the release valve and blasted him with a heavy stream of water. "Your common ass always needed a bunch of bitches!" she screamed, spraying him with another deluge.

Victoria bombarded her husband with vile epithets, "motherfuck" this and "motherfuck" that, as he cowered and shielded his face.

"What in the hell is wrong with you?" he shouted. "Have you lost your damn mind?"

She dropped the metal hose and dashed into the house. Before he could catch her, Victoria dead-bolted the door. Marsh stood outside, leaning on the doorbell, hammering on the door with his fists, and calling her name.

"Torie, please!" he cried.

She finally relented. Marsh, soaked from head to toe, walked cautiously into the foyer.

"Can we talk now?"

"There's nothing to talk about," she said with a smirk.

"I want to tell you everything."

"What's left to say?" she said, screwing off her wedding set and chucking it at him.

"Don't do this," he pleaded, extending his open palms.

"You did this!" she said, jamming her finger in the air. "This is all on you!"

Against his better judgment, Marsh followed his wife down the hallway and into the master bedroom.

"Fuck this shit!" she screamed.

A lead crystal lamp suddenly hit the bedroom wall and blew apart on impact. A barrage of nineteenth-century African wood-carved masks—trailed by a Bose Wave radio, two speakers, several hardback books, and a framed photograph of them that had been taken on their last anniversary vacation—swiftly followed.

"Fuck this and fuck you!" Victoria shrieked again. "You don't get to do this to me!"

Marsh attempted the impossible, to explain it all away under the guise of a failing marriage. He murmured something that sounded like contrition but stumbled over his words.

She exploded again.

"Get out!" she shouted, hurling another round of books.

Marsh rushed in and grabbed her up with both arms.

"Let me go! Damn you, I said let me go!"

"Settle down, baby," Marsh said, his voice growing softer with humiliation as he released her.

Victoria was crying now. A torrent of angry tears spilled down her cheeks. She went to the master closet and dragged an armload of his clothes, still on the hangers, out to the center of the bedroom floor.

His shoulders slumped. "I needed somebody," he said pensively. "She isn't—" he started to say, before he caught himself.

"She isn't what?"

Marsh didn't respond.

"Answer me! She isn't what?"

Marsh answered with more silence.

"Get your shit and get out," she said, jamming her finger toward the heap of clothes.

"I'm not going anywhere."

"You must think I'm weak and dumb enough to let your sorry ass stay here."

"You're launching the campaign in three days. How will that look?"

"I don't need you, Marsh. I swear I don't."

"And that's always been your problem. You don't need anybody."

"Don't you fucking dare put this off on me," she said, hauling an oversized suitcase out of the closet. "You're out here wining, dining, and screwing dime-store whores, and I am to blame for that? This bitch has got you feeling yourself, doesn't she?"

"I can't tell you that she doesn't mean anything to me. I can't lie like that."

Victoria dropped the luggage. She fell over the open suitcase, crumpled up, and sobbed.

"Torie, baby, we have to work this thing out. I'll end it, I swear," he said, kneeling beside her. "I won't leave you. I won't leave our girls. I won't leave this house."

Victoria raised her head and said, "Then, motherfucker, you better not sleep."

The package, now safely locked away, contained ten full-color photographs and a high-definition DVD that Victoria could not bring herself to watch. Her husband's transgressions were painstakingly detailed in a three-page, time-stamped dossier that covered a week's worth of his sins. A rendezvous in a hospital parking lot, another at the Buckhead Ritz-Carlton, and two more in a room she could not readily identify. A printout of his cell phone records revealed hundreds of calls and text messages, extending back over at least a year. Victoria was already drafting the divorce petition in her head.

There had been other women, she knew, some before they married and at least one after. That was the "Atlanta Way," she kept telling herself over the years as one girlfriend after another watched their husbands run off with a mistress. There had been marriage counseling and a teary reunion, and then the twins were born.

She'd combed the pages for a mention of the woman's name. Her face was hauntingly familiar, although Victoria could not immediately place where or if they had met. And then, as she waited for Marsh to come home, it dawned on her. Samantha Jones-Geidner, the thirtysomething reality television star and ex-wife of a record label executive, had been introduced to her by a mutual acquaintance at an Atlanta Medical Association reception two years ago. At the time, she was still married to Stony Geidner, a sixtysomething Jewish entertainment lawyer who invested his fortune on a stable of rap artists. Stony made no secret of his predilection for women of color, and Samantha was as black as she was beautiful.

Victoria found Marsh in the kitchen, nursing his face with a bag of ice. There was a deep gash in his hairline.

"I'm going to need some stitches."

"Samantha Geidner?"

Marsh didn't answer.

"I don't want you here tonight," she said quietly.

SIXTEEN

That was a mighty fine sermon you preached last Sunday, Reverend. I caught it online."

"I do appreciate that, Mr. Loudermilk, and I appreciate your invitation."

"No, please. Call me Virgil. And have a seat. Rest yourself."

The Reverend Dr. Rudolph Goodwin sat down in the black leather chair. He was an impressive creature by any measure, down to his tailored suit, silk socks, and platinum cuff links. The preacher was tall and lean, and Virgil marveled at his chiseled face. No flashy jewelry either, Virgil noticed, just a silver wedding band. Goodwin had a regal, statesmanlike air about him.

"I hear you started your congregation in a school cafeteria. Five original members, right?"

"Including my wife, yes."

"Like the Jackson Five."

Goodwin chuckled, though Virgil felt his reserve. The church boasted over twenty-five thousand members now, live-streamed three services every Sunday, and even had a weekly broadcast on a Christian television network. The plain truth was, Virgil knew near 'bout everything there was to know about the preacher and his humble beginnings. He'd asked J. T. King to develop a full dossier on the pastor, which made for good reading.

Young Rudy Goodwin was raised in a second-floor, cold-water flat with no central heating, on land that later became the Georgia Dome. His daddy worked at Atlantic Steel for thirty years, making metal fencing and wiring for "Mr. Tom" Glenn, while his mama sold hot plates off the back porch at two dollars a whop to pick up the slack. Neither had ever owned a car or anything else, as far as King could discern. A lawyer by training, King was good about these things, in addition to helping to craft solid messaging.

It all made for a splendid rags-to-riches story. A man of meager beginnings, the good reverend now tooled around town in a drop-top Bentley coupe and made use of a private jet. Still, there were problems to be worked out, King advised, though nothing scandalous that would result in unpleasant headlines. Yes, Goodwin was as perfect as his mama's meat loaf. Virgil leaned in and eyed him like a pan of banana pudding fresh out of the oven.

"There is nothing more important than having a family that supports you. I can promise you that," Virgil said, his southern drawl more prominent now. "I like a self-made man. Reminds me of my father. I truly respect what you've built out there."

"We've got six campuses around the country, praise God."

"I picked up one of your books over the weekend. I'm only through a few chapters, but it's off to a good start."

"I'll have my secretary send you the others."

"Oh, when I said 'picked up,' I meant off my shelf. I have all eight of your books."

"I'm working on a new one now. We do our own publishing, and all the profits go to our family foundation."

"You don't say?" Virgil said, already aware of the financial arrangements.

"The proceeds fund our mission trips and college scholarships endowed in my wife's name. She worked her way through Georgia Tech and graduated in three years, you know."

"So I've read," Virgil said. "I'll forgive her for not going to UGA. Y'all have quite a story."

This was their third meeting. The first was at City of Faith, in the pastor's office, and though he was not usually prone to such things, Virgil had been downright mesmerized. The second was in Goodwin's home, equally splendid and situated in a gated south Fulton County subdivision, where Virgil met his charming, dutiful wife, Esther, and their two teenaged sons, Rudolph, Jr., and Ephraim. Some rapper Goodwin called "T.I." lived a few doors up, which meant next to nothing to Virgil.

Now sitting in the Club at Chops, an ultraexclusive, member-only dining room on the lower level of one of the city's premier steak houses, Virgil was sure he had his man. He'd decided on that during their second meeting, over tall sweaty glasses of sweet tea. Goodwin would be his pick, even before his brethren in the League had a chance to lay eyes on him. Try as he might to keep things hush-hush, word leaked out and raised the ire of Victoria Dobbs. He'd been advised, by those paid to look after such matters, that she was moving fast. Big-name consultants were hired out of Washington, and a new field director, recruited from the DNC, was already in place.

His brother, Whit, objected to the latest salvo, but he knew as well as anybody what had to be done. Dobbs had to be stopped. Even so, Virgil hadn't expected a sitting mayor to bash her husband over the head like that. A private detective provided a detailed report of the fisticuffs. The good doctor had four stitches and was now holed up in his cousin's penthouse at the Atlantic off Seventeenth Street near the old steel mill, according to the latest dispatch.

"I apologize for dragging you all the way out here, especially at this late hour. My wife has a houseful of guests, or I would've invited you over for a proper meal. She isn't nearly as agreeable as your Esther, unfortunately."

"I am sure she is lovely," Goodwin said. "The Good Lord doesn't always give us what we want, but He gives us what we need."

"A lot of things describe my Libby Gail. 'Lovely' isn't one of them. She gets downright ornery when I mess with her plans. She'd come in third runner-up to a bullfrog, if it came to a contest, so I hope you don't mind the venue. A few of my colleagues wanted to meet you in person," Virgil said. "I assured them that you were the right man for the Fifteenth District; however, it's an expensive proposition, and we all want to make sure that we're backing the right candidate."

"I value your consideration, Virgil. Losing Congressman Hawkins was tough on all of us."

"It was indeed, and I like your graciousness, seeing as how you and Hawkins got along like two polecats scrapping in the brush."

Goodwin raised a brow, smiling to hide his uneasiness, and said, "He was a good man."

"I suppose you want to ask me how I know that."

"It's no secret that Hawkins asked a congressional committee to investigate my church. We welcomed that."

"That's true enough, though I know it ran deeper than that," Virgil said, sipping a glass of sparkling water. "I hope you don't mind the vetting process. It ensures that we don't encounter any surprises."

"No, no. I expected as much. Like you said, this is a big investment. Is it true that you backed Mayor Dobbs in her reelection?"

"We don't generally talk about whom we have and have not supported, Pastor. But, yes, Mayor Dobbs and I have long been friends. I knew her daddy, a fine man if ever there was one."

"And now?"

"And now I have other interests," Virgil said. "She does call you Reverend Cash Flow, you know."

"Cheap and petty."

"Dobbs can be petty, sure enough, but she doesn't come cheap and neither do you."

"I am a good steward of my many blessings."

"Does that include that private jet?"

"I'm not a pauper. I'm a preacher. I assure you that our books are in order. I do have to say that you have an impressive track record."

"Meaning?"

"Getting Pfeiffer into the mayor's office, for starters. You have to admit throwing your weight behind Boney Jeffries wasn't exactly prudent, though."

"You can't win every day. But, like I said, we don't generally discuss what or whom we decide to support. Democratic voters tend to get their tail feathers in a tangle when Republicans get involved in their affairs. I'll be straight with you. We never meant for Boney to win. His problem was that he talked too much and couldn't control his zipper. And, well, Pfeiffer turned out to be a crook, as we all know."

"So why back him in the first place?"

"We needed heavy turnout numbers that year, so we could win those four city council seats. They got in and promptly shut down any and everything Pfeiffer put his paws on. We snatched the cake right out of his mouth. He was mayor in name only by the time we got through with him."

A server came by, took their drink orders, and hurried off.

"Boney was a real trouper, and to tell you the God's honest truth, it took more effort than we expected to beat him the next time he stepped up to the plate. He was no match for Dobbs, but he did manage to force her into a runoff. She whipped him good the second go-round and near about ran him out of the city."

"I've got seven thousand members who are voting residents in the Fifteenth District, not counting those who will volunteer on the campaign. There are fifteen thousand people on my rolls."

"Oh, don't I know it! We counted. Ran all the names through the secretary of state's voter registration log. You'll need every one of them. If they can't vote, they can walk door to door."

"How did you get our membership list?"

"That's what we call 'margin,'" Virgil said, rearing back in his chair. "With all due respect, Reverend, you ask too many questions."

"I like to do my homework, same as you apparently do. This is my life we're talking about."

"I have to agree with you there."

Virgil settled in and began regaling Goodwin with one of his favorite campaign stories.

In 2009, after forty-two-year-old Atlanta businessman Cecil Yancey, the only other meaningful candidate, dropped dead of a heart attack before he could sign the election qualifying papers, local lawyer and gadfly

Bonaparte "Boney" Jeffries took a second bite at the apple and signed up to run for mayor against State Senator Victoria Dobbs. As anticipated, she took the early lead based on name ID alone and was already picking out new draperies for the ceremonial room in the executive offices. Jeffries refused to back down and the polling numbers narrowed. The Dobbs campaign was stunned when she didn't clear 50 percent, forcing a runoff. Boney trailed her by just under 1,700 votes in the first heat.

The following week, during the three-week runoff, an outfit called Reclaim Atlanta launched a wave of negative television, starring a strategically darkened photograph of Jeffries. They hit urban radio too.

A six-figure media buy, narrated by a distinctly African American voice, ran on V-103's morning drive show, calling him "Phony Baloney Boney." Their slick brochures, itemizing his alleged tax-dodging schemes, turned up in mailboxes in the largely white, Northside precincts. Church parking lots were papered with flyers, with a fake union bug logo, all but accusing him of tax fraud.

"Reclaim Atlanta? That was you?"

Virgil clasped his hands over his belly and answered with a grin.

"And will be again, if you decide to run," Virgil said. "Tell me about Yvonne Ingram."

"She's the executive director of my family foundation."

"And?"

"What are you asking me, Mr. Loudermilk?"

"You know what I'm asking."

"The situation is settled."

"I'll trust your word on that," Virgil said. "Until you give me reason not to."

Thirty minutes into their conversation, Cordie Russell, Bertram DuBose, and J. T. King arrived through the private, members-only side entrance. Whit was running late. Virgil decided to move ahead without him. After a heavy dinner of bone-in porterhouse wagyu steaks and plenty of Chilean pinot noir from Virgil's reserved locker, they got down to business.

King started in immediately, peppering the minister with policy questions. Where did he stand on entitlements? Did he support abortion? Whom did he vote for in the last presidential election? Tort reform, immigration, gay marriage, gun control? King, a former lobbyist turned health-care magnate, covered the gamut like a speed-dating champion. Goodwin took most of it in stride, offering thoughtful answers that seemed to please his inquisitors.

"I like what I'm hearing. That being said, you know if he says any of this out loud, he'll lose in a landslide," King said finally. "The Fifteenth is and always will be deep blue. That's the deal we cut to keep Hawkins in office and keep four black Democrats in Congress."

"J.T., my man, that's what we have consultants for," Virgil chimed in with a laugh. "Reverend Goodwin here is a Democrat, at least on paper. As long as he wasn't caught with a small boy or a dead girl, we can clean it up."

The men chuckled, but Goodwin maintained a serious expression.

"I will not bear false witness," the preacher interjected.

"We don't expect you to lie, son," Virgil assured him.

"Son?"

"I didn't mean it like that. Chalk it up to my country ways."

Goodwin shook it off.

"There are ways to position these things, and most of it will never come up," King said. "Because you are running as a Democrat, most folks will assume you're on their side. We aim to keep it that way."

"Is Dobbs the only opponent we expect?" Goodwin asked. "What about the general election?"

"There won't be a general. This is a come-one, come-all special election, and no Republican with all of their marbles would think to sign up for this," King said.

"True enough. But there is no telling who else might decide to toss their hat into the ring. I hear Sarah Mitchell is toying with the idea of running. That's why we plan to go early and hard," Virgil said. "It'll keep the noise down. If need be, we'll flood the zone with more candidates to dilute the vote."

"I don't even have a campaign manager," Goodwin said.

"You will by morning. We've got everything you need, ready to go," King said. "We'll put together a briefing team and hire a speechwriter."

"My wife, Esther, writes all of my speeches."

"We'll let her look over things," King assured him. "We'll want to make certain the message points are in line with your voice. She can help with that."

Goodwin relented. "Okay, okay." He tossed his napkin onto the table and straightened his tie.

"So, you're in?" King asked.

"My wife and I prayed over this. We believe this is our divine purpose. The answer is yes."

Virgil called for the server again and ordered up a round of cigars and double-malt Scotch.

"Gentlemen," he said, standing under the muted gold lighting. "Meet the next United States congressman from the Fifteenth District of Georgia!"

Whit Delacourte wandered in as the men raised their glasses. "Well, he sure does have nice teeth," he quipped.

SEVENTEEN

The open-invitation party at the downtown Hyatt Regency hotel got off to a grand start. A raft of direct mailers topped with marquee names and a heavy social media push delivered an overflow crowd. Bartenders poured rounds of wine and uncapped ice-cold beers at ten dollars a pop as hundreds of revelers squeezed into the Centennial Ballroom well before the program was scheduled to begin. A banner stretched above the empty podium, emblazoned with the newly unveiled campaign slogan that simply read: BELIEVE.

Reporters roamed between the high-top tables festooned with blue and white balloons, searching the crowd for interviews. Lobbyists, representing big-money interests, chowed on bounteous bowls of chips and nuts, mingling among neighborhood activists bedecked with campaign buttons. B-list politicos and a handful of nameless preachers jockeyed for positions close to the stage while a throng of volunteers checked in attendees on iPads and dutifully handed out self-sticking name tags.

Pastor Melham from Ebenezer, dressed in his finest linen suit and a freshly shaven head, strode in with his wife, Suzanna, and an entourage fit for a king. Melham immediately began chatting up Beau Easley, the president of Central

Atlanta Progress. A dispatch of plainclothes security guards lined the exits, studying the crowd. Another flank covered the podium perimeter.

The woman of the hour remained sequestered in a presidential suite on the twenty-second floor. Earlier that day, Marsh and Victoria had their first meal together since the brouhaha, and the laceration appeared to be healing nicely. The thawing had begun only because Rosetta put her foot down, made the lunch reservation at Canoe, and demanded that they ride together in the same car.

"You're not getting up on that stage without your husband," her mother scolded. "And I don't give a damn how much of a low-down son of a gun he is. Living with your father was no bed of roses, I can tell you that."

"Mother, tell me Daddy didn't."

"Yes the hell he did, and that ain't all of it neither. You can kick Marshall's behind again later, if you want to, and I'll be right there with you, but tonight you've got a race to win."

The Atlanta Way.

Marsh was now quietly flipping through the TV channels in the master bedroom of the hotel suite while a team of makeup artists and hairstylists worked their magic on Victoria in the outsized dining room area. Her mother and the girls were holed up with the remaining family, including in-laws and a host of cousins, in two spacious adjoining suites down the hall.

Victoria hadn't spoken to her brother in the days since she told him that she was bringing on a new campaign manager. Chip didn't take the news well, but given the ugliness touched off by revelations of his connections to Richard Lester, it had to be done. She'd called him twice, at Rosetta's urging, only to be sent to voice mail. She was less concerned about her brother than what she would wear that night.

She'd chosen a belted winter-white St. John suit, coupled with a pair of closed-toe, cross-strapped Gianvito Rossi slingbacks, for the occasion. Her mother's twenty-fifth-anniversary pearls were the perfect complement. Her campaign manager, Roy Huggins, who was hired only five days ago, ran through the announcement speech again before running off a new copy on a mobile printer.

"It's all here," he said, handing her the scripted remarks. "Criminal justice reform, public education, jobs, wage inequality, renewable energy, smart development."

"You know nobody in Atlanta gives a hoot about an energy policy, Roy," Victoria said, interrupting the briefing.

"Except Georgia Electric," he responded. "Clay Robinson is expecting to hear something tonight."

"Fine, keep it. But pare back the language. Clay is a good lobbyist and an even better friend. He'll understand. Add more about social justice, mass incarceration, and gun control. Oh, and comprehensive immigration reform. We need a preemptive strike on Rudy Goodwin and to hit Governor Martinez where it hurts at the same time. Invite Clay in for a one-on-one tomorrow morning."

"But the Concerned Black Clergy breakfast starts at eight A.M.," Roy complained. "Reverend William Barber and the president's faith coordinator are flying in. Dr. Bernice King said she likes to start on time."

"Well, now it starts at nine. We're talking about a bunch of preachers. They'll be late anyway. And you don't know Bernice like I do."

"Who's going to tell Pastor Lowery?"

"You, of course."

"Okay, but remember we've got to get white independents to win. This isn't a Moral Monday rally."

"You're right, this is moral every day. This is a referendum. Change the speech," she said, as the makeup artist began applying false eyelash strips. "Stay around here long enough, and you'll soon realize that there are no independents in Georgia. This isn't California or Michigan. We take sides down here. I can fit all the so-called moderates around here in a shoebox. Make the revisions and get me a fresh copy. I fully intend to defend the Fifteenth District."

"Ma'am, we've got twenty minutes."

"That's just enough time for these lashes to dry," said Victoria, eyeing him warily. "Never mind, I'll do it off the cuff."

"The whole speech?"

"Absolutely."

"But we've spent days—"

"Remember my speech at the Democratic Convention in 2012?"

"Of course I do. Studied it, line by line."

"I never looked at the teleprompter?"

Roy grinned and nodded.

The door clicked open, and Sal Pelosi stepped inside, tailed by her brother, Chip, who was beaming from ear to ear. Chip was a good-looking man, not unlike his father, and dressed to the nines in a Tom Ford suit and slip-on loafers.

"Look at you!" he exclaimed. "Fine as hell, looking just like Mama."

"I'm so glad you came."

"I cain't wait till the niggas see you!" he said, stumbling over a corner table. "Where's that husband of yours? Nigga, where you at? Get on out here, so I can see that split in your wig!"

Victoria immediately soured.

"You're drunk!" she said, jamming her finger at Chip.

"I ain't been drinking, I swear to God, on Daddy's grave."

"You're going to need Jesus, John, Peter, and Paul to keep me from whipping your behind tonight, if you don't turn around and walk out that door."

"We've always been niggas, always gone be, straight up out of SWATS. Believe that."

"Our father didn't raise us on that and you know it. If Mama was in here, she would've popped you in the mouth."

"Daddy is dead and Mama, bless her heart, ain't long behind him."

"You better pray she lives a good long time. Mama is the only thing standing between you and the gutter."

"You're everything Daddy always said you would be. You do know how to count those coins, though, huh? Big house and fancy cars went right to your head. You don't even go by Vicki anymore. Don't sound quite as rich as Torie, eh? Tor-eeeeeee Dobbs. Sounds like some white sorority girl. Or is it Victoria? Which is it now? I wanna make sure I get this right."

She was out of her seat now, draped in a hotel robe with a head full of pin curls, and charging toward Chip. Pelosi stepped into her path. Marsh emerged from the back room and grabbed her left arm before she could plant a fist in her brother's jaw.

"You gone bust me in the head too? No need in holding her back, Doc," Chip said dismissively. "She's full of shit now and always has been. Where your water hose at?"

"If it wasn't for me, you'd be sleeping under a bridge or cooling your heels in the state pen. Never forget that I'm the only reason you aren't in shackles, eating dry oatmeal and soggy toast."

"You ain't never been about shit."

"Get him out of here, Sal. Make sure you keep him nailed down for a few hours."

"You're going to detain me? Under what law?"

Pelosi parted his suit jacket and let Chip get a good look at the revolver strapped to his side.

"You're fool enough to think I need one," Victoria said.

"Oh, so that's how you do your only brother? I'm your blood. You're going to put your goon squad on me? I ain't no hood rat."

"Hood is as hood does."

"You don't want it with me. I'm the last person to want to step to and you know it. I know where your bones are buried. Remember, I helped dig the graves."

"Are you threatening me again?"

"Look at you, clowning like you're some kind of saint. With a cold-blooded-ass wife like you, I get why your husband got him a little taste on the side!"

Victoria resisted the impulse to dive-choke him on the spot.

"Shut the hell up and get sober, Chip, and I might find you a new job. And stay away from those dope boys. Keep messing around with Dickey, and you'll wind up sharing a jail cell."

"You weren't calling him a dope boy back in the day. I was all gravy when you were driving his fancy cars and shopping on his credit cards, right?" Chip shot back. "Queen Victoria, who knew you still had a little ghetto left in you? When the smoke clears, remember it was niggas like me that got you where you at."

He smoothed his suit jacket and strutted out. Pelosi radioed a second man near the elevator.

"Keep Mr. Dobbs on ice," Pelosi ordered. "I'll tell you when to let him go." He turned and said, "Clear this room."

Victoria suddenly found herself alone with Marsh.

"What was that all about?" he said quietly.

"It's just like Chip to get out of pocket. He's out of control."

"So what, he said a word we don't use in our house? If I had a dollar for every time you uttered something foul, I could buy you a whole closetful of Hermès bags. What were you thinking?"

"I wasn't," Victoria said.

"That's clear."

"He deserved it after what he said to me. He wants to destroy us."

"We'll get through this," Marsh said, his voice breaking up and trailing off. He stopped, palmed her face, kissed her forehead, and said, "I want us to get through this."

"I don't know how we do that," Victoria whispered. "I'm being honest. It's going to take more than a nice lunch. This is hard."

"You need to go after your brother. Talk him down. He has to be on that podium tonight. He's been with you the whole way, and you need him on your team."

"I can't afford to have him in that room tonight."

"If he isn't there, people will talk."

"They are already talking."

"So, you're going to throw him out on the street like that? He's family."

"He'll be my brother until the day he dies, but I don't know what Chip is hopped up on this time, and there is no telling what he might do or say. How does he even know what happened at the house? I can't afford to take that chance."

"He didn't seem inebriated to me. A little riled up, that's all," Marsh said, "and you are still my wife, even if you don't want to be, and no matter what we go through, he is ours."

Victoria let out a deep, knowing sigh. She went to the door, opened it, and poked her head into the hallway. "Sal, go get him. My husband and I need to spend some time with my brother. Roy, tell Pastor Melham to start the prayer."

"He might not ever stop talking."

"That's the point."

EIGHTEEN

The rear doors opened and the ballroom erupted. Roaring applause, punctuated by whistles and joyful shouts, as the mayor and her family entered the ballroom just after 8 P.M. Standing room-only, the waters parted as they made their way through the throng and toward the stage. Victoria hugged and glad-handed well-wishers along the way. Her husband was sporting a small bandage on his head. According to the official statement from the mayor's office, there had been a boating accident out on Lake Oconee. A sail whipped around, struck him in the forehead, and knocked him out. Hampton found it curious, if not unbelievable, that the mayor and her husband had taken a road trip only days before the campaign launch.

She was among her people tonight, Hampton thought as he rolled his way around to the right side of the podium and pulled the brake on his wheelchair. The circular configuration was something new, strategically built to allow her to address the indoor rally like a town hall. Dobbs understood the value of good stagecraft. Rumor had it that True Blue Strategies, a team of highly successful campaign consultants out of D.C., was the mastermind behind the work.

Hampton spotted the lead man, Roy Huggins, following closely behind the Dobbs-Overstreet family. Huggins, according to his research, had been dispatched from the Democratic National Committee. That, in itself, was usual given the prevailing wisdom not to get involved when more than one Democrat would be on the ticket. The new website was a glory to behold, and there was a new field director too. While most of the paid staffers were Georgia-bred, the influence of Washington-based advisors was clear. There was no sign of Chip Dobbs, her wayward brother. Hampton figured she'd tossed him out like a load of dirty laundry.

This was going to be less of an announcement than the kickoff of a four-week coronation, though Hampton was sure she would run every day like she was twenty points down. The mayor once made the mistake of taking a state senate election for granted and nearly lost. Mabel Darnell famously called Dobbs a "show horse," and Dobbs quickly paid her back by leaking the incumbent's tax returns, a sealed civil judgment, two misdemeanor assault charges dating back fifteen years, and documentation of a county lien on her house. Dobbs knew how to sling a bucket of mud and come up clean. The one-sided race went down as the most expensive statehouse campaign in Georgia history. Darnell got drubbed and Dobbs danced her way to the Gold Dome.

Hampton checked the battery levels, stuffed his tape recorder into a breast pocket, and waited for the speech to begin. It would be a spectacular show, even with Pastor Melham's lackluster opening. Dobbs, despite her questionable ethics and ofttimes coarse demeanor, was one of the best stump speakers in all the land.

Despite the electricity that filled the room that night, the fight to replace Congressman Hawkins would be nothing short of an all-out donnybrook. Dobbs was stepping into the ring, dukes up and chest out. The Reverend Dr. Rudolph Goodwin was said to be gearing up and had hired a small team that same morning. There was no firm word on timing, but the announcement was expected to come in days, along with a promised lineup of marquee endorsements. A crop of social media pages was in play, and someone was already posting under @RudyInTheHouse on Twitter. Almost as quickly, a spate of bloggers, no doubt hired by the Dobbs campaign, published video clips from his sermons.

Goodwin was a televangelist who gallivanted around the globe on private jets. It was no secret that he sunned in Costa Rica and pushed "prosperity gospel" to his flock of largely working-class black people, who dutifully gave up a tenth of their earnings. The good reverend called it "sowing a seed," but Goodwin seemed more interested in lining his pockets with millions in tax-free dollars. His gated McMansion in South Fulton and a private jet had been a gift from his congregation. In multiple self-published books, he touted "joyful submission" for women and zero-tolerance for the "abomination" of gay marriage. A YouTube video of him and his pastoral staff running through a pile of money spread out over the altar went viral. Some of the videos had been scrubbed from the internet, citing copyright violations, proof that Goodwin already had a small army of high-end lawyers working to polish his reputation.

Hampton had gone to the sprawling church, City of Faith Christian Ministries, the previous Sunday morning and listened to a decidedly less controversial but markedly political sermon. There was less talk about purifying fires and more about the stewardship of voting, as if it were an eleventh commandment.

Hampton scribbled down a few notes, capturing the sights and sounds, as he listened to the magnificent choir sing and watched the collection plates circle the luxurious sanctuary. He wondered how many of the congregants actually lived inside the Fifteenth District, when the church itself stood to the south of the legislative line and squarely in the Thirteenth. The Fifteenth, a straight shot across the City of Atlanta and Fulton County, lay to the west side of the Fifth, represented by Rep. John Lewis, and to the north and east of the Thirteenth, which was helmed by Rep. David Scott.

State Representative Sarah Cohn-Mitchell was said to be rounding up support. Mitchell, a divorcée who still lived like a housewife, was a real surprise. A fiscal conservative and social liberal hailing from Neighborhood Planning Unit A, Mitchell was the ex-wife of Leland "Lucky" Mitchell, minion of one

Virgil Loudermilk. That was one complication that Hampton had not predicted.

Hampton ran out of fingers and toes counting up the potential candidates. Mitchell, who talked faster than a midnight drag race up Buford Highway, was probably running out of sheer boredom, he figured. She had too much money and too much time on her hands, but she knew her way around a good piece of legislation.

Goodwin, the megachurch pastor who bathed himself in the blood of Jesus, was a political neophyte. He had never declared his party allegiance before, though word had it that he would run as a Democrat and Virgil Loudermilk was pulling the strings. Hampton wondered why Loudermilk had jumped ship in a race that would be like sledding uphill in a mud storm. But that was a question for another day, Hampton thought to himself.

Hampton filed an eleven-hundred-word story about Goodwin's rumored political ambitions, complete with both on-the-record and anonymous sources. It was set to go live the following morning.

He scanned the ballroom for other missing faces. City council president Keyes Jordan was notably absent. Jordan was a member of Goodwin's church, and the street chatter had it that he, too, was a closet Republican who ran as an independent to keep his nonpartisan seat. Sadie Brooks-Newkirk, the newly elected chairman of the Fulton County Commission, was also missing, as was H. Milsap Stallworth, the president of the 100 Black Men of Atlanta. Stallworth's absence was odd, given that he never missed a moment in the spotlight. Where one or more television cameras were assembled, one could count on finding Stallworth in the midst.

Perhaps more curious, there was still no sign of Chip Dobbs. The mayor's brother was a political liability, so it wasn't surprising that Dobbs had put him out to pasture. According to the morning headlines, Richard Lester was out on a five-million-dollar cash bond, under house arrest with a court-issued ankle bracelet, and awaiting trial. Chip hadn't been charged, though Hampton figured it was only a matter of time before he cut a sweet deal—if he hadn't already. There were three unnamed informants listed in the Lester indictment.

Hampton watched with intensity now, as Mayor Dobbs traded hugs and air-blown kisses with volunteers and shook hands with a scrum of preachers and assorted business leaders. The ballroom was packed, but even now she had a way of making you feel like she knew you personally and that your deepest troubles were her own. There was real substance under her pretty words, Hampton admitted to himself.

There was big, little, and no money in the room, more than enough to carry an election, by Hampton's estimation. The script would be easy, Hampton surmised. A couple of perfunctory lines about her mentor, Ezra Hawkins, and maybe a few strategically placed tears as she memorialized her decades-dead father.

The entourage continued making its way through the masses. Music filled the air as they hoisted their daughters onto the stage. The mayor's twin daughters, named in honor of Mahalia Jackson and Maya Angelou, wore matching blue taffeta dresses with marvelously large bows cinched at the waist. They were the spitting image of their mother. Their silk-pressed hair flowed down their backs like cascading waterfalls.

Here I am, baby!
Signed, sealed, delivered, I'm yours!

The Dobbs-Overstreet family was a beautiful lot, postcard perfect. Hampton couldn't help thinking that the mayor looked a lot like a movie star as she strode onto the stage, waving like Miss America. She was surrounded by assorted business leaders, selected clergy, and other high-profile supporters squeezed in shoulder to shoulder behind them—a coalition of the willing and powerful, all eager to be caught in the camera shot. Congressmen John Lewis and Hank Johnson were among the chosen few who stepped onto the podium. He spotted David Scott too. Dobbs was stacking the deck.

Pastor Benjamin Melham took to the microphone again. Hampton checked his recorder for a second time. Littering his introduction with praises to the Almighty, the preacher let his voice boom over the audience. Then came Congressman Lewis, his trademark southern drawl and peculiar inflections still prevalent years after the civil rights movement, when he had been kicked in the head by a horse during a protest.

"She did not come to be served, but to serve!" Lewis exclaimed. "Ladies and gentlemen, I bring to you the next congresswoman from the Fifteenth Congressional District. My sister, my leader, my friend—"

BOOM!

Lewis flinched. Hampton reflexively covered his head as the floor rattled beneath him. The lights flickered and the crowd flooded toward the exit doors, clambering to get out.

BOOM! BOOM! BOOM!

The building shook. A team of security guards ushered the mayor, her family, and all three congressmen from the stage and guided them out a side door just as the lights went out. Hampton heard crying and shouting in the darkness. Emergency lamps kicked in, dimly relighting the room. Hampton could see burly security guards pushing people out the bank of doors. He released the hand brake on his chair and gripped his wheels.

For all his grumbling about the APD, Hampton was relieved when a uniformed officer grabbed the handles of his wheelchair and pushed him into the crowded hallway. The escalators had been shut down.

"Any idea what's going on?"

"Fire in the parking deck," the officer said. "The elevators are out. We'll take the stairs."

"Seriously? Anybody hurt?"

"That I don't know, sir."

The officer flagged down a second, and together they carried Hampton up three flights, in his chair, and into the atrium-capped lobby. He could smell the putrid smoke now. The fire alarms screeched. A firefighter shouted orders over a bullhorn.

Outside, Peachtree Street was already lined with frightened hotel guests, employees, and nosy tourists. First-responder vehicles came from every direction. Plumes of thick gray smoke billowed from the front valet drive, which descended into the underground deck. Hampton caught sight of a slender boy blowing by on a skateboard.

Babyboy404?

They locked eyes briefly as the teenager paused, then hiked up his jeans and zoomed away. Hampton noted his dreadlocks tied back in a knot, his narrow jaw and cocoa-brown skin.

Babyboy404?

Hampton felt an urge to give chase, though he was immediately glad he couldn't afford to pay for hotel parking and had left his minivan in a metered spot, a block over on Portman Boulevard. The story was already writing and rewriting itself in his head as he arrived at a Starbucks near the corner of Seventh and Peachtree.

NINETEEN

Rosetta was telling her son all about the ladies over at Starr's Beauty Palace, and how she suspected Mrs. Lorna Boone was cheating at bid whist, when an orderly walked in. He greeted her respectfully, as if she were a head of state, and placed a clear plastic bag on the nightstand. Chip was still unconscious, but Rosetta was sure that he could feel her presence.

As he drew closer, Rosetta realized she found the hospital attendant oddly familiar. There were sprigs of gray along his temples and he had soft yet serious eyes.

"Mama Dobbs, you don't remember me, but I ran track and played football with Chip at Mays. We're all pulling for him," the white-clothed orderly said. "I'm going to the prayer vigil at Elizabeth Baptist, if I can get off work early."

She hesitated, then asked, "What's your name, son?"

"Roger, ma'am. Roger Thompson. They used to call me Skeeter in school. Still do."

"Well, praise Jesus. You're Willie Thompson's boy, right? I see it now. You talk like him too."

"Yes, ma'am."

"How long have you been working down here?"

"Going on twelve years now."

"Pray for my son, will you?"

"Yes, ma'am, I will," Roger said. "And we're praying for Vicki too. She's come a long way since we graduated from high school. I knew she'd make good."

"Indeed. I hope you will vote in the special election."

"Yes, ma'am. I remember when I cast my first vote for mayor. Maynard Jackson. They don't make them like that anymore."

"I imagine they don't," Rosetta said.

"He made this city. White folks ain't like it none, but Maynard was our man."

"Indeed, he was."

"Sam Massell fired a thousand garbage workers after a thirty-seven-day union strike. Maynard stood shoulder to shoulder with men like my father, and they helped him take the mayor's office."

"You know your history, son. Too many have forgotten."

"Now this city is changing. All those people moving into all those big high-rises," Skeeter lamented. "I hope you don't mind me saying, white people."

"Speak your heart, son."

"Westside don't even look the same. Fancy restaurants and condos, full of happy white folk. I got on a MARTA train last week to get down to my part-time gig at the airport and I was the only black face on there. They buying up the whole Westside too. Cain't even get a studio apartment off Northside Drive with a whole month's pay nowadays. Ain't that something?"

"That's a shame," Rosetta said. "Folks oughta be able to afford to live in the city if nowhere else."

"Vicki is on our side. She's one of us too. My mama packed up and moved out to Villa Rica five years ago. Sold her house on Oglethorpe Avenue over by West End Mall. The buyer was some real estate development company out of Germany. They paid cash."

"Sure enough?"

"Yes, ma'am," Skeeter replied. "They say if it keeps going on like this, with everybody moving up and out, the next mayor will be white too. I'ont mind that, but I cain't even get tickets to a Falcons game, and the Braves moved to Cobb County. They blew up Atlanta–Fulton County Stadium and built a new ballpark, but we never got the development they promised, and now that's gone too. My daddy's sister got a nice check to move off the Hill, but she's staying with my mama now because the money ran out. Hurts my heart."

"She ain't by herself. Too many families can tell the same story."

The Atlanta Way.

Rosetta was thinking now about the Grand Bargain, about the deal cut between black political power brokers and wealthy white business leaders. Dating back to the early '70s, and further if she admitted it to herself, the unwritten treaty assured black leadership in a majority-black city, even if they didn't hold the purse strings. The biracial partnership kept the city on a solid business footing, winning an Olympic bid and a torrent of economic development over nearly a half century. It spelled the difference between St. Louis, Cleveland, or Chicago—deeply segregated cities where black people living in decimated neighborhoods wielded little in the way of political power. For decades, Atlanta had fought to maintain the balance of race and class, of wealth and poverty, but people living on the margins mostly lost out.

Even Skeeter, a nine-dollar-an-hour orderly at a public hospital, knew the math. And Rosetta knew it too. Her late husband, the Reverend Dr. Park Dobbs, had been an early proponent, an architect of the political landscape on which their daughter now stood. The fight had been hard, blood had been let, but a new generation of beneficiaries—black and white alike—knew little of that legacy. The lone hope lay with her daughter, Rosetta lamented, not to turn back the clock but to right the road ahead. She prayed that her husband's dream would be enough to stave off the winter she knew to be coming, that Victoria would continue to embrace that hope.

"She's one of us," Skeeter said again.

"Indeed," Rosetta replied, deep with measured regret.

"I won't keep you. I'm praying for Chip," he said.

What was left of her youngest child's charred suit lay inside the bag.

Rosetta rose from her chair and took hold of it. Skeeter disappeared down the hall.

The Marcus Trauma Center at Grady Memorial, named for Home Depot cofounder Bernie Marcus, has fifteen beds, including seven dedicated to resuscitation. Chip had arrived by ambulance with complex solid organ injuries, including a perforated kidney and liver. The left side of his skull was crushed, and if he survived, they said he would need reconstructive surgery.

The facility, situated along the downtown connector on Jesse Hill Drive, was less than a mile from the downtown Hyatt, a brisk walk across Woodruff Park and through the Georgia State University campus on a pleasant day.

Victoria found Rosetta there, in a heavily guarded room in the "red" section of the trauma center, still clutching the plastic bag of clothing.

"Mama?"

"They say he might not ever be the same."

"None of us will come out of this the same."

The breathing machine hummed and a heart monitor let out pulses in the oddly odorless room. Victoria could see a patrol officer's heavy leather shoes under the separation curtain, which gave her slight relief. She was satisfied that Grady Hospital security knew how to handle high-profile patients, and there were dozens of APD officers stationed in and outside the hospital. Even so, there were plans to move him once he'd been stabilized and placed under federal protection.

The regional ATF director and Agent Clearwater from the GBI briefed her that afternoon. An explosive device was rigged to Chip's remote key fob. Chip was four parking spaces away when the police sergeant sent to retrieve him called his name. He heard his name and spun around, but not before clicking the keyless entry button.

Click, click. BOOM!

Chip unwittingly detonated the switch tied to the wireless locking system, and the matte-black Porsche 911 exploded. The force of the first blast knocked him forward, rendering him unconscious as his head planted against a concrete pylon. A second and third car caught fire, igniting the gas tanks, kicking off another round of blasts.

The sergeant, badly burned himself, radioed for help as he dragged Chip by his armpits into the glass-fronted motor lobby. Within the hour, the fires were contained and ATF agents sealed the deck and two floors that housed conference rooms above it. Guests were rebooked at surrounding hotels, leaving the Hyatt dark and empty for the first time since it was built in 1967.

"We seized ninety-six hours of surveillance footage, and every parking attendant has been questioned," Clearwater explained. "We ran every license plate through the state DMV. We're interviewing the owners, one by one."

As the joint task force waded through reams of evidence, Chip clung to life with burns to over two-thirds of his body. It took three surgeries to repair his liver and kidney. His face was fully wrapped in gauze, leaving openings for his eyes and the tracheal tube. A central line was attached to his chest.

If only I hadn't made him leave in the first place. If only I had not . . .

Victoria struggled through the blame, reliving the horrible fight with the brother she loved. He'd been right about a lot of things last night. How she regarded herself as above it all, though still desperate for public approval, even denying her husband the respect of taking his name.

Now sitting with Rosetta, cupping her veiny brown hands in her own, Victoria remembered how she'd spent her whole life protecting her brother and now thought God seemed to have been protecting him from her.

"This is my fault, Mama. I let this happen."

"Enough with that. I won't let you sit up here and talk like that," Rosetta protested. "I heard about that foolishness up in that hotel room."

"I'm sorry, Mama."

"No need in that. No right or wrong as far as I can see. You two have been at it since the day your father and I brought him home from the hospital. You bucked and hollered more than he did."

"Did I really?"

"You didn't even like me holding him. You wouldn't let me nurse the boy in peace."

Victoria allowed herself a pained smile. She spotted a wrinkled envelope, singed at the edges, on a tray table next to a sweating cup of ice.

"Where did that come from?"

"It was in his suit coat pocket," Rosetta said. "There's a fancy piece of construction paper in there, shaped up like a bird or whatnot. I think little Chippy might've made it. You remember that boy Skeeter Thompson from school? He brought it in here with your brother's clothes."

Victoria went numb. Her legs stiffened.

"What is it, dear? Are you alright?"

She shook her head and said, "Yes, Mama. I'm fine. And I remember Skeeter. I got him a job down here back when I cochaired the Fulton-DeKalb Hospital Authority."

Victoria grabbed a pair of latex gloves from a box on the counter and carefully opened the envelope. Suddenly there was a knot in her throat, and she could not breathe. Her thoughts drifted back to Ebenezer, the Sunday morning when Ezra Hawkins was killed. Gunshots echoed in her head like a cascade of fireworks. Her mother's voice began to roll in the background and echoed through the haze as though it were coming from the other side of a mountain. It looked like a bird, maybe a dragon, just like the one she'd found in the congressman's Bible. The origami was a message of some kind, she knew. One she did not understand. Victoria now felt like there was a target on her own back.

She'd collected more than her share of political enemies. Be it somebody who didn't get a city contract, somebody she beat in an election, somebody else she didn't endorse, or still others who simply did not like her hard-boiled, take-no-prisoners style. That was the cost and tax of doing business. Victoria could number and name all of them from rote memory. But things were different now.

For his part, her brother always wandered too far over to the other side of the proverbial tracks, hanging out with hustlers, petty thieves, and dope boys in one strip club or another. She'd warned him, time and time again. But there was little Victoria could do to keep him from that life. Though now, she couldn't put away the suspicion that the car bomb was tied to the carnage that unfolded at Ebenezer, and that it had everything to do with her. She suddenly felt like a sparrow trapped in a gilded cage.

Her brother was now lying mutilated in a hospital bed, in a medically induced coma, unable to speak or breathe on his own. A central venous catheter, pumping barbiturates into his body, protruded from his chest. The mechanical ventilator and feeding tubes were keeping him alive.

"Mama, the prayer service is starting soon, and I think I should go," Victoria said, trying to hide her trembling hands. "Lieutenant Pelosi will see to it that you get out to the house. Your room is ready and my officers will stay with you. Two in the house, two in the driveway. Promise me that you won't leave here with anybody but Sal."

"I need to stay right here with my son."

TWENTY

Hampton hadn't been over to Manuel's Tavern since before the accident, and if he had his druthers, he wouldn't be going now. It took more than three days and a barrage of emails and phone calls to reach her, and when she finally picked up, Valerie Norbreck-Haynes was plainly annoyed.

"The only people who chase me down like this are publicity hounds, telemarketers peddling fake car warranties, and reporters looking for work. If it's a job you're after, we don't have any openings," she said abruptly, before he could explain why he needed to talk.

"I'm not looking for a job," Hampton said.

"You should be, from what I hear," she said dryly. "What do you want, Mr. Bridges?"

"A few minutes of your time. I need to run something by you."

"Well, spill it. I've got three reporters on deadline, and I'm staring at a fifteen-thousand-word rough cut of a Sunday magazine piece that my boss plucked out of the slush pile and flung onto my desk. Claims it has Pulitzer potential, but I'd rather set myself on fire than edit another mini tome about white America's opioid crisis. Damn thing reads like a botched version of *War and Peace* without the French invasion, so make it quick."

Hampton let out an audible sigh.

"Sixty seconds."

"Not over the phone. Can we meet in person?"

Valerie relented and suggested that they meet at Manuel's Tavern on Highland Avenue. Hampton wanted to balk. Being around alcohol, months into his sobriety, wasn't exactly a good idea. Sleep came easier now, and the ugly hangovers were all but a distant memory. He was a more peaceful man, Tucker would say, although he certainly could live without Hampton's wiseass sense of humor. Most of the progress, of both the mental and physical variety, was due to his ex-wife's prodding. Seeing her made him feel alive again. And he cautiously hoped she was feeling something too.

One day at a time.

Hampton took his first shot of whiskey chased by a swig of beer when he was fourteen, the summer after his freshman year in high school. Jimmy Lee Bridges, in his infinite wisdom, said getting his boys drunk would build up their tolerance for later. He lined up a row of shot glasses, a pint of Jim Beam, and a six-pack of Stroh's on the kitchen table and talked girls, sex, and booze. Florence vehemently objected to the proceeding, which didn't end until both boys were splayed out on the linoleum-tiled floor, laughing like a pair of feral hyenas. Her husband claimed he was getting Hampton and his young brother, Jason, ready for the real world, such as it was.

Hampton knew his probation officer would surely frown on his excursion to the bar, even if it was technically a work-related meeting, and one bad night with a decent bottle of bourbon could land him back in jail. If there was one thing Hampton hated more than his daddy, it was spending six nights in a county lockup and the six months of court-ordered, twice-weekly Alcoholics Anonymous meetings that soon followed. He'd fallen off the wagon just once since his arrest, to awaken on his toilet, still drunk, with his pants around his ankles, and soaked in his own vomit.

He arrived just after 5 P.M. and found Valerie perched at the front bar, sipping on a bottle of Red Brick, a craft beer that Hampton was once fond of. He felt a pang in his throat and swallowed hard. Back when they were married, Claire always kept the refrigerator stocked with Red Brick and canisters of High Road ice cream, two of his favorite local creations, and only now had he come to appreciate that. She'd cooked up a plate of broiled fish tacos and black bean salsa and delivered them personally last night.

That she'd called about Inman was not a surprise, given how much she'd loved their mutt, and he silently hoped she had some love left for him. He'd said both too much and too little, he lamented. He was still in love, he had to admit, with the one woman who made him want to be a better man.

Claire promised more visits and more food. She'd even paid to get the muffler and alternator on the minivan repaired and the grinding brake rotors replaced. Hampton wouldn't let himself feel bad about that, despite his previous infidelities, seeing as how the divorce cost him every dime he had and the spare pot he pissed in.

It was a Saturday evening and slow by Manuel's standards. Regulars populated the booths on weekdays after work. Hampton and Valerie traded casual banter until he asked about a string of stories she'd published about Congressman Hawkins. She suggested they take it to the back room.

"You smell better than you did the last time I saw you," Valerie said with a playful sniff.

The Eagle's Nest, situated in the rear, was up a short flight of stairs. Hampton navigated the risers, carefully shifting his weight on his crutches.

"Need some help?" Valerie said, placing her palm on his back as he wobbled up to the landing.

"I'm good, thanks. I know it doesn't look it, but this is getting easier. I hear they're going to renovate this place soon, rip it up and start again. Maybe there'll be a handicap ramp."

"I heard about the accident. Sounded like it was pretty bad."

"It was, but here I am. Fresh as a daisy," Hampton said as he struggled into the booth. "See? No worse for wear."

"You're a really good writer," she said. "I'd put you right up there with some of the best local reporters around the country. Your stuff reads like a Fleetwood Mac revival."

"Thanks, and thanks again for coming," he said. "Like I said, I'm not looking for a job."

"They probably would have fired you if you weren't on modified duty. You know, with lawsuits and all."

"I would've fired me too. I spend every day re-earning my job. Strange as it sounds, that sometimes means taking some risks."

"I hear you're difficult."

"That's a generous assessment. But what reporter worth their salt isn't? Half the job is nailing the story. The other half is fighting with a snot-nosed lawyer to get it published."

Valerie nodded in agreement.

"The news business has changed," she said. "Walter Cronkite didn't have to worry himself about some 'citizen journalist' with a half million Twitter followers going after network advertisers to get him canned. Can you imagine Peter Jennings doing battle with some college dropout slurping ramen noodles and chugging Red Bulls, who posts conspiracy theories from his grandmother's basement between rounds of *Call of Duty*?"

"It's a different ball game, for sure."

"Most days, especially when I make appearances on cable news, I don't have the stomach to look at my social media mentions. Nefarious players aside, this is now a multilateral conversation. Our very credibility is under attack."

"More like a firing squad."

"Learn to endure the lawyers. Keep writing. Let it be bold, but get it right."

There was nothing fancy about Valerie, Hampton noted. She was a straight-shooter, he knew, at once jaded, deeply invested, and protective of their profession.

"We're the Fourth Estate," Hampton said. "Though I wonder how long that will survive."

"We're guardians," Valerie added, "and the barbarians—ugly, bloodthirsty, and armed for war—are at the gates. But we will survive."

She'd come dressed in a dowdy light blue blouse and a frumpy dark brown skirt, looking more like a meek, bespectacled librarian than a sword-wielding general defending the final bastion of journalism. Her long, blunt-cut brunette bangs fell just above her eyebrows, which Hampton figured had never been plucked. She reminded him of his fifth-grade social studies teacher. Valerie, like Mrs. Bateman, eyed him seriously, if not with a healthy dose of suspicion and contempt, over her wire-rimmed eyeglasses.

"You've been around here, what, eight or ten years now, right?"

"Who's counting?" Valerie said with a shrug. "Longer than I thought I would be."

"It's an interesting city, wouldn't you say?" he said, trying to break the ice.

"About as interesting as a pile of lug nuts most days," she said. "And then there are days like this."

"Tell me about it. Can I ask you something off the record?"

"Depends," she said, pursing her lips.

"You remember that big transportation bill that got killed up in Washington?"

"Of course. There hasn't been a fight like that around here in years. One would've thought it would sail through like syrup on a snow ski."

"That was quite a dustup," Hampton said. "I thought for sure the Georgia congressional delegation would hold together on that one. The plan would've changed the entire face of the region. And Atlanta would have been the biggest beneficiary, no doubt. Got killed in committee."

"We like our cars around here. Even more surprising was the way that state senator from East Atlanta teamed with the North Fulton County Tea Party to fight it," Valerie said. "What's his name again?"

"Horace Moreland. He claimed that not enough black-owned businesses were getting a piece of the pie. Moreland still can't get a ticket to the Mayor's Masked Ball, not that he wants one. All that corporate money in one place would probably make him break out in hives. I hear he's been popped for speeding at least four times since the vote, and the city keeps tagging his house with obscure code violations."

Valerie took a swig of beer and said, "Yeah, that's the one. Appears he barked up the wrong tree."

"I thought Dobbs was going to knock his teeth out of his mouth," Hampton said, sipping his Arnold Palmer. "Ezra Hawkins came out against it too. I can't remember a time when he and Dobbs were on opposite sides of anything. Any idea why?"

"Off the record?"

"Off the record."

"You've got me on that one," she said. "What I can tell you is that Hawkins got a big payout for initially supporting it. Went straight to his foundation. Then he flipped."

"Come again? We're talking about the same Saint Ezra, right? Resident do-gooder with a dozen streets, schools, and federal buildings named in his honor?"

"They bought him, rest his soul," Valerie said. "He took their money, and then changed his mind for some reason. Said it was the minority contracting thing, but I never believed that."

"Must have been a hefty sum to pay off somebody like Hawkins. Who bought him?"

"Not so much as one might think. And the same people who will fire you if you keep asking questions."

Hampton's head started twirling. Of course, Hawkins was in bed with the League, and that meant Virgil Loudermilk would've been calling the shots. However, the notion that Delacourte Enterprises was somehow involved in a direct payoff to a sitting member of Congress didn't seem to line up with how they did business. It would explain why Tucker summarily killed his story pitch about the independent expenditure campaigns they ran.

"Let me get this straight. Somebody associated with Delacourte Enterprises bribed Hawkins for his vote and then got stiffed?"

"That's my hunch, but you didn't hear me say that."

"Please tell me you're kidding."

"I do not kid, Mr. Bridges. You have to know that by now. It appears the good congressman was having second and third thoughts about his vote and decided he could support the bill with a few conditions. I have the draft language of an amendment he was going to introduce before he was killed."

"Saying what?"

"One of the big points was stripping the sole-source contract language of the legislation. That meant, if passed, every procurement contract would have to be placed out for public bid by an independent, community-controlled commission, and the mayor's office would have no say in the process."

"So Hawkins was sidelining Dobbs?"

"And her brother."

"That's right, Chip Dobbs used to run the city contract and procurement office."

"Until you went and got him fired."

"The question is why put them out of the game?"

"That's the question for the ages," Valerie said. "There's also the question of whether she received any cash for her support."

"Can I see the draft amendment?"

"I've got a hard copy," Valerie said. "I'll scan and email it over."

"No, no," said Hampton, shaking his head vigorously. "Can I come pick it up?"

"That's a lot of trouble to go through when I can send it to your personal email account."

"I'm not so sure that's a good idea."

"Okay, fine," she relented. "You can drop by to pick it up Monday morning."

"One more thing. Why would Delacourte Enterprises care about a transportation bill?"

"Well, there's another good question. If I knew, I would've put a reporter on the story. No way our legal team clears a piece like that without hard evidence of a bribe. Answer that, and I might have a job for you after all."

"Thanks, I'll keep that in mind. By the way, how'd you get the Hawkins Amendment?"

"You know better than that," Valerie said. "I'm only giving it to you because there are a dozen other ways to get it and you're, well, infirm at the moment. Call it a professional courtesy."

It was getting on eight o'clock, and if he made good time, Hampton could make it out to the prayer vigil for Chip Dobbs. He thanked Valerie again and said he'd swing by her office to pick up the document. As he made his way over Freedom Parkway and onto the downtown connector, Hampton racked his brain. A once tightly stitched alliance was now coming undone at the seams, and decades-long allies were turning on each other—one was dead, another clinging to life, and still another was about to mount a bid for Congress. He needed to figure out what the Delacourtes wanted with that transportation bill and what, if anything, Victoria Dobbs had to do with it.

TWENTY-ONE

The mayor's caravan floated over I-20, passing the Hamilton E. Holmes Drive exit, toward the westerly edge of the city. The evening traffic was sparse, even for a Saturday, and she felt alone in the back of the Suburban as the downtown skyline disappeared over her shoulder. She felt the walls of the vehicle tighten around her, the air suddenly dense and suffocating. Her lips quivered and she felt her body shudder as they made the exit onto I-285 and merged into a southbound lane.

"Take the Cascade Road exit, Sal," Victoria said finally. "Hang a right and pull into the Publix parking lot."

She called Chief Walraven from her cell.

"I need to ring you back," he said in a low voice. "We're wrapping up a task force meeting."

"It's urgent."

Minutes later, Victoria was pacing the shopping center parking lot, never veering far from the two plainclothes FBI agents who'd exited their car and stood near the rear of the SUV. Another stood on either side of the nose. Sal stayed behind the wheel. Her cell phone buzzed.

"I think I found something," she said, cupping her hand over her mouth. "I don't know what any of it means."

"I'm listening," Walraven replied. "Go ahead."

"I think whoever tried to kill my brother shot up Ebenezer too."

"Caleb Vasquez is dead, Mayor Dobbs," said Chief Walraven. "Feds ran the ballistics. It was a clean match. Everything we've got says he was just a guy who caught a bad break on his military discharge and couldn't get into the VA."

"That happens too often, but listen," Victoria said firmly. "He didn't do this alone. I promise you that. Somebody sent him, and I don't think they're finished."

"Ma'am, did you know your brother was going to testify against Richard Lester?"

"He would've told me."

"Your brother was protecting you."

"From what?"

"He was a government informant against a major drug cartel. Your brother knew what he was into."

"And you think Dickey blew up Chip's car? We went to high school together, for Christ's sake. I've known Dickey all of my life."

Victoria started pacing again, walking in small circles as she talked. Richard "Dickey" Lester had been her high school sweetheart, even though her parents forbade her from dating. They met up at Greenbriar Mall back in the day, stealing kisses in the parking lot when nobody was looking. Good-looking and smart, he was always dressed to the nines, even starching his jeans, and drove a brand-new Mazda RX-7. Dickey was a star athlete, netting three state titles in track in his junior year. Everybody called him "Dickey Phoenix" because he seemed to fly around the curves and blow through the finishing line tape. The word was, some college recruiter bought the car and paid off the mortgage on his mother's house.

Outside of practice, Dickey didn't spend much time around school that Victoria could recall, but he somehow still managed to make the honor roll. He'd show up on test day, ace the exam, and leave before the last lunch bell rang. When he did show up for a full day, they sat next to each other in AP American History. Victoria was dazzled by the way he spat out answers before Mr. Demby could finish a question. Even then, everybody knew Dickey sold weed, though he never did anything in front of Victoria. He used to call her "Big Time."

"You're going places, Big Time," he told her a few months before graduation. "You don't need me holding you back."

Victoria was heartbroken when Dickey showed up with Ericka Borders to the junior-senior prom. She had gone alone, dropped off and picked up by her father, while Dickey and Ericka came in a stretch limousine after a fancy dinner at Mr. Hsu's downtown. Wearing a floor-length, shimmering sequin gown, Victoria beat back tears as she and Dickey walked the aisle together and were crowned Prom King and Queen.

"Don't cry, Big Time," he told her as they danced to Keith Sweat's "Make It Last Forever" under the crepe paper streamers and rotating disco ball. "I'm with Ericka tonight, but I'll always be with you."

That fall, during her freshman year at Spelman College, Dickey popped up on campus in a two-door, drop-top, white-on-white Mercedes-Benz. She wanted to ask him where he'd gotten the money, but thought better of it. Besides, when she started dating a Morehouse premed student named Marshall Overstreet, Dickey stopped coming around.

Some years later, there had been a rendezvous in Chicago during the '98 DNC Convention, when Dickey showed up unannounced at Midway Airport and ferried her to dinner in a gleaming red Maserati. She was a twenty-three-year-old Harvard Law first-year back then, and Dickey, who'd finished three years at Georgia State before dropping out, was running strip clubs in Atlanta. The Gilded Kitty was doing good business, with lines cascading out the door and a VIP check-in reserved for various professional athletes and chart-topping rappers. He was in Chicago, scouting a new location, Dickey explained. He'd opened another in Miami and one in Houston too.

They spent their first and last sunrise together in a suite at the Waldorf-Astoria on the Magnificent Mile. An outsized bouquet of long-stemmed red roses, a chilling bottle of white gold Dom Pérignon, and two champagne flutes awaited their arrival. Dickey, she noticed, paid the bill with a black American Express Centurion Card. The next morning, they went for a leisurely walk along Lake Michigan and talked about a future together for the first time. Victoria had been taken with his attention to detail, how he'd spared no expense to ensure her every comfort.

Make it last forever.

She was in love and had been from the first time she laid eyes on him. There were more dates, more cities, and more than a few promises she knew he could not keep. There were other women, Victoria knew, and making a life with Dickey seemed foolhardy. The breakup happened while they were on vacation in Nevis and came as suddenly as a midsummer island rain. There had been an argument, fueled by questions he refused to answer.

"I won't lie to you, Big Time. You gotta stop asking about things you don't really want to know."

Victoria got on the plane alone.

Soon after that, she rekindled her romance with Marsh. Dickey went ghost again, and it would be another two years before Victoria heard from him. By then, Marsh had proposed. Dickey sent an engagement gift, a beautiful oil painting of the newlyweds that Marsh refused to hang in their house. It was common knowledge, even then, that Dickey was running a drug ring and laundering cash through his nightclubs. He was still known as "Dickey Phoenix" on the street.

"Richard Lester is the biggest heroin dealer in the Southeast," Chief Walraven reminded her now. "He's cutting it with straight fentanyl too, and we've got the bodies to show for it."

"We had our differences, but Chip wouldn't agree to testify without telling me about it, and Dickey wouldn't lay a hand on him."

"You're talking like you still know him. He isn't the same young man you went to high school with."

"Some things are hard to let go," she admitted. "It's been more than a few years since I last talked to him."

Dickey had meant something to her, at least then, and her to him. That she knew for sure. It seemed like a lifetime ago. Spilling everything for Chief

Walraven didn't seem wise. At least for now, Victoria decided not to mention the origami she'd found in the congressman's Bible or the one her mother discovered tucked inside Chip's clothing. The figures were both red, pressed together the same way, and looked like birds.

A phoenix?

"Mr. Lester is a dangerous man," Walraven said.

She'd long suspected the nightclubs were a front. There was too much money, and too few office hours. Despite her warnings, Victoria also knew that Chip maintained a relationship with him long after her own had ended.

Mr. Lester is a dangerous man.

"Mr. Lester hurt a lot of people, and some of them didn't live to talk about it. One of his foot soldiers was lit up like a Christmas tree last year, coming out of his mama's house in College Park. He bled out on her front porch. And don't forget one of his lieutenants was charged in that arson case nine years ago. A woman, her three kids, and a firefighter died in that fire over in the Bluff. The only reason Lester hasn't been convicted of anything yet is because prosecution witnesses almost never make it to the courthouse."

"The woman out on Alexander Boulevard? She was connected to Dickey?"

"She was a prisoner in her own home. She had key-lock burglar bars on the windows and doors. A squadron of firefighters got in right before the roof collapsed."

Situated in the English Avenue–Vine City corridor, the Bluff spans roughly ten square blocks and sits in the shadow of the Georgia Dome. Despite every crackdown and every attempt at urban renewal, the open-air drug market flourished. Sonia Hill, according to news reports at the time, died with her children in 2005. They were huddled up under a mattress.

"Lester was behind that, we know," Chief Walraven said. "All because Ms. Hill owed one of his punk-ass dealers seventy-five dollars and couldn't pay him fifty-cent on the dollar in interest. She was murdered over a hundred twelve dollars and fifty cents. We got the guy who set the fire, but he never put it on Lester. Wouldn't even speak his name. Six months after the conviction, they found him hanging by a bedsheet down at Jackson State Penitentiary."

"You're saying Dickey had her killed over some pocket change? You can't even buy a ticket to a Falcons game on money like that."

"We couldn't tie him to it, but, ma'am, that is how Lester does business. No way to make it to the top of that pyramid without spilling a lot of blood. By the time the ATF raided his house in Alpharetta, he was running everything north of Florida and south of Virginia, stretching west all the way to the Mississippi–Louisiana border. They used the RICO Act to confiscate nine cars and four houses, one of which is a mansion down on Sea Island."

"And you think he tried to kill Chip?"

"Whatever your brother knew, it was enough to put twelve ranking members of the Sex Money Murder gang behind bars. The lead indictment against Mr. Lester was sealed until the gang unit could build the cases and get the remaining suspects into custody. Once it went public, the bodies started dropping. Your brother was the last remaining witness."

"Then why in the hell wasn't he in witness protection?"

"He refused. Two weeks ago, he stopped talking altogether."

"Right after our godfather was murdered."

"And you think the two are connected?"

"I don't know what I think anymore."

"The GBI traced a green Camaro that was seen parked close to your brother's vehicle. Pulled out fifteen minutes before the explosion. The Camaro was reported stolen down in Dublin. Carroll County sheriff's deputies found it torched over on the west side of Villa Rica early this morning. ATF took a suspect into custody a couple of hours ago. His cell phone records tied him to Rochelle Charles. She lives over off of—"

"—Camp Creek Parkway," Victoria said, cutting him off.

"That's her. The suspect is her fourteen-year-old son, DeVonte. It's his second arrest inside of two weeks. Got picked up for shoplifting at Lenox."

"She is Dickey's half sister," Victoria said almost inaudibly, leaning on the grocery store buggy in the parking lot. "DeVonte is his nephew."

Victoria felt the numbness washing over her and she did the math in her head. Dickey's younger sister, Rochelle, was a year behind them and pregnant before she hit junior year. She had three kids now, and DeVonte was her youngest son. If DeVonte was involved, Victoria thought to herself, then so was Dickey.

"Chief, are you sure about all of this?"

"The device was far too complicated for some fifteen-year-old middle school dropout to configure," Walraven said. "He was probably just a lookout. But, yes, we're fairly certain Lester was behind this."

"Rochelle lives over there with her mother, Miss Gloria, and her stepfather. The bigger Atlanta gets, the smaller it is. Are you going to bring her in?"

"We brought Rochelle in for questioning this afternoon. Neither she nor her son are talking. Bond hasn't been set yet, but as I understand it, his grandmother offered up the deed to her house. The feds seized Lester's assets under RICO when he was indicted, but I'm guessing the lawyer is pro bono since he's DeVonte's uncle. Dickey's older brother Riley Lester damn near beat us to the interrogation room."

"Dickey's very own in-house legal counsel."

"I assume he's simply a placeholder. Right now, it's only stolen car and arson charges. If your brother dies and they can pull the case together, the state will put him on for first-degree murder. He's too young to face the death penalty, but twenty-five to life is a big bargaining chip."

"To make him talk?"

"That's the calculus," Walraven said. "But if I'm DeVonte, I'm more afraid of my uncles than a jury."

TWENTY-TWO

Half the 1994 graduating class of Benjamin E. Mays High School showed up to the prayer vigil at Elizabeth Baptist. This was Chip's church "home," even if he rarely found his way into its pews. His college roommates from Morehouse, Scooter Taylor and Kevin Harvey, sat next to Althea, Chip's live-in girlfriend, who was weeping and clenching a small white Bible. Despite conflicting reports of his death, Chip was still on life support at Grady Memorial Hospital. No doubt, somebody somewhere was writing his obituary.

As the mayor entered, walked down the aisle, and ascended the stairs to the platform, the sanctuary fell into a hush. Four FBI agents stationed themselves on opposite sides of the altar, and four more stood near the rear entrance. There were others outside, sweeping the parking lot, she knew. As she scanned the faces in the sanctuary, she could not shake the feeling that she was being watched.

She'd come to this pulpit before, both in gladness and in mourning, as both a candidate and as mayor. She started by formally thanking the pastor for opening the doors on such late notice and the ushers for standing duty on a

Saturday night. She extended her gratitude to the investigators and the medical team, and that drew a hearty amen.

Victoria surveyed the mass of people before her. Some had been present the evening before, awaiting the thundering campaign speech that never came. Others were long-missed friends from the old neighborhood, her Spelman sisters, rows of Morehouse men, colleagues from the state legislature, her mayoral staff, and still other people she saw too little of. There were political allies and onetime foes alike pressed in among the fold. News cameras lined the upper balcony. CNN carried the service live.

Her husband, Marsh, sat off to the right, in the first pew on the lower level, his arms stretched out and embracing Mahalia and Maya on his left and right. He'd braided their hair himself, Victoria could tell. The crooked partings and messy plaits were visible even from a distance. On any other day, she would have been embarrassed and chided her husband for bringing the girls out in public like that. But Marsh was filling in the gaps, and tonight she was grateful.

She grinned painfully at Althea and her nephew, Chippy, with whom she had rarely visited. She didn't even know what kind of ice cream he liked or the name of the stuffed bear he was holding on to. She knew he was four years old, but couldn't recall his actual birth date if her very life depended on it. That would change after tonight, she swore to herself. Like Victoria, Chippy shared his grandmother's light, caramel-brown skin. Chippy had his father's wide, nickel-sized eyes; full lips; and long, lanky body and was likewise prone to bursts of excitement.

"Auntie Vee!" he called out. "Mama, Mama! That's Auntie Vee!"

Althea quickly shushed him and pulled the slender boy onto her lap. Victoria bowed her head in silent prayer, the audience following suit.

"Amen," she said after a few moments.

When she opened her eyes, she spotted Hampton Bridges on the far right end of the balcony. His presence was no surprise. Even though she abhorred him, Victoria was growing accustomed to Hampton's being among the press corps again.

"The doctors say it doesn't look good," she said solemnly. "They say he is lucky to be alive, even for this long. They asked me what kind of man he is. Was he the type to give up and give in? They wanted to know what kind of will he has. They said his survival depends on that. I said: 'He's a Dobbs.'"

The church roared. Victoria spotted Riley Lester seated in the third row and swallowed her breath. Their eyes met. She did not flinch. That he had come to this place, knowing that his own nephew would almost certainly be charged in connection with the bombing, was obscene. Victoria nodded in Riley's direction. If he had come with a message, and it seemed clear that he had, she sent one in return. And so, it began.

"My brother came into this world fighting, and he won't leave here without one—"

The church thundered again with rolling applause. Victoria waited for a cool spot and continued on.

"So, then, I stand here tonight not only with a heart of sadness for his current condition, but also in a gladness that only hope can bring. I rejoice in the miracle yet to unfold. We are a believing family. Ours is a radical love.

"Those of us who know Chip best also know how much he loves this town. You are his ATL, the city that gave birth to him, and the city that raised and educated him. You lifted him up when he was right and busted his backside when he was wrong. I know something about that too, amen," she said with a grin and a small laugh.

"Our mother is with him now, holding his hand, praying for him as he wanders through the valley. His Atlanta, and ours, is a city of many hills— Peachtree Street Hills, Garden Hills, Summerhill, Druid Hills, Castleberry, Brookwood . . . ," she said. "But for every hill there exists two valleys."

"Amen!" somebody shouted.

"Storms will come. Tough winds will surely blow. Though even as the earth shakes, together as a people, as a city, as one family, we will stand resilient in the face of the evildoers," she said, glancing at Riley. "We will not shirk nor shrink nor wither on the vine. We will not turn back."

"Amen!" came another voice from the pews. "Go 'head, sister!"

"We will not run and hide away in our houses or shutter our storefronts. We will not stop congregating in hotels and church houses. We will not stop living and loving. We will not give you this city!" she bellowed, jamming her finger in the air.

In a single breath, she said, "To the bomb planters, to the snipers mounting rooftops, to anyone who attempts to terrorize, murder, and maim, to rain down evil across this land, I say this: Like a tree planted at the water's edge, we are one people and we shall not be moved!"

They were on their feet now. Marsh pumped his fists, beaming with pride.

"I am married to an extraordinary man and the mother of two girls that I could not live a single day without," she went on.

Victoria locked eyes with her husband. Marsh nodded his head as if to say, "Tell them."

She paused then, glanced down at the empty lectern, and gathered herself.

"God of our weary years. God of our silent tears," she uttered.

Victoria looked out over the sea of people, who were still standing, waiting for the word they knew was coming.

"I am mayor of this great city, born and bred not more than a mile from this church house, and with God's blessing, I will one day soon walk the halls of Congress in your name."

Hampton sat straight up in the pew. The mayor was on fire now, like she was preaching a sermon. Riley stood, clapped politely, and grinned.

"I will carry your water to the highest hill in the land and back again! What was meant for evil, the Lord above meant for good!"

"Hallelujah!" a man called out from the back.

"Praise be to God!" came a woman's voice.

"Selah!" shouted another.

The rear double doors parted, and Sal Pelosi appeared, holding it open as Victoria's mother stepped into the sanctuary. She paused, stood breast out and dignified yet solemn. It was the same look Victoria remembered from the day they buried her father.

Rosetta began to sing.

Why should I feel discouraged?
Why should the shadows come?
Why should my heart feel lonely
And long for heaven and home?

Her impassioned voice grew in strength as she made her way toward the pulpit.

When Jesus is my portion,
A constant friend is He.
His eye is on the sparrow
And I know He watches over me.

The masses joined in with the second stanza. Victoria left the lectern and met her mother center aisle. She melted into Rosetta's breasts. The gathering, still singing and some now crying, raised their hands to the heavens.

"It's alright, dear heart," Rosetta said softly but assuredly, rubbing her daughter's back. "He's gone, baby. Your brother passed on. To be absent the body is to be present with the Lord."

"God is close to the brokenhearted," Victoria whispered, quoting Psalm 34:18. "He is my rescue."

TWENTY-THREE

Virgil and Libby Gail spent much of the day touring some newfangled winery over in Rockmart, Georgia. Lunch was a dry and ungodly arugula salad tossed with withered strawberries, pecan crumbles, and feta cheese. There wasn't a decent cut of meat in the whole place, including some overbaked, tough-as-shoe-leather chicken drowned in an indiscernible mix of seasoning. Virgil swore the "summer wine" tasted like swamp water. Why anybody with the good sense of a greylag goose would attempt to farm grapes in Northwest Georgia was beyond his understanding.

"We drove damn near to Alabama," Virgil protested as they pulled into the driveway, "for a plate of burnt yardbird!"

"Well, I enjoyed it," Libby Gail said dismissively. "Next time, I'll leave you at home."

"By all means, please do!"

By midafternoon Sunday, Virgil was still mad and teetering on the brink of starvation. He fished through the cabinets and discovered nothing worth eating aside from a sleeve of focaccia party crackers and a slightly questionable container of crab dip. He stuffed his jowls until he wasn't mad anymore.

Thanks to her meddling stepsister, Libby Gail was on another raw food diet, and there was nothing else in the house but root vegetables and a pile of fruit that he didn't want any part of. He thought about ordering delivery, but quickly realized he'd never so much as called for pizza without Libby Gail's help.

Harold, the houseman, was out back helping Libby Gail rearrange the yard furniture for the second time that week, and Virgil was told they were not to be disturbed. He wanted to raise a stink, but he knew that would only get him another lecture about his own eating habits, a discussion he'd avoid at near 'bout any cost. Virgil decided it was better to sleep it all off.

He woke up just past nightfall, tucked what was left of a 750-milliliter bottle of Bulleit Bourbon under his arm, and headed to the theater room on the lower level. Virgil tossed back a shot, relaxed deep into a stadium-style recliner, and cued up a series of newly produced campaign spots. He grinned as the first video lit up the wide screen.

He lit a cigarillo, taking several long drags as he admired his handiwork. Reverend Goodwin was simply magical on camera, just as Virgil had imagined, and that lifted his spirits. The pastor's broad shoulders and compassionate yet strong demeanor were everything Virgil dreamed they would be. Goodwin was a son of Atlanta and a man of God. Virgil hated to think that he might one day be disappointed in the pastor. He didn't worry so much about the issues as he did holding the line on Goodwin's narrative as a family man. There were problems, he knew, given the reverend's purported extracurricular activities. Laying aside rumors that Goodwin had a Velcro zipper, the minister was still his best shot at taking down Dobbs. Virgil worried that a "bimbo eruption," as he liked to call such matters, might spoil his plans. Goodwin swore everything had been put to bed, so to speak. Still, he trusted preachers less than politicians, and this one was as slick as week-old bacon grease.

Recruiting a viable candidate to mount a bid against Dobbs in the special election, other than the customary yahoos and suit-fillers, had been tough sledding. The pickings were slim. No small thanks to his own doing, Dobbs was Hawkins's heir apparent and had been for a dozen years. Few others had the name recognition, the fund-raising prowess, or the courage to take her on. Backing Dobbs in previous races was Whit's idea, but despite millions spent on one election or another, the anticipated payoff never came to fruition. The alliance was troubled from the start. Her loyalties had always been as questionable as the week-old crab dip rumbling in his stomach.

She took courtesy meetings, but did little to advance legislation of any direct benefit. Sure, Dobbs tossed a few crumbs their way. However, when it came down to it, she did just as she pleased. Truth be told, Hawkins delivered much of the same. The late congressman outright refused to place their pick for the Federal Communications Commission on the president's desk. That deciding vote, a ruling that regulated ownership of multiple media outlets in the same market, had been costly. And killing so-called net neutrality, a hard-fought issue involving pay-for-play internet speeds, had nearly busted the deal. In the most recent skirmish, an omnibus transportation bill that failed in committee after Hawkins refused to sign on, Virgil watched billions turn to dust. There were rumors that he was about to file an amendment that would revive the legislation before his untimely demise. The proposed legislation would have cut Dobbs out of the deal, and Virgil was certain she would fight like an alley cat to keep it off the floor.

Virgil would take pleasure in her political demise. Dobbs was, at least in his mind, too big for her proverbial britches.

No permanent friends, no permanent enemies.

People disappear when they die, he thought with another puff. Such is true about politics too, Virgil reasoned. One minute you're at the top of the heap; the next, you're lying supine in a cheap pine box. If he had his way, this would be the last election for Victoria Dobbs. She'd quit or lose. Virgil didn't care which. That little housewarming gift he'd ordered sent to her house was the first salvo. He was armed and ready to unleash a treasure chest full of her indiscretions.

Bet on black.

Rudy Goodwin was good enough, as far as Virgil was concerned. In only a few days' time, he'd assembled a small staff and created an aggressive campaign calendar. An email blast would hit a hundred thousand voters at mid-

night, followed by a press release due out by 4 A.M., just in time for the
morning news producers to get a bite. Goodwin, surrounded by a thousand
supporters, would be on the Capitol steps by noon, in time to make the midday local newscasts. Virgil personally looked over the speech and decided it
was nothing short of magnificent. The preacher's wife had a few inconsequen-
tial revisions, and he let them pass. Virgil knew the value of a happy wife.

Happy wife, happy life.

The national networks would show up too, given the nature of the race
and the death of Hawkins. The first round of campaign ads would hit the air-
waves with the 5 P.M. newscasts and keep rolling through until the late-night
talk shows came on.

"All lives matter," Goodwin said in one thirty-second spot. "Yours and
mine, from the cradle to the grave."

Of course, the unstated message was that Goodwin was pro-life and supported the death penalty, but according to the high-priced consultants who
were paid to study such things, voters would read different things into it.
Goodwin wanted to say "womb" instead of "cradle" and demanded that he say
"life" instead of "lives," but J. T. King, who had been assigned to personally
handle Goodwin, swiftly rejected the idea during the videotaping session. Virgil thought the pastor was going to storm right out of the studio. He knew
King could have a hard edge.

King was a tall, slender, bookish-looking man who always got down to
the point. It was his job to keep the preacher in line and on message. Virgil
watched as he ran his fingers through his shock of jet-black hair and tried not
to let his frustrations get the better of him.

"I'm with you on that," King said, "but you've got to remember who lives
in the Fifteenth. This is one of the most solidly blue districts in the country."

"I am who I am," Goodwin responded.

Virgil was forced to remind the preacher that this wasn't his pulpit.

"Our team at Aristotle Strategies tested 'all lives matter' and determined
a clear majority of colored folks find it more favorable than 'black lives,'" Virgil said.

"Colored?" Goodwin said.

His discomfort was clear. Goodwin was half out of his chair and appeared ready to bolt.

"Oh, I apologize," Virgil responded, correcting himself straightaway. "I meant to say 'African American.' Blame my head, not my heart. I came up in another time."

"I prefer 'American,'" Goodwin said, retaking his seat. "One nation, one people."

"This is Atlanta," King said with measured annoyance. "You can be 'black' or you can be 'African American.' Pick one."

"You're going to lecture me about race?" Goodwin shot back. "I've been a black man all my life. I was born in this skin and I will die in it, but I won't ever be 'colored' for him and nobody else."

"Pastor, I meant no disrespect," King said, lowering the temperature. "You have to understand the political landscape. Some things won't go over well with African American women, and they represent a substantial part of the electorate. They will decide this race."

"Indeed," Goodwin said. "I'm married to one, you know."

"And you're running against one," King said. "Hell, Victoria Dobbs knows half of them by name."

Virgil remembered how the remark seemed to poke Goodwin in the chest. It was clear that he didn't like being lectured by a white man. But, even after all of the haggling, the commercials turned out pretty good as far as he was concerned.

Virgil trained his eyes on the theater screen. There were three commercials featuring Goodwin. A fourth and final ad, starring Victoria Dobbs, began playing as Lucky walked into the media room. Photos of the mayor; her brother, Chip; and Richard "Dickey" Lester leered ominously from the screen. A folky, unmistakably southern black female announcer said, "Are these the kind of people you want representing you? We're better than this, Atlanta."

Lucky entered the theater room, folded his arms across his chest, and silently watched. By the time the voice-over said, "Paid for by Reclaim Atlanta," Lucky was fit to be tied.

"We can't run that," Lucky said. "Haven't you heard the news?"

"What is it now, Lucky? How much bad news you got in those britches of yours?"

"Prentiss Dobbs died last night."

"You don't say? Well, that is an unfortunate development. We'll send flowers."

"Did you hear what I said? You have to get the boys to edit him out of that video."

Swigging the last corner of his shot and pouring another, Virgil said, "We bought up every station in the city, plus a big radio buy on 750 AM and V-103. I aim to box her in and make her fight. And we all know what she's like when she's teed-off. Remember, that broad started this fight."

The video included a still photo taken from a Mays High School yearbook, with Dobbs hugging up on Richard "Dickey" Lester like young, sex-starved lovers. Her brother was grinning in the background.

"Virgil, I said he's dead. It's all over the news. You cannot run that like it is."

"Tell me again like I didn't hear you the first time," he said, sucking on the last of the butt and extinguishing the cigarillo in an armchair ashtray.

"Who cares if you got your feelings hurt? I might've cussed you blind too."

"She's disloyal," Virgil said with a belch. "I tried to tell y'all that when we put her in office the first go-round. Whit, bless his heart, still has a soft spot for that gal, and who could blame him? If he had it his way, she'd be sitting in the Oval Office right now, scorching everything we've built. I cannot convince my long-suffering brother that she's anything short of a saint. A damn disgrace is what she is. And her brother was too."

Virgil recalled meeting young Chip at a National Black Arts Festival reception some years back. Prentiss Dobbs spared not a single breath before he informed Virgil that he was the son of the late Dr. Park Dobbs. Even with that, how the dimwit got into any reputable college, let alone Morehouse, was a mystery, Virgil thought. He used to joke that he could hear the rocks clanging around in Chip's head when he entered a room.

His sister apparently inherited all the brains, Virgil surmised, though in his mind, both had less grace than a hairless pygmy possum. But whatever he lacked in intellect, young Chip more than made up for on the street. If one wanted to win an election inside of I-285, it was common knowledge that Chip Dobbs was your man. His stock skyrocketed when his older sister won the mayor's race.

"Is she going to suspend her campaign?" Virgil said with a sniff. "One would think she'd put the whole thing on ice at least until the funeral is over."

"Heck, there's only four weeks until the election, and the clock starts ticking Monday when qualifying closes," Lucky said. "You have to reckon she won't waste a day."

"And neither can we, my friend. We damn sure can't wait until they put that boy in the ground to get things going. When's the funeral, anyway?"

"It hasn't been announced," said Lucky, shaking his head at the empty popcorn maker. "We can't run the one with Lester in it until we know for sure. Maybe we should think about letting Goodwin put out a condolence message and suspend active campaigning until after the burial."

Virgil pulled on another shot of whiskey. "I think we should position it all as a potential drug hit and let the media run with it."

"We can't do that," Lucky said. "It will make her look sympathetic to the voters."

"Who says we can't? Who's going to be sympathetic to a drug-addled miscreant who had the keys to the city contract department?"

"Every mama in Atlanta, that's who. Between that and Hawkins, and then to find out her husband has been pussyfooting around with some TV gal, Dobbs will come off looking like a victim," Lucky said. "We don't have any proof Chip was taking dope."

"And there's no proof he wasn't."

"I'm only saying that I've been knocked flat on my ass by a lot less."

"Don't go losing your shit on me now, Lucky. I told you this one would get rough. Might be a real barn burner. Hey, speaking of that, you remember when we snuck off down to Bainbridge for that cockfight in '71?"

"How could I forget? I won us a grip of money."

"You always knew when to lay your cash on the table, and I'm telling you that it ain't no time to fold now."

"I'm only saying that I'm not sure how much else she can stand."

"We 'bout to see," Virgil said, eyeing him wearily.

Virgil and Lucky had roomed together at University of Georgia back in the mid-'70s. Lucky didn't fuss much when Virgil hatched a plan to kidnap the team mascot, a bulldog named Uga III. They drove five hours through the night down to Savannah and waited outside the owner's house until a housekeeper let the pooch out into the yard that morning. The first shot from the pistol that whirled past his ear took Lucky by surprise. He scampered under a car parked on the street and watched as Mr. Frank "Sonny" Seller upbraided Virgil, whom he'd caught inside the wrought iron–fenced yard and held at gunpoint.

Whit, then in school at Emory University, was forced to drive down there and bail them both out of the Chatham County jail before their father found out, which Virgil admitted would be much worse than getting shot.

Virgil re-cued the tape and ran the last spot again. It was problematic, just as Lucky had advised. Virgil turned off the DVR and checked his watch.

"Fine," he relented. "We'll edit Chip Dobbs out of the spot and hold the others for a few days."

"What about Lester?"

"What about him?" Virgil asked.

"He won't like seeing his mug on television. This could be dangerous."

"He's under house arrest. Feds are watching his every move, and you've been watching too much Netflix."

It was a quarter past ten, and Libby was in all likelihood fast asleep. She wouldn't like all this tomfoolery, as she called it.

"Lucky, let's say you and I grab a bite to eat. I've got a hankering for some barbecue, and One Star Ranch over on Irby Avenue is still open."

He clicked an intercom button on his armrest. "Harold, pull my car around."

"Yessuh, Mr. Loudermilk. Will that be all for the evening?"

"You can go on home now, Harold. I'll see you in the morning, first thing."

Lucky sucked his ribs clean and got wasted on a pitcher of tequila punch while Virgil soaked up a bowl of sauce with a thick slice of Texas-style garlic toast. Virgil ordered up another beer, his fourth of the night, not including the whiskey shots back at the house, but cut Lucky off. After a while, he got tired of feeding Lucky quarters for the jukebox and listening to him belt out a string of country songs out of key. Among other things, Lucky was tone-deaf. He was blathering on about the lovely Latina, who currently had his nose swinging wide open like a barnyard door.

"A good woman will make you break all the rules, Virgil. Make you wanna sing all night long!"

"You should save that singing for the shower, and by 'good,' you mean 'beautiful.'"

"That too!" Lucky said gleefully.

"Pipe down. You're making a spectacle of yourself."

"There's nobody in here but us. My Gabriella sure is good to me, I can tell you that," Lucky replied in a slurred whisper.

"She's good for putting a dent in your wallet."

"I'm a good find!" Lucky said in protest, swaying in the restaurant booth, barely able to keep his balance.

"That's what your last two wives said, Lucky," Virgil said.

"I'd spend my last dime to make her happy, and she knows it."

"It might come to that if you don't get a prenuptial agreement this time around. I'll put it to you like this: Do you think Gabriella would spend more than ten minutes with you if you were dead broke?"

"Heck, Virgil, I could ask you the same thing about Libby Gail."

"And you'd be right. Only I know exactly why my free-spending wife married me. She burns through more cash than a Silicon Valley start-up. I don't have a good-looking bone in my body. Hell, I ain't easy on the eyes, but Libby

Gail has been mine since the day I picked her up for the Swan Ball in my daddy's new Cadillac."

"Gabriella loves me just fine, car or no car."

"I'm sure she does, Lucky. I'm sure she does."

"I can't imagine being with anybody else. You ever once think about stepping out on Libby Gail?"

"You mean with another woman? Hell no. Libby Gail Smoot would skin me alive."

"Not even once?"

Virgil shook his head vigorously and replied, "No, not even one time."

"What about Whit? I hear he was quite a scoundrel in his day. He must've had the pick of the litter."

"Whoever told you a thing like that?"

"That's what they say."

"Who is this 'they' you're talking about?" Virgil said, perking up. "Gossip is worth less than a plug nickel."

"You know how the women are. My ex-wife used to talk about it all the time. You know how Sarah is when she gets a little Scotch in her. It doesn't take much."

"And what did she say, exactly?"

"Only that Whit was a man about town. Even liked black women back in college. Sarah said he used to sneak off down to Spelman to see some gal."

"Sarah should mind her own business."

"So, it's true?"

"I'm not saying it is. I'm not saying it ain't."

"Well, I'll be damned."

TWENTY-FOUR

S hit! Shit! Shit!"

Hampton banged the keys and cursed the blank screen. He'd begged Tucker for a new laptop, only to get another rambling admonition about how he should be glad to still have a job when city papers around the country, big and small, were scratching for profits like a one-legged cat in a sandbox.

"Shit!" he shouted.

Hampton blew out a gust of air and started praying out of desperation. The full of his professional career, including an unfinished manuscript and years of investigative notes, hung in the balance. After a hard boot, the monitor took its time lighting up again. Hampton groaned, plugged in a spare external hard drive, and waited for the system to back up. He'd scrubbed the house, looking for his old drive, upending boxes, tearing through laundry baskets and kitchen cabinets, but came up empty. He'd been forced to buy a new one, which required getting an extension of the gas bill, but couldn't help wondering what he'd done with the other one. After a string of Hollywood celebrities got hacked and their nudes were posted all over the internet, he didn't trust virtual storage spaces and word-processing websites. His Google Docs account had been hacked twice in the last year.

He watched the files transfer as he gnawed on a fried bologna sandwich and swigged a warm cranberry Red Bull. Claire was working late, and he didn't want to bother her for another care package of her delicious food.

He'd spent most of the evening laying out the League's dirty work, half admiring the way they stayed within the confines of state statutes and federal campaign finance law while aggressively buying up elections. To what end, he did not yet know. If there was a political ideology, Hampton couldn't find one. Although now that he had the Hawkins Amendment, his suspicions only deepened.

He'd written a spate of stories about Reclaim Atlanta, which was now back in business and about to run a second round of television commercials, according to his sources, but his editors refused to print a syllable. It was clear, at least to Hampton, that the League was behind Reclaim Atlanta the first time, and had chosen Mayor Dobbs at least twice before. But according to his sources, they had a new dog in the hunt now: the Reverend Dr. Rudolph D. Goodwin, a televangelist with a doctorate of divinity from a diploma mill out of the Cayman Islands and an honorary degree from Blessed Heart University. It was a curious choice, given Goodwin's nonexistent political track record and previous silence on any issue of note. Goodwin came out of the gate swinging.

The death of the mayor's brother complicated matters. Goodwin issued a statement and suspended his campaign out of respect for the Dobbs family. Hampton went to the prayer vigil, despite Claire's admonitions that it would be disrespectful to go inside the church. And it was a good thing he did, especially since Dobbs announced her candidacy from the pulpit that night. In any other race, any other candidate might have postponed active campaigning, he noted in the story that he would file the following morning. It was a damn good speech, he had to admit. However, the special election would last only a few weeks, and this was Victoria Dobbs, he reminded himself, a woman who saw a political opportunity in nearly everything.

Hampton did not want to think like that now, no matter how much he personally despised her. But Mayor Dobbs was ruthless, just as Chanel Burris warned. Hampton knew that firsthand. It had been less than a year since he was on the receiving end of her fury. He was dead sure that Dobbs was behind his car accident, not to mention the nasty rumors that had circulated about him on the blogs while he was still handcuffed to a hospital bed, even if she hadn't hiked up her silk skirt and crawled under the hood of his car herself.

Eighteen months back, when Hampton first shared his suspicions about the existence of a political loose group operating out of a post office box in Buckhead, Tucker figured it was a pint of whiskey doing the talking and told Hampton so. He ordered Hampton to shut it down.

"Maybe Boney Jeffries isn't such a lunatic after all," Hampton said, pleading his case.

"Listen here, Boney could find a reason to start a fight in an empty broom closet," Tucker said, dismissing the story without so much as reading beyond the lead paragraph. "And here you are, chasing conspiracy theories like a two-dollar whore on nickel night."

There was some truth to that, Hampton mused as he tapped the keys on his laptop. Riding the wave of a four-pack of energy drinks, he'd been waiting hours for a call to come in. He tried to forget that he was home alone without even his dog to warn him if something else went down. The locks had been changed and burglar bars installed, none of which gave him any lasting comfort. He could think of a dozen ways to die, all of which were better than getting shot up in a home invasion. Hampton figured nobody would come looking for him, save for Claire or maybe Tucker, and then only if he botched another deadline. He'd been targeted in that robbery. He knew that for sure, but figured the whole story would get him laughed out of an APD station house.

Nigga, we whatn't supposed to kill no fuck-ass dog.

Hampton was startled when his smartphone buzzed a little before 11 P.M.

"Sorry it took me so long. I had a gig last night and I didn't really see anything," the woman said apologetically. "They stopped talking every time a server walked back there. They ordered the room sealed around eight o'clock. They wouldn't even let Ole Karup inside, and he all but owns this place."

"Ole is still around, eh? He must be two hundred years old by now."

"White cowboy hat and all," she said, referring to the unofficial reigning King of Buckhead. "Ole was pissing bricks. He tore out of the valet line in a white drop-top Bentley."

"And this was last Thursday night? Tiffany, did you recognize any of them?"

"Yeah, J. T. King, Bertram DuBose, Virgil Loudermilk. They come in all the time. There was some black guy I didn't recognize. Dark complexioned like Wesley Snipes and short. Maybe around fortyish."

"I'm betting that was Cordell Russell."

"The waffle guy?"

"One and the same. Pretty sure."

"The preacher man got here first," Tiffany, his all-time favorite snitching hostess, said. "I recognized him from television."

Oh, how he missed her deliciously warm lips and the way she wrapped herself around him. Tiffany had once been his favorite pastime.

"He came in by himself, checked in at the desk, and waited by the oyster bar until Mr. Loudermilk arrived."

"Anybody else?"

"Oh, and there was a Mr. W. Whitney Delacourte," she added. "I only know because he paid the bill and I got a peek at his credit card. He went to the upstairs bar for drinks after the meeting broke up. He looked real sad, though. Didn't talk to anybody except the bartender and the bottom of a double-malt Scotch. He didn't leave until after last call. The bartender called him Whit, like they were old friends."

Hampton's tongue knotted up in his mouth.

"I know that name," Tiffany said. "Why does it sound familiar?"

"Does Delacourte Enterprises ring a bell?"

"Oh, right. Right. Isn't that the family that owns your newspaper?"

"That and twelve more. They also own a chain of one hundred and fifteen television and radio stations around the country. DCI is probably your cable and internet provider too. It stands for Delacourte Cable and Internet."

"Dang, that's rich!"

"He lives in a twenty-five-thousand-square-foot mansion up on Garmond

Drive. One of the biggest private residences inside the city limits, second only to Tyler Perry's house on Paces Ferry Road."

Hampton long suspected that Whit Delacourte was an active member of the League, though he should've put two and two together, since Loudermilk was involved. No one could ever place Delacourte in the room, though, until now—and at least according to the official campaign disclosure reports, he hadn't made a single personal contribution to any politician anywhere since 1975, when he gave five hundred dollars to then-Governor Jimmy Carter's presidential campaign exploratory committee. By Hampton's calculations, Whit Delacourte was a few years out of Emory Law and a junior associate at a big-name firm around that time.

"Sorry I couldn't get more. We were pretty busy that night."

"You got more than enough, thanks."

Hampton's stomach rumbled. Maybe from the greasy sandwich, maybe from the confirmation that with a single keystroke, somebody like Whit Delacourte could end his career.

He'd met him only once, at a company-sponsored holiday party, and found him kind, if aloof. Hampton traded pleasantries with his wife, Patricia, whom he found just as lovely and everybody called Patsy Jo, while her husband raised a toast to another good year. Nobody mentioned the coming layoffs, of course.

Hampton found last year's annual filing for the Ezra J. Hawkins Foundation, but there was no mention of any especially large donation from any Delacourte company or family members. The W. Whitley and Patricia J. Delacourte Family Foundation wrote a $200,000 check after the congressman's death to help underwrite the memorial expenses and establish a scholarship fund in his name, said a press release that Hampton discovered on the nonprofit's website. He spotted a $100,000 gift from something called the Liberty Fund, but could find no trace of it other than a one-page Articles of Incorporation, a reference to its address in Ball Ground, Georgia, and its registered agent: Elizabeth G. Smoot.

He searched the secretary of state's corporate database again, using the name of every Delacourte he knew. He cross-referenced the Ball Ground address for the Liberty Fund, which turned out to be a home titled to ESG

Enterprises, an LLC incorporated by Elizabeth G. Smoot. Who she was and why she was interested in Hawkins escaped Hampton, until he remembered Loudermilk's wife, Libby Gail. He quickly found his wedding announcement in the *Atlanta Times-Register* online archives. The house and everything having anything to do with the Liberty Fund was held in his wife's name.

Whit's son, Coleman Delacourte, had a partial interest in a construction company known as Resurgens Properties, though Hampton didn't find it consequential and the entity didn't appear to have any financial ties to Hawkins. According to tax records, Resurgens built multifamily housing complexes and a few strip malls.

"What's this about? Are you writing a story?" Tiffany asked.

"I can't really say."

"When am I going to see you? I've got a chilly bottle of wine with your name on it."

"I'm sure you do," Hampton said, and then demurred. "I don't drink anymore, and I haven't dated in a very long time."

"Who's talking about dating? A little fun, that's all. I'll do all the work."

"Hey, um, I'll check in with you next week and see what you've got going on, okay?" he said, wriggling away.

Tiffany Lullwater was a pretty girl, twenty-six and banking on a singing career that hadn't come to fruition. She had long tanned legs, long flaxen hair, and a sweet Tennessee accent that used to make Hampton's heart race. It had been a long time since he had a woman, any woman, let alone one like Tiffany. Hampton realized he didn't want to be that man anymore.

Seeing Claire again, eating her glorious food, listening to her melodic voice, made him miss her touch. She'd clearly moved on, and he'd tried to convince himself that one day he would too.

"You still miss your wife, don't you?"

Hampton didn't answer. Instead, he thanked Tiffany, said good night, and got back to work. Between the League, Delacourte Enterprises, and Dobbs, Hampton had his hands full anyway. And now, there was the matter of ESG Enterprises and Resurgens Properties.

His files on Mayor Dobbs had grown to a healthy thickness over the years.

State Senator Victoria Dobbs-Overstreet was sworn in under the Gold Dome three days shy of her thirty-sixth birthday. By all accounts, she worked twenty hours a day, every day of the forty-day legislative sessions, making friends on both sides of the aisle. During her tenure, her name was near the top of every important piece of legislation signed into law. She lorded over the Democratic caucus with an iron fist and knew well how to cut a deal with Republicans, who now controlled both chambers—even when there seemed to be nothing up for negotiation. Dobbs seemed to find political leverage where none was thought to be had and used it like a sledgehammer.

Speculation had it that Dobbs wielded a dossier on nearly every sitting member of the state legislature, some information more personal than others, and on Governor Martinez, too. Dobbs kept a rumored blacklist, and anybody on it was politically dead or soon would be. She was more feared than revered in some quarters, Hampton knew, though the governor wouldn't waste a breath before she clocked Dobbs over the head if she got a clear shot.

Over the years, he'd met with more than a few sweaty-palmed lawmakers who were looking to drop the dime on Dobbs. None of them had the goods to make an ethics charge that would stick. Hampton figured that nobody, not even Virgil Loudermilk and his pay-for-play preacher, could stand in her way. If anything brought down the Great Torie Dobbs, Hampton surmised, it would be Dobbs herself.

He scooted closer to his desk, pulled up and replayed the audio of a 911 call. It had come from a blind email account and was encrypted with a passcode that arrived separately. No APD detective, outside of the official public affairs spokesperson, would dare talk to him on or off the record these days, so the method of delivery was not surprising. What it contained, however, was another matter altogether.

Seems a neighbor on Andrews Drive called in a domestic dispute of some sort, nearly a week ago. The yelling outside woke her from a cold sleep. From a second-floor window, Mrs. Gaffney said she could see two people fighting in a driveway below. She never said who they were, but the address matched the Dobbs-Overstreet residence. A dispatcher assured her that a squad car was heading to the scene, though there was no record of a response included in the message. Hampton thought back to the campaign event and remembered the bandage on Dr. Overstreet's head and the statement put out by her office to explain it all away.

"Must've been some boat she hit you with," he said, gleefully pecking the keys on the computer.

TWENTY-FIVE

Six pallbearers marched along the brick walkway toward the Potter's Field, a dark metallic gray casket hoisted onto their suited shoulders. Pastor Melham stood at the center, far edge of the enclosed portable tent, wearing a long black cassock and a matching ceremonial stole. He nodded as the coffin was lowered onto the silver brace and secured. His freshly shaved head glistened in the midsummer heat. A barefoot woman, dressed in a black leotard and flowing gossamer skirt, performed a liturgical dance, her palms stretching to the heavens in silent praise, as the family took their places.

Althea took little Chippy onto her lap, making room on the row of satin-covered foldout chairs for Miss Rosetta and their kinfolk. Victoria, her husband, and their twins filed into the seats beside them. Melham offered Marsh a pitying glance, and then bowed his head in prayer.

"Some wounds heal over time, though even in our grieving we must embrace the lesson of our scars," he began.

He concluded with a few words about a merciful God and how only the righteous would see the face of Jesus.

"There will be a full accounting," Melham said. "And yet, an equal portion of grace has been afforded to us all."

When the preacher was done gently chastising the living about the ephemeral nature of life and the abundance of grace, Victoria rose from her seat. She stepped to the foot of the coffin. With a warm soul-soaked voice, she began to sing.

> *May the works I've done speak for me,*
> *May the works I've done, oh Lord, speak for me.*

Her alto voice was strong and wonderful. The mournful mood seemed to lift. There was no organ and no choir, no cheering band of campaign supporters. Her arms outstretched, lifting her eyes over the steely gray casket, adorned with an array of white roses and lilies, and into the sky, this was between her and her God.

> *May the life I live speak for me,*
> *May the life I live speak for me.*
> *When I'm resting in my grave,*
> *I want to hear my Master say,*
> *May the life I've lived speak for me.*

As Victoria retook her seat to a round of soft amens, the history of the burial ground unspooled in her head. Oakland Cemetery, situated along Memorial Drive and not more than a mile outside of downtown Atlanta, was the final repose of the city's founding fathers, political leaders, and other dignitaries who littered the history books. Her father was buried here, as were golfing legend Bobby Jones, author Margaret Mitchell, and Maynard Jackson.

Victoria surveyed the extravagant mausoleums and sculptures that harkened back to a time when wealth and race followed one to the grave.

The mourners were surrounded by more than seventy thousand graves, including those of Confederate soldiers. Some were memorialized by towering, ornate sculptures and others marked by a simple marble plate. Over the years, some people reported hearing a man's ghostly voice calling the names of those who died in battle. Victoria could hear nothing but the whispering winds.

She had come here in middle school on a field trip. In her second year at Harvard Law, she buried her father no more than a few paces away from where she now stood. Victoria returned twice more as a member of the Georgia state legislature and a third time as mayor. She never forgot the story of the first documented African American burial since she heard it in seventh grade. Each time she came, including this day, Victoria visited the boy known only as "John."

In 1853, the fourteen-year-old Negro boy was laid to rest in what was then called Slave Square. Victoria found his master's name, William Hearing, listed on the official paperwork. Victoria and John shared the same birth date, according to the document, and were born 127 years apart—he on March 23, 1839. Victoria was born on the same day in 1966.

"Over twelve thousand black people are buried on the grounds," the cemetery director once told her. "Most of them were children. They were interred in the back section next to Potter's Field."

Some of the remains were unearthed, years after they were first laid to rest, and reinterred in the area called the "colored pauper grounds," to make room for wealthy white families and war veterans, the director went on explaining. He'd pointed to the "whites only" section, which left the then–state senator feeling like a "colored gal."

"Only two bodies, those of Georgia Harris and Catherine Holmes, remain buried over there."

Securing a plot for Chip so close to their father took some political wrangling. It required getting special permission and buying out the family that owned the adjoining plots, as there was little ground available for new interments. Westview, a historic interdenominational cemetery in southwest Atlanta that was home to both "the famous and the ordinary," was Rosetta's second choice. Coca-Cola founder Asa Candler and iconic mayor William Hartsfield, for whom the airport is named, were buried there. But Victoria vowed that, no matter the price or political tensions, her brother would be buried in Oakland alongside their father.

The prayers were brief. The eulogy was no more than twenty minutes in length. Chip, who had known no lasting peace in his living days, wouldn't have wanted to be prayed over for too long, Melham said.

Some of the womenfolk, toting pillbox purses and showy hats, fanned themselves with their summer church gloves. There were strong-faced men, dressed in obligatory black suits and tightly knotted ties. Victoria, seated between her daughters, cradled a bouquet of long-stemmed white lilies, and her mother held a small shovel across her lap.

Pastor Melham read a closing scripture and recited the same benediction he always said in church, and it got the same hearty amen it always got. When the final prayer was complete, Victoria stepped forward and placed the bundle of flowers onto the coffin lid. Rosetta then got up and walked to the head of the casket.

"You can let it down now," the old woman told the funeral director.

Together, the mourners watched as suited men from Murray Brothers Funeral Home lowered the beautiful box into the ground. When the coffin reached the bottom, Rosetta said, "Hand me that shovel, young man."

She gripped the handle with both hands and began to fill the hole. Her brother, Tommie Byrd, tried to stop her, but Rosetta went on.

"I brought my child into this world. I will see him out of it."

She dug into the pile of dirt and lifted the first pitch into the grave as a pair of doves were released. Women began to shriek and wail. A man shouted, "Glory, glory!"

Not even Steve Weisenhunt, Chip's pickup basketball teammate, could keep his eyes dry. Scooter Taylor and Kevin Harvey locked arms with the other pallbearers and began to pray. Katherine "Kick" Hartsfield, Rosetta's elder and only surviving sister, slumped over in her chair, her arms thrashing back and forth. "Holy Father!" she shouted again and again.

Rosetta kept working, the sweat pooling on her brow. She pulled off her hat and looked up to the sky. "I will keep nothing from my Father," she said to the heavens. "I surrender unto God all that He has given unto me."

Rosetta may as well have been preaching rather than shoveling, the way the people carried on under that tent. When he'd seen enough and began to worry about Rosetta's health, Pastor Melham stepped forward and gently took hold of her hands.

"Your work is done, Mother Dobbs," he said with assurance. "Prentiss is at rest in the arms of our Heavenly Father. There will be just one funeral today."

Rosetta caught her breath, nodded, and stepped away from the pit. One by one, each member of the family took turns praying over the grave and exited the site. As they turned to walk away, Pastor Melham beckoned Victoria and Marsh to wait.

"A word?" Melham said, waving them back to their seats.

"I need to spend some time with you," he said in a low, serious voice. "The devil knows where to cast his temptations. Don't let this earthly world take away from you what Christ Himself has anointed and ordained."

Marsh shook his head in agreement, silently acknowledging his infidelities. Victoria stared off into the distance.

"Father, forgive them," Victoria said to the heavens. "For they know not what they do."

The pastor was immediately perplexed. Melham may have been confused by the mayor's reference to the crucifixion, but Marsh understood his wife perfectly and braced himself.

Victoria rarely quoted Scripture. But when she did, it meant she was readying for a fight.

TWENTY-SIX

Hampton watched live coverage of the funeral procession on the newsroom monitors. The caravan of cars, led by four freshly polished limousines, moved eastward over Memorial Drive, and then made its way silently and alone northbound along the downtown connector. State patrol vehicles secured the on-ramps, holding midday traffic at bay as the mourners made their passage. All four local news choppers captured the entire scene.

The final destination, an anchor said solemnly, was the mayor's home in Buckhead for a private repast.

Hunched over his cubicle, a dozen miles away, Hampton thumbed through the Hawkins Amendment again. He hadn't yet told Tucker about the congressman's plans. The resulting public contracts for new highways, rapid rail expansion, and other developments from the initial legislation would have been worth billions, and Mayor Dobbs would have no say in who won the contracts. The way Hampton saw it, one thing was clear: The language in the amendment was designed to strip contracting powers from the mayor's office and hand them to a bipartisan community-led commission. If somebody was trying to buy public bids through her office, the legislation was cutting them off, too.

Hampton could find no direct connection to the Delacourtes or Louder-milk, save for the Ball Ground house and the younger Delacourte's small construction company. But if Valerie Norbreck-Haynes was right, there was a reason they spilled so much cash on Hawkins. Now Hawkins was dead and his amendment was dead too. The mayor's brother, who once led the city's contract procurement office, had just been carted across town in the back of a hearse.

The measure would've almost certainly drawn the support of the Republican-controlled House Committee on Transportation. The Hawkins Amendment would've sailed through both the House and Senate chambers with ease, and there was no way the president could refuse to sign it. All of that left Mayor Dobbs, and anybody on her side, hanging out with the wash.

Hawkins was locking them all out. But why?

Dobbs and Hawkins were still tight as twine when the congressman was killed, though Hampton now wondered if their accord was more like a leash. The congressman's decades-long alliance with the League, dating back to the mid-'70s, had gone up in flames, and Hampton now wondered who else got burned. He studied a stack of existing and pending city contracts, but found nothing.

The altercation outside the mayor's Buckhead mansion was something altogether different. Back-fence talk chalked it up to the good doctor's philandering with a woman named Samantha Geidner. Hampton rang her phone a dozen or more times, though she never once picked up. According to a publicist out of New York, Geidner was on a planned vacation somewhere in the Caribbean and would have no comment on the matter.

Hampton understood the mayor's temper better than anybody. He'd heard about the incident out at the Buckhead Diner and now wondered if Virgil Loudermilk was behind the mysterious package that was supposedly delivered to her house. If true, that meant Loudermilk and Dobbs were in the midst of an all-out war. Hampton's gut told him the special election was simply a proxy battle. There wasn't a chance he'd get to ask Dobbs about it. Munching on a bag of Honey BBQ Fritos, Hampton could only imagine the mayor's response if he asked for a one-on-one interview.

Kathy Franco, the senior crime beat reporter, wandered in and plopped down in a chair beside him. "I've got an early birthday gift for you," she said, reclining in the ergonomic swivel chair.

"You know how much I adore surprises. Wha'cha got?"

Franco slid a slim stack of paperwork onto his desk. "Medical records from Northside Hospital," she said. "Happy birthday!"

Hampton scanned the top sheet. "How'd you get your hands on this?"

"Magic, my friend."

The top page was an emergency room discharge sheet for Marshall L. Overstreet. The record said an attending physician patched him up with four stitches and an allotment of painkillers and muscle relaxers. The CT scan was negative, according to the notes, but the patient had a number of abrasions about the head, neck, and forearms. The document was signed and dated the day after the so-called boating accident.

"From the looks of things, she knocked the hell out him, and I think I know why," Hampton said.

"She's got the makings of a real prizefighter," Franco said. "If Mayor Dobbs doesn't win this election, she could jump on Floyd Mayweather's Money Team."

"That's exactly why she's going to win this thing. It'll take more than a slick preacher to bring her down," Hampton said. "Her bite is bigger than her bark."

"Seems like she did everything except bite him. Says here that he had bruised ribs, multiple contusions, and a fractured thumb."

"Can you write this up?" Hampton said.

"Sure, what's up?"

"For starters, she might burn my house. But I'm working on something big, and my plate is full."

"Bigger that this? Mayor Dobbs couldn't possibly hate you any more than she already does."

Hampton's desk phone was ringing. "Indeed, and I'm about to test that theory," he told Franco, picking up the receiver. "A visitor for me? Yeah, who is it?"

He paused, turned toward Franco, and said, "Hey, I've got to run. I'll shoot you some stuff on that domestic incident in a bit. I have a 911 call from a neighbor. Already transcribed for your reading pleasure. There's something about a man getting blasted with a pressure washer."

"The kind they use to clean building exteriors?"

"That's what it sounds like. Word on the street is an unmarked package arrived at the mayor's house, containing proof that her husband was cheating on her," Hampton said. "I think that's what set her off."

"Any idea who sent the package?"

Hampton ran an imaginary zipper across his lips. Franco grinned and scooted away.

"Don't send her up. I'm coming down," he told the security guard over the phone, "and make sure she doesn't leave."

Minutes later, Hampton hobbled into the lobby using forearm crutches. He barely recognized Chanel at first. She wasn't wearing her usual getup, and there wasn't a stitch of makeup.

"Can we go somewhere and talk?" she said in a low voice. "Privately."

"Sure, we can do that," Hampton said. "What brings you here?"

"I ain't have no place else to go."

"What can I do for you?"

"We need to talk," she said, fidgeting, "in private. Is there somewhere we can go?"

He gazed into her eyes. She'd been crying. Hampton looked around and said, "Okay, I'll sign you in."

"Don't put my name on the books."

"Um, okay, sure. Follow me."

He'd never known Chanel to hold her tongue, but on the elevator ride she was quieter than a Tibetan monk on a sojourn to Nepal. Hampton found an empty, darkened conference room on the sixth floor, out of sight and earshot of the newsroom two floors below. Chanel trailed him inside. Hampton hit on the light switch and pulled the blinds.

He waited patiently as she took a seat across from him.

"Listen, I didn't tell you everything," Chanel began. "I couldn't. I need you to understand that."

"I've always known that," Hampton said. "So, where do we start?"

Chanel opened her purse and placed a piece of shiny construction paper on the table.

"What is this?" Hampton said, picking it up. "Origami?"

"It's a message."

"A message?"

"An omen. Do you have a tape recorder around here?"

"Sure, do I need one?"

Hampton placed his smartphone on the table and clicked on a voice recording app. Chanel stared down at the device and said, "I might not live long enough to repeat myself."

Four hours and three cups of coffee later, Hampton and Chanel pulled up alongside the Amtrak station on Peachtree Street. He handed Chanel a sack lunch and a one-way ticket to Michigan under the name "Tracy Cantrell." Over his father's objections, his mother, Florence, agreed to open her home to "Tracy."

"They're good people. My mother is, anyway," Hampton said. "She'll take good care of you. My mama will see to it that you get three square meals every day, and you'll have a roof over your head while we sort this out. I hope you don't mind sleeping in my old room."

"Thank you," she said, almost inaudibly.

"We should call the police. I've got a couple of friends at the GBI."

For the third or fourth time that day, Chanel said, "No."

"If even half of what you told me is true," Hampton said, "somebody belongs in prison."

"If I thought I could trust the police, I would've gone to them a long time ago, and maybe Ezra would still be alive."

You don't know what kinna people you messing with.

Hampton suddenly didn't like sitting out on Peachtree Street. He wheeled around to Deering Avenue, parked along the curb, and watched a wave of people exit the train station in his rearview mirror.

"Did he tell you anything about who he thought was after him?"

"Never would say," Chanel said. "He just kept on talking about that amendment and all that money up for grabs. Ezra thought if he could get it passed, then that would save his life."

"And he said that to you?"

"Not in so many words, but, yeah, he was scared."

"Why didn't he just vote for the initial bill?"

"He said his heart wouldn't let him. Said the people elected him to do a job, and as long as he was breathing good air, he wouldn't quit doing it."

"Why do you think these people want to kill you?"

"Because they know what I know. They sent him that same red bird before they had him killed."

"Who is 'they'? Who sent it to you?"

"I don't know."

"You don't know or you won't say?"

Chanel spoke in even tones now. Hampton studied her face. She told him how afraid she'd been when she heard about Chip Dobbs and the bombing at the hotel. "He wasn't shit in high school, but don't nobody deserve to get burnt up like that."

"They arrested a suspect, right?"

"They got Rochelle Charles's boy on lockdown, but he don't know nothing about making no damn bombs. His uncles sure as hell do, though."

"You know them?"

"Rochelle went to school with us too. And so did her older brothers Riley and Dickey."

"Richard Lester?"

"That's him. He goes by Dickey," Chanel said. "Him and Vicki used to fuck around in high school. Had everybody thinking she was a virgin, but I knew better than that. They say Chip was helping Dickey run money through his nightclubs and turned state's evidence to keep his own ass out of jail. They say that's what got him killed, but I don't believe that's all to it. They could've just clipped his ass coming out of Phipps Plaza."

"What is it that you do believe?"

"I think the same people that killed Ezra got to Chip. That's what they're saying out in the street, anyway. This is big, even for Dickey. If he in it, he ain't in it by his damn self. Ezra kept his ass out of jail more than once."

"And you think the car bomb is somehow connected to the church shooting?"

"The only thing tying them together is Vickie and them city contracts," she went on saying. "If you don't hear from me, promise you'll take that envelope I gave you straight to her."

"Why Dobbs?"

"She might be the only person who can save my life."

Hampton had more questions, but the look in Chanel's eyes said she was done talking. He nodded, reached into the backseat, and handed her a prepaid cell phone and an overnight bag stuffed with new clothes.

"There's some cash in the side pocket. That should hold you until you get to Flint."

"Tell your wife that I said thank you," Chanel said, opening the passenger door. "She don't know me from Adam's house cat."

"She's my ex-wife, and she's better than anything that I ever deserved. Call me at the number I gave you from every stop."

Chanel opened the passenger-side door and got out. As Hampton watched her disappear into the terminal, her words kept replaying themselves: *I am a transgender woman. My mama named me Malik.*

That night, Hampton bolted the doors to his house and rechecked the window locks. He scanned the high school yearbook again until he found a class photograph of Malik Townsend, wearing a tuxedo jacket and bow tie. He was awarded the "Best Lead Actress" prize for a school rendition of *Dreamgirls*. It was a small, high school production, but Malik, dressed in a sequined gown and fake eyelashes, stunned in the role of Effie White. Hampton went through the arrest records from 1985 again and found a mug shot of Malik that matched Chanel's date of birth.

This was the kind of scoop that reporters waited their entire careers to get. It had to wait, though, Hampton knew. He was thinking about an unfinished manuscript now and how Chanel had unwittingly rewritten everything.

"And Congressman Hawkins?" he remembered asking Chanel.

"We were in love," she said, "until the day he died."

TWENTY-SEVEN

Inside Goodwin's campaign headquarters, situated in a strip mall on Piedmont Road near the Lindbergh MARTA station, the phone bank bustled with volunteers. Every call was scripted and the responses were tallied on a whiteboard that covered the span of the back wall. A live feed, chronicling the social media buzz and managed by a three-person team, spooled down a vertical flat-screen monitor, punctuated with soft beeps.

Virgil Loudermilk came up with the campaign slogan himself: One Atlanta. The communications team found it brilliant, but they were paid handsomely to believe such things.

A smattering of applause broke out when the Reverend Goodwin walked in. He'd been out door-knocking for most of the day, and judging by his dour demeanor, the neighborhood canvassing had not gone well. He dug deep and greeted the room with a decidedly upbeat speech, though it was difficult to hide the disappointment on his face.

"The tide will turn," his campaign manager assured him. "Our opponent has near one hundred percent name ID, and right now she's the sentimental favorite. The good news is you've got over a hundred thousand Twitter followers."

"How many of them did we buy? How many of them are going to vote for me? What are the real polls saying?" Goodwin asked.

"Paid social media advertising is good campaigning. The numbers look good, but the only poll you need to worry about is the one they take on Election Day."

"It doesn't feel good out there right now."

"It's still early, Pastor Goodwin."

"We've got less than two weeks to go. Early is late."

The truth of the matter was Robbie Newkirk had been shipped in from Florida to run things because no reputable local talent wanted the job and every available campaign manager out of D.C. balked at the chance to flush their professional life down the drain. In his brief career, Newkirk had two congressional wins and a handful of local elections under his belt. Even so, the DNC refused to take his calls, and he privately accused the national chairman of pressing his thumb on the proverbial scale.

"The mayor has a lot of friends in Washington. It isn't over until it's over," Newkirk assured Goodwin with a hearty pat on the back. "We're halfway in. Let's get you some coffee. The briefing team is setting up in the back."

"Briefing team?"

"You have an editorial board meeting at the *Times-Register* in three days, and the first debate comes right after that," Newkirk said. "Your wife dropped off some comfortable clothes, if you want to get changed."

"I'm fine," Goodwin responded, pulling off his tie. "Just don't send me to see another Mrs. Renfro."

"Renfro?"

"A white lady over on St. Charles Avenue in the Virginia-Highland," Goodwin said. "She called me an Uncle Tom right to my face and told me to get the hell off her porch."

"We won't win every vote," Newkirk said. "As long as we keep Dobbs under fifty percent, we can force a runoff and reset the clock."

"How does that help us?"

"Turnout is always low in a special election, but it's even lower in a special election runoff. It will come down to that."

"You're assuming we can beat Sarah Mitchell and make that runoff."

"Pastor, I assume nothing. All I can promise you is that we're putting everything we have into this."

Goodwin followed Newkirk through the maze of makeshift offices and into a conference room. J. T. King was handing out bundles of position papers and gave one to Goodwin as he stepped through the door.

"Take a seat, Reverend. We've got work to do," King said. "Robbie, order up some supper. We might be here a good long while. How's the yard-sign planting coming along?"

"Slow but good. It's a steady build out there," Newkirk answered like a platoon sergeant. "We're taking this thing block by block."

Goodwin struggled through the talking points. When it became clear that he was having trouble with policy details, the group took a break, scarfed down dinner, and moved on to debate prep.

"Robbie here will play the role of Mayor Dobbs, and I'll be the moderator," King said.

The debate opening statement had to be rewritten three times before Goodwin caught the rhythm. "This doesn't sound like me," he complained time and time again. "I wouldn't say it like that."

"We want you to be comfortable," Newkirk said. "Take your time, Reverend."

When they got to Black Lives Matter, Goodwin stopped and slapped the table.

"It isn't that I necessarily disagree with Dobbs on this," he said warily. "My own sons have been stopped for no good reason. My oldest boy got locked up in Fayette County for driving six miles over the speed limit and missed his lacrosse match. We should take a hard look at police accountability, especially when somebody dies. I don't care what color they are. These police unions—"

"—are among your best allies," King said, cutting him off. "You're getting a lot of donations from the police and fire unions. They're out there knocking on doors and putting flyers on every parked car that they can find."

"I understand that, and I am grateful for every one of them," Goodwin said. "I also understand that when an officer fires their gun, the people deserve to know why they did it. Nobody here can argue with that. And the way I see it, neither will the people of the Fifteenth District."

"Alright, alright, let's come back to it," King said.

"Fine," Goodwin responded, scanning the page. "Let's talk about these guns."

Newkirk sat up in his seat and arched his aching back as Goodwin rambled on about mass shootings and the need for an assault weapons ban. King slumped down in his chair. He'd have to explain it all to Loudermilk, who wouldn't be pleased to hear that Goodwin was about to get mollywhopped by Victoria Dobbs in the first debate. It was plain to see that he was no match for her agility on the issues and wouldn't be able to counter her ability to dive deep into the minutiae and deliver policy solutions that everyday people would understand.

"Dobbs is a Harvard-trained, former state lawmaker and two-term mayor who has been preparing for this moment every single day of her life," King said finally. "Remember, you've been doing this for a few weeks. For Dobbs, it's like mother's milk."

The door clicked open, and Virgil Loudermilk appeared. Lucky tagged along behind him.

"Good evening, gentlemen!" he boomed. "How's it going, Rev!"

The men traded perfunctory handshakes.

Newkirk stood and offered him his seat. "No, please, Mr. Loudermilk. I will stand."

Lucky, who hadn't eaten since noon, gobbled up the last Styrofoam plate of fried chicken salad while Virgil held court.

"They're putting me through my paces," Goodwin said. "But I've got to stay true to myself and my values."

"Reverend Goodwin, this is the best team that good money can buy," Virgil said, folding his hands over his belly and rearing back on the chair's hind legs. "I don't suspect you'll agree with everything, but we ain't got but a few days to get you ready for the fight of your life."

"I understand the editorial board is a tough bunch."

"No, that'll be easy. It's Victoria Dobbs whom you need to concern your-self with."

"She's that good?"

"Did you look at the game tapes we sent over to your house?" King asked.

"Not yet," Goodwin admitted. "The campaign calendar has been full, sunup to sundown. My wife is already complaining about the hours."

"It'll take everything you've got and then some," Virgil said. "And, yes, Dobbs is that good. She sings talking points better than a church choir. It's a real humdinger when she takes it off the cuff. Pardon my language, but she can cajole the shit out of a snake and raise the dead from a grave. Now, the editorial board will take it easy on you."

"How do we know that?"

King smiled.

Virgil chuckled and said, "Because I own them."

TWENTY-EIGHT

Her cell phone blared on the nightstand, rousing Victoria from what had been the first good night's sleep she'd had in weeks. She rustled in the blankets, huffed, and rolled over. Marsh was awake then too, clearing the crust from his eyes.

"I thought we agreed that you were going to turn it off at night," he said.

"You agreed," Victoria said with a yawn. "You know I can't do that."

Their girls, nestled between them in the king-sized bed, were still sleeping like freshly nursed, three-day-old puppies. The rumbling stopped and started again. Victoria was annoyed.

"Who's calling here at this hour?"

"I'll get it," Marsh said.

His expression turned grave as he said, "Uh-hun, uh-hun. Thanks for letting us know."

"Who was that?"

"Roy."

"My press secretary?"

"Where's your iPad?"

"On top of the dresser. Why?"

"Hold on."

Marsh eased out of bed, retrieved the tablet from atop the mirrored dresser, and began tapping the screen.

"What's your password?"

"The day we met."

"Help me out here."

"You don't remember our anniversary?"

"C'mon, Torie. Not now."

"February twelfth. Add three zeros."

Thumbing through the tabs, he blew out a heavy gust of air. "Baby, this isn't good."

"What is it now?"

"Your second favorite roving reporter is out with a new story this morning."

"Kathy Franco? About what?" Victoria said, sitting straight up.

"Us."

"What do you mean 'us'?"

Marsh waved her into the bathroom. "Look at this," he said, handing over the tablet. He sat on the edge of the sunken bathtub, bare chested in his pajama pants, and buried his face in his hands.

Victoria immediately soured as she read through the lengthy story, which listed a string of anonymous women who had allegedly slept with Marsh. There was a studio photograph of Samantha Geidner, the reality television starlet whom Victoria had come to loathe the sight of. Franco had quotes pulled from a 911 tape and even had a firsthand account from Mrs. Gaffney, their neighbor. Victoria reread the last line: "Repeated calls to the mayor's office went unanswered."

Victoria scrolled through the story twice. "This is a hit job."

"What are we going to do about it?" Marsh asked.

"Nothing," she said dryly. "We aren't going to do anything."

"I know you better than that."

"We aren't going to do anything, Dr. Feelgood. You'll screw anything walking, won't you?"

"C'mon, Torie. That's not fair."

"Damn, if it ain't. You got us into this and I'll get us out," Victoria said. "Just keep your damn mouth shut and your pants up. I'm going to need your call history. Pull the cell bills."

"What?"

"I said pull the goddamn itemized bills," Victoria demanded. "I don't care what's in it. Pelosi will review invoices and make certain your little harem stays in check. Get him a list of names."

She reached into the shower, turned on the jets, slipped off her nightgown, and got in.

"And call Roy back," she ordered over the smoked-glass stall. "Tell him to draft a statement. No press conference. And ask him to bring the policy briefing book he put together."

"So you're actually going to that editorial board meeting?"

"You bet your wayward ass I am."

"What are you going to tell them?"

"Everything."

The mayor was still reeling when Pelosi picked her up from the house. Victoria admired his sturdy bearing. A barrel-chested Italian with a severe Brooklyn accent and jet-black eyes, Salvatore Pelosi had a commanding presence, even though he rarely spoke more than a few words at a time. It took some cajoling and promises she knew she had to keep, but wrangling him away from Congressman Hawkins's staff was decidedly one of the best decisions she'd ever made.

"You can't buy that kind of loyalty," Hawkins once told her. "Treat him right, and he'll protect you with his life."

Victoria knew that now. Pelosi had proved himself indispensable on more than one occasion since she hired him onto the APD and stationed him in the mayor's office. A former Defense Intelligence agent, he quickly went about the work of setting up an internal security detail, an off-the-books squad of officers whose only job was protecting the mayor and her interests.

Each member of the special unit, comprising eight men and two women, received counterterrorism training under Pelosi's supervision and remained embedded within their respective zone commands. Not even their shift supervisors were aware of their dual assignment to the Special Operations Corps or that the unit itself existed. The mayor had a public security detail, though none of the SOC members were officially appointed to it. Even with the feds on protective duty now, the circle around her remained intact. Everything moved on Pelosi's command.

Last spring, soon after word of the secret squad leaked to a blogger at DrivingGeorgiaRight.com, the missives abruptly stopped and the articles disappeared after two plainclothes members paid a predawn visit to a house on Land O' Lakes Drive in northeast Atlanta. Eric Byrne was startled to find them standing in his bedroom when he awoke one morning. He hurriedly tapped the keys, deleting files and sweating like a Coke can while they looked on.

"Who are you?"

"The important thing is we know who you are, Eric," one of them answered, dropping a thumb drive in his lap.

Byrne was immediately confused. "What's this?" he asked.

"It's your next story. Publish it by midnight."

That night, at exactly 11:59 P.M., the first revelations about Hampton Bridges, his drinking proclivities and penchant for young coeds, went live.

It had been an especially crafty SOC unit officer, a freshman recruited from a GBI surveillance team, who tracked down that 911 call from Mrs. Gaffney and determined which dispatcher had handed it over to an investigator working out of Zone 2. Detective Shaun Haverty, a twelve-year veteran, was hauled into police headquarters for questioning, and at first denied knowing anything about the call or who sent the message to a reporter.

The detective kept demanding to see his union representative, until Pelosi entered the interrogation room and snapped on a pair of leather gloves. Through a one-sided window, the mayor stood stone-faced and folded her arms as she watched Haverty stiffen.

"I am going to ask you one time, Detective Haverty," Pelosi said. "Who do you work for?"

"I don't understand the question, Lieutenant. I am employed by the City of Atlanta. I have a part-time job directing traffic for Sunday services up at Peachtree Road United Methodist. I'm saving up to buy a new house," he nervously explained. "My wife is due in December."

The blow to his right eye came quick and without notice. Victoria flinched as blood splattered and the detective fell backward in his chair, nearly tipping over. Dazed, Haverty looked up into the ceiling fan and mouthed something indiscernible. Victoria could not tell if it was a prayer to God, a plea to Pelosi, or both. Tears rolled down both sides of his inflamed face. The mayor swallowed and steadied herself. It was an unusual request, but she had demanded to see the interrogation in person.

"Once again, Haverty, who do you work for?"

Pelosi's words were firm and more deliberate now. He punctuated every syllable with a pause.

"I want to see my lawyer," Haverty mumbled.

Pelosi snatched him up by the throat with one hand and clocked him in the jaw with the other. Haverty spat out a glob of blood.

"I don't have all motherfucking day, Detective. Make it plain and you can go."

Victoria watched Haverty closely from the adjoining room. His eyes darted left to right, and then pinned on the viewing window.

"She's out there, isn't she? Mayor Dobbs, ma'am, please. I'm going to lose my job and my pension, either way."

"I'm afraid more than your paltry pension is on the line. You can walk out of here with your head up, go home to your wife with your integrity intact, or I can roll a stretcher in here. The choice is yours," Pelosi said. "Game's over. Give me the name."

A second officer, a hollow-eyed woman with a pageboy haircut named K. L. Wade, handed Pelosi a nightstick.

"Put your hands on the table," she said coolly.

Haverty was visibly trembling now.

"Tell me what you want me to say, and I'll say it," he said, slumping down in the metal chair.

"I said put your hands on the table."

"They are going to kill me."

TWENTY-NINE

He took his time. There was no need to rush now. He traced his fingers down her spine and over the small of her back—that gentle touch lovers do when they want to stay with you a little while longer. Marvin Gaye was on Pandora, singing something about morning dew and throwing away his pride.

"Just relax," Hampton whispered, tenderly pressing the meat of his palm into her back.

You're all, all the joys under the sun wrapped up into one
You're all, you're all I need
You're all I need

Claire let out a soft moan as he slipped on top of her, firmly massaging the back of her neck with his thumbs.

"I've missed this," she said.

Hampton swore to himself, with every thrust and as the thrills exploded through his body, that he wouldn't let go this time. He was becoming a new man, the kind of man Claire married. When it was over, when they had given all there was to give, he caressed her shoulders and nibbled on her neck as they walked to the shower. Claire turned on the water and nudged Hampton in first.

"Go ahead," she said. "Let me take care of you. I'll grab some fresh towels."

She slipped into a silky white kimono and knotted the belt at her glorious waistline.

"I like you better naked, you know," Hampton said with a sly grin. "I'm going to tell your grandmother that you took advantage of me."

"She wouldn't doubt a word of it," Claire said with a snicker, pausing to lean on the doorframe.

Hampton loved the way she laughed.

It was morning now, and Hampton had been up working all night.

"Oh, and hey, thanks for the cash and clothes," Hampton said. "I'll pay you back as soon as I can."

Claire waved him away. "I'll get us some coffee," she said.

"Cream and no sugar, please?"

"As if I forgot. I know everything there is to know about you, James Hampton Bridges."

"Then you know that I love you."

Claire smiled and turned away.

"Hey, what's that on your back?" Hampton called after her, getting out of the shower. "What is that fancy design on your robe?"

"This is a kimono," she said, twirling around. "And it's a Japanese dragon. You remember that big assignment at the U.S. Embassy? I got it in Tokyo. I would've brought you something back too, but you were a naughty boy."

Claire dropped infrequent reminders about his previous infidelities, but Hampton let it pass. They were together now, and that's all that mattered.

"It looks sort of like something my source gave me," Hampton said, drying himself. "It scared the hell out of her. And me too, if I'm being honest."

Hampton wrapped a bath towel around his waist, went back to the den, and relistened to a portion of his interview with Chanel. He yanked off his earbuds.

"Shit."

"What's wrong?"

"My source said something about a small, upstart construction company, and I think I know which one. The CEO is Whit Delacourte's son, Coleman."

"Cole?"

"You know him?"

"Yeah, he runs Resurgens Properties and his company just won a piece of an Atlantic Station project," Claire said. "He's a nice guy. They beat out six other firms in the city procurement process. They rang in late with the lowest bid. It's almost like they knew the numbers. You know how these things go, right?"

"I guess I do."

Hampton opened his laptop and tapped the keys.

"For a relatively new player, they've got an impressive track record, even with all the connections," Claire said, hovering over his shoulder. "I've seen their capabilities statement. New commercial projects in three states, and a handful of government contracts. Fifty-one percent minority-owned."

"Coleman is still white, last I checked," Hampton said. "Who's the minority?"

"Coleman's wife, Rafaela. Cuban, I think. Mostly silent, though. She only shows up for big presentations. Everybody calls her Raffi."

"My source didn't remember the name of the company, but I'm sure that's the one."

"And you trust this source of yours?"

"Yeah, mostly. And look here," Hampton said, pointing to a PDF he downloaded from the company's website. "Prentiss Dobbs is listed as cochairman of the community advisory board."

Hampton did a quick Google search on Rafaela Delacourte. He pushed himself back from the desk.

"Her maiden name is Vasquez."

"So?"

Hampton started tapping the keys again. He found a ten-year-old obituary in the *Times-Register* for Gloriella Vasquez, who had eight surviving children. Among them were Rafaela and Caleb, who was then a sergeant in the U.S. Army. Hampton kept clicking until he found Caleb's name in the archives on the *Stars and Stripes* website. Sergeant Vasquez was a highly decorated scout sniper, with several tours in Iraq and Afghanistan, according to a story posted three years ago.

"If this is the same Caleb Vasquez, and I have every reason to think it is, he was killed in that SWAT team raid a month or so back."

"The guy who shot up Ebenezer Baptist?"

Hampton clenched his teeth and stared at the screen as he did the mental math.

"I shouldn't be telling you all of this," he said.

Caleb was the brother-in-law of Coleman Delacourte, who was the son of Whit and the nephew of Virgil Loudermilk. Suddenly Hampton understood why the Delacourtes might've been interested in that transportation bill and the construction contracts that came along with it.

"You don't honestly think they killed anyone," Claire said, reading his thoughts. "Well, do you?"

"I don't know what to think right now," Hampton said without looking up. "All I'm saying is that it was a fuck of a lot of money to watch go circling down the drain. The only thing standing in their way was Ezra Hawkins, and now he's rotting in a grave out in east Georgia."

"And Chip Dobbs too?"

They traded somber glances.

"I don't know. My source seems to think they are connected. But Chip Dobbs had a bunch of enemies. Let's not forget that he was tied up in that drug gang too. I published a story about him and a kingpin named Richard Lester last year, right before my accident."

"Who's this source?" Claire asked.

"I can't say right now."

"Okay, fine. Let's forget about Richard Lester for a minute. For the sake of argument, let's say this guy Caleb was working for the Delacourtes and murdered Ezra Hawkins. Chip Dobbs was helping them, right? Why kill him too?"

"I don't know, Claire."

Claire frowned. "This sounds crazy," she said. "You know that, right?"

"Tell me about it," Hampton said. "Tucker has been saying the same thing for years."

"He knows about this?"

"He gave me the green light to follow the money trail, but Tucker has no idea about any of this."

"You should be talking to the FBI or the GBI right now."

"I don't have enough, and I promised my source I wouldn't go to the police. Anyway, they'd laugh me right out to the street and bolt the door behind me."

"Well, if people were tailing your source, don't you think they know that you've been meeting with them?"

You don't know what kinna people you messing with.

He dug into his backpack and pulled out the piece of construction paper.

"Hand me your kimono," Hampton said.

Claire slipped off the sheath. Hampton laid it out over the desk, then matched the curious design with the origami Chanel had given him.

"What's that?"

"My source called it a bird, but it looks more like this dragon," Hampton explained. "You're the professional designer. Which is it?"

Claire shrugged.

Hampton checked his watch. It was after 10 A.M., and Chanel's train should've made it into Chicago by now. He hadn't heard from her since the train crossed into Indiana.

"This is what your book is about, isn't it?"

Hampton didn't respond. He let his head fall into his hands.

THIRTY

Victoria felt a familiar surge of adrenaline as she stepped from the SUV with blacked-out windows and onto the curb in front of 235 Perimeter Center Parkway. Though she had weathered far more than a dozen editorial board meetings over the course of her public career, this one promised to be more contentious than all the others combined. She would be asked pointed questions and forced to defend her record; in turn, she would demand that they defend theirs.

There would be questions about the omnibus transportation bill that died in a congressional committee, despite her previous assurances that passage was all but guaranteed. She had done the hard work, she'd tell them, of crossing the aisle to work with Republican leaders in the statehouse and members of the Georgia congressional delegation. They wanted, quite frankly, more than she was willing to give. Questions about the city's contracting practices and her late brother's conduct in the procurement office were also likely to come up.

Roy Huggins was nervous about her plans to push back on the morning's story, and he'd said so at least twice along the ride up Georgia 400. Roy had spoken to the managing editor, Tucker Stovall, earlier in the day and briefed the mayor on their conversation as they drove to the meeting. The decision to publish the Franco story was made after consulting with the in-house legal team, Roy explained. Their chief counsel, Virgil Loudermilk, signed off moments before it went live.

"Stovall is satisfied with the sourcing," the press secretary said as they exited on Abernathy Road. "He says it's rock solid."

"That's because it is," Victoria admitted. "The problem is the rock they turned over to get it."

"You actually hit Dr. Overstreet?"

"With everything I could lay my hands on."

"So the public statement your office put out about that boating accident was a lie?"

"It isn't something I came to easily."

The news was out, and she'd put away any hope of getting the *Times-Register* endorsement, despite the fact that Whit Delacourte was still chairman of the umbrella company. He was a decent man, she told herself, unlike his wayward cousin-brother.

Victoria once counted Whit as a friend of her administration, a bridge she could count on in troubled waters. It was Whit Delacourte who stepped up with the first check, for $200,000, written to the Ezra J. Hawkins Memorial Foundation after the carnage at Ebenezer. Even so, Loudermilk would almost certainly see to it that Reverend Goodwin, the slick-as-duck-fat televangelist and political neophyte, got the nod from the editorial board. She'd wanted to cancel the meeting and ordered Roy to make the call the night before. The morning paper changed everything.

Hours after Detective Haverty was forced to turn in his badge and service revolver, the mayor arrived for the scheduled 3 P.M. meeting sporting a fresh suit and a devil-may-care attitude. The day had finally come when she could extract a long-overdue pound of flesh.

Situated in a glistening office tower, behind a sprawling shopping center and luxury condominiums, the new home of the *Atlanta Times-Register* was a departure from the aging, concrete-faced mid-rise it had once inhabited downtown on Marietta Street. Victoria had led the delegation that lobbied against the move to the suburbs. Dunwoody boasted cheaper rents, and the lion's share of subscribers lived north of the city limits.

Victoria folded and tucked the day's paper under her arm. Huggins followed her up the walkway and through the revolving doors. She waved happily at two security guards seated behind the reception desk.

"Good afternoon, I'm Mayor Dobbs, and I'm here to see Tucker Stovall," she told them cheerily.

Minutes later, she got off the elevator and entered the bustling newsroom, where she was greeted by a news assistant, a familiar young face not more than a year or so out of college.

"Hi, Mayor Dobbs. I'm—"

"Olu Gatewood!" she said, beaming. "It's good to see you."

"You remember my name?"

"Of course I do. That was one heck of a valedictorian speech you gave last year."

"Morehouse was good for me, ma'am."

"And you were good for Morehouse, young man. Did you pledge?"

"Yes, ma'am. Alpha Phi Alpha."

"Good choice. You're a Morehouse man now, walking in the footsteps of giants. My father was an Alpha."

"Yes, ma'am. The editorial board is waiting in the conference room, if you will follow me. Can I get you some coffee? Maybe some water?"

"Water would be good, thank you."

"Done deal. I'll get you situated in the fishbowl and bring you a bottle."

"The fishbowl?"

"Sorry, I mean the conference room," Olu said. "We call it the fishbowl because it looks like one."

"Naturally."

The newsroom fell into a hush as the mayor made her way through the cubicles and into a second corridor lined with glass-enclosed offices. The mayor waved courteously at some and nodded menacingly at Kathy Franco, the crime-beat reporter who'd written not one but two stories about the incident at her house.

The "fishbowl" was a beautiful box fronted with semi-frosted glass. The floor-to-ceiling windows offered a clear view of Stone Mountain to the northeast and Kennesaw Mountain to the northwest. Every seat, save for one, was occupied by stern faces along the table that stretched the full length of the room. Victoria reflexively raised a brow when she spotted Hampton Bridges seated on the left.

A knife fight in a phone booth.

Huggins took a seat among a bank of reporters who were stationed along a wall in overflow chairs, while the mayor greeted each of the attendees personally. She circled the table, shaking hands and trading niceties until she came to her last stop.

"Mr. Bridges," she said, extending an open palm. "Please, stay seated. Don't stress yourself."

"A pleasure to see you, Mayor Dobbs," Bridges said politely.

Wish I could say the same.

"Likewise," she said. "Glad to see you're back on your feet."

Victoria took her appointed seat at the head of the table and clasped her hands. She placed her right hand over the left, guarding the six-carat diamond wedding set against gawkers. Taking it off would've confirmed their suspicions. The questions came gently at first, with Stovall flinging the initial round like hardened pellets of cat shit that missed their mark. Bridges chimed in with a few relatively innocuous queries.

It went on like that for an hour or more. Victoria studiously answered with a litany of talking points as the reporters furiously scribbled on their notepads. A digital recorder positioned in the center of the table captured every word. She stuck to her script, mostly, veering away only to make a side joke here or there, to which she received respectful laughter. Stovall thanked her for her time.

"If you will indulge me, I have a few questions of my own."

Stovall frowned and scanned the room.

"Shall we take this to my office, Mayor Dobbs?"

"That won't be necessary, Mr. Stovall. In fact, I think your full team should be present. For reporting purposes, of course."

Stovall was visibly bothered. Bridges readjusted himself in his seat.

"I had the displeasure of speaking with my police chief about a personnel issue this morning," she began. "Detective Shaun Haverty has been employed with the Atlanta Police Department for sixteen years. Over at least the last two, as far as we can determine, he has been splitting his time conducting, shall we say, undercover work."

Bridges was wide-eyed now, Victoria noticed.

"I have recused myself from the process. However, I can tell you that Detective Haverty has been placed on administrative leave pending a departmental hearing, and I expect that soon after that, he will be terminated. City Attorney Armand Daou will ask both the Fulton County prosecutor and the U.S. district assistant attorney general to review the case and take any evidence to a grand jury. A separate investigation, led by the GBI, is being launched as we speak."

"Mayor Dobbs, what is this about?" Stovall asked.

"It appears that Mr. Haverty has admitted sending Mr. Bridges here a copy of a 911 tape from one of my neighbors, Mrs. Edna Gaffney. Now, I won't dispute the legality of the disclosure. I'll let that go out with the wash. A simple Freedom of Information Act would have given Mr. Bridges access to that recording at some point, if he knew to ask for it."

Stovall chimed in again. "Our story was well sourced and you are a public official who, it appears, was involved in a domestic violence incident. Kathy Franco is one of our very best."

"That is true enough," Victoria said in return. "However, this is more about your chief legal counsel, J. Virgil Loudermilk, who we believe orchestrated the disclosure."

"That is a serious allegation, Mayor Dobbs," an opinion columnist, Deanna McCaskill, interjected.

"Absolutely. And I would not make it if I did not have definitive proof of his actions. Let me tell you a story, Ms. McCaskill. A little more than two weeks ago, two days before I formally announced my candidacy, a package arrived at my home. It was addressed to me and contained, I am sorry to say, incontrovertible evidence of infidelity by my husband."

"Is this on the record?" Bridges asked.

"You can print every word of it, Mr. Bridges. Keep the tape running."

Victoria stood and began walking around the table, gesturing with her hands as she spoke, as if teaching a classroom full of schoolchildren.

"As this paper reported," she said, pointing at Bridges, "there was indeed an altercation that night. My husband never struck me, as Ms. Franco implied in her article. I was angry, as any wife would be, and I hit him, and, yes, I sprayed him with a pressure washer. There was no boat accident. I asked my office to issue a preemptive statement in an attempt to protect my family's privacy."

"Did an officer go to your home that night, Mayor Dobbs?" McCaskill asked.

"No, I took a call from Chief Walraven and assured him that all was well. The security detail was told to stand down and my husband declined to press charges."

Victoria stretched her neck, let it crack, and continued. She had their full attention now.

"My husband and I have begun the difficult work of putting our marriage back together. We are committed to what we know will be arduous but personal work.

"That being said, I was curious about some things. I wanted to know, as you well might, who sent that package to my home and who then leaked the story to Mr. Bridges and Ms. Franco. I wanted to know who violated federal privacy laws by disclosing my husband's medical reports.

"Now, I understand as well as anyone that politics is not for the faint of heart. Proverbial as they made be, shots get taken and fired. But I wanted to know how my private life showed up on your front page this morning with such perfect timing, in the midst of my campaign for Congress, hours before this editorial board meeting was set to begin. These are the questions that you should be asking yourselves."

Stovall stood up and abruptly ordered the reporters from the room.

"No one writes anything until I see it first," he said as they filed out. "Bridges, stay seated."

Victoria drew a sheet of paper from the briefing book and continued, walking through the bullet points. The page was used merely for show. Victoria had memorized every line.

"This morning, Detective Haverty answered those questions, Mr. Stovall. He turned over his banking records, showing cash deposits in various increments dating back two years. If necessary, Chief Walraven's office will provide you with redacted copies for your review. Haverty claims that he was being paid by Mr. Loudermilk to monitor the actions of various public officials, including myself and at least four unnamed others. He tailed my husband for at least a week. A GPS tracker was attached to his car.

"Mr. Haverty somehow accessed my husband's cell phone accounts without a warrant and took photographs that remain too painful for me to look at. He also sent Mr. Bridges a passcode-protected email message using a proxy server. The last deposit, forty-five hundred dollars, was posted this morning after the story went live on your website last night and in time for the print edition.

"My press secretary tells me that your internal legal team cleared the story and that Mr. Loudermilk personally reviewed it."

Stovall was blinking rapidly now. Bridges didn't make a sound. McCaskill was strangely impassive, clicking her pen on the table in a steady rhythm.

"So that I am clear," the mayor continued, moving in next to her, "we believe Mr. Loudermilk paid a member of law enforcement, a city employee, to spy on my family, sent me the product of his illicit behavior, and then promptly fed the story through that same city employee to a reporter at this newspaper, which of course is coincidentally controlled by his family. And if that were not enough, Mr. Loudermilk reviewed and gave the story his Good Housekeeping seal of approval."

The Atlanta Way.

Feeling a spate of satisfaction with herself, Victoria turned toward the window and perused the wondrous skyline. The milky clouds that floated over Stone Mountain seemed to liquefy under the midday sun. She looked at them again. Then, staring into Stovall's eyes, she said in a single breath:

"And now, you expect me to believe—even after answering a flurry of pedantic policy questions today—that I stand a chance of earning your endorsement, not that it means anything anymore. Mr. Loudermilk used to tell me that he owned this editorial board, and now I know that to be true."

She was visibly angry now. Roy Huggins stood up. Victoria raised her palm before he could part his lips.

"I was frustrated when this paper went after my brother with unfounded, sordid allegations and, even as he lay in a burn unit, clinging to life, one of your reporters thought it right to come to his church and stalk our closest friends and family. I was disappointed when an obituary supposedly written in honor of Congressman Hawkins was littered with decades-old, unsubstantiated rumors. I understand that you have a job to do and that this is a for-profit enterprise. I do not expect you to parrot my speeches or give me a free pass. However, what I do expect is that you will honor your obligation to this city and to your readers. I expect fundamental fairness, not a hit job at the behest of a profiteering political arsonist with an axe to grind!"

Victoria collected her Chanel handbag from her chair and swung it over her shoulder.

As she and Roy began to leave, Victoria turned and said, "Ms. McCaskill, I fully expect that you will call Mr. Loudermilk to personally inform him of my allegations. You should know that my lawyers are drafting a federal civil suit, specifically naming you and Mr. Loudermilk among the defendants. I know that you are his point person in this newsroom and I will prove it. Who can say if there will be criminal charges? I imagine, though, that you're going to be spending a bit more time with your beautiful family."

The once-stolid McCaskill looked panic stricken. The notion that she was one of only two syndicated black women columnists in the country, as well as an Alpha Kappa Alpha and Spelman sister who had grown up in Mechanicsville, was not lost on Victoria. She could take no pleasure in taking McCaskill down.

"And, Mr. Bridges, don't fret," the mayor said dismissively. "It looks like you were just a patsy and it doesn't appear that you have anything worth taking, other than what's left of your pride."

THIRTY-ONE

The storms erupted over Atlanta. Virgil took cover at his compound located due south of the Chattahoochee National Forest in Ball Ground, Georgia. Besides the torrential rains slicking interstate highways, filling creek beds, and flooding residential enclaves, the chatter class was alight with back-fence talk about the political warring going on. There were simply too many people in that editorial board meeting for word not to get out, and Atlanta was, and always had been, the biggest small town on earth. For the most part, Victoria Dobbs came out smelling like a rose, and Virgil could think of better things than hearing his name swish around in the mud.

There were some, at least according to Libby Gail, who were bursting with delight over the mayor's latest predicament, and this was music to Virgil's ears. It was all too perfect: the husband, the children, the big house in Buckhead, the fancy cars and European ski trips. Her storybook life was falling apart, and that was due cause for celebration.

Pacing the paved circular drive, Virgil pulled back the sleeve of his summer windbreaker and rechecked the time. It was unseasonably rainy and cool for mid-July, but with yet another tropical storm system coming up off the Atlantic coast, Georgia didn't stay dry for more than a few hours at a time.

If you don't like the weather in Atlanta, wait a few minutes. It'll change.

The same could be said for the politics. For now, Virgil was more concerned about Hurricane Victoria than a forecast that promised flooding. He hadn't expected her to go quietly, given her predilection for histrionics, but her latest salvo was clearly intended to burst the dams. There had been a time when she was more amenable, even likable, Virgil recalled. Victoria was a smart woman, he knew, and stunningly beautiful even when she was in a huff.

He'd been introduced to Victoria, then a young lawyer working in a forgettable department somewhere in the City Hall Annex, not long after she graduated from Harvard Law. The daughter of Park and Rosetta Dobbs was gorgeous if not more than a little presumptuous. Still, he'd been taken with her sure-footed brilliance and, at the urging of Ezra Hawkins and his brother, Whit, Virgil agreed to take her under his wing. When she later needed campaign cash, for one political pursuit or another, Virgil had been Johnny-on-the-spot with every dime she needed and more. If there were strings to be pulled, he pulled them. If there were political bones to be buried, he was handy with a shovel.

Well, it wasn't long before his precious little peacock fattened up, fanned her feathers, and began strutting about the political yard. He'd expected as much. Truth be told, keeping Dobbs in line all those years had been more than a piece of work. Be it not for Whit, Virgil would've cut her off before she got out of the statehouse. Now, the Great Torie Dobbs was the sitting mayor, running for Congress and threatening to personally set him on fire.

It was near 'bout 2 P.M., and the chopper had not yet arrived. He scanned the densely clouded sky, half regretting that he'd sent Lucky on such a critical errand. He worried the helicopter might not make it off the ground with the weather around Atlanta being so bad and all. The flight up from the city was a dead twenty minutes in clear skies, at best, but he hadn't heard from Lucky in well over two hours.

The Loudermilk estate, situated along Hawks Nest, was an impressive spread, not unlike his house in Atlanta or the chalet down on St. Simons Island. The twenty-thousand-square-foot main house stood on a six-acre lot surrounded by lovely pastures and once belonged to Big Whit and given to his adopted son and his wife upon his death. Virgil immediately quit-claimed the deed to Libby Gail, calling it an anniversary gift. He'd spent millions renovating the place over the years, under Libby Gail's supervision, of course. A spectacular master suite now overlooked the bi-level swimming pool, red clay tennis courts, and a private lake. A helipad sat on the left end of the front pasture. The five-seat Agusta A109C helicopter had been a gift to himself spring before last.

"Goddamn you, Lucky," he grumbled, cursing the whipping winds. "Where in the sand hell are you?"

Thanks to the circus act the mayor put on, there were decisions to be made. Live news trucks currently surrounded his house and office in Atlanta. Libby Gail complained that a reporter from the Associated Press kept calling her cell phone and some fella from CNN showed up at the Buckhead Diner, hoping to find him there in his usual spot.

Of course, the Delacourte Enterprises corporate communications director issued a perfunctory statement, promising a full investigation that Virgil knew would never come to fruition. The *Times-Register* editorial board published a joint opinion column proclaiming the virtues of independent journalism and called for his immediate ouster. They would have no choice but to endorse Dobbs now, he figured. McCaskill resigned, over his fervent objections, and Virgil knew he might have to step aside, at least for a while.

Mud dries and flicks off.

Until then, he was content to stay at his luxury farmhouse and far away from the shutterbugs and rubberneckers. Besides, the refrigerator and wet bar were fully stocked. And, at least here he wouldn't have to listen to Libby Gail's mouth. His brother, Whit, was another matter. He'd driven up earlier that morning, and the two argued until Virgil agreed to relinquish his role as chief legal counsel and give up his seat on the board of directors. Both of which would be temporary, Whit promised, assuming their contingency plans worked out.

"What in the hell did you do this time?" asked Whit, immediately tearing into Virgil before he'd made it out of the car.

"I said I would take care of it."

"Take care of it? Is that what you call this?"

"She can't prove a word of it," Virgil said. "My hands are clean."

"Your hands haven't been clean since you took a mud bath in that plastic swimming pool Daddy had out in the backyard."

"You approved this mission yourself."

"I didn't tell you to go bribing a cop. That's a federal offense!"

"And the least of our worries right now. I said I would take care of it. You have my word on that."

Red faced and huffing, Whit was beside himself. Virgil made every attempt to pacify him, but his brother wouldn't hear it.

"C'mon in the house, and let's talk this thing out," Virgil pressed. "You didn't drive all the way out here to stomp your feet across my driveway."

"No, I came out here to kick you in your fat ass!"

"Settle down, Whit," Virgil said. "This'll all blow over. We'll win the race, and everything at the company will be sausage, grits, and gravy."

"You think I give a damn about that right now? I'm tired, Virgil. Enough is enough!"

Virgil leaned against the porch column, lit a cigarillo, and took a long, studied draw.

"Put that out," Whit demanded, waving the smoke away.

"This is my house, and you might run things down in Atlanta, but I'm the king out here. Daddy left this place to me. You and Baby Sister got a majority stake in the company and I got the house. Nice bargain for you, if you ask me."

"Goddammit, I said put it out!"

It wasn't like Whit to holler like that. Virgil's usually mild-mannered brother had always been slow to anger. Whit seemed to be letting him have it for transgressions old and new, Virgil reckoned. He hadn't seen his brother like that since they were in grade school when he mixed up some vinegar, peroxide, and baking soda and tried to blow up a model airplane that Whit had spent all summer painting and admiring. Then there was the girlfriend he stole from his brother in the ninth grade. Virgil had a knack for making Whit's ass itch.

"Fine, fine," Virgil said, extinguishing the butt in the wet grass. "We're in this together. You remember that."

"Until we ain't."

"What is that supposed to mean?"

"You know what it means," Whit said. "I've been pulling your ass out of a ditch since the day your daddy dropped you off at our house on Sycamore Avenue, and there's only so much more I can do. I promised your mama, rest her soul, that I'd see after you. But if she knew you like I did, she'd dump your ass off at the nearest Greyhound station. The sun didn't rise in her eyes until your incorrigible ass woke up in the morning."

"I'm only trying to see after Cole. You and I know that poor boy of yours ain't got a lick of business acumen," Virgil said. "We set up that construction company and gave him a heap of money. Him and that wife of his rolled through every bit of it. Before I knew it good, he tried to buy up every distressed commercial property from here to Mississippi, and he can't keep Raffi out of Phipps Plaza, not that he tries real hard."

Whit nodded in agreement.

"Every time I turn around, they're jetting off on shopping trips on Delta private charters," Virgil said. "He doesn't have our daddy's mind for money. Hell, he spent his entire trust fund inside of seven years. I did what I had to do to keep them afloat. Now, I cut off his jet account last month like you told me to. But, he's burning a hundred grand a month in expenses on God knows what."

Whit nodded again, waved the lingering fog of smoke away, and hesitantly agreed to take the discussion inside. He followed Virgil across the hardwood foyer and into the cedar-paneled great room.

"You know the doctor said I can't be around tobacco smoke," Whit said.

"Dr. Kessler told you to lay off fried pork chops and red-eye gravy too, but you're still eating them."

"A man's gotta have something to hold on to. What do we know about that detective of yours?" Whit said, resting his bones on the oversized sofa. "Would he testify?"

"There won't be a case. Anyway, Lucky sent the wire transfers from the Cayman account. It's his word against mine, and we know how that will go. We'll do what we have to do."

"There won't be a case? Are you going to buy off a U.S. district attorney too?"

Virgil scanned the ceiling and said nothing.

"That's exactly what I'm afraid of," Whit said, studying the deep wrinkles in Virgil's jowls.

"I'll take care of Haverty," Virgil said. "The wheels are already in motion."

Virgil called for a housekeeper and had her bring a bottle of Bulleit Bourbon up from the cellar and two shot glasses. It wasn't noon yet, but he figured a little liquor would help smooth things out.

"You have to step down," Whit said, wincing and tossing back a glass. "The least you can do is take a leave of absence while we sort this thing out. Wilma agrees with me."

"Baby Sister always sides with you," Virgil protested. "That doesn't mean diddly-squat."

"That's fifty-six percent of the voting shares. We might have to terminate your employment contract. We've got to protect our interests here."

"This is my daddy's company too," Virgil said. "I'm still a shareholder."

"Don't make me exercise the morality clause."

"You can't be serious about this. Take your time and think about what you're saying."

"And we'll need to shut down Resurgens too."

"That's all he's got. Cole doesn't have any marketable skills, other than picking out women's shoes at Neiman Marcus, and you know it."

"Maybe we can sell it," Whit said. "Private transaction. Get his name off of it, set him and Raffi up in another business. I don't care if it's a food truck. I'll put him on an allowance."

"Any sale, private or otherwise, will draw fire for sure. I say we leave it as it is for right now."

"And what about our mayor?"

Virgil poured another round. Whit, waiting for an answer, didn't touch his shot glass.

"What are we going to do about Victoria?" Whit asked again. "She's threatening a civil suit and a criminal investigation."

"Empty promises," Virgil said. "There's no way she'd put her own neck on the chopping block like that. She'd swell up like a puffer fish if they ever put handcuffs on her."

"I'm nobody's prosecutor, but I can't see where she's broken the law," Whit said.

Again, Virgil said nothing.

"Alright, leave her alone," Whit said. "If she wins, she wins. If she loses, it'll likely be her last race. I'll ring her up and see if I can get her to agree to a cease-fire."

"Do you honestly think she'll listen to you?"

"She might. Her mother and I have always been on good terms."

"I ain't taking that chance. I'll handle your mayor."

"I said leave her alone. What about our silent partner?"

"There are some things you don't want or need to know. Not now, not ever," said Virgil. "We've always been clear on that. If anybody takes a hit, it'll be me. I'll step down for ninety days or so until the dust settles. Maybe even six months, if that makes you feel any better. But if Victoria's little outburst in that editorial board meeting was any indication, she's gunning for a fight, and I aim to give her one. We'll carry it right out into the street, so the good people of Atlanta can see what she's really made of, if we have to."

"This has to stop," Whit said, gripping the small glass. "It's time to call a truce and unwind this thing."

"It's too late for that, Whit, and you know it."

Whit went to swig his liquor and instead lobbed it at the cedar-paneled wall.

"Well, hell, deep down you two are just alike, aren't you?" Virgil said. "You always were the kind to get blinded by a piece of ass."

"You stop right there, Virgil!"

"You put this whole damn thing in jeopardy on account of your bleeding heart. You don't owe her a goddamn thing," Virgil shot back. "She could spend a thousand years thanking you a thousand times a day, and it still wouldn't be enough for all you've done for her."

"I said let it be! Shut it down right now!"

Whit got up, stormed out, and slammed the front door behind him. Virgil leaned back and assessed the situation. There were moves to be made, he knew. Despite Whit's fussing, his latest plan was already in motion.

He'd planned for the possibility that Dobbs might link him to the detective at some point, especially with that secret cop squad of hers and all. He figured Haverty must've started flapping his gums the minute Pelosi got hold of him. The fact that Dobbs had already spilled it all to the editorial board left him flat-footed.

Half the day had gone by, and he hadn't heard a peep out of Lucky. Virgil clicked the button on his Bluetooth headset and tried calling again. Right about the same time, he heard the propellers slicing through the winds over the main house. He stepped outside and walked to the edge of the helipad. The air grew cooler as the chopper descended onto the tarmac. Lucky, the pilot, and a third man, Riley Lester, stepped out, ducking beneath the slowing blades.

Virgil greeted his guest straightaway. "Glad you could come all this way," he said. "How's your family?"

"Everybody is fine, under the circumstances," Riley replied.

"Indeed."

"Weather's ugly. We could've met down in the city," Riley said, tipping his nose toward a bank of rain clouds. "We've got a half dozen safe houses still operating. My brother said this was urgent, so here I am."

"I appreciate the courtesy."

If he was feeling uneasy, Virgil figured Lucky was trying not to let on. But Virgil, having known him for the full of his adult life, spotted the hesitance in his eyes. Lucky motioned to the pilot to wait in the chopper.

Virgil escorted his guest inside. They traded small talk as they waited to be served a supper of pan-seared duck breasts, roasted potatoes, and collard greens. It would be the first and last time he and Riley would ever meet, he figured, so Virgil made sure the meal was something special. He had been accustomed to talking to his brother in person, but the situation was different now. Dickey Lester was wearing a court-ordered ankle bracelet, and his calls were no doubt being monitored. Virgil regretted getting into business with them, given their proclivity for violence, but the brothers were sitting on prime property, and those acres were key to his plans for Resurgens. When the time was right, he'd kick Cole and Raffi to the curb and walk away with billions in construction contracts. Then too, knowing what he knew about Dickey and Victoria made his plans all the more delicious.

Lucky picked over his plate until it was cold and indigestible. Riley ate slowly and methodically until the plate was scraped clean, like he was dining at a five-star restaurant. He dabbed his mouth with a cloth napkin, folded his hands across his lap, and waited. When Virgil was satisfied that his dinner companion was full, he stuffed his jowls with the last corner of sweet bread and tossed his napkin onto his plate, signaling he was ready to get down to business.

"You sure you wanna stay around for this?" he asked Lucky.

Lucky got up abruptly, leaving his chair pushed back, and left the room.

"A glass of wine? Maybe a cocktail?" Virgil offered. "I've got a full bar."

"No, thank you. I don't drink when I'm working," Riley replied. "My brother is a generous man. He sent a gift for you." He reached into his jacket pocket, pulled out a small black box, and slid it onto the dining room table.

"What's this?"

"An external hard drive."

"What's on it?"

"Everything Hampton Bridges has been working on for the last six years." Virgil patted the top of the case and grinned. "How much will this cost me?"

"Again, my brother is a generous man."

THIRTY-TWO

Hampton settled in for the fireworks. The first and only debate of the campaign cycle was about to get under way in studio 1A at Georgia Public Broadcasting. The theater-style, cushioned armchairs were brimming with local boldfaced names.

Tom Houck, an ever-present, loquacious, gravel-voiced politico, who had had the ear of every sitting mayor dating back to the mid-'70s, was seated behind him, trading guffaws with Maria Saporta, who published a widely read blog about the politics and business of Atlanta. Next to them sat Alexis Scott, a legendary journalist in her own right whose grandfather founded the nation's first black-owned newspaper in the twentieth century. Hampton greeted them gingerly. He was, after all, the same reporter who'd gotten into a drunken car accident with a barely legal mistress not so long ago, and the embarrassing shine hadn't quite worn off. Scott, as is her custom, was most gracious, while Houck eyed him warily. Saporta, with her shock of long gray-streaked brown hair and toothy smile, offered a consoling glance.

He had been one of them, Hampton lamented, a high-flying political columnist and statehouse bureau chief, glad-handing and swigging craft beers

at Manuel's Tavern, until his untimely downfall. The whispers among his colleagues had been especially hurtful, though he was learning to live with that
now. Valerie Norbreck-Haynes camped out in an empty seat next to him.

To Hampton's surprise, Whit Delacourte appeared near the rear doors,
wandered down the aisle, and sat at the end of the first row. There were no
security guards and no assistants. He had come alone, dressed in a weathered
polo shirt, a pair of neatly pressed khaki slacks, and well-worn dock shoes with
no socks, all of which Hampton found odd. His presence caused a stir among
the press corps, but Delacourte seemed oblivious to the chatter. Hampton
watched as he crossed his long legs, dangling them over the aisle, and settled
in. Saporta near 'bout ran out of her shoes getting over to greet him. Delacourte traded niceties until she apparently got the message that he wanted to
be left alone.

Hampton turned his attention to the glorious stage. It was outfitted with
blue and red draperies, a row of faux Roman columns to give everything a
regal effect, and three freshly polished podiums. The klieg lights were still
dim when the moderator, Buzz Landry, ambled in to a smattering of applause
and took his place at a fourth lectern situated at a safe distance to the left of
the others.

At 7 P.M. sharp, the stage lit up and he opened the televised event.

"Ladies and gentlemen, welcome to the Atlanta Press Club Debate, presented by Georgia Public Broadcasting," he said. "I am Buzz Landry, your
moderator for the evening. Tonight, you will hear from the three major candidates in a special election for Georgia's Fifteenth Congressional District."
There was another smattering of applause.

Landry then paid his respects to the late Ezra Josiah Hawkins, asked for a
moment of silence, and laid out the ground rules before he got down to the
business of introducing his prey for the evening. As her name was called,
Mayor Dobbs strode onto the debate stage wearing her signature St. John suit,
a Georgia flag pin, and an above-it-all attitude that was hard to miss. State
Representative Sarah Mitchell made her entrance, wearing bookish glasses
and waving like the second runner-up in a beauty pageant. Pastor Goodwin
followed her in, dressed to the nines and grinning like he'd been invited to a

neighborhood potluck. Hampton wondered how much he paid a cosmetic dentist for that glorious smile. The trio shook hands and awkwardly paused for a group photo.

Mayor Dobbs made sure their revelry wouldn't last long. She delivered a rousing opening statement that brought half the audience, which was packed with her own supporters, to their feet. She invoked the name of Congressman Hawkins at least four times inside of one minute, so much so that Hampton lost count.

Over the next ninety minutes, Hampton watched as Dobbs shellacked the preacher like an old coffee table before she kicked his wobbly legs out from under him. For her part, Mitchell stayed on message and was turning in a passable appearance. Neither she nor Goodwin was any match for Dobbs. The bats hadn't been that hot since the Braves beat the Cleveland Indians in the '95 World Series. Dobbs came out swinging and kept the bases loaded, but her defense was the real showstopper.

When Mitchell got up the nerve to challenge Dobbs over her high school relationship with a now-indicted drug kingpin, the mayor seemed to leap over the outfield wall and snatch the ball into her glove.

"Maybe we should stroll through your yearbook," she said, turning to face Mitchell straight on. "Maybe we should talk about your college sweetheart and first husband, Jefferson Chait, who is now doing time in a federal camp for insider trading and wire fraud. Or maybe you'd like to talk about your second husband, Leland Mitchell, who gambled away the family fortune on every poker table from here to Vegas and back. Perhaps we shouldn't discuss your father's unceremonious ouster from Southern Bank and Trust for spearheading a mortgage fraud scheme that put more than three thousand Georgians out on the street."

Dobbs had come ready to bust out every pane of Mitchell's glass house, if need be. Mitchell looked positively dumbfounded as she gulped a waiting glass of water.

"And as for you, Reverend Goodwin," the mayor said, pivoting on heels and swinging her head in his direction.

The moderator stepped into the fray before Dobbs could get her well-manicured hands around the pastor's neck. Whatever she had on Goodwin would have to wait for the next round of questions.

Through the years, Landry had toppled more than his share of politicians—including a sitting governor, two candidates for secretary of state and a west Georgia pediatrician who had his eyes on a congressional seat. Dr. Art Felix had not expected questions about a decades-old divorce that included allegations of adultery, statutory rape, and witness tampering.

Landry was a tough customer, Hampton knew, and delivered his fastballs with a disarming silkiness that you couldn't see coming until they hit their mark. His southern accent was as thick and smooth as the waterfalls cascading through Tallulah Gorge. Somewhere north of sixty-five years old and still anchoring a morning-drive newscast on public radio, the white-haired reporter seemed to hit a new stride with every election cycle. Hampton eyed him closely now, wondering what manner of devilment he had up his sleeve.

Moments later, without warning, Landry lowered the boom.

"Pastor Goodwin, this query is for you. Your opponents have both released their tax returns, yet despite repeated promises, you have not opened your books. However, charitable filings by your foundation show that you paid yourself and members of your family at least six million in fees since its inception just four years ago, while making grants of less than ten percent of its revenue. It appears that the largest—and in two of those years, the only—beneficiary was the Goodwin family. First, will you release your personal tax filings? And second, how do you explain taking nearly ninety percent of your foundation's dollars for yourself and your family?"

Measuring his words, Goodwin responded, "I am a servant-leader. My wife and two sons work full-time at our foundation, and since 2010, we have awarded more than six hundred scholarships to college students around the country."

"Yes," Landry said. "By my math, Reverend, that would make each one worth about a thousand dollars, or about the same amount you billed the foundation for a single dinner in New York last summer. Mr. Goodwin, if your donors cannot trust you with their money, how can the people of the Fifteenth District trust you to do their business in Washington?"

The preacher stammered and coughed, but there was no answer.

Down goes Frazier! Down goes Frazier!

Hampton noticed Goodwin gripping the podium to steady his shaking hands. He'd written about the fake charity and the eye-popping $250,000 payment that went to his eldest son, R.J., who was fresh out of college. The story was languishing in the legal department, waiting for the final go-ahead.

"He seems to be at a loss for words," Mayor Dobbs chimed in unexpectedly. "So then, let me answer for him. The fact is, while Pastor Goodwin has been jetting around the globe, preaching the good word to poor people about sowing a seed to gain riches, he was enriching only himself. For the money he raised, that foundation could've funded an entire four-year degree for every single member of the current Morehouse, Spelman, and Clark Atlanta freshman classes. The only street paved with gold is the driveway leading up to his house. He could have paid to expand and repave all forty-two miles of I-285."

The crowd burst into laughter. The time-limit bell sounded, but the mayor kept going. Dobbs rolled her shoulders back as the reverend stared down at the empty lectern.

"And one more thing, Pastor," she said. "I noticed another foundation beneficiary in the records. It seems a woman named Yvonne Ingram received in excess of two hundred thousand dollars a year, beginning almost two years ago. The same Yvonne Ingram gave birth to a baby girl in April of 2012."

Ding! Ding! Ding!

"Pardon me, Ms. Overstreet? I don't know what you're implying. Yvonne Ingram is a loyal member of our church and the executive director of our family foundation. She is a good and faithful servant, and she earned every penny of her salary."

"It's 'Mrs.,' thank you, and the question is who and what she was serving."

Holy Mother of God!

Landry stared at Pastor Goodwin as if he were the devil incarnate coming to collect innocent souls. The audience didn't make a sound, and whoever was operating the time-limit bell didn't see fit to interject. Mayor Dobbs continued with the waylay. Hampton waited for the kill shot.

"It is my understanding Miss Ingram is a member of your church, as you duly noted. However, as head of your family foundation, she had no official duties other than cutting checks, and she had been, in fact, funneled over half a million dollars to keep her illicit relationship with you and your child together out of the public eye."

"How dare you, ma'am," Goodwin feebly protested.

"Dare I do, Pastor Goodwin. We can ask her about it, if you wish, since she's seated here in the audience tonight."

Hampton watched the blood drain out of the preacher's face as he spotted his mistress among the spectators. He flipped his notebook open and said, "It's all over but the shouting now."

THIRTY-THREE

Victoria trailed Marsh through the kitchen door, down a side hallway, and into the master bedroom. Her bones were aching, but the day was behind her now. A warm bath, a little music, and maybe a half tablet of ibuprofen were the perfect prescription. The prospect of running for reelection felt like a woolly coat in the summertime. She could not imagine doing it again every two years, as Ezra had. He'd been thirty years her senior and in Congress nearly as long, running every election like he was a newcomer fresh out of the sticks. She missed him now. His long veiny hands and smooth-as-cake-batter skin, the way he chuckled when she chided him over his packed schedule.

Run every day like you're running from behind.

Where he got the vigor, she did not know. Ezra never knew a day without the work. He was always in the fight, sunup to sundown and every moment in between.

Stay ready. Sometimes the fight comes to you.

On nights like these, she leaned on that.

Sometimes the fight comes to you.

They'd stopped briefly at the central campaign headquarters, she and Marsh, located along the Peachtree–Brookwood split in the heart of Midtown. There were four campaign offices in all, two to the south and another situated in a strip mall in far-north Fulton County, but this was the nerve center, the guts of the Dobbs campaign, where decisions were made. Volunteers and staffers greeted them with thundering applause.

"Don't come for me unless I send for you!" one volunteer shouted.

"Twirl on that!" Roy Huggins chimed in.

They raised a toast of cheap champagne in their Styrofoam cups while Miss Rosetta sat quietly at a corner table with her purse in her lap. A driver was dispatched to carry her home. Victoria broke away from the well-wishers to hug and kiss her mother good night.

"You are your father's child. Remember that, Victoria," she said. "He was in that room tonight, even if you couldn't see him."

"I know it sounds crazy, but I could feel him, Mama," Victoria said. "I want him to be proud of me."

"He might not've liked all that mudslinging. But your daddy loved your every breath. He's watching over you, even if you don't always know it."

"Mama? Are you proud of me?"

Rosetta paused and said, "Of course I am, sweetheart. Win or lose, you don't have anything to prove to me. You never did. You can rest your mind on that. Do the next right thing."

Bleary eyed and exhausted, she'd made quick work of Pastor Goodwin and shut down Mitchell before she could get any fancy ideas. But Victoria was uneasy about her mother's words. She could feel Rosetta's disappointment. For the first time, despite the cheering masses, she felt her mother's shame, even if Rosetta refused to say it out loud.

Victoria longed for her bed now.

Run every day like you're running from behind. Stay ready. Sometimes the fight comes to you.

In a few short hours, she was due back out on the street. For all practical purposes, the city government was thankfully running on autopilot and, save for a few executive orders and perfunctory ribbon-cuttings, she devoted most of her time to the congressional race and increasingly frequent appearances on cable news.

NBC's Chuck Todd, ever the skeptic on such matters, had already anointed her the clear winner before a single vote had been cast and tallied.

"You are the heir apparent," Todd said. "What are your priorities?"

"I don't believe in political inheritances," Victoria responded. "When all is said and done, my priority is now, has been, and will always be the people of the Fifteenth District. That means fighting for criminal justice reform, equal access to affordable health care, and meaningful jobs at meaningful wages. That also means making sure every child—black, white, and brown—has the right to a quality basic education and that a college education is available to every American who wants one."

"You sound a lot like Congressman Hawkins," Todd said. "If he were here now, what advice would he have for you?"

"He would tell me that nothing is promised. He would tell me to work hard to earn every vote and to keep earning them long after, if so honored, I am sworn into office."

Victoria was in her element under the klieg lights. Her rise to a national platform, her position among the country's most highly recognized big-city mayors, had long since been foretold, and she had prepared for every moment. Even so, as she stepped into her marvelous home, her precious daughters asleep in their beds, it all felt fleeting, as if it could be snatched away by a thief in the night.

Marsh had not said a word along the drive to the impromptu party nor on the ride home. He was her one true love, the man who would forsake everything to buy her pardon. But now, Victoria could feel the disgust radiating from his bones as he stripped out of his suit and flung it onto a mahogany valet stand. He'd been cordial enough to her campaign team and had, at least, spared her the embarrassment of a public upbraiding. Marsh fought with his silence, and tonight was no different. He went upstairs, dismissed the nanny for the night, then returned to their bedroom.

Victoria didn't have the heart to ask her husband what he thought about the debate. She already knew. Marsh couldn't be more different from Rosetta.

He wasn't the kind to hide his candor for very long. He could not simply tuck his disappointments away. If pressed, he would not duck behind pretty words. It wasn't his way, she knew, and at some point, he would make his displeasure known.

He'd been stoned-faced in the first row that night, clapping politely when she hit a good beat. The *Atlanta Times-Register* poll would be released the next morning, and Victoria, despite Todd's pronouncement, already knew she was under 45 percent. She had a narrow lead over her opponents, and the race was within the margin of error. With less than a week of active campaigning left, the real fight had begun, and she knew voter turnout was everything. She tried not to worry about the numbers now. Marsh was standing across the room, but it felt like her husband was oceans away.

She watched him slip on a pair of cotton drawstring lounging pants, gather his pillow, and pull an extra blanket from the linen closet. Marsh was never the kind to preen, but even now he was a beautiful man, built like a modern-day Adonis with sculpted pectoral muscles as if he had been carved from stone. In that moment, she imagined herself running her fingers over his closely trimmed, extended goatee and through the gentle curls.

Right then, right there, she wanted her husband to love her again, to feel his skin pressed against hers. She missed the way he kneaded the small of her back with his knuckles, the way he tugged at her nightgown until it fell to the floor, the way he lifted her chin and sucked at her lower lip until her fingers began to tingle. The words to their wedding song danced in her head.

> *Can you just feel how much I love you*
> *With one touch of my hand?*
> *Can I just spend my life with you?*

"We knew this would be a tough election," Victoria said finally. "I had to take them down. They came for us first, remember?"

"Yeah, yeah," he said dismissively. "Don't come for me, unless I send for you. That's what they said, right?"

"Please don't do me like that."

"Like what, Torie? Like you've been doing me? You've been out there conquering the known world, but what about us? Did you ever once think about us?"

"Every minute of every day."

"I knew you were still in love with that Dickey character when we met. Just when I thought he was out of our lives for good, here comes a bunch of TV ads to remind me. And that damn painting is still in the basement."

"He's under house arrest, sporting an ankle bracelet."

"And if he wasn't? I've stood by you through everything, Torie, for better or for goddamn worse. But I won't do this."

"You are my everything," she said tearfully. "You and our girls, you are my known world."

"Then it sounds like you have a decision to make."

"So, you're saying you want me to quit?"

"I would never ask that of you, but I want you to get that damn painting out of our house," he said. "I want you to be the woman who said yes to me, yes to our life. I fell in love with you the moment I laid my eyes on you, and I swear I've never stopped. Where was that woman tonight? What happened to her? You wouldn't even deny that man onstage tonight."

"You married a public servant. I was born to this. I made a specific choice to live out that promise. And, yes, it comes with a fight. That's the deal I made when I put my name on that first ballot, and that's the commitment I reaffirmed when I filed the qualifying papers to enter this race. That's the woman you saw on that stage tonight. That's the woman you married, and I am that woman every day."

"Are you? Because this one only seems to be worried about winning, no matter the price or who has to pay it. You had no right to talk about that man's family like that. You don't know their marriage, just like they don't know ours."

"Ours was in the damn newspaper!"

"And you helped to keep it there!"

The fire in his eyes was unmistakable, but Victoria was unmoved. She folded her arms across her breasts and said, "When were you going to leave me? Tell me. Before or after that trip you and Samantha booked for Anguilla?

Oh, you didn't think I knew about that? It was never going to be a boys' trip. You can tell her that I'm sorry I spoiled her weekend plans with my husband!"

"I don't have to take this shit from you. You don't need me. You can keep playing with your own pussy, if that makes you happy."

The blow took him by surprise. His head swung sideways as she planted her open palm across his cheek. His eyes watered. Whether out of anger, sadness, or disappointment, Victoria could not tell, and in that moment, she did not want to care.

"Never do that again," Marsh said.

"Or what? You'll leave me?" she shouted. "You left here years ago. You leave me every time you walk out of here to go fuck one of your bitches. Every moment you spend with a dime-store whore is another moment you miss with our daughters."

"You just couldn't leave Maya and Mahalia out of this, could you? I would set myself on fire for those girls and you know it, but it's all about scoring cheap points for you, right? Anything for the win."

"You want a divorce? Then file the goddamn papers! Take your shit and get the fuck out of here!"

"Don't think I haven't thought about it, Torie. But between your parents and mine, they were married a hundred years. Real marriages, strong marriages take work. And I cannot hold this one up by myself."

"Ain't nobody asking you to! You ain't in this by yourself," Victoria shot back. "My mother is as strong as they make them. She sat in my daddy's church for years, knowing there were three, four, and five women in that congregation on any given Sunday who would suck my daddy's dick on demand. Your daddy wasn't no saint. I'm sure your mother put up with more shit than a little bit. My mama told me to stay with you, like she stayed with my father, but I'm not my mother or yours. You won't make a fool out of me!"

She was in his face now, standing breast to chest. "You want out? Then, motherfucker, get out! Ain't nothing holding you back but your silly fucking pride."

"Stop it, Torie!"

"Oh, gosh, Marsh, what would good people think? What will this do to the

Overstreet name?" she said, sarcastically. "Keep blaming a stupid painting, if you want to. But I will be damned if I let you put that on me while you're screwing some trick on a call-room cot in the emergency room!"

"Fuck you!"

Victoria reared back, balled up her fist, and lunged forward. Marsh caught her by the wrist before she could take another swing at him. She felt the intensity of his grip. Still holding her arm, he darted his eyes back and forth, searching her face with a smoldering rage she had not seen before. They locked eyes. And then, he let go.

"Hit me," she said, sneering. "Goddammit, I said, hit me!"

Marsh shook it off, released her from his grasp, snatched up the blanket, and said, "I've never laid my hands on you, and so help me God, I never will."

"Let me find out you're still fucking with that bitch. Let me find out that your punk ass is still in these streets, and so help *me* God, I will bury you next to your own whoring-ass daddy. Now, twirl on that."

"You've lost your mind. I'll sleep upstairs."

Victoria was immediately sorry. She tried desperately to quiet the storms in her head. In the days after the congressman was murdered, she'd struggled to maintain her balance. Marsh's infidelities, long known to her, were suddenly staring her in the face. Then, after her brother was killed, she felt herself falling apart. Victoria responded the way she always had, by lurching forward, by throwing herself into her work. That had been her way, and Marsh, knowing her proclivities better than anyone, had to understand that. There were both political and personal costs, much more than she had anticipated, much more than her decidedly fragile marriage might be able to withstand.

Sometimes the fight comes to you.

There was a time when she thought she could not live a day without him. His quiet confidence had been an anchor in rough seas. But in the years since, there had been brutal fights, times when the distance between them spanned the seven seas. She wondered now how long they would be able to hang on.

She'd wanted to tell him how much she missed his touch, but thought better of that now. Instead, she let him walk out and drew herself a warm shower. When the race was over, she thought, maybe they could patch things up. But for how long, she did not know. The blood was seeping through the bandages again, and they had been unable to stanch the flow. She could surely raise their daughters on her own, but in her heart of hearts, Victoria still believed there was something worth saving. She wanted him to believe that too.

They had once known love in its fullness. But the playful text messages and surprise floral bouquets were a distant memory now. So too were the stolen glances, weekend getaways, and Sundays in Chastain Park watching their daughters frolic on the swing set. Marsh spent more late nights at the hospital, and there were many more when he didn't come home at all. She'd stopped asking where he was going or where he'd been, and Marsh didn't even bother making excuses anymore. Pelosi had offered to put a tail on him and report back.

"That won't be necessary," Victoria told him. "Wherever my husband is, that's where he wants to be."

For Victoria, it felt like the last cup of sugar had been spilled out onto the floor. That sweetness was gone now. She had been unable, if not unwilling, to catch it in the fall. She lay in bed that night, uncomfortable, for the first time, in her own skin.

Do the next right thing.

Sometime around 3 A.M., she felt her husband crawl into bed beside her and pull her in close. She was startled, but allowed herself to fold into his steely arms.

"I couldn't sleep," he said, lifting her hair at the nape.

Can I just see you every morning when
I open my eyes?
Can I just feel your heart beating beside me
Every night?

"I'm sorry," she said. "God, I'm sorry."

Victoria felt his soft lips on her neck. She let out a gentle sigh, turned and allowed her lips to touch his, and whispered, "I don't want to let go."

THIRTY-FOUR

I t took two hours to get him on the phone, but by the time Virgil reached the preacher, the decision was already made. Goodwin and his wife prayed into the wee hours of the morning, he explained, and concluded that he would end his bid for Congress. The media avail was set for 1 P.M. in the main sanctuary at City of Hope. A revival service would immediately follow.

"This is what's best for our family," Goodwin said. "It's in the Lord's hands now."

No matter what the numbers said, the way he saw it, Goodwin had a better chance of beating Usain Bolt in a footrace down Spring Street than toppling Victoria Dobbs. That didn't quell his sore belly. He listened to millions burn up like a skillet of corn bread.

"Why didn't you tell me about all of this when I asked? I gave you the chance to come clean before we got into this thing. You could've saved us some trouble."

"I figured you knew when you asked me about Miss Ingram. You seemed to know everything else about me."

"Oh, I knew about the affair and a lot of other things," Virgil said. "But a baby? Now, that's another matter altogether. If you'd have said something, maybe we could've worked something out. I've dealt with worse, believe me. We could've gotten her out of town for a while."

"We didn't want that. My wife and I made that decision long before you came knocking," Goodwin said. "This is something we worked out two years ago when Rania was born. Esther, bless her, stepped in and made sure Miss Ingram was provided for and that my daughter got everything she needed."

"Your wife knew?"

"The relationship was brief. My wife and I were separated at the time, and I didn't know about the pregnancy until Miss Ingram asked to meet with us one Sunday after church. We said we would do the right thing. We gave her a job and bought her a house."

"You could've said all that at the debate."

"I'm a man, Mr. Loudermilk, but I've never cheated on my wife and I'm not the crook they tried to make me out to be. We were separated at the time and had already agreed to get a divorce. When we decided to reconcile, I broke things off with Miss Ingram, and that was that—or so I believed. She was something special, but I wanted the wife God prepared for me."

"And you thought Dobbs wouldn't find out and use it against you?"

"Again, we thought we were doing the right thing. Besides, the mayor has her own bones rattling around in the closet."

"Don't I know it."

"She really gets your goat, doesn't she?"

"I suppose you could say that," Virgil replied. "But that's neither here nor there right now. We spent a lot of money trying to get you elected, but I'll let that go out with the wash."

"Do you ever pray, Mr. Loudermilk?"

"Not in a very long time, Pastor. I don't reckon God likes me much."

"You should get to know Him."

"You're a true believer, ain't you?"

"I cannot count the miracles that have unfolded in my life," Goodwin answered. "Even now, in the midst of these things, I know He has a plan for me."

Virgil wanted to be angry with Goodwin, but he couldn't find it in himself to get worked up about that now. With the preacher out of the race, Dobbs would almost certainly sew up his support and win the special election outright without a runoff. That wouldn't be the end of it, Virgil knew.

They'd been close, once upon a time, plotting various political schemes and cutting backroom deals, before Dobbs got full of herself and turned on him. They were chest deep in the sauce now, and he knew it was a real possibility that they'd both get drowned at some point.

"I am heading to a meeting with the campaign team now," Goodwin said. "They need to hear it from me before I make a public announcement. I appreciated your support, but we're on our own now."

"I suppose that's true."

"Mr. Loudermilk?"

"Yes?"

"Will you let me pray for you?"

Virgil fell silent as Goodwin spent the next few minutes beseeching the heavens in his behalf. He ended it with a solemn amen.

Lucky wandered in as Virgil wished the pastor well and hung up. He went to the wet bar to fetch another drink, his third of the day.

"Don't you think you oughta slow down? It ain't even noon yet."

"We've got a problem," Virgil said, chucking down a bourbon cocktail laced with orange bitters. "Want one?"

"How long are you going to stay up here? Libby Gail keeps asking after you. Says you won't pick up her calls."

"Until the winds quit blowing."

"That might be a while, Virgil. You kicked up quite a storm."

"Goodwin prayed for me just now. Imagine that."

"He should've poured a bucket of holy oil on your head. You could use a little healing," Lucky said with a stuttered laugh.

"What I need is this here drink."

"I heard about Goodwin quitting today. J. T. King called me with the news on my way up. The way I see it, he doesn't have a choice. Wouldn't be the first time you bet on a dead horse."

"Oh, I ain't worried about that sorry bastard," Virgil said. "I'm more concerned with Hampton Bridges right now."

"The reporter?"

"Despite my best efforts, he's still digging around, and this time I think he might become a real problem for us. Seems he was writing a book featuring yours truly, among others. He had a timeline running back to 1973. If Whit knew about that, he'd run us both to the woodshed. We've got that hard drive, but that ain't accounting for what's in that reporter's head."

"He's relentless. I'll give him that much," Lucky said. He sucked in as much air as his chest would hold and blew it out hard. "Maybe I'll have that drink after all."

"You know where the glasses are. There's some ice in that bucket over there on the bar."

"Tell me something," Lucky said, pouring himself a shot of whiskey over two cubes of ice. "Why not walk away now? Maybe Whit's right. Maybe we oughta fold up the tent and call it a day."

"It ain't that easy, Lucky, and you know it."

"So what's the plan? What're we going to do about Bridges? How much does he know?"

Virgil scoffed at the questions. "You know what we've got to do."

"Can't we just sue him and shut it down?"

"Too late," Virgil said. "The ball is already in play."

"I was afraid you might say that."

"Hey, what's his wife's name again?" Virgil said, tipping open the wood blinds, eyeing his still-muddy pastures.

Lucky was immediately confused. "Whose wife?"

"Bridges. You know, the architect?" Virgil said. "They got divorced last spring, but I hear they're heating up the sheets again. What's that gal's name?"

"Ruby Claire Tolsen."

THIRTY-FIVE

Hampton figured Tucker wouldn't like it, but the lede to his latest story was already written and the rest was unspooling in his head. Despite his previous missteps, this was the only way he knew how to do the job. Give it everything you've got and let the chips fall where they may. There had been few rewards in that, not even an attaboy from his editors, other than his professional pride. The powers that be hadn't seen fit to nominate him for a single journalism award over the years, and if Hampton was honest, he was still annoyed about that.

He hadn't expected this in journalism school. He'd come to reporting when the Golden Age of Journalism was still afloat and the pay was better than decent. Hampton enjoyed those early years, before the crash came and reporters were treated like used-car salesmen. He blamed the internet and smartphone technology for that. Citizen journalism had its upside, but, generally speaking, Hampton loathed the thought of what it had done to his profession.

This new story would be another stake in the ground, and if Hampton had his way, it would run front page, above the fold with a two-inch headline. That was a pipe dream, he knew. But his sourcing was solid, even if most were anonymous. Fearing reprisals, few would agree to go on the record.

Documentation was everything, and he had enough to paper the way to the Georgia–Florida line and back again. He stayed up all night, strumming out and fretting over the draft copy, then hit the Submit button around 4 A.M.

He clutched Claire as she slept and felt her soft breaths whisper over his arms as the midday sun poured through the bay windows. He stroked her warm belly, nestling his chin over her shoulders, and let himself dream about settling down with her in a nice house with children.

Maybe, if they were lucky and their hearts allowed, there would be a new dog. So much had been lost, including Inman, whom they'd adopted four days after their wedding, and only now had he let himself hope for more.

Hampton was on his feet now, a man in full, walking without crutches. She was here, and that was good enough for the time being, though Hampton knew nothing about their lives would be the same once the next story was published. Even now, he knew there were things he could never tell her.

With Chanel sequestered away in Flint, she had begun to speak more freely and could not stop talking about Reclaim Atlanta. Hampton believed every word she said. The shadowy political action committee, as he suspected, was being operated out of a Buckhead post office on Pharr Road, and the League had been quietly buying up elections going back nearly forty years. Election law changed over the years, and thus, they shifted strategies.

Hampton rose quietly, dug his digital recorder out of his backpack, and listened to their conversation again.

"Ezra ain't like doing business with them," Chanel said. "But, he said that's how things work. They bring the money. We bring the votes."

"They? We?"

"White folk, black folk. Northside, Southside."

"I thought that's what you meant."

"Only Ezra said that's all changing now," Chanel said. "Young white folks are filling up all these fancy condos, y'know? They're taking Atlanta back."

Reclaim Atlanta.

"And you think they did business with the mayor?"

"Her and everybody else."

Hampton suggested that they might've been financing Goodwin.

"I don't know nothing about no scheming-ass preacher man," Chanel quipped. "My cousins used to go to his church. He wouldn't use the benevolent fund to help people unless they were members and could prove they paid tithes for two years straight."

"The church required bank statements?"

"No, but the church clerk down at City of Faith made my cousin bring in her tax returns after her apartment building burned down. Said he was praying for her, but she needed to give God the first of her harvest, and there were consequences for disobedience spelled out in the Scriptures. She don't make but nine dollars an hour, plus food stamps."

"That's a shame."

"Damn sure is. Heard about that baby of his too," Chanel said. "With all these rumors floating around, wasn't no way to say if it was true or not. I guess we know now."

Chanel met Virgil Loudermilk once, she explained, maybe two or three years ago when she stumbled into a meeting at the congressman's house one Sunday night. Hampton pushed for an exact date. Chanel said she couldn't remember, but it had to be year before last.

"It was five or six of them sitting there in his living room. Vicki was right there with them," Chanel said. "They were talking about the next governor's race, and I heard them talking about who they could put up against Governor Martinez."

"What did they say?"

"They hushed up when I walked in. I thought for sure Vicki recognized me, the way she kept looking. Ezra told them I was his housekeeper. I ain't like it, but I went along with it so people wouldn't get to talking about us. Anyway, they were trying to find somebody to run for governor, and Ezra told me they all but begged him to do it."

"That would've been one helluva race."

"He turned them down real quick. Ezra ain't even need to think about it, not for one second. Told me he didn't think no black man could win a statewide race like that, and really, no Democrat could after the last one left office."

"He was probably right about that."

"Probably, my ass," Chanel said. "I'm being real with you. I don't know nothing about no politics, but these folks ain't gone let no black man in the governor's mansion unless he's coming through the back door. He said Vicki thought about it, though."

"Running against Martinez?"

"Yeah, but Ezra talked her out of it."

"What do you remember about Mr. Loudermilk?"

"Fat, white, and smelled like old money. His dusty ass used to call Ezra every other day, looking for a favor. Ezra ain't like him, and to tell you the truth, I didn't neither. Ezra said he was an evil old bastard. Anyway, what they really wanted was to get some big transportation bill passed up in D.C."

Hampton sat straight up in his chair and pressed the phone closer to his ear. "What do you know about that?"

"All I know is they waved a lot of money around until they got Ezra, Vicki, and a bunch of black state legislators on their side. Ezra said that without them, the president wouldn't sign it. They wanted Ezra and Vicki to lobby Congress too. The deal was done, but Ezra ain't wanna go through with it. He told them he wasn't for sale and that they could have their money back."

"How much did they pay him?"

"More money than he'd ever seen before."

"As I understand it, he gave it back."

"Not exactly."

"What do you mean?"

Chanel went silent.

"I am going to ask you something, and I need you to be honest with me." After a long pause and no answer, Hampton took a breath and said, "Do you think they had Congressman Hawkins murdered?"

"Real talk, though, I never did believe the news about no lone wolf. Ezra used to say people could get strange over a piece of change, and we ain't talking about no nickels and dimes. After he got that envelope at his house, he ain't even wanna go to church that morning. He said he knew what it meant, and it had him fucked up in the head."

"The bird?"

"Uh-hun."

"Did he tell you what it meant or where it might've come from?"

"I like Miss Florence and all," Chanel said, moving the subject. "She keeps putting holy oil on my forehead and says she's blessing me. My edges can't take all that."

"I can't say it helped my father either. Is he still drinking?"

"All day, every day," Chanel said. "He ain't bothering nobody, though. I can't stay here long. I ain't gone sit around and wait for somebody to put a bullet in my head. I paid too damn much for this weave," she said with a nervous chuckle.

"Maybe you should cut it off," Hampton said.

"Cut what?"

"The wig. Nobody would recognize Malik."

"I ain't doing that. This is who I am."

"I don't want anything to happen to you," Hampton said. "I'm sorry if I offended you."

"We straight," she assured him. "It's all good."

"There's something you're not telling me. Where did the money go?"

Before he could utter the next word, she said, "I gotta go."

Hampton stuffed the recorder into the backpack, leaned in to kiss Claire's temple as she slept, and put his clothes back on. Here he was, in love again and chasing the biggest story of his life. And it felt like both were chasing him.

Paid for by Reclaim Atlanta.

Thanks to the fisticuffs at the debate, despite buckets of cash wheeled in by the League, Goodwin was out of the race now. Hampton was at the press conference down at his church. He'd watched as the preacher confessed his sins surrounded by a throng of his members and a smattering of community activists. His wife, Esther, stood next to him, clutching a Bible and weeping. All of his children, including an eighteen-month-old, apple-faced baby girl, were present. Goodwin explained his predicament, publicly asked for forgiveness.

Hampton felt sorry for him. Even so, he did not let the opportunity to pose a direct question pass.

"What is the nature of your relationship with Virgil Loudermilk?" Hampton shouted from the back.

"I am proud to say that many of Atlanta's business leaders invested in our campaign," Goodwin responded. "We were honored to have their support."

"Did he or any of his associates ask you to run for Congress? Were they running your campaign?"

"Jesus was in charge, then and now. Offering myself for public service, we believed, was the will of our God, and as Christians, we are bound by that."

Hampton held back on asking more questions. He didn't want to give his story angle away to his colleagues in the press scrum.

Claire was beginning to wake. Hampton went to her. She reached up and intuitively massaged the knot in his neck. He thought of Esther and how she'd cried that afternoon. He'd hurt Claire like that too.

"I love you," he said. "Will you love me?"

"Forever and always," Claire whispered. "We're in this together."

His phone was buzzing. The caller ID was Tucker's cell number.

"It's okay," she said, looking away. "Answer it."

"We're rolling with it. Check your email for edits," Tucker said. "Get me the updated copy, and we'll post it within thirty minutes. Make it tight."

"And legal?"

"It's been cleared," Tucker said. "How many installments in this series?"

"This thing is still writing itself."

Hampton was all but certain now, especially after Dobbs walked in and blew the place up, that the corporate minders at Delacourte Enterprises had snuffed the first stories he pitched about Reclaim Atlanta and the League. Tucker was simply doing as he was told back then. But now the company was formally distancing itself from Loudermilk, McCaskill had quit, and Hampton had the leeway he so desperately craved.

"By the way, I sent you a link to a video the Dobbs campaign posted on

YouTube. It's a showstopper. Write a wrap, and I'll get the digital team to embed it into your story."

"What's it about?"

"Reclaim Atlanta."

Hampton knew the League funneled money into Goodwin's now-defunct campaign, and he had the documentation on Reclaim Atlanta to prove it. There was more, but his hard drive had gone missing, and he was still recreating the records.

Hampton's latest piece revealed that Virgil Loudermilk was behind every dime. He had an anonymous source saying there was active coordination with the Goodwin campaign, a clear violation of federal law. According to another source, Loudermilk and J. T. King were spotted at the campaign office out on Piedmont Road and had spent several days prepping the minister for the Press Club debate and the *Times-Register* editorial board meeting. They'd written his speeches and recruited a campaign manager out of Florida, who turned out to be nothing more than a boy Friday, to run the outfit. It obviously hadn't done a lick of good, since Goodwin hadn't seen a good message he couldn't trample.

The legal team pored over his copy to make sure nothing was in it that would get them sued. Hampton wasn't so much worried about a lawsuit as he was about Chanel's safety. And, if he was being honest with himself, he was worried about his own. The break-in at his house still haunted him. Hampton was beginning to think his hard drive hadn't walked away by itself. They had come looking for something.

Nigga, we whatn't supposed to kill no fuck-ass dog.

The newly installed burglar bars didn't make him feel any better. He thought about asking Claire if he could stay with her for a while, but if Chanel was right, that wasn't exactly the best idea. Being here in her house, even now, felt risky. Though Chanel's latest revelations were confusing, Reclaim Atlanta was still in business and running the same playbook she described.

There was money in the wind. He figured Chanel knew exactly how much and where it was. Then too, somebody lost a shot at billions in transportation funds, thanks to Ezra Hawkins, and Hampton was convinced that somebody's last name was Delacourte.

Chanel talked in circles and shut him down when he got too close. She was avoiding something, he knew. There was at least one more player Chanel would not name.

You don't know what kinna people you messing with.

THIRTY-SIX

I have loved this city every day of my life," Victoria said, looking straight into the camera. "Together, we are building a better tomorrow for ourselves, for our children, and for the generations yet to unfold. Come Election Day, I will need more than your votes. I need you to stand with me, shoulder to shoulder, as we work for change in our communities, in our city, and in our nation. That won't be easy. There are people who don't want to see that change, people who want to turn back the clock of progress.

"In the coming days, you will hear a lot more about a group that calls themselves Reclaim Atlanta. But don't let them fool you. I know who they are, and they are not on our side. They are not on the side of smart growth, affordable housing, and equal pay. They are not on the side of equal access to affordable health care and eradicating poverty. They want to shred the social safety net, and they answer not to you, but to their Wall Street bankers. They are not on the side of criminal justice reform, safe streets, or making sure the American Dream is available to you and your children. They are not on the side of public education, for voting rights, for equal protection under the law. When an unarmed suspect is gunned down, they do not seek accountability and transparency. They do not weep for our sons and daughters.

"I believe there is a better way. When we fight, together we win. And I am asking you to believe."

The video closed with a montage of Victoria Dobbs. Photos of her volunteering in a food bank, reading to a classroom of children, and addressing throngs of supporters flashed across the screen. "We are in this together, because we believe."

She'd spent hours sweating over the draft script. Marsh joined Roy Huggins to help with the edits. And then she abruptly threw it away, rewriting every line until she was satisfied.

"You will always be a Dobbs," she told herself. "Stay true to that."

Do the next right thing.

The video had more than two hundred thousand unique views and counting now. Clips were played on the nightly newscasts.

"Win this clean," Marsh said as they left the last television interview of the day. "Be the servant-leader you were called to be."

"And if I can't?" she said. "What if this is the final ride?"

"A servant always finds a way to serve."

Team Dobbs staked out the Peachtree–Piedmont Road intersection. A second group headed to the north and set up shop on the Buckhead Loop between Lenox Mall and Phipps Plaza. A third went deep into Mitchell territory and situated themselves at the corner of Roswell and Mount Paran Roads above tony Tuxedo Park in far north Buckhead. Sarah Mitchell's forces fanned out across the near west side and even put a few yard-sign-waving volunteers along Joseph E. Lowery Boulevard near the Atlanta University Center. Tellingly, both campaigns largely ignored southwest Atlanta, the heart of Dobbs Country, leaving the precincts uncontested.

A fistfight between campaign volunteers made the midday news. Local NBC Atlanta anchor Blayne Alexander was broadcasting live from the scene of a weekend fair, when a shoving match got going outside Antioch Baptist Church North.

"We can't afford this right now," Victoria said. "Get them off the street. Roy, issue a statement. I will call Sarah Mitchell and apologize."

"For what?" Roy protested. "Her people popped off first. We'll look weak."

"We will apologize."

She personally ordered a campaign aide to identify the volunteers involved in the fight, dismiss them, and fire the precinct captain. Althea, Chip's girlfriend, delivered his old campaign files. Victoria combed through them. She studied the get-out-the-vote map Chip had drawn up and dispatched her remaining ground teams to major shopping malls, busy cross streets, and key residential neighborhoods Chip identified in his plan.

On her command, just as Chip had prescribed, they traveled in groups of ten and twenty. The Dobbs campaign doled out cash allotments for sign-wavers. Everything over one hundred dollars was noted on the campaign disclosure report to ward off questions.

Win this one clean.

"Momentum is everything," she told her senior team on an early afternoon conference call. "We've got a week to go, and we're going to deny them every opportunity."

Around 2 P.M., Victoria laced up her running shoes, donned a DOBBS FOR CONGRESS T-shirt, and headed out to the streets. With Pelosi behind the wheel, her advance man navigated them from post to post until Victoria was sure that everything was in good order. In three hours flat, she toured Castleberry, Brookwood, Eastlake, Old Ivy, Habersham Valley, Ansley, Peachtree Battle, Ormewood, Cabbagetown, West End, Cascade, Piedmont Heights, and half of Midtown, pausing to greet supporters and give a brief rousing stump speech.

"You gotta believe!" she shouted.

Her final destination, just before 6 P.M., was Foundry Park in Atlantic Station. The open lawn, along Seventeenth Street on the west side of the downtown connector, was jam-packed with cheering masses. A sound truck blasted music from speakers, and a wave of volunteers was handing out T-shirts when she arrived. Victoria snapped open a Diet Coke, took a swig, and mounted the stage.

"You gotta believe!" she shouted from the microphone. "With your help, we're going to turn this city around!"

The crowd roared.

"In recent days, this city has known the fullness of grief," she said solemnly. "We laid my mentor and friend Congressman Ezra Josiah Hawkins to rest. Then they took my brother from me," the mayor said. "I prayed. Lord, what hath Thou done? Can this be Your will?"

The masses fell silent. It was the first time she'd spoken, in public or private, about her brother since the funeral. She missed their late-night strategy calls and the way he laughed from his belly. She still regretted their last fight, but nothing had been more painful than to watch Chip get caught up in a game she knew he would lose. He was in over his head, she told him repeatedly. If she could turn back the clock, she would've grabbed him by the collar and shaken some sense into him. She would've told him to stay the hell away from Dickey too. Her own relationship with Dickey had already cost her too much, and now her marriage was falling apart. The possibility that he'd had Chip killed still haunted her. She would win this race, but Chip wouldn't be there at the finish line. Victoria wanted somebody to pay for that. Even and especially if that somebody was Dickey Lester.

"He answered, I am here to tell you," she said as the moon rose behind her. "They meant evil against you, but our Lord God meant it for good! They cannot take away what our Father hath provided! Let this rock be your stepping-stone!"

Another round of ovations broke out. The applause escalated as her husband, daughters, and mother stepped underneath the grand Millennium Gate archway and joined her on the platform. The family hugged as Pelosi stood a few paces away, stone-faced and silently surveying the crowd.

A new tracking poll was in, and with eight days left in active campaigning, Victoria had well over 50 percent. Not even Virgil Loudermilk could stand in her way. He'd been sidelined and was likely still holed up at his Ball Ground,

Georgia, estate, and Reclaim Atlanta was about to be shut down by a judge's injunction. In a few days' time, Loudermilk would be lucky if he wasn't staring at a federal warrant. She could thank Hampton Bridges for that, at least in part. His story about Reclaim Atlanta shook the earth like tectonic plates shifting along the Brevard Fault Line.

Her team of attorneys found the nearest judge and pressed for a hearing on the campaign finance matter. The first was set for the following Monday morning. Loudermilk, Goodwin, and Mitchell would be forced to testify. All of which would make great fodder in a federal indictment. If Loudermilk wanted a fight, she swore he'd do it in a jailhouse jumpsuit, cuffs, and leg shackles.

"You gotta believe!" she shouted.

As she exited the stage, Pelosi tugged her elbow. "We have a situation," he whispered, cupping his hand over her ear.

"Now?"

"Yes, ma'am."

Victoria glanced around and made eye contact with Marsh, who quickly looked away. That morning, she'd told him bits and pieces about Shaun Haverty and how the detective had been taking payoffs to spy on them. Marsh listened to every syllable of every word. He'd taken her face by both hands, looked her in the eyes, and said nothing.

"We have to go," Pelosi said again.

In the darkness, work crews wearing safety vests gathered on a narrow bridge over the Chattahoochee River along Paces Ferry Road. The body, naked and partially encased in black Hefty trash bags, had been spotted floating by in the waters below. Six teenagers, all seniors from the Lovett School, had been out white-water rafting. They were each questioned and released to their parents.

The cadaver hadn't been in the river more than six to eight hours, the medical examiner on the scene concluded. The victim's tongue had been cut out, his knuckles broken, and his face badly bruised, but otherwise, the remains were intact.

"It's him," Pelosi said.

Still dressed in a pair of jeans and a campaign T-shirt, the mayor watched as the body was loaded into the back of a waiting vehicle.

"Tell me we didn't do this," Victoria whispered.

"No, ma'am," Pelosi said. "I can assure you that it wasn't us."

Victoria stepped in front of a scrum of waiting reporters situated at the rise of the bridge beyond the crime scene tape.

"Our investigators will work tirelessly to make a positive identification and to determine the person or persons responsible," she said. "To be honest, I am frustrated and angry that someone's life was taken, and frankly, that this can happen in our community. Unfortunately, we have no further information at this time. We will provide hour-by-hour updates as we have them."

She turned and walked away without taking a single question.

Agent Jason Clearwater cut her off at the pass. "He took a real beating before he was dumped out there," Clearwater said.

"It's an unfortunate tragedy."

"I understand you met with him recently."

"Whoever told you that is mistaken," she said dismissively.

"Then you won't mind coming in for questioning."

"I'm willing to help in any way that I can."

"I understand he was about to be fired from your department."

"An internal investigation is under way, but I guess you know that," Victoria said with a smirk. "Haverty was a decent man. He was tied up with the wrong people."

"People like you?"

"Excuse me?" Victoria said. She could not hide the flash of anger. "Put your cards on the table, Agent Clearwater. Don't talk about it. Be about it."

"Detective Haverty was allegedly involved in a bribery scheme."

"So, you read the paper. And?"

"And you should expect to be questioned about that."

"Here's what you won't do," she shot back. "I am perfectly willing to answer all the questions swirling around in your head, but you won't attempt to interrogate me on an open roadway."

"This isn't an interrogation," Clearwater said. "Yet."

"Don't play with me, son."

"Or what?"

"I've got bigger fish to fry than you, Jason Leland Clearwater. Keep going, and you'll be reassigned to the GBI file room before the sun comes up."

"Are you threatening me?"

"I don't do threats, young man. You should know that by now."

She spun on her heels and walked away, leaving Clearwater standing in the middle of the street.

Pelosi met her at the southerly base of the bridge. "What was that all about?"

"That little Yankee bastard had the nerve to imply that I am somehow in-volved in this. Are you sure the SOC unit didn't move on Haverty?"

"We got all we needed out of him. He was better for us alive than dead."

"Clearwater knows something."

"Don't let that rattle you. He's on a fishing expedition."

"Then make him cut bait."

"No need. We're clean."

"Who would've wanted Haverty dead?" Victoria whispered, staring down into the dark embankment.

"You mean other than Loudermilk? Haverty was playing a dangerous game. He was as dumb as a bag of frog hair, but he knew that much."

"A cornered dog is a dangerous thing. And this one has a billion dollars."

Pelosi shook his head knowingly. "What now?"

"We tell the GBI all we know about his dealings with Loudermilk. Spill it all," Victoria said. "I've got to get some rest and get back to the campaign trail in the morning. I've got six churches to do tomorrow. Once we get the go-ahead on releasing his name, I'll have my office issue a statement."

"He was still one of ours," Pelosi said.

"Indeed. No matter what he did, he was still one of us," Victoria answered. "We'll stop the termination papers, and he'll be buried with full honors. I'll see to it that his wife gets his pension and the city's insurance payout. She shouldn't have to scrape to get by, and I'll make sure the city council votes my way on that."

As she turned toward the waiting SUV, Pelosi stopped her again.

"Ma'am, the coroner said his mouth was stuffed with paper," he said.

"Debris from the river?"

"Not likely. The detective said it was caught in his windpipe. Looked like a folded airplane. Red construction paper."

The mayor stopped and said, "It's a paper god."

"What does that mean?"

"It means this isn't over."

"This?"

"Promise me that you will protect my family."

THIRTY-SEVEN

"G et on 'way from me now. Scoot!"

Virgil leaned against the freshly polished balustrade, overlooking the double-story grand foyer, and examined his options. He'd been forced out of his compound, his expansive estate in north Georgia, to deal with the latest salvo from Victoria Dobbs. The Loudermilk house on Blackland Drive was empty, save for Libby Gail's cat, who was now yowling and rubbing up against his leg.

"I said scoot, gawd-damn it!"

The cat ignored him, as usual, and threw herself belly-up at his feet as if begging for a stroke. The full-white Persian had taken the opportunity to piss all over a mound of dirty clothes. Due vengeance, Virgil figured, for the overflowing litter box and the lack of food in her bowl. He'd caught her licking water out of the commode, which was fine by Virgil, so he left the toilet seat up.

He went down to the kitchen and scrounged around in the cabinets until he found an old can of tuna. He pried it open with a paring knife, dumped the contents onto a porcelain saucer, and set it on the floor. He lit a cigarillo and blew smoke rings in the air. Libby Gail would pitch a fit about him smoking in the house and feeding her cat table food on her good plates. At that moment, Virgil could think of little that he cared less about. The body in the river had been positively identified, and the name was released that morning.

They'd first met, he and Haverty, some thirty-odd years back, when the detective was fresh out of the police academy. Virgil always knew Haverty liked his bread toasted and buttered on both sides. In a den of thieves, that kind of greed was to be expected and even admirable, the way Virgil saw it. The plan was to make sure the detective didn't say any more than he already had and to keep him away from Pelosi and his goons. That didn't include being fished out of the Chattahoochee wearing nothing but a garbage bag. Now Haverty was as dead as a week-old pastrami sandwich, and Riley Lester hadn't returned his calls.

There was an unfortunate paper trail tying Virgil to Haverty, and thanks to Victoria Dobbs, it wasn't long before the GBI came knocking. He'd declared his innocence, of course. Virgil explained that Haverty had been employed to provide private security, which was the God's honest truth.

On top of that, he'd been served with a subpoena to appear in state court for alleged campaign finance violations. The process server, escorted by no fewer than eight sheriff's deputies, had come all the way up to Ball Ground to find him. Virgil could surely think of better things to do with his Sunday than spend it reviewing his testimony with a pack of lawyers who billed in fifteen-minute increments. He couldn't find it in himself to give half a damn about an injunction against Reclaim Atlanta, seeing as how Goodwin had already quit the race and Virgil would rather eat a flame-broiled bullfrog swimming in cream sauce than put a dime behind Sarah Mitchell. Dobbs wanted his testimony on the record, under oath, so she could use it later, he figured.

He'd known Sarah for years. After all, Virgil was the best man when she married Lucky back in '89. Virgil knew the union wouldn't last. He also knew Sarah was a wily creature who wouldn't let a sack of bad poll numbers sway her. A few years back, she won a comeback election for the statehouse against a sitting incumbent when conventional wisdom said her goose was fried. Last night, the Mitchell campaign posted reams of financial disclosures on her website, along with a press release tallying all the money she'd gotten from Virgil and his friends over the years.

Sarah had enough moxie to choke the life out of a grizzly, but she was still no match for the Great Torie Dobbs. The press release didn't even get a response.

The injunction against him and the League, which he fully expected to be ordered, wasn't worth a pot of dry pinto beans, now that Goodwin had quit. Getting a temporary sanction was a tactical move, just as her tirade at the editorial meeting had been. However, with her law school classmate Darius Highsmith leading the team, the mayor was clearly angling to extract a pound of his flesh by putting him on the witness stand. Highsmith was a Southerner by birth and a real firebrand when it came to courtroom theatrics. A fourth-generation Missionary Baptist preacher, when he wasn't chasing skirts up the courthouse steps, Highsmith could sing the ABC's and a jury would swoon and swear he was quoting Shakespeare. His petition to the court, which Virgil had the displeasure of reading, sounded like a Twain novel.

Mayor Dobbs specialized in warning shots, the kind that whizzed over your head, coming close enough to split your hair right down the middle. But this wasn't that. Behind all that pretty talk about uniting Atlanta, Dobbs was a shrewd operator. Long on charm and heavy on guile. Virgil liked her better when they were on the same side.

She had outgrown her satin britches long ago, and he'd warned Whit more than once about giving her too much rope. If Virgil had his druthers, she'd be hocking watermelon slices out of a pushcart on Peachtree Street. To his chagrin, she was now likely headed to Congress in a landslide.

The most recent public polling had her at over 50 percent, but the internal numbers were even uglier. By J. T. King's math, independents were breaking in her favor, and she was now hovering around 62 percent. She was clearing all the milk and bread off the shelves like a snowstorm was coming. Mitchell was stuck with the crumbs. Where the election was concerned, the proverbial fat lady was warming up in the wings, preparing for an encore performance.

The mere thought of throwing all that money behind Goodwin made his belly ache. King and Bertram DuBose took the news in stride. Neither of them had quite so much skin in the game. And now, there was a preliminary hearing and various in limine motions to deal with. It was likely the last rodeo for the League and their PAC. Loudermilk was preparing to shut down the whole shebang.

The petition had been filed on behalf of Dobbs for Congress, and a second complaint was submitted to the state board of ethics. That meant the legal fees were coming out of her campaign account, which Virgil knew to be a hefty sum. In the end, he'd pay a civil fine and be done with it.

Virgil looked down at the cat, who was circling him again like a vulture in heat.

"What in the hell do you want now? I swear, you eat better than I do."

Virgil was stuck with the cat, whose name he did not care to know. His wife was off in South Carolina, staying with her stepsister and her do-nothing governor husband, and their son was still off seeing the world with his bride. He hadn't seen Libby Gail that mad since he forgot their twentieth wedding anniversary.

"How dare you embarrass this family like this!" she'd shouted. "Hell, I can't even take tea at the St. Regis without folks stopping by my table to tell me how sorry they are. The damn clerk at Dior turned her nose up at me, and Juanita Milner asked me to step down as cochair of the Crescendo Ball. And Harold quit, you know? Didn't even give me any notice. Just up and quit."

"Gal, it'll all blow over soon enough."

"John Virgil Loudermilk, you can't fly right to save your life. Can you? Doling out all that money to those politicians was one thing. Now they're saying that you bribed a police officer, for heaven's sake! They're going to put you in prison, and where will that leave us?"

"It'll be fine, I said. I ain't going to nobody's jail."

"I've kept my mouth shut for years on your account. I don't generally involve myself in your affairs, Virgil. But you dragged us all into this, and I expect you to make this right."

"Stop being dramatic, will you? It ain't like I killed anybody."

"Well, that detective is sure enough dead."

She stormed out, got into a waiting town car, and rolled up the window before he could get another word in edgewise.

Hours later, the house was hot and Virgil couldn't sleep for sweating like a mule. Virgil couldn't figure out how to work the air-conditioning unit without his wife's help, so he stripped off his clothes, plugged in a fan, lay in the bed naked, and let the breeze flow over his girth. In the middle of the night, he felt a rumbling in his stomach. Before Virgil could make it to the bathroom good, he threw up all over the carpeting. The next morning, he was still passed out crossways over the bed when Lucky found him.

"Let me help you up."

"I'm alright, Lucky. Cut on the air-conditioning."

"Where's Libby Gail?"

"She packed her bags and went up to Columbia to stay with her sister."

Lucky grabbed one of Libby Gail's house robes from the bathroom and threw it on top of Virgil.

"Here, cover your ass," Lucky said.

"To tell you the truth," Virgil said, "I'm worried about that hearing."

"They can't shut down what's already dead."

"Dobbs is hunting for something else. She's got Highsmith carrying her water on this one. She's trying to put my ass in a sling."

"Well, I'd wanna hang your ass too. Or whatever Libby Gail left of it."

"She had smoke coming out her ears when she left here yesterday."

"Speaking of smoke," Lucky said. "You smell like a furnace. Where's Harold?"

"Quit."

"Quit?"

"Yeah, that's what Libby Gail says."

"How long's he been working for y'all?"

"Fifteen years or so."

"Maybe you should call him. Offer him a raise or something."

"If Harold was worried about money, he wouldn't have been working for us in the first place. Can't say we ever paid him what he was worth. That man is like family. Hell, I miss him more than I miss Libby Gail right now."

"Family don't wash your cars, take the garbage out, fetch your dinner, or run your bathwater."

"You know what I mean."

"No, Virgil, I don't," Lucky said. "He ain't property."

"Harold is a good man."

"He'd have to be to put up with your mess this long."

"I'll call him," Virgil said, slipping on Libby Gail's powder-blue chiffon robe. "We never did give him a Christmas bonus. Maybe a little money will help matters."

"It looks good on you. Spin around so I can see it."

"Cut it out," Virgil said.

"Take it easy," Lucky said. "You're gone give yourself a heart attack."

"Lucky, I don't know what I'd do without my wife. She's been shoveling my shit for years. Now, I've never stepped out on her, not even once. But I've put her through some things, and this might be the straw that breaks the camel's back. She all but accused me of killing Haverty."

Lucky arched his left brow.

"That wasn't in the plan," Virgil said.

"Libby Gail will be fine," Lucky said. "It's you I'm worried about. All that drinking and smoking will kill you, sooner or later. We ain't kids anymore, you know? When's the last time you've seen a doctor?"

"You sound like my wife. I'm fine."

"No, the hell you ain't. You've got to put an end to this thing between you and Mayor Dobbs before it kills you," Lucky said. "It's eating you up. And put them damn cigarillos down."

"She declared war the minute she decided to run for Congress."

"You knew she'd do that."

"And now, she done went and sent the damn GBI after me."

"What do they wanna talk about?"

"Haverty."

THIRTY-EIGHT

Hampton hobbled into his house, kicked off his flip-flops, and went to the refrigerator for a cranberry Red Bull. Claire didn't like his latest addiction, but the hours had been long and he needed something to keep pushing. Claire was stuck in the office, and aside from a few text messages, he hadn't heard from her all day. It was four o'clock when he sat down at the kitchen table, opened his laptop, and watched the news clip. He immediately dialed his editor.

"Damn!"

"Damn is right," Tucker said from the speakerphone. "This is the same cop Dobbs was talking about at the editorial board meeting."

Hampton couldn't take his eyes off the monitor. The video from the local ABC News affiliate showed a black bag being dredged from the Chattahoochee River just shy of the Cobb County line. The anchor said the body had been in the water for a few hours, but other than that, few other details were released.

"Yeah, that's him. Detective Shaun Haverty."

"Franco turned in the story on it this morning," Tucker said. "I need you to stay clear for now, seeing as how you might be a part of the official investigation."

"Me?"

"Haverty sent you that 911 tape. You might have to testify about that at some point."

"You know good and well I'm not going to talk about a source, dead or alive. Besides, I didn't know he was the one who sent it until Dobbs said so."

"And the legal team will have your back. For now, we need to make sure every hand is clean on this. I am already sitting on an order to retain our records."

"What did the mayor have to say?"

"Only that Haverty was still officially employed by the Atlanta Police Department when he died, so she will make sure his pension is paid out to his widow."

"Well, that's surprising."

"It's a political calculation, for sure."

"Isn't it always?"

"Apparently, the city can deny the claim. It's discretionary, since the internal investigation was ongoing. Stay on the campaign trail."

"Fine," Hampton said. "But I think this is tied to my story."

"Hold your fire for now, at least until I can set up some time with the lawyers. What about Mitchell?" Tucker asked. "I have to say, I'm stunned by the polling numbers."

"What about her? She's going to lose. She's getting mollywhopped," Hampton said.

"I always thought it would be closer, but this is Victoria Dobbs we're talking about."

"Madam Bell could've have predicted this one," Hampton said, referring to Atlanta's most infamous, albeit dead, fortune-teller.

"I haven't heard that name in ages."

"Her real name was Judy Marks. Made millions reading palms for Atlanta's rich and not-so-rich out of a house on Cheshire Bridge Road," Hampton said. "She drowned in a reflecting pool near the Buckhead Ritz-Carlton back in '97."

"She should've seen that one coming."

Hampton wanted to laugh, but he let it pass. He figured that Dobbs was sitting on a load of opposition research about Mitchell. Unless the numbers tightened again, and that didn't seem likely this late in the race, he figured Dobbs would leave it on ice.

"Expect something from me tonight on Mitchell, and I'll go to the Loudermilk hearing in the morning. You know how much I enjoy fireworks in the summertime."

"That's what I like to hear," Tucker said. "By the way, how's Claire?"

"I'm a lucky man, Tuck. A very lucky man."

"Ain't that the damn truth."

Around ten thirty that night, two hours after filing a story on Mitchell's misfortunes, Hampton was munching on a tub of Brunswick stew and a thick slice of sweet corn bread. It was a much-needed break. The house band was between sets, and the line for the next one stretched out the door and around the building. The music was good. But the food at Fat Matt's Rib Shack, which was delivered in wax paper, Styrofoam cups, and grease-soaked brown sacks, was truly divine.

Hampton scraped the bottom of his bowl with a spork and tried to forget about the election going on. It had been three days since he'd last spoken to Chanel, and he worried now that he might never hear from her again. According to his mother, Chanel said something about going to visit a sister in Illinois. Only she'd never once mentioned having a sister to him, or any brothers, for that matter. Maybe she'd decided to cut and run. After all, that's what he would've done. Out there on her own, riding an Amtrak through the Midwest, she probably got a taste of freedom for the first time and liked it.

He was beginning to think Chanel knew exactly how much money Congressman Hawkins got from the League and where to find it.

Hampton wanted to be free too. He'd grown tired of the horse race, tired of the political infighting at the newspaper and chasing down ne'er-do-wells posing as public servants. If he had his way about things, and he rarely did, he'd be living in a hut in Costa Rica with an internet connection and a coffeemaker, and a couple of bestsellers under his belt. Claire would be there too, of course, wearing nothing but a nice tan.

Just when he'd gotten used to living without her, their love was alive again. An he felt alive again too. They both hated working on Sundays and promised each other they'd meet back at her place by midnight. The drive up to Alpharetta from Midtown was a clean forty-five minutes without the weekday traffic, leaving him plenty of time to enjoy a plate of ribs and all the fixings.

He chugged the last of an Arnold Palmer, shook the ice in the cup, and went for a refill. Shady Lane and the Westside Boys took to the low-flung stage and lit up their microphones. Hampton ordered a second slice of sweet potato pie. He dug in as the blues trio hit the first notes to B.B. King's "Please Love Me."

I was in love with you, baby,
Honey before I learned to call your name.

He'd been lovestruck and out of his mind once before in life, when he first met Claire, and here it was again, fresh and new like the sun coming over Stone Mountain. Hampton's cell phone buzzed just as he was gobbling down the last bite of a pie. The number on the display had a 312 area code. He couldn't figure out what anybody in Chicago would want with him. He hesitated, then answered on the last ring.

"Hey, Hamp!" the cheery voice chimed.

"Who is this? I can't hear you?"

"It's me, Chanel!"

"Wait, hold on," he said, taking the conversation outside. "Who is this again?"

"It's Chanel!" she said.

"Thank God. I was worried about you. Where are you calling from?"

"I'm in Chicago at a coffee shop down on East Randolph. Nice place. They let me bum their phone. It's called Intelligentsia, I think."

"You can't stay there. You have to get back to Flint. When does the next train leave?"

"I don't know," Chanel said. "Chicago is really pretty. The water is so blue. One of these days, I'm going out on one of those boats. There's a Ferris wheel too. I've never been on one before. It's beautiful at night."

"You lied to my mother. You're an only child."

"I ain't want her worrying after me."

"Where's the phone I gave you? You have to answer when I call."

"I lost it on the train coming over here," she said. "I appreciate er'thang you doing, but I ain't never had no daddy, and I ain't got one now."

"Listen to me, Chanel. You have to go back to Flint."

"Nobody knows I'm here," she said.

"It's late. Check into a hotel for the night. I can wire you some cash. Promise me you'll get a new phone and hop on the first train out in the morning. I'll get my daddy to pick you up."

"Is everything okay? You don't sound right."

"I'm fine," Hampton said, picking the meat out of his teeth. "I'll be better once I know you're back in Flint with my mother. It isn't as pretty as Chicago, but you'll be safe there until we get this all sorted out."

"I heard about what happened to that bitch-ass cop."

"Haverty?"

"Yeah, a real bastard."

"You knew him?"

"You can say that," Chanel said. "He was the one who busted me back in '85. He was just a rookie back then."

"Nobody deserves to die like that."

"I ain't sending no flowers that way. My mama used to say sometimes bad things happen to good people and the other way around. But you know what? Sometimes bad people get what's coming to them."

"Why would he do that?"

"It was a long time ago."

"C'mon, Chanel, we've come this far together. You don't trust me?"

"I don't trust nobody after what happened to Ezra. No offense."

"None taken."

"All I'm saying is he was the cop who locked me up, now he's dead and I ain't sorry."

"Alright, fine. Tell me about that envelope again. Where did you find it?"

"It found me. It was sitting on my kitchen counter when I came in from work, like I told you," Chanel said. "It scared the shit out of me. Ain't nobody had no keys to my apartment except me, my landlord, and Ezra. When I opened it and saw that bird, I nearly died right there on the spot. It's just like the one they sent Ezra before he got killed."

"Get on that train in the morning," Hampton said. "Please."

THIRTY-NINE

Atlanta City Hall remains a splendidly beautiful place. Like an aging and forgotten beauty queen clutching her jeweled crown and scepter, she carries a pained smile in hopes that someone will look beyond her years, beyond the crow's-feet and the botched face-lifts, and still see her loveliness.

Situated a block from the Georgia State Capitol on the southerly edge of downtown, the original neo-Gothic structure was completed in 1930. The new annex, which houses the executive suite and city council chambers and faces Trinity Avenue, was added six nearly decades later, in 1989. Architects preserved the western face of the building, designing a new multistory atrium complete with a marble-laden stairwell and a water fountain.

But now, with its outdated adornments and weathered carpets, the interior looked like every other '80s throwback, Victoria thought. The once-spectacular indoor fountain has been dry for at least two decades and counting, and despite new coats of paint, the place smelled like the ever-shrinking municipal budget. There was a surplus now, the first in years, thanks to tough negotiations with various unions over the city's pension fund and airport leases.

That Monday morning, Victoria took the back elevator up from the private parking deck and arrived in her office without notice. The hallway entry walls were lined with oversized oil paintings of the men who had preceded her. Among them were Ivan Allen, Maynard Jackson, and Sam Massell. Giants, one and all, though Victoria knew that this had also been a place where devils and their fallen angels resided in comfort.

"Good morning, ma'am," the receptionist greeted her cheerily.

"Good morning, Miss Judith. How're those grandbabies?"

"Perfect as the day they were born. Growing every day. My youngest grand is talking and walking now."

"Kiss them for me?"

Victoria disappeared behind the security door that led to the mayoral suite. She stepped through the flag-draped receiving room and took refuge in an adjoining wood-lined library. Seated at the long table, she glanced at a collection of memorabilia: law books and coffee mugs, signed biographies from various luminaries, a baseball bat and a weathered glove gifted to her by Hank Aaron. There were various gold shovels from groundbreakings, framed newspaper clippings, as well as photographs with celebrities and heads of state. They were gentle reminders of how far she had come.

It wasn't yet 10 A.M., and she was already exhausted beyond measure. There had been victories in this room, though not enough to stave off the sadness she felt now.

A knock at the door broke through the memories and startled her.

The mayor's chief of staff, Holly Cochran, poked her head inside. "I apologize for the interruption, ma'am."

"Come in," Victoria said, batting away tears. She sat up straight and composed herself.

"Are you okay?"

"It was a long weekend. I'm sorry. What do you need?"

"We need to run over your public calendar. I did my best to coordinate the schedule with Roy Huggins."

"I'm sure it will all work out," Victoria said, waving her into a chair. "I'm all yours."

Holly flipped open a binder and walked through the coming days, noting the tight schedule.

"I'm not sure how you're going to make it all work. I can make some adjustments," Holly offered. "We can cancel some of this and send a surrogate, if we need to."

"It will all work itself out. Always does, right?"

"I do have a press request," Holly said. "It's from Hampton Bridges, and he says it's urgent."

"He's on our blacklist."

"Understood, but he keeps calling, and it's driving the communications team insane."

"That's what we pay them for. Keep him on ice."

"Yes, ma'am."

"Is that all you have for me?"

"Yes, ma'am."

Holly scooted back from table, paused, and said, "I've never lived in D.C., but if you will have me, I'd like to join your congressional staff."

"The race isn't over yet. There will be many more miles before any of us can sleep. Is the Haverty statement ready?"

"Yes, ma'am. I will have the press office send you the draft. And if you don't mind my saying, I've got faith in you. We all do. You're like that phoenix," Holly said, pointing to the gold-embossed city seal on her binder. "You keep rising from the ashes."

"Indeed. Thank you, Holly."

"If you will excuse me, I have a meeting with the council president."

"About?"

"He wants to rename a street after Christopher Bridges."

"Ludacris? He's from College Park."

"Yes, ma'am."

"Well, that's one Bridges I happen to like. Which street?"

"South section of Whitehall."

Victoria rolled her eyes and said, "Tell the council president he has my blessing. Just tell him not to go trying to rename anything after Yung Joc, Stevie J, or Gucci Mane until I leave this office."

"I will inform him," Holly said with a broad grin.

Before she got to the door, Victoria stopped her.

"I want you to know that I am grateful. You could be out there making a lot of money at some big law firm, but you gave up a great job to work for me," she said. "So, whether I am still mayor or I take that congressional seat, there is a place for you. I need people like you at my side."

"Thank you, ma'am."

A lot of things in Atlanta carry the city seal or at least some version of it, Victoria was thinking as Holly closed the door. It was inscribed with the word *resurgens*, Latin for "rising again," and Victoria knew the history well. A bronze monument now located in Woodruff Park, in the center of downtown, was erected in 1969 to memorialize the city's hundred-year recovery after the Civil War. The sculpture, a gift from the Rich Foundation, depicts a woman being lifted by a bird from the flames—a phoenix. Victoria felt like that statue now, naked from the waist up and hoisting a mythical phoenix overhead.

Staring at the seal, she was reminded of her duty to her city. What she had always feared now stared Victoria in the face, demanding a reckoning. Taking down Virgil Loudermilk, tying him up in court, and sending the GBI his way were only the beginning, she knew.

Do the next right thing.

Gathered in the bowels of City Hall East on Ponce de Leon Avenue, in their cavern floors beneath police department headquarters, the mayor's SOC team listened as she pieced together what she knew. When she was finished, Victoria let her chest fill with air and blew out a hard gust. She placed two ziplock bags that contained two red pieces of origami on the table.

"My brother was carrying this one the night his car exploded," she said, lifting the corner. "Congressman Hawkins received the other. I found it in his Bible."

"I'm confused," Pelosi said. "Slow down and tell me again. You think some-one sent these to Ezra and Chip just before they were killed?"

"Yes. And they left one balled up in Haverty's mouth," Victoria replied. "Every time I see one, somebody dies. It's a sign of rebirth, but, of course, the victims don't rise again. Whoever is behind these believes their own power is ascendant."

Pelosi eyed her closely as she spoke. A tear wet her cheeks.

"I know who did this," she said. "And if I'm right, this isn't over."

"Let's say, for the sake of argument, that you are right. Have you said any-thing about this to Chief Walraven?" Pelosi asked.

"You and I both know my police chief doesn't have the stomach for this. I should've fired him a long time ago, and the GBI is still chasing its own tail. If I'm right, it won't be enough. I am a dead woman walking."

"We've got a security detail covering your entire family."

She was visibly shaken, still tearful, but kept her hands planted on the metal table. "This won't end until he takes everything from me."

"Who, Loudermilk?"

"This is bigger than him. I should've listened to Ezra." She broke down. Tears flooded her face. "God, I should've listened to him. He'd still be here now. And Chip too. This is my fault. But I was naïve. I could've stopped him."

"Stopped who?"

Victoria said nothing. Her lips quivered.

"I'm not into conspiracy theories, but let's play this one out," he said. "Some-body get me a list of everything that carries the city seal or any part of it. Anything with a phoenix or the word *resurgens*," he said finally. "What else do we have, Detective Delacourte?"

"There's a million companies with *resurgens* in the name. But I looked up the symbol online," she said, "and I think it's called a chronepsis."

"What in the hell is that?" Pelosi said.

"The dragon god of fate, death, and judgment," the mayor interrupted.

"As in *Dungeons and Dragons*?" another officer said.

"Fill us in, Whitney," Pelosi said.

"Yes, sir, Mayor Dobbs is right. In the virtual game, the chronepsis is silent and dispassionate. Only interacts with those who are dead or dying."

"I have an old friend who was into that sort of thing," Victoria said.

Pelosi scratched his head. "Dragons or murder?"

"Both. And there's only one company that matters. It's a commercial development firm owned by Coleman Delacourte."

"Who's this friend?" Pelosi said.

Victoria wiped her face and said, "A word in private."

Pelosi ordered the room cleared.

FORTY

The Monday morning court hearing ended almost as quickly as it got going, and Virgil walked away with what he called a pyrrhic victory. An injunction against Reclaim Atlanta was ordered, but despite Highsmith's chest thumping, Virgil testified to little more than he had to. He rang his secretary to say he wouldn't be in as planned. He ordered his calendar cleared.

There was some testimony that Virgil preferred not to have on the record, including his role in the Goodwin campaign and two other candidates in prior races. Specifically, he was forced to confirm the members of the League and exactly how much money each of them had given directly to Pastor Goodwin's now-defunct campaign. Highsmith wasn't nearly so good as his reputation, but good enough to drag his good name through the mud. Donors to Reclaim Atlanta were protected under both state and federal law, but Judge Sheehan decided he'd heard enough about the League's monkeyshines and ordered the questioning stopped.

It didn't matter that Virgil went to law school at University of Georgia with Rufus Sheehan, who was only the second African American in its history to graduate. Virgil had even written a glowing letter of recommendation back in 2002, urging the governor to appoint Sheehan to a vacancy on the state supreme court. Much to his relief, the hearing was over almost as soon as it started.

At precisely 10:45 A.M., Virgil entered a Starbucks near the corner of Fourteenth and West Peachtree Street, a few doors down from the Four Seasons Hotel and in the heart of Atlanta's row of high-priced law firms, and ordered a double-shot Venti vanilla latte. He settled into a hard-back chair in a far corner and unfurled a newspaper. The second rush hour was petering out, but there were still too many customers in the coffeehouse for his tastes. He took three sips, quickly forgot it, and lost himself in the business section of the *New York Times*.

He enjoyed the anonymity. No one here knew his name, let alone what was unfolding. He savored the quiet moments. His cell phone buzzed and he let it. Virgil was drowning in the soup now, he admitted to himself. Between Victoria's legal plays and the silence from Riley Lester, he felt the walls closing in. There was no way to predict what one or the other might do. He'd dialed Riley that morning before the hearing got under way but got no answer.

The partnership had paid good dividends, but the brothers and their penchant for violence could not be controlled. He wondered now if his head would be the next one on the platter.

There was no way he could explain this to Whit, not that he gave diddly-squat about his huffing and puffing right now. He tossed the nearly full latte and the newspaper into a waiting garbage can and left the coffeehouse. Virgil drove aimlessly about the city for a bit, thinking through his next steps. Lucky arranged for a private security team, and he was due to meet with the lead man within the hour.

Ten minutes later, he was tooling along Piedmont Road, headed north toward Buckhead, when his cell phone started buzzing again. It was near 'bout noon, and he'd missed his favorite truffle deviled eggs drizzled with honey and topped with fried chicken skins. The caller ID on the dashboard said it was Libby Gail.

"You ready to come on home yet, gal?"

"How're you keeping yourself?"

"Barely," Virgil said. "Without Harold around, I ain't eating good."

"You can order takeout."

"We've been married thirty-five years, and all I can get is takeout?"

"I'm sure the Buckhead Diner will bring you something."

"Pulling in there now."

"That figures."

"Ain't you gone ask me about how the hearing went?"

"You got yourself into this, Virgil, and you'll get yourself out," Libby Gail said. "I read about it already. Anyway, that isn't what I'm calling about."

"Well, don't wait. Give it to me, gal. Tell old Virgil what's on your mind."

"Stop calling me 'gal.'"

"Never thought it bothered you."

"You remember Rose, don't you?"

"Rose?"

"Rosetta."

"Park Dobbs's wife? The mayor's mama? Sure enough."

"She called Whit last night, saying she needed to meet with him."

"How do you know this?"

"Patsy Jo told me, of course. She took the call at the house when it came in."

"What does she want with Whit?"

"You and I both know what she wants."

"Does my sister-in-law know that?"

"If she does, she's never uttered a word to me about it. Never once in all these years."

"What else did she say?"

"Don't know. Patsy Jo didn't hear all of the conversation. Said Whit just kept nodding and saying 'uhn-hun.' Then he took it to the den. He should know good and well, a secret like that won't hold forever. Not in Atlanta."

"Listen here, Libby Gail, I only told you because you're my wife. It ain't no time to start flapping your gums to Patsy Jo or anybody else."

"It has never been my place to say," Libby Gail said.

"I've got some calls to make. I'll ring you back in a while."

"Virgil, honey, this is a mess. If this ever gets out—"

"It won't unless you start talking."

"Big Whit is rolling over in his grave. You know that, right?"

"You and I both know my daddy would've done everything I did and then some. He knew all about this."

Libby Gail suddenly went silent.

"You still there?" Virgil said. "Hello, hello?"

"Yes, I'm here."

"Something else is on your mind. I can smell it."

She paused and said, "Did you kill Haverty?"

"I figured that's what you had twirling around in your head. No, I didn't, Libby Gail."

"Did you pay somebody to do it?"

"No, and if I did, I wouldn't tell you about it."

FORTY-ONE

Hampton dialed Chanel again, for the fifth time that night. His mother, Florence, hadn't heard from her either.

"Come on, Chanel, pick up," he said, pecking at the keypad on his smartphone.

Another call rolled straight to voice mail. No greeting, just two beeps.

She'd been anxious on their last call. Talking in circles and then coming to a dead stop when he got around to the subject of money and who might've killed Ezra Hawkins. The notion of a lone wolf hadn't set right with Hampton either. After all, the congressman didn't sit on the Armed Services Committee or Veterans Affairs. There was no indication the shooter had ever once called his congressional office or made any contact via social media.

According to the FBI, the gun found in the house was a clean match to the murder weapon. Caleb Vasquez was dead, and the investigation was officially closed.

Hampton wondered now if Chanel might've been right. She clearly knew more than she was saying.

Sending her to Flint seemed like a good idea, or at least the best he could think of at the time. Going to the police with such a flimsy story felt like a fool's errand. He hadn't the stomach to tell Tucker what he suspected, and he hadn't uttered a word to anyone about the congressman's affair with Chanel.

He'd heard rumors about Ezra Hawkins over the years. The scuttlebutt was that Hawkins frequented a gay nightclub on the Westside, where he had a reserved room. The congressman never married and had no children, but the notion that he had been in a three-decade-long relationship with a transgender woman was still more news than Hampton saw fit to print.

The revelation, if he ever told it, would make for an explosive headline. But Hampton wouldn't write about it—not for Hawkins's sake, but for Chanel's— at least for now. If everything she said was true, meeting with him meant jeopardizing her life. She was smart and streetwise, but obviously scared. Now he thought she'd gone and done something they'd both regret.

It was well after 11 P.M., and the story about Shaun Haverty had been all over cable news again that day. Hampton was sure the detective was behind the mysterious email he'd received, just as Mayor Dobbs suggested. Hampton looked up at the smiling set of headshots posted on the wall. Loudermilk was tacked to the middle of the fray, which he called the "wall of shame."

Dressed in a banker's suit, with a silk tie and a starched white shirt, Loudermilk looked like any other lawyer. That he was Whit Delacourte's cousin-brother complicated matters. Hampton realized that he had always been afraid of this moment, afraid that his story was about more than buying up elections. In the early days, he thought the League was just a group of rich Buckhead businessmen pouring money into their chosen candidates in exchange for city contracts. Hampton had been doubtful, at least before Haverty was discovered in the river with his tongue sliced off, that they'd actually kill somebody to get what they wanted. And if they had Haverty murdered, why not Prentiss Dobbs and Ezra Hawkins? What was once too absurd to believe made perfect sense now.

You don't know what kinna people you messing with.

He stepped out onto the rear porch and relit a menthol cigarette, a Newport, the eighth one that night and seven more than he'd had since he was seventeen, and smoked it down to the butt. Hampton's chest was burning, but his head was clear. His calculations had been deliberate, the accounting for the money and connections precise, but he had not banked on what he was looking at now. There was a failed transportation bill worth billions, a Delacourte family–owned construction business, and a trail of bribes. And now, there were bodies, at least seven of them by his count: Chip Dobbs, Haverty, and four others who were killed at Ebenezer along with Congressman Hawkins. Hampton was possessed by the idea that the League might be behind it all.

He steadied himself and walked back inside. The mayor was involved in some way. Her fingerprints were all over that transportation bill, and he was certain, despite the scant documentation, that the League had funded every campaign of her political life. His disdain for Victoria Dobbs was not a matter of debate, and he still believed that she and her band of thugs were behind his car accident. Even so, he couldn't wrap his head around the notion that she was involved in a string of killings.

He rang her press secretary a dozen or more times, unable to get an interview. Hampton wanted to look her in the eye and ask the mayor about Reclaim Atlanta. Her books were clean. Still, Hampton had his suspicions.

He fished through Chicago's local news, hoping he wouldn't find her among the weekend's shooting victims. It was a relatively light weekend in the Windy City. Four people had been murdered, according to the *Tribune*, and another three wounded. None matched Chanel's description or the names "Malik Townsend" or "Burris." He tried "Tracy Cantrell," the pseudonym he gave her, but came up with nothing.

He rang four hospitals that night and even put in calls to the Cook and Lake county morgues. No one matched the description he gave, not even when he mentioned that the potential victim was a transgender woman.

He laid his head on his desk, still gripping his cell phone, and began to weep. The tears quickly became sobs.

Claire was here now, fast asleep in his bed. She'd been feeling sick, vomited twice, and turned in early. They joked that she might be pregnant.

"Wouldn't that be a hoot," she said.

"A beautiful hoot," Hampton replied.

Around 2 A.M., he crawled in beside her and cupped her warm body in his arms. She had a slight fever and slept fitfully. Hampton rose again around 4 A.M. His smartphone, the ringer turned on for the first time in months, lay on the bedside table. He checked the display. No calls.

He started to pray. Hampton hadn't talked to God about much of anything in years, even as he lay half-dead after the accident. But pray, he did. He prayed for Chanel's life, for answers to all the horrific questions floating around in his head. Hampton looked up at the ceiling and wondered if anybody was listening.

Inside his makeshift war room, Hampton began walking through every word Chanel ever told him. He leafed through the mound of campaign finance disclosures again, looking for something he might have missed. He printed pictures of Cole and Rafaela Delacourte and added them to the array on the wall. Raffi was a gorgeous woman, with serious eyes, just as Claire had described. He found an image of Caleb Vasquez, in Army dress uniform, and added him to the mix.

Then there was the matter of Babyboy404. Hampton was sure the boy on the skateboard outside the downtown Hyatt Regency hotel was the same teenager he'd seen getting arrested out at Lenox Mall. He signed on to Twitter. He pulled up the profile for a @Babyboy404 and got nothing. He tried an alternate spelling: @Babyboi404.

The photo avatar smiling back at him was the same face of the person who shot Inman. The day of the break-in, his house was dim, but there was no mistaking it. This was Babyboi404. He printed the photo and pasted it on the wall. *Damn, kid.*

Staring at the image, he shouted, "Who are you, and what were you doing in my house! Why did you shoot my fucking dog?!"

Claire awoke with a start. "What's wrong? Are you okay in there?"

"Everything," he called back. "Every fucking thing!"

Hampton was shaking now, fearful and angry, as he felt Claire's arms around him. Wearing a tattered Northwestern University T-shirt, she tried to calm him. He pointed at the photo.

"He's just a boy," she said, eyeing the brown-faced kid. "How old is he?"

"Old enough to break in this house and kill Inman. I swear I saw him out-side the Hyatt the night that car blew up. He was riding a damn skateboard."

He checked the smartphone again.

"Malik never called?"

"Her name isn't Malik," Hampton said, recounting the story. "It's Chanel, and now she's missing."

Claire listened as Hampton rambled on, pointing and shouting like a man on fire. Hampton was spitting out a volley of words that made little sense.

"When did you last hear from her?"

"She called from Chicago a few nights ago," Hampton said. "I begged her to get on the first train out to Flint the next morning. My mother said she never got there. My father waited outside the station for hours."

Claire went to the kitchen and brewed a pot of tea to settle her stomach as Hampton continued punching the keys and surfing social media profiles. He was looking for something, anything, that would make it all make sense. Just as he was about to give up, Hampton found a story on the *Atlanta Times-Register* site.

Babyboi404 had a name: DeVonte Charles. He was fourteen and had been arrested on car theft and arson charges. The story, filed by his colleague Kathy Franco, said the boy was also charged with shoplifting at Lenox Mall several weeks back. His case was moved from juvenile court into the adult system. He was being held without bail in federal detention, a curious thing, thought Hampton, given that arson was a state charge.

Why are the feds involved?

A few more clicks, and he found a press release on the U.S. district attor-ney's website. DeVonte Richard Charles was facing an indictment on inter-state drug trafficking and tied to the Sex Money Murder clique operating out of southwest Atlanta. The same drug ring run by Richard "Dickey" Lester, the mayor's high school boyfriend.

"Shit!"

"Baby, what's happening?"

"I don't know."

Claire set her teacup down and wrapped her body around his. He could feel himself quaking in her arms.

"I have to find her," Hampton said.

Hampton grabbed his cell phone. He tried Chanel again, and still, there was no answer. He was grasping at straws now, which seemed to light up and burn to dust in his hands.

Using an online directory, he located a phone number for a Dorothy Burris in the 1700 block of Avon Avenue.

"I'm sorry to bother you, Mrs. Burris," he said delicately. "But I'm looking for Chanel."

"Who is this?"

"My name is Hampton Bridges, and I'm a friend."

"You mean Malik," she said. "I haven't heard from my son in years," the old woman said. "If you see him, tell him that I love him."

"Yes, ma'am," Hampton responded. "If you hear from her, will you ask Chanel to call me?"

The line went dead.

FORTY-TWO

Victoria uncrossed her legs, stood up, and stretched her hands above her head. The day's campaign events were scuttled and the mayoral calendar was cleared. It was Tuesday night, the week before the election, and the day's local newscast noted her absence from the campaign trail. She let the pundits roar.

The ad hoc meeting in her living room had started at 7 P.M. and gone on for at least three hours. The queries were gentle but vigorous. The floor was open and the full SOC unit was present. An officer was directed to record audio. When something needed to be asked or said off the record, the lieutenant dutifully turned it off but kept notes at Pelosi's instruction.

Pelosi studied her face and locked gazes with her. She glanced away.

"Take your time," he said. "You have to tell us everything you know. And anything you think you know. We need to fill in the gaps."

Victoria sat on a barstool, away from the others, and ran her fingers through her hair. She was afraid now, she admitted to herself. Her mother's voice echoed in her head.

Do the next right thing.

"You can turn it on now," Victoria said. "I'm ready."

The story began slowly, around twenty years ago, after she graduated from Harvard. The plan was to come back to Atlanta, practice law, and run for office at some point. Things unfolded quickly, after a statehouse incumbent decided to step down. State Representative Evelyn Lottier changed her mind and put her name on the ballot, though not before Victoria announced her candidacy. Both refused to drop out, and Lottier regarded it as an act of betrayal. The result was a political pummeling, the likes of which Atlanta hadn't seen since then–City Councilman Bill Campbell trounced Fulton County Commission Chairman Michael Lomax and six other candidates in a bruising 1993 race for mayor.

Right after Victoria was sworn in under the Gold Dome, her father, Ezra Hawkins, and Virgil Loudermilk went about laying the groundwork for the road ahead. Soon, Victoria was taking lunch with many of the city's luminaries and making frequent overnight trips to Washington and New York. It was in Manhattan at the CORE: club, a members-only establishment on East Fifty-fifth Street off Park Avenue, where she first met Virgil Loudermilk in the months leading up to a rematch against Lottier. He was hosting a fundraiser for a cringeworthy U.S. Senate candidate from Ohio and invited her to join them. After the event, a small group traveled in two town cars to Peter Luger Steak House in the Williamsburg section of Brooklyn for a late-night meal of two-inch steaks and red wine.

"He wrote me a check that night and said if I was ready to play ball, there was plenty more where that came from," Victoria said. "Only, I never put it in my campaign account. When it didn't clear his bank, he asked me out for coffee to explain why. I wanted the campaign funded by the people I was going to serve. He nodded and told me how brilliant he thought I was, even for a twenty-seven-year-old.

"I didn't want the people in the statehouse district to see that kind of money coming from the Northside. Besides, my opponent would've used it against me. Lottier was already waving my family name around, like I needed a crown knocked off my head, and I wasn't about to give her any more fuel."

"What about Chip?" Pelosi asked.

"I put my brother in charge of the finance committee. Donations rolled in from around the house district. I told Chip to make sure there weren't any out-of-district checks and to vet every contributor. To my knowledge, nobody from Loudermilk's loose group ever made a direct contribution to any of my campaigns. But he created an independent expenditure campaign to support his pick of candidates, including me. They call themselves the League, and they funnel everything through the same outfit. Reclaim Atlanta. Loudermilk hired Chip to help engineer media buys and recruit street teams. Between that and what he was getting from Dickey's strip clubs, Chip was pulling down serious cash. I told him he was in over his head, but he refused to quit. I had no choice but to fire him when that first story broke last year."

"He got himself killed," Pelosi said. "You were smart not to take Loudermilk's money."

"I didn't say that," Victoria said. "I said my campaign never took his money.

"After my father died, him and Whit Delacourte pledged to endow a scholarship in his name at Morehouse," she said, glancing at Marsh. "I still had a bunch of student loans from undergrad and law school. One day, I got a consolidated statement in the mail with a zero balance. I was confused at first, so I called the bank. A lump-sum payment had been made to the account, and the payer was the Delacourte Trust. I told my mother I needed to pay it back, but she kept telling me not to look a gift horse in the mouth. Loudermilk said he didn't want me to have to worry about debt while I was running for office."

"I thought I paid that off," Marsh said.

"I put your money into the girls' college fund."

Marsh sighed. "What else is there?"

"It went on like that for a long time, even after I got elected to the state senate," she continued. "He didn't ask for much. Sometimes I'd take a courtesy meeting with someone because he asked, but for a long time, that was about the size of it. Every once in a while, after I won the first mayor's race, he'd ask me to withhold my endorsement from a candidate he didn't like or to appoint somebody to a community board. I supported him when I thought he was right and went the other way when he was wrong. I personally shut down his bid to control the FCC, but I backed the transportation bill last year because it was the right thing to do for the region."

"Ezra didn't agree," Pelosi said.

"We didn't agree on everything," Victoria said. "And he respected that."

Marsh was confused. "If you never did anything for him, why was Loudermilk sending money your way?"

"He was keeping a promise he made to my father," Victoria said. "He didn't get anything more than an open ear. I heard him out and made my own decisions. When I decided to run for Congress, out of respect, I went to tell him face-to-face. I already knew he had Goodwin on a string when I walked in. He needed somebody he could use to revive that bill, and Goodwin was the perfect patsy."

"But you were supporting the bill. Why not use you?"

"Because Ezra intended to introduce an amendment that would cut Loudermilk and his minions off at the knees. If the contracts didn't come through the city, my administration would have no control over the procurement process. That meant Resurgens Properties, owned by Coleman Delacourte, would lose out. Chip didn't like it, but I was going to back the amendment. He spent every breath he had trying to convince me to back down. I'm sure Loudermilk was paying him for that.

"The potential contracts included highway expansion, commuter rail from here to Chattanooga and down to Columbus, and at least two billion in commercial and residential developments along the path. Only I never agreed to send a dime their way. Cole's little upstart firm didn't qualify for half the projects they'd already won, and I wasn't about to sole-source billions more to them. Chip was taking their money and making promises in my name that he couldn't keep. When I fired him, he went ballistic. He joined their board of directors after he left the city payroll. That amendment would have put an end to it, once and for all."

"And you think that's why Ezra was murdered?"

"I know it is," Victoria said. "The shooter was Caleb Vasquez. He was Rafaela Delacourte's brother. I knew who it was the minute I saw that house on the TV. He didn't deserve a trial after what he did in our church. Ezra hadn't been dead ten days, and Loudermilk was already threatening to put a bunch of baseless rumors about him on the street."

"Sergeant, turn off the tape," Pelosi said, raising his palm.

Pelosi cleared his throat and ordered the SOC team members out of the room. Marsh remained seated.

"Dr. Overstreet, sir, this is your home and I respect that. But Congressman Hawkins was my friend, and I need to discuss something in private with your wife."

"No problem," Marsh said, getting up.

"No, honey, you should stay," Victoria said. "Sal, we're in this thing together. I want my husband to know everything."

"Those rumors were true," Pelosi said.

"What're you talking about?"

"Congressman Hawkins was gay. I don't know if that's the word for it, but that's the only one I've got."

"No, he wasn't. I don't care what you call it, and I wouldn't give a damn if he was. He would've told me."

"No, ma'am, he wouldn't have. I used to drive him over to a private club at least twice a week when he was in the city," Pelosi said, "and it's more complicated than that."

"Complicated?"

"You remember the prostitute he was caught with thirty or so years ago?"

"Yes, what about her?"

"This is hard to say," Pelosi said, turning his back on Victoria and Marsh. "The prostitute was a young man named Malik Townsend, and—"

"Malik from high school?"

"Yes, and their relationship didn't end there. They all but lived together," Pelosi explained. "The housekeeper you saw at his house a few years ago? That was Malik."

"That wasn't a man," Victoria said, confused. "Whatever Ezra's sexual proclivities were, this isn't anybody's business, and I don't think it's relevant."

"Let me finish before you say that," Pelosi said. "He spent a ton of money on a series of sex-change operations and even put the money up for a name change. He put up nearly every nickel he had for those surgeries. Even took out a second mortgage on his house. He was flat broke and he needed money.

"Loudermilk showed up with a suitcase. In exchange, Ezra said he'd support that transportation bill, then he changed his mind and drafted that amendment. Only, I don't believe money ever made its way back. Malik goes by Chanel Burris now. I believe she knows where the money is. She was with him the night before he died."

Pelosi paused, turned around, and said, "He would've married Chanel, if he could have. I am sure of that. He knew he couldn't do it, but he wanted to give Chanel a life.

"I'm sorry you had to hear this from me," Pelosi went on. "I tried talking to Chanel after the funeral. She wouldn't take my calls. I went out to her job at Lenox Mall. The manager said she quit without notice. Never even picked up her last paycheck. Her apartment looks like she just walked away."

"Any idea where Malik is now?"

"If she's smart, she's hiding," Pelosi said. "By the way, Shaun Haverty was the same officer who arrested her years ago. I've always believed Loudermilk was behind the bust at the motel and he was hanging it over Ezra's head."

Pelosi sat across from Victoria, wide-legged with his hands clasped between them, and waited.

"I know where the money is," she said finally. "Chanel doesn't have it."

"Fuck," Marsh said reflexively. "How much are we talking about?"

"Ten million."

FORTY-THREE

The Delacourte house on Garmond Drive sits on a hill, high above the winding streets and lesser mansions in Buckhead, and there was no finer residence within the city limits. Surrounded by brick columns and wrought-iron fencing, it was nearly twice as large as both neighboring homes and covered the span of four adjoining lots. Whit ordered the custom home built in 1996, and it took two years to construct.

A buzzer sounded and a twelve-foot gate swung open. Virgil eased up the long driveway, through the soaring pines, and parked his car, nose against the garage. He noticed a white Lexus pulling in behind him. He didn't recognize the man behind the wheel. Rosetta Dobbs was in the passenger seat.

"Good morning, Rosetta. How're you getting along today?" he said, extending a bent elbow.

"Virgil," she said dryly, and ignored his waiting arm. "Fair to middling. I wasn't expecting to see you."

"Like a bad penny, I guess," Virgil said.

"On that, we can agree," she said, stepping out of the vehicle.

"I'd say we're off to a good start."

"We haven't spoken in twenty years, and it would be twenty more if I had my way about it."

"I'll try not to be offended."

"I should hope that you are," Rosetta said.

The left-side garage door clicked open and Whit appeared. He was standing between the tail end of a pearl-white Bentley coupe and a matching Range Rover, both of which belonged to him. His wife's Mercedes wasn't in its usual spot.

"It's been a long time, Rosie," Whit said, advancing toward her.

Virgil watched Rosetta's disposition soften. They embraced like old friends. In that moment, whatever had come between Whit and Rosetta over the years was gone.

"You're still as pretty as the day we met," Whit said, cupping her chin and pecking her on the cheek. "Time has been mighty good to you, Rosie."

"I'm sorry to come out here like this," she said. "I mean no disrespect."

"There's nothing for you to be sorry about," Whit replied. "I was in love with you then, and forgive me for saying, I always will be. Time hasn't changed that."

She drew back her sunglasses. Virgil could see the dew in her hazel-green eyes. She'd aged some, but, then again, they all had. Some better than others.

"I see you're eating well," she said with a slight grin. "You're not still smoking, are you?"

"Doctor made me give it up."

"Good on him."

Virgil knew then why his brother always had a soft spot for her, and even now the connection between them was unmistakable.

"It'll take more than a pack of Marlboros to slow me down."

"Or a swift kick in the behind," Rosetta said with a muted laugh.

Virgil watched Whit kiss Rosetta on the forehead and take her by the hand.

"Let's go inside and talk some," his brother said. "It's been too long."

"Come back in an hour," she instructed the driver.

"Who was that?" Virgil asked as the car pulled away.

"None of your damn business," Rosetta said.

"What concerns my brother, concerns me," Virgil quipped.

Rosetta ignored him.

"Why is Virgil here?" she said to Whit. "I said we needed to talk alone. If there's a better time, let me know and I'll come back."

Whit paused and said, "You have to trust me on this, Rosie."

She relented and he led her through the garage and into the back of the house. Virgil shuffled in behind them.

"You have a beautiful home," she said to Whit.

"Thank you, Rosie," he said. "We don't need this big house. Only my wife isn't interested in moving."

"Patricia is a good woman," Rosetta said.

"She'll never be you," Whit said. "I was never ashamed of what you and I had."

"I always knew you'd be something," she said, twisting her wedding band.

"I had a better start than most."

"Forgive me for calling so late in the evening. I suppose I should've expected Patricia to pick up the phone. I hope it wasn't any trouble."

"None at all, Rosie. You are welcome to call on me anytime. Take a seat and I'll get some coffee going. How do you take yours?"

"I'll take some tea, if you have it, and a little cream will do me just fine."

Whit wandered off to the kitchen and left Rosetta and Virgil alone in the great room.

"We're not enemies, Rosetta. I ain't got nothing against you," Virgil said.

"You don't have a reason not to like me. I never gave you one."

"Fair enough."

"You're going to leave my child alone. That I know for sure."

"You don't know your daughter like you think you do, Rosetta. She came out swinging. What did you expect?"

"I didn't expect you to try to bust up her marriage," Rosetta said.

"I hear that ain't the only thing that got busted up."

"I knew you were behind that. Then, you went and bought off that preacher. She whipped his tail, like I knew she would. My husband trusted you, but I never did. The last thing I wanted was to see my daughter mixed up with you."

"The last thing I wanted was to see my brother mixed up with you. That daughter of yours bit off more than she could chew."

"You won't sass me about my child, Virgil. I don't give a damn who you think you are."

"She's definitely your child," Virgil said. "Ain't no two ways about that."

"She's mine," Rosetta said, "and don't you ever forget that. She doesn't trust you and neither do I."

"Who needs trust when you can have power?" Virgil said. "Nobody knows that better than the Great Torie Dobbs."

Virgil knew Rosetta had a backbone. The first time he laid eyes on her was fifty years back, in the fall of '64 after the Georgia–Georgia Tech football game. It was Whit who couldn't stop looking at her. She caught him staring, flashed a smile, and his brother was positively smitten.

"I'm going over to talk to her," Whit had said.

"Don't you dare," Virgil said. "You can't take that gal home."

"Who's talking about taking anybody home? What Daddy don't know won't hurt him."

"It ain't Daddy I'm worried about. Your mama will pitch a fit. Since when are you into colored gals?"

"She ain't colored, she's beautiful," Whit said. "I'm going over there. Hold my Coke."

As it turned out, the pretty girl was a nineteen-year-old biology major at Spelman College. Soon enough, word got out that "some rich white boy" from Emory University was coming on campus to see Rosetta. They got on hot-and-heavy for a while, sneaking off to Lake Lanier on the weekends, until Rosetta abruptly broke it off. Apparently, her parents didn't approve either. And besides that, she had a new boyfriend. Parkland Dobbs was a seminary student at Morehouse.

At the start of senior year, when Rosetta informed him of her engagement, it broke Whit's heart. She and Park got hitched right after graduation. The ceremony made the pages of the *Atlanta Times*, the *Daily World*, and *Jet* magazine, and the reception was held at the Georgian Terrace Hotel. Later that year, in 1972, her first child was born: a daughter. A son came soon after.

Even so, Virgil knew that Whit's feelings never gave up the ghost. In time, he met Patsy Jo and they got married. After a year of trying, Cole was born in 1976.

Sometime in the early '80s, Virgil bumped into Rosetta and her husband, Park, at the airport. He'd completed his PhD and been named senior pastor of a church on the south side of town, Park said proudly. They were off to some theology conference in Kansas City, he explained, and Virgil was coming in from San Francisco. They traded pleasantries, and Rosetta showed him photos of their two young children: Victoria and Prentiss.

Virgil took one look at her flowing hair and telltale toothy smile, and said, "She's a beautiful little girl."

Park politely promised to keep in touch, and the couple hurried off to catch their flight. As far as Virgil could tell, the young pastor didn't know then that it was Whit whom Rosetta was sneaking around with in college or that they'd kept in touch even after they traded their vows. Now Park was dead, Rosetta was sitting in his brother's house, and that beautiful little girl was currently mayor of Atlanta.

Through the years, Virgil pressed Whit on the matter, only to get stiff-armed and brushed off. He thought the whole thing was behind them, until his brother showed up at his law office in June of '95. Park Dobbs had been laid to rest that spring.

"Are you sure this is what you want?" Virgil said at the time. "Surely, there is another way."

"Ain't but one right way," Whit said. "I need to get my affairs in order."

Virgil got up and pulled the blinds. It took them four full days to hammer out a document that satisfied Whit. He was specific about the wording. They lied and told their wives they'd gone on a fishing trip, none of which would be believed, but Patsy Jo and Libby Gail let it all go without question.

"You've always been reasonable," Virgil said to Rosetta. "I didn't like it then and I don't like it now, but my brother did what he thought was right. You always did have a good head on your shoulders."

"You do too," Rosetta said. "Don't give me a reason to knock it off."

"Let's bury that hatchet," Virgil said, "for old times' sake."

"Fine. Until you dig it up again," Rosetta said. "I don't wanna have to bury it in your neck."

Whit entered carrying a tray of coffee cups. Rosetta set her purse down on the sofa next to her and forced a smile. Whit placed three settings, including cloth napkins and polished silver teaspoons, on the table.

"The middle one is yours," he told Rosetta. "It's raspberry. I hope you like it."

Rosetta reached down, drew the porcelain cup to her mouth, took a sip, and said, "Whatever we say stays between here and that gate out there."

"You have my word on that," Whit said. "Virgil?"

"Forever and always," Virgil responded with a smirk.

"Well, then, let's get to it," Whit said. "Rosie, what's on your mind?"

The meeting was brief and Rosetta did most of the talking.

"My daughter is the most important thing in the world to me," she said. "And, Whit, I appreciate everything you've done for her. I know where that student loan money came from and all the rest, even if Virgil was the one who wrote the checks. I also know Virgil has been up to some devilment around here."

Virgil reared back in the lounging chair, cupped his hand over his chin, and waited.

"If anything should happen to her, and I don't care what it is, I'm going to blame you," she said, looking at both men, "and I will spend the rest of my days making sure you pay for it."

"She'll win the congressional race," Whit said. "The polls look good. It'll be a landslide."

"No harm, no foul," Virgil said.

"I'll be the judge of that," Rosetta quipped. "Whit, you know I'm not talking about no damn election. You promised me you would look after her, and I expect you to make good on that, even if it means Virgil here won't always get what he wants."

"What is it you think I want?" Virgil said. "Give it to us straight, gal. How much do you want? How much will it take?"

"Don't test me, Virgil Loudermilk," she said.

"The way I see it, that daughter of yours is doing all the testing," Virgil said.

"Shut up, Virgil," Whit said. "Let Rose have her say."

Rosetta's expression turned dour. "Is the paperwork in order?" she said.

"Yes," Whit said. "Everything is spelled out just the way I told you. If any of my beneficiaries challenge it, they get nothing. Virgil drafted the document himself."

"I need a copy. If anything should happen to you, I don't trust Virgil with our business. He's liable to burn it up."

Whit offered her a plaintive glance and scratched his meaty neck. Virgil watched his shoulders slump.

"We never told her the truth," Rosetta said, "even when the kids teased her in school. They kept saying she was the milkman's baby. Came home crying all the time."

"She didn't deserve that," Whit said, "and I'm sorry it had to be that way."

"She didn't deserve half the things your family has done to her," Rosetta said. "I've stayed silent many years, because that was the best thing. But I will burn this house down to the bricks, if that's what it takes.

"You can take that to the bank, Virgil," she said, gathering her pocketbook. "Thank you for your time, gentlemen. I'll see myself out."

"Hold on, Rosie. We can work this out," Whit said. "Hold your fire."

"That decision is yours, Whit," she said.

"It all stops now. Right, Virgil?"

"Whatever you want," Virgil said.

"Well?" Rosetta pushed. "When will I have it?"

"So be it," Whit said. "Virgil, get her a copy of the document and send me a duplicate so I can get it to an attorney."

"I am your lawyer."

"Not on this, you're not," Whit said. "Not anymore."

"A piece of money doesn't mean anything to me. My husband gave me a good life," Rosetta said. "She's my child and I aim to see after her."

Whit nodded thoughtfully. "She's mine too," he said, "and I aim to see after her."

FORTY-FOUR

There was a low hum in the newsroom that Thursday morning. Hampton managed to clear his email in-box, return a couple of phone calls, and get some copyedits in. He'd been summoned to Tucker's corner office, something he came to loathe, and braced himself for an upbraiding. He was relieved to find out that he was getting his weekly column back.

"This isn't a gift. You earned it," Tucker told him. "The opinion page is missing your voice. Your first column will go up Monday night, the day before the election. I'm thinking you already know the subject."

"Honestly, I didn't think I'd get another shot," Hampton said. "Does it come with a pay raise?"

"I'm not Mother Teresa. I don't do miracles. But it does come with an assistant, and I've got the perfect one for you."

"She didn't either. Who's the assistant?"

"Olu Gatewood," Tucker said. "Wait, aren't you Catholic?"

"That's my mother. I am, well, let's just say I'm agnostic. I just pray and hope something good comes of it."

"I never knew that."

"Mostly out of habit or desperation. I'm hedging my bets, so to speak."

"You can teach young Olu a lot. Just don't teach him any bad habits."

"He's a good kid and he writes like a song."

"You were a good kid when I met you."

"He's better than I ever was."

"One rule," Tucker said. "I need this job and so do you. Don't get us fired."

Hampton smiled and stood up with a slight stagger. He gripped the arm of the chair to steady himself. It had been only weeks since he gave up the wheelchair, and he was using the forearm crutches less and less these days. He wanted Claire to see a man standing on his own two feet, like the day they were married. She'd cautioned him to move slowly, to take his time. His physical therapist agreed. There was more work to be done.

"Thanks again, Tuck," he said. "As for getting us canned, I'll do my best."

"That's what I'm afraid of."

Sometimes, when he was tired, he felt his knees wobbling. Being able to take a piss standing up was its own reward. It wasn't like he was going to run a marathon. Hampton was never into that kind of thing, anyway. He did long to hurl Claire onto his back and give her a piggyback ride again. He wanted to hear her giggle over his shoulder and feel her legs strapped around his waist.

He was glad to be back in the swing of things at work too. Somebody saw fit to give him a paycheck for writing, and meager as it was, that was worth something. Claire was always the breadwinner, something his father frowned on. He couldn't wait to tell her the news.

Aside from the time when he dreamed about playing shortstop for the Detroit Tigers, Hampton couldn't remember wanting to be anything else. While some of the guys he grew up with went to work at an automotive plant or for a parts maker, he was studying for the SAT with hopes of getting into a great journalism school. He'd been wait-listed at Columbia.

He would have done things differently, he was thinking that morning as he walked out of Tucker's office, if he had the chance to do it all over again. There would be fewer drinks and he wouldn't have cheated on Claire. Tucker had every reason to fire him at least three times over, and he wouldn't have been able to blame him if he had.

Hampton left Tucker's office almost skipping through the cubicles. He went looking for Kathy Franco, and he found her in the breakroom, hunched over her laptop and nursing a cup of coffee.

"Hey, Kathy, what's up?"

"Putting in the work. You know me."

"Yes, I do. Can I ask you about a story you wrote?"

"Sure."

"There's a kid name DeVonte Charles. In federal custody on interstate drug charges."

"My favorite car thief. What about him?"

"You tell me," Hampton said.

Franco waved him over to a table near the window.

"I've been looking into the Sex Money Murder clique for a while now. They run the Bluff and every other heroin trap in the city. They're tied to the Bloods. DeVonte is fourteen, coming up on fifteen, but the feds say he was born into the business. Started as a lookout for his uncle when he was still in grade school. Now, among other things, he's a wheelman. He's up on big charges, and he doesn't even have a driver's license."

"Who is this uncle?"

"Well, that's where it gets interesting. His uncle is Richard Lester."

"That lines up with my thinking."

"They moved the car theft and arson charges from state to federal court. Unless DeVonte starts talking, and fast, he's going to spend the next forty years in prison. If he turns state's evidence, that's his ticket to freedom. Why're you interested in him?"

"For starters, I'm sure I saw him the night the car bomb went off at the Hyatt, and I don't think that was a coincidence. He was outside the hotel, rolling by on a skateboard, scanning the crowd."

Franco raised her eyebrow and said, "That's interesting."

"I have a feeling the feds think he's the link to the bombing that killed Prentiss Dobbs."

"Keep going."

"Prentiss was freelancing for Richard Lester. I was out at Lenox when his nephew got pinched for shoplifting too. And that car they found burnt up in Villa Rica matches the description of the one I saw parked in my driveway last month. I was at home when three guys broke in my house. They sped off in a green Camaro."

"You weren't hurt, were you?"

"No, but one of them shot my dog. Killed him right in front of me."

"Inman? Are you fucking kidding me?"

"No," Hampton said. "And I think DeVonte is the one who shot him."

"What did they take?"

"I didn't think they took anything, at first. Not that I had much to get," Hampton said. "But I haven't been able to find an external hard drive. It had a lot of research on it for a book I'm writing."

"The one about Reclaim Atlanta?"

"Something like that. I thought maybe it was all a coincidence. But this kid just kept popping up."

"So, you think the guys who broke in your house were looking for that hard drive?"

"Yeah, it's starting to look that way. I've been talking to a source about some of this, and I think it's connected."

"DeVonte wouldn't do anything without his uncle's approval. He is being groomed for bigger things."

"That's what worries me, to be honest," Hampton said.

"So, if the feds think Lester was behind that car bomb, and if that was actually his nephew you saw outside that hotel, they're probably right. You might be the only one who can place him at the scene."

"Any idea why Lester might want to kill Prentiss Dobbs? They've known each other since grade school, and it's true he once dated the mayor."

"He was going to testify against him," Franco said. "At least that's the word on the street."

"There's another piece to this. I can't talk about it right now. I'm not even sure how it fits."

"Hope I helped."

Hampton's phone buzzed. It was a message from Claire.

Stayed home from work. Sick.

"Hold on a minute, Kathy."

Are you OK?
No. Vomiting. Fever is back.
On my way.

"Can we talk again later? I have to run up to Alpharetta to see my wife."

"Claire? I thought you two were divorced."

"Something like that. Can we talk about this later?"

"Sure thing."

Hampton collected his backpack, hurried to the elevator. His feet hadn't moved that fast in a long time. He called Claire from the car as he sped up Georgia 400.

"I feel really dizzy," she said. "I can't stand up."

"Just lie down, baby. I'm coming."

The house was quiet when he arrived, and there was no sign of Claire. Hampton began checking the rooms, one by one.

"Claire! Ruby Claire!" he called out. "Claire!"

He heard the sink water going in the master bathroom and poked his head inside. He found her wearing her kimono, slumped over on the tiled floor, wedged between the toilet and the double vanity. Hampton shut off the faucet. He shook her, but she did not wake.

"Claire, baby, wake up."

He shook her again, this time with more force. Her head flopped and her body was limp. Hampton checked and found a weak pulse on her neck.

"Nine one one, what's your emergency?"

"Please send an ambulance. My wife is unconscious. She might've fallen, I don't know. She's been sick with fever and vomiting."

"Your name, sir?"

"James Hampton Bridges. It's 2204 Easthaven Place, Champions Overlook subdivision."

"A unit is headed your way, sir. Is she breathing?"

"I think so."

Two paramedics dispatched from a North Fulton firehouse entered the house less than seven minutes later. Hampton met them at the door and directed them to the bathroom, where Claire was still splayed out.

He watched one of them apply chest compressions and cup his mouth over Claire's, forcing air into her lungs. She didn't respond.

"Don't leave me, baby," he kept saying. "Don't leave me."

FORTY-FIVE

D r. Overstreet, please!" Hampton yelped. "I need to talk to her!"

A patrol officer from the overnight detail pinned him, knee to back, facedown in the grass. A second cop stood two or three feet away, pointing his service revolver, while another attempted to apply handcuffs.

"Please!" Hampton screamed again.

"Do not move! Stop resisting! Stop resisting!"

Blue strobe lights lit up her living room window. Victoria flipped on the outdoor lights and waited inside. Hampton's polo pullover was ripped at the collar. A shoe fell off in the scuffle. Victoria could see the crack of his pale ass.

"Son, do you know what time it is?" Marsh said. "You couldn't wait for morning to call the office?"

"I'm sorry, I tried," Hampton cried out, hawking up more blood. "I'm really sorry. I need to see her."

"It can't be worth all of this."

The reporter was bucking and thumping his chest against the ground, his legs kicking wildly. His body suddenly went limp.

"Okay! Okay!" Hampton relented.

The cuffs were snapped on. Victoria stood at the bay window, arms folded and stone-faced. A patrolman patted him down and another searched his backpack. Hampton was still on the ground, talking in rapid bursts now, and appeared to be shouting. It was not yet first light, and Victoria, still hazy, could only guess what he was saying.

Hampton fucking Bridges. What in the hell are you doing in my yard?

She walked outside in her bare feet. Marsh was standing in the driveway, dressed only in a pair of scrub pants, giving a statement to one of the officers.

"Morning, gentlemen," Victoria said. "How did he get by you?"

Before any of the officers could answer, she said, "Never mind, tell it to your section chief."

She turned her attention to Hampton. "What're you doing here, Mr. Bridges?" Victoria said. "Is nothing sacred? You're going to mess around and get yourself hurt out here." Her voice was stern, not with anger but imbued with pity.

"We'll book him on trespassing and assault, ma'am," the officer said.

"That won't be necessary. He's harmless. Uncuff him," she said. "Give him his shoes."

Hampton stood up and said, "I'm sorry, Mayor Dobbs."

"What do you want?"

"They tried to kill my wife," Hampton said, lowering his head in submission.

"We're still on that? First, you said I tried to kill you," Victoria said, rolling her eyes, "and now you're saying somebody went after your wife? Now, why on earth would anybody want to do that?"

"I thought maybe you would know."

"Get his ass out of here."

"Wait, please. I need to show you something. It's in my bag."

"You're trying what's left of my patience, Mr. Bridges. I don't have time for your schemes."

"Please. Let me show you."

"Fine."

"It's clear," a patrolman said, tossing him the bag.

Hampton dug inside and pulled a piece of origami from an interior pocket. Victoria noticed his hands trembling.

"She told me that if anything ever happened to her, I should bring this to you."

Victoria couldn't see what he was holding at first. She stepped closer and immediately froze. Her eyes widened. She opened her mouth, but nothing came out.

"Who gave you those?" Marsh asked.

Hampton didn't respond.

"Answer him!" Victoria shouted. "Where did you get them?"

"Her name is Chanel Burris. Ma'am, I think you know her as Malik Townsend."

Victoria paused and said, "Handcuff him and bring him inside."

"Ma'am?" an officer said in protest.

"I said put the cuffs back on him and bring him in the house."

"I can wake the girls and take them to Rosetta's," Marsh said.

"Honey, I think we need to stay here."

Hampton was seated in the living room, handcuffed to a high-back king chair when Pelosi arrived fifteen minutes later. The SOC team pulled up, two by two, in separate cars. The overnight detail was dismissed.

"There's a squad car on Miss Rosetta's house," Pelosi said. "We also locked down your Aunt Kick's house, as a precaution."

"Thank you, Sal," Victoria said. "Do you think that's enough?"

"We've taken other measures."

"Understood."

"What about my wife?" Hampton said. "She's at North Fulton Hospital in ICU."

Claire was on life support with ethylene glycol poisoning, he explained. The attending physician said it was touch-and-go. There was major organ damage, but she was conscious now.

"We're there," Pelosi said.

Hampton was confused.

"What does that mean, you're there?"

"It means we're there," Pelosi said.

Hampton hadn't slept all night, he said. Claire had been sick for several days.

"We thought it was a stomach virus or food poisoning. I was hoping she was pregnant. She seemed to be getting better, then she sent me a text at work yesterday afternoon. I got there as fast as I could. She was unconscious on the bathroom floor when I found her. The doctors initially thought it was the flu."

"Your wife ingested antifreeze, Mr. Bridges," Pelosi said. "Any idea how that happened?"

"Claire didn't have an enemy in the world."

"But you do."

Hampton swallowed hard.

"Whoever tried to kill your wife put antifreeze in something she drank. Who's been in that house other than you?"

"Nobody. Claire lived alone," Hampton said. "Can we take these handcuffs off now?"

"Sure, why not?" Pelosi said. "It's not like you're going anywhere. I'll put a bullet in your head if you try, and the way I see it, you can't run very fast."

"I'm not going anywhere," Hampton said with a deep sigh.

"It doesn't take much," Marsh said. "Two to eight ounces. It usually acts within twenty-four hours. She's still alive and that's a good sign."

Pelosi placed a bottled water on the table in front of Hampton.

"Drink up," Pelosi said. "We're going to be here awhile."

"I didn't poison my wife."

"I know you didn't," Pelosi said. "Mr. Bridges, do you have keys to her house?"

"Yes."

"Hand them over," Pelosi said. "Delacourte, head out there now. We need every glass in the kitchen. Check the dishwasher and the trash. Pull every container of liquid in the refrigerator."

"Her address is—" Hampton said, before Pelosi cut him off.

"We know where she lives."

"Roger that," the SOC officer responded. "What if I run into Alpharetta or Fulton County PD?"

"Call me," Pelosi said.

"Wait," Marsh said. "How long did you say she was sick again?"

"Several days. Three or four, at least," Hampton said, thinking back. "It started late Sunday night."

Pelosi looked at Marsh plaintively. The doctor shrugged.

"Hard to say. I'm a heart surgeon," Marsh said. "Could have been administered in small doses over time. It had to be consistent, though, so the body wouldn't have time to break it down. Somebody wanted her to suffer."

"Or watch you watch her suffer," Pelosi said, tipping his head toward Hampton. "The target was you, Mr. Bridges. I'm sure of that. Whoever did this didn't want to kill your ex-wife. They wanted you distracted. What are you working on right now?"

"I can't say," Hampton said nervously.

Pelosi got in his face and barked, "Mr. Bridges, I don't have time for journalistic ethics and neither do you!"

"You're investigating me, aren't you?" Victoria said.

Hampton looked down at the carpet and rubbed his damp hands together. He'd sweated out his armpits, and his face was misty like he'd run a country mile.

"My head hurts," he said. "Can I get something for my head?"

"It's me, isn't it?"

"Yeah, something like that."

"Spit it out, goddammit!" she shouted.

"Fine," he said. "I've been looking into the League and your connections to Virgil Loudermilk. I have been tracking political donations going back thirty years."

"My records are clean."

"As a whistle," Hampton said. "But you and I both know better than that."

"You want my help, then start talking," Victoria said. "If you think you've got something on me, I will personally drive you over to GBI headquarters and drop you at the curb."

"Chanel is missing," he said finally. "I put her on a train to Flint. She was staying with my mother. She got spooked after Haverty turned up in the Chattahoochee and took off on her own. The last time I heard from Chanel, she was in Chicago at a coffee shop."

"How long ago was this?" Pelosi asked.

"Almost a week ago. I gave her money for a hotel and a new burner phone, but she never checked in. I need to find her."

"Why did she tell you to come to me?" Victoria asked.

"Never would say exactly," Hampton said. "She told me you were the only person who could save her life."

"I haven't seen Malik in years," Victoria said.

"Her name is Chanel. She told me about the League and all the money," Hampton said. "She told me about that transportation bill and said that's why Congressman Hawkins was killed. Somebody sent him a message."

"What kind of message?" Pelosi asked.

"One of those red paper birds," Hampton replied. "Chanel got one too. I helped her get out of town."

"That's probably the only reason she's still alive," Pelosi said. "If she's still alive."

Hampton broke down sobbing. "Ma'am, please help me," he muttered. "Help me find her."

Victoria nodded to Pelosi, giving him the go-ahead.

"We'll do what we can," Pelosi said. "I've known Chanel for many years. She's special to me too."

Marsh uncapped a bottle of pain relievers and handed Hampton two gel caplets.

"Tell me everything Chanel said. Walk me back, minute by minute," Pelosi said. "Don't leave anything out."

"I can't do that."

"You can and you will," Pelosi said.

Hampton stood up and paced the room, gesturing with his hands as he recalled the events in specific detail from the moment he first met Chanel. When he was finished, he scanned the room.

Hampton said, "The tapes are in my backpack."

"We believe you," Victoria said. "I have the paper god that was sent to Congressman Hawkins. I found a second one in my brother's clothing. They are exactly like the one you showed us."

"Paper god?" Hampton said. "You know who did this, don't you?"

"I may be the only person who can stop him."

"Loudermilk?"

"Unfortunately, we aren't that lucky," she said. "Believe it or not, there are bigger devils in the world."

They traded knowing looks.

FORTY-SIX

Virgil was knotting his tie, watching from an upper window as three Ford Excursions and a blacked-out Ford Taurus pulled into the parking deck entrance below. He'd been expecting them. His lawyers were stationed in the conference room. Wearing a pair of simple khakis, a plaid button-down shirt, and some nicely broken-in leather loafers, he'd forgone the pretense of putting on socks.

"Come on in, boys," he whispered to himself as he watched them enter the building.

There would be no arrest, he surmised, but there would be a volley of questions, and he was well prepared to answer them. The ginger-haired avenger led the way.

"Good morning, Mr. Loudermilk," he said, stepping into the penthouse suite of offices. "I'm Special Agent Jason Clearwater."

"Good morning, Agent Clearwater, it's good to finally meet you even under these unfortunate circumstances. Shaun Haverty was a friend of mine. But I guess you know that."

"I suspect you will fill me in."

"Absolutely. I've got nothing to hide," Virgil said. "At least not an indictable offense. Come on in the conference room. Rest a spell."

The questioning went on for two hours. There were six agents in all and three attorneys, including Virgil.

"I hired him to perform some private duties. He was a security consultant for my family. Everything was by the book," Virgil said, "Nothing wrong with that, right?"

"I need to ask you about some of those duties," Clearwater said, taking a side chair. "Let's call them extracurricular activities."

"Oh, you mean that little package I sent to the mayor?"

"Tell me about that."

"I've always liked Victoria. Her husband was running around on her, and I thought she oughta know."

"You admit to hacking her husband's cell phone records?"

"Heavens no," Virgil said with a chuckle. "Haverty did that on his own. It was an ugly piece of business, I must admit. But that ain't what I paid him for."

"I'd ask him, but he's dead," Clearwater said. "And leaking that 911 tape to a reporter. Did he do that on his own?"

"Wasn't my doing," Virgil said. "I asked him to take a few pictures, that's all. If he was here right now, he would tell you that."

"Only he isn't."

"I fired him the minute I found out," Virgil said. "I sent Haverty an email and told him how disappointed I was in his untoward behavior. He was always a bit overzealous."

"And you have this email?"

One of Virgil's lawyers slid a printout across the table.

"This is time-stamped the morning the *Times-Register* story was published," Charlie Stewart said blithely. "And this is a copy of the server records."

"I'll need his hard drive," Clearwater said.

"You'll need a warrant," Stewart interjected.

"Mr. Stewart, when I need to produce one, I will," Clearwater said dismissively. "Mr. Loudermilk, tell me about Reclaim Atlanta."

"Not much to tell you," Virgil said. "I testified in a hearing earlier this week. It's all on the record. I'm sure you can get the transcript."

"We had an agent in the courtroom."

"Is that so?" Virgil said. "And what, pray tell, did this agent learn?"

"You're a smart man, Mr. Loudermilk," Clearwater said. "I'll let you think about that."

"You're not from around here, are you?"

"Does it matter where I was raised?"

"Well, see, that says it all," Virgil said. "You didn't end that sentence in a preposition like a Southerner would. Now, tell me, where'bouts you from?"

Clearwater shrugged and said, "Seattle."

"That's what I thought."

"Meaning what?"

"You think we Southerners are stupid, don't you? You wound up down here, working out of sunny downtown Conyers, Georgia, because you couldn't find a job anywhere else. I'm sure the FBI has plenty of openings. Why didn't they hire you?"

"Mr. Loudermilk, we pulled a body from a river last week. The man was an officer of the law. You must know that we will turn over every rock to find out who put him there."

"I expect you will," Virgil said.

Stewart stood up and said, "This interview is over. Unless and until there is a warrant, there will be no hard drive."

"Mr. Stewart, take your seat. We're searching his residence right now."

Virgil was immediately uncomfortable. "Which one?" he asked.

"All of them. Blackland Drive, Ball Ground, and Sea Island. Here are copies of the warrants," Clearwater said, sliding an envelope onto the table. "Now, about that hard drive. I have a warrant for this office and everything in it. That includes every file and computer."

Virgil near 'bout swallowed his shirt.

"We have your phone records," Clearwater added. "The good people at your cell service provider were gracious enough to hand them over."

Virgil was blinking now like a flashlight with low batteries.

"Show me an indictment and we'll talk," Stewart said.

"I'm not quite done," Clearwater said. "Tell me about Resurgens Properties."

"We're done here," Stewart said.

"It's alright, Stew," Virgil said. "It's my nephew's company. We gave him some seed money, drawn from his trust fund, to get started. Other than that, my brother and I don't have any hand in it."

"If only I believed that."

"Suit yourself."

"Mr. Loudermilk, tell me about Richard Lester."

"The drug dealer?" Virgil said with a laugh. "Never met the man. Read about the mayor's boyfriend in the papers. Sounds like one bad dude."

"I know you don't think much of us Yankees," Clearwater said, standing up. "But this one doesn't go fishing in barren waters."

Virgil stood up and said, "Take a look around, son. *Mi casa es su casa.*"

Clearwater unlocked his cell phone and tapped out a text message. Within minutes, a team of blue-jacketed GBI agents swarmed the office.

Virgil was forced to open his safe. He sat in his own lobby while the search was conducted. He buried his face in his hands as one agent walked by holding a plastic bag with an external hard drive inside.

FORTY-SEVEN

A yo, nigga, what's good?" he shouted. "Get'cho mu'fucking hands off me!"
The nondescript, two-story house in a quiet neighborhood off Cascade and Fairburn Roads was oddly staid for someone of his purported wealth and reputation. There were no fancy cars in the drive, and inside the rooms were sparsely furnished. A half-eaten plate of collard greens mashed up with corn bread sat cooling on the coffee table. ESPN played silently on a small television.

"Stand up, turn around, and place your hands behind your back."

"Not until I call my lawyer. I am not leaving here until I talk to my lawyer."

"I'll spare you a quarter later," the officer said.

There were eight of them. All wearing ski masks, four carrying AR-15 assault weapons.

He was wearing a white sleeveless T-shirt, a pair of oversized basketball shorts, blue Adidas flip-flops, and an ankle bracelet. Music blared from the surround-sound system.

Pull up to the scene with my ceiling missing!
Middle finger up to my competition!

"Shut it off," one officer ordered another.

The sole woman in the squad drew her weapon, pointed it at the man in the easy chair, and said, "Now do I have your attention, Mr. Lester?"

"Shoot me, then, bitch."

"I have no problem blowing your damn head off," she said calmly. "Face it, Mr. Lester, I bet your mama won't even cry when you're gone. Nobody will march for you. There won't be a parade. Go ahead. Twitch."

"Who are you? Ain't no damn federal agent up in here with masks on."

"This chambered round is the only law you need to recognize," she said with a shrug.

"You don't know who you fucking with," Dickey said.

"Stand up and turn around. This is the last time I am going to ask you."

Dickey cursed, rose from his seat, laced his fingers behind his head, and turned around.

"Where are you taking me?"

She ignored his question. His legs were shackled, and they shuffled him out of the house. There was a black van with blacked-out windows parked at the curb. Suddenly Dickey understood his predicament and began to fight, throwing his shoulders and bucking his body.

"Fuck that! I ain't getting in no mu'fucking van! Y'all can kiss my black ass."

Two men lifted him off the ground and tossed him into the rear. He yelped as he hit the floor. "Y'all ain't gone buckle me in?"

"She wants to see you," the woman said. "Enjoy the ride."

"Who sent you to get me? Ain't no bitch got that kind of power."

"Victoria Dobbs."

"Pussy, heroin, and guns," Pelosi said.

"I don't know what the fuck you talking about," Dickey said.

"Come on, now, Dickey. Don't play me small."

"I ain't never ran no bitches."

"I didn't say you were into prostitution. You just like pussy too much, and that's what got you caught up. You couldn't think of a better cover than running strip clubs?"

"Man, fuck you."

Victoria watched from the other side of the two-way mirror. Bringing him here to the SOC Unit squad room had its risks, but she had no choice. She hadn't seen Dickey since she left him in Guanacaste, Costa Rica. He was good-looking, still, despite the rap sheet and the federal case against him. He licked his full lips and arched his heavy brows.

That morning, she'd finally given in and had the painting removed from the house. A SOC officer was tasked with destroying it.

"I have to end this," she'd told Marsh. "Highsmith made the transfers this morning. All ten million."

"Where is it going?"

"Arjana Global Ministries is a church-run nonprofit in Soweto, South Africa. The bishop agreed to use it to build a school for girls. Loudermilk won't miss it where he's going. I have to deal with Dickey now, and I have to do that face-to-face."

"Do you think he'll talk to you?"

"We're going to find out," she said.

Do the next right thing.

"We don't have a lot of time," she said. "The feds will come looking for him, and he's wearing a court-issued monitor."

She steadied herself and clicked open the door leading to the interrogation room.

Dickey was sitting calmly at the far end of the table. Pelosi was in the corner, arms folded across his chest.

"I'll leave you two alone," Pelosi said, walking out.

Victoria took a seat on the opposite end of the table and waited. She tried to ignore his hard leg muscles and his beautifully chiseled face. He'd run track in high school, the hundred-meter dash and hurdles. In her mind's eye, she could still see him, chest out, snapping the finish-line tape.

Dickey picked up the nickname "Phoenix" in high school for his speed. He shattered regional athletic records at one meet after another. College scholarship offers poured in, but Dickey got hurt in the state championship race during their senior year. His hamstring separated as he cleared the last hurdle in the two hundred meter. The tendon tore from the bone. He collapsed onto the clay track. Victoria remembered the agony on his face as the medics carted him away. He was still known as "Dickey Phoenix" on the street.

"It's been a long time," she said. "You know why we're here."

"I'm waiting on you," Dickey said. "You sent for me. We're on your dime."

"I don't want to ask you why," she said pensively. "If you ever cared anything about me, why do this?"

"I've always been about my business, Big Time. How you think I was flying you around the world?"

"You said you'd never let it touch me."

"And you said you'd never leave me," he said. "You think it ain't hurt me to see you get on that plane?"

"I did what I had to do," she said. "You had to live your life and I had to live mine."

"He don't love you like I do."

"Love?" she shot back. "Is that what you call this? Ezra and Chip are dead. Y'all killed a cop."

He looked her in the face and didn't flinch.

"After everything Ezra did for you—the parole letters, the suspended sentences—you had him killed. Five people died in that church. That ain't business," she said, sneering. "That little boy bled out in my arms! An innocent woman is fighting for her life right now, and that's on you too! I know you tried to kill that reporter last year."

Dickey twisted his neck and let it crack. "What yourself."

"If that's love, I don't want it," she said, stroking away tears. "You killed my brother, and I won't ever forgive that!"

Dickey shrugged. "The feds got to Chip. Punk-ass snitch. I had him living right. Put him in nice cars, got him courtside seats at the arena. I even sent that nephew of yours to the best damn day school in Buckhead."

"At what price? Maybe Chip was tired of paying. I got sick of watching him run behind you like a wet-nosed dog," Victoria said, looking up. "What's up with Loudermilk?"

"Chip introduced us some ways back," Dickey said. "I was looking for some new business opportunities, and his nephew was getting into the construction game."

"The Delacourtes don't need your money."

"Nah, they don't," Dickey said. "But Virgil needed me to make that paper work. I had some land he wanted to get his hands on."

"What property?"

"The west end of the old rail yard off Seventeenth Street."

"Atlantic Station?"

"All the way over to Joe Lowery Boulevard. He wanted what I had in the Bluff too," Dickey said.

"The new football stadium."

"I still own the title to the land where the overflow parking lots will be built. I took a piece of his nephew's construction business in exchange."

The math came together quickly in Victoria's head. That proposed commuter rail would have run south out of Marietta and down to the Gulch, just outside the new stadium. Whoever owned the right-of-way stood to make millions. According to public records, most of it was held by the Renaissance Group.

"So you're Renaissance?"

"Me and my investors, yes," he admitted. "Virgil expected you and Ezra to go along with everything. That transportation bill was my payday. I would sell to Resurgens and get out with my money before they broke ground."

"How did you evade federal seizure?"

"My name ain't on nothing," he said. "You know me better than that."

"I never cut a deal with Virgil. No matter what Chip told you, I never agreed to sell any construction contracts."

"That's all well and good. You took the money, though," Dickey said. "Bribery is a federal crime."

"I never touched it. I didn't know where it came from."

"Ain't no jury gone believe that lie," Dickey said. "You've been rocking with Virgil for years. Watching y'all squabble was better than that time Tyson bit off Holyfield's ear."

"I donated every dime to a charity."

"You always did have a soft heart. You on term limits, though. I would've bought me a new mayor. But you think he's going to let you get away with that? Come on, now, Big Time, that's ten million dollars."

"He wants more than money. He wants to destroy me."

"You honestly don't know, do you?" he said, leaning back and smiling. "You're going to be Atlanta's first black billionaire."

"Billionaire?"

"Your mama never told you? That's just like Miss Rosetta," he said. "Always worried about what the good people of Atlanta think about her."

"What does my mother have to do with this?"

"Ask Miss Rosetta," he said. "She made sure you got taken care of. Real talk, though."

"Meaning?"

"She went over to Whit Delacourte's house and had it out with him and Virgil."

"My mother loves me."

"Don't ever question that," he said. "Don't you ever question that."

"We don't have a lot of time," Victoria said finally. "The feds will come looking for you, and, well, they didn't approve this meeting."

"You had me snatched out of my house. Virgil always said you had some real goons on your payroll."

"Turns out I needed them, thanks to you."

"If I wanted you got, you would've been got."

"Did you mean it when you said you loved me?"

"You woke up this morning, right?"

"Tell me what the paper gods are," she said. "What do they mean?"

"It's a phoenix. This Asian dude I bunked with in the state pen taught me how to fold them up."

"Dickey Phoenix, I figured that much out myself," she said. "I understand the GBI got search warrants on Loudermilk. The deal is over. The GBI raided his houses and offices."

Dickey shrugged again. "That's what I hear. And you sent them, right?"

"Help me end this."

"Ain't but one way to do that, Big Time."

She looked away and shook it off.

"Tell me, can you kill a man? Can you live with that?"

"'When justice is done, it is a joy to the righteous,'" she said, staring him in the eyes, "'but terror to evildoers.'

"Proverbs 21:15."

FORTY-EIGHT

Hampton sat in the dimly lit hospital room and watched her sleep. Claire was off the respirator, and that was good. She woke infrequently, but still could not eat solid foods. He'd fed her ice chips and clear broth, fondly remembering how she had cared for him when he was recovering from the accident. They would have a new life, he promised himself, and he was thankful for that. It was cloudy and raining out, the droplets of water ran down the windowpane, and Hampton thought that was good too.

"The greatest danger is not to set a target too high and miss it, but to set it too low and reach it," a woman's soft voice said.

"Michelangelo," Hampton replied.

"Ha, more like Mrs. Florence Bridges!" the woman exclaimed.

Hampton was startled. "Chanel?"

"In the flesh, sweetness."

"Where've you been?"

"At my mama's house," she said. "I figured whatn't nobody gone come looking for me there."

"Isn't that the truth," Hampton said.

"Except Sal Pelosi," she said. "Followed my mama right on home from the grocery store."

"How did he know you were there?"

"Ain't too much Sal don't know," Chanel said.

"Right again. I swear that man is a magician."

"More like a thief in the night," Chanel responded.

"I had the pleasure of seeing his work up close," Hampton said. "He plays rough."

"And then some. You ain't seen what that man is capable of. Be glad for that," Chanel said, stepping into room. "How is she? I got up here as soon as I could. Security is tight. They ain't even wanna let me in."

"She's good," Hampton said. "It was rough there for a while, but she's good. It'll take some time, but she'll be fine."

Claire was sleeping peacefully, lulled by a cocktail of sedatives. There was no major organ damage, the doctors said, but the telltale crystals in her stomach confirmed that she'd ingested poison. The investigators had come and gone, and after a brief conversation with Pelosi, Hampton was free to go. A pair of uniformed officers were left stationed outside the hospital room. Visitors required specific clearance.

"She's beautiful," Chanel said. "I know what you see in her."

"It's what you can't see that's so special. She deserves better than me."

"I used to tell Ezra that," Chanel said. "He loved me when nobody else could or would. Sometimes he loved me better than I loved myself."

The heart monitor beeped in steady rhythm. Hampton clutched Claire's hand and felt her gripping his. She smiled, opened her eyes slightly, and murmured, "I deserve you."

"Claire, I want you to meet my friend Chanel," Hampton said. "Chanel, this is Claire."

"I'm glad you're okay," Claire said. "We were worried about you. Where did you go?"

"I wanted to ride that Ferris wheel," Chanel said. "So, I stayed in Chicago for a while."

"I thought you might do that," Hampton said. "You've always been a hopeless romantic."

"I ain't, really. But I went down to Navy Pier after I talked to you. Then I walked to the Amtrak station and got a ticket to come back home. I was tired of running, and to tell you the truth, I missed my mama."

"I called her," Hampton said. "She told me that she hadn't heard from you in years."

"My mama don't tell no lies," Chanel said. "She told you she hadn't talked to Malik. I was sitting right there at her kitchen table, eating a plate of banana pudding."

"He's writing a book about this, you know," Claire said.

"Just make me look pretty," Chanel said.

"That'll be easy," Hampton said.

That same Monday morning, the day before the election, all of Georgia's fourteen U.S. congressmen issued a joint media alert stating their unified support for House Bill 423—an omnibus transportation bill that included the Hawkins Amendment. Simultaneously, both sitting U.S. senators from Georgia released a statement affirming their support and pledged to introduce the legislation on the first day of the new Congress at the start of the fall session. The entire delegation, Democrat and Republican, signed on.

Victoria was sitting in her campaign office when Roy Huggins came running in with the news.

"How in the heck did you pull this off?" Huggins said, thumping the press releases.

"There are a lot of things that divide us," Victoria said. "But every one of us wants what's right for this state."

"All fourteen House members and both senators?" Huggins said. "There's no way it won't pass."

"That's the beauty of it," Victoria said. "Getting them all on a conference call was rough. I was forced to call on Governor Martinez."

"She despises the air you breathe. She picked up your call?"

"No," Victoria said with a laugh. "I went to the governor's mansion."

"Unannounced?"

"I hear that's how things get done these days."

"You're going to make a great congresswoman. It will be a pleasure serving you."

"Time will tell, my friend," Victoria said. "For now, we've got a race to run. It isn't over until tomorrow night, and Mitchell has been on the street, going door-to-door, all week."

"She doesn't make it easy."

"Mitchell never does," Victoria said. "If we're lucky, maybe she'll run for mayor."

"You think Atlanta is ready for a white mayor?"

"The demographics have changed a lot over the last few election cycles. More black folks are moving to the suburbs, where they can get a bigger house and better schools. And, well, the city is full of new condominium complexes."

"And gentrification."

"Yes, and gentrification," Victoria said.

"I assume you've heard the news about Richard Lester?"

"Feels like forever since I saw him," Victoria said. "It doesn't make it any easier. We were close in high school. Never thought he'd end up like that. It's a shame, really. He could've been sitting right here in this seat. Dickey was always smarter than me."

"He wasn't in the lockup for three good hours," Huggins said. "Somebody must've wanted him bad."

"Dickey had a lot of enemies, and he earned every one of them."

"We've got to get going. You've got a round of television interviews on your calendar this morning, and then we're packed with campaign stops until late tonight."

"I'll be out in a minute," Victoria said. "I've got a call or two to make."

Huggins closed the door, and suddenly Victoria was alone again. She reached into her desk, pulled out a manila envelope, and emptied out the contents. Her daughter Mahalia had been right the first time.

A paper god.

She'd spent weeks trying to discern their meaning, unable to wrap her head around what was happening. She'd been caught up in the horror of it all and hadn't even trusted her own police chief with her suspicions. She never loved Dickey, she knew that for sure now, but the fact that he openly admitted to being behind the murders took her breath away. He'd talked about Ezra and Chip like he was knocking pawns off a chessboard.

She ran her fingers across the fine edges and admired her own craftsmanship. She'd chosen black silk paper. She was overcome with its graceful silence, the finality of it all.

At exactly 8 A.M., Victoria strode into the E. Rivers Elementary School gymnasium on Peachtree Battle Avenue. A bank of cameras followed her in as she signed her name on the roll, presented her driver's license, and stepped to the ballot box. Marsh was in the booth next to her. There was one race on the ballot, the special election for U.S. Congressional District 15, and two names.

She said a silent prayer and checked the box next to her own name.

Rosetta and their twin daughters waited near a checkout table while she and her husband collected their stickers.

"I know who you voted for," he said with a broad smile.

"It's a secret ballot, Dr. Overstreet, protected by the Constitution."

They kissed for the cameras and she waved to supporters as she exited the building.

"You gotta believe!" a man shouted from the parking lot.

Victoria raised her fists in the air and pumped them. "You gotta believe," she said.

"Honey," she said, turning to Marsh, "I've got a stop to make. I'll see you back at the house later."

"What time should we get to Centennial Park?"

"We canceled the concert," she said. "We're going back to Ebenezer. We can have dinner at home first."

"I started looking at homes in the District," he said. "I found a few you might like, and I made a call to Sidwell Friends too. The admissions officer is eager to meet Maya and Hallie."

"I think we should stay right here in Georgia," Victoria said. "I'm not interested in taking the girls out of school, and you've got to be here to run your practice. I'll commute. Let the work fall on me."

Eleven minutes later, Victoria entered the Cathedral of Saint Philip through the forward sanctuary doors. The glorious room, with its polished hardwoods and stained-glass windows, was more wonderful than she had remembered. She'd been here only once before, for a christening some years ago.

The long narrow center aisle, lit up by candles, led to the pulpit. She took a seat in the end row, rested against the wood, and watched a man as he knelt at the altar.

Dickey was dead now, by her order, and she was at peace with that. There had been a struggle, she was told. He was found in his bunk with a sheet wrapped around his throat, just hours after he'd been booked into the jail. By the time the federal transport van arrived, Dickey was already in the morgue.

No one came to claim him.

"Forgive me, Father," she whispered.

Victoria could hear the man on the altar praying, uttering something indiscernible from the distance. She watched as he lifted his hands toward a cross draped in purple sheeting. That they were here, together now, in this church, weighed on her. Pelosi had begged against it, but there were some things that she had to see through for herself.

When justice is done, it is a joy to the righteous, but terror to evildoers.
PROVERBS 21:15.

She crossed her heart, stood up, and walked down the aisle. As she approached, the man continued to pray. She could hear the longing in his voice now, the tearful pleadings of a broken spirit. He saw her and immediately recoiled. He had been crying, she could tell. His face was swollen with grief. She wanted to feel something, but found nothing.

"God works in mysterious ways," she said.

"We have some things to work out," he said.

"You've run out of things I want," Victoria said. "I worked things out with Dickey."

"You killed him, didn't you?"

Victoria let the question fall away and said, "Sometime next fall, a new school will open in South Africa. I thought you would want to know that I endowed the academy in your name: The John Virgil Loudermilk School for Girls."

"This war between you and me is over as far as I'm concerned," he said.

"You always were the kind to confuse the battle with a war," she said. "I come in peace, yours and mine."

She pitched the folded black dragon at his feet and walked away.

"God help me," he said.

EPILOGUE

I t took some doing, but Whit Delacourte had the day to himself. Thanks to the shots of bourbon he'd had after supper last night, his stomach was in knots. Between that and the dull throb in his head, Whit thought the day could only get better. Besides, the Good Lord saw fit to let it rain and kept Patsy Jo's mouth shut long enough for him to get a decent night's sleep. He knew little about what his wife had planned that day, except that she was on the way up over to Phipps and his accountant was likely to get an itemized bill from American Express, spelling out the damage, at some point. His wife was no doubt behind the wheel of her convertible CL Mercedes, her glorious mane of silver-gray hair flowing in the wind.

It was late morning when he finally crawled out of bed, slipped on a pair of drawstring pajama pants, and reluctantly parted the balcony doors. Blinding sunlight poured into the bedroom, creeping over the furniture, casting hard-edged shadows. He propped himself against the doorjamb, squinting just hard enough to see his twin granddaughters, Maya and Mahalia, play hand-clapping games under the pagoda.

I wish I had a nickel, I wish I had a dime,
I wish I had a boyfriend to kiss me all the time!

His lungs craved smoke, though he denied himself the pleasure of heading over to the filling station for a fresh pack of Marlboros. It'd been six months since he had his last cigarette. For the first seventy-two hours, he thought he was going to jump clean out of his skin. It took everything he had not to go digging around in the kitchen trash in search of discarded butts with at least two good puffs left on them.

Whit was convinced that Dr. Kessler had it in for him. He was, after all, the same Trip Kessler who'd lost his high school sweetheart to Whit two days before the '67 Westminster High School prom. The girl in question was Patricia Jolene Lindsey. Whit picked her up in his daddy's brand-new Cadillac, married her six years later, and spent nearly every day since wishing he could give her back. He wasn't thinking any better of his beloved the day she dragged him over to Kessler's office for a checkup. Dr. Kessler told Whit that if he kept living like there was no tomorrow, pretty soon one day there wouldn't be.

"You must have some kind of death wish," Dr. Kessler had said, looking up from the patient chart.

"So, I got a little winded on that fancy machine of yours," Whit said. "A man my age ain't got any business running anyhow."

"I'm recommending drug therapy."

"Well, write me a prescription and I'll be on my way."

"You'll have to change your diet and start exercising too."

"Here we go," Whit said, twirling his muddy brown eyes in the air. "I'm going to eat what I'm going to eat. The next thing you're going to tell me is that I can't have fried pork chops."

"And work a little less," Dr. Kessler said.

Whit shrugged again and said, "That'll be the day."

"And quit smoking."

Whit let out a hard grunt. "I'm trying," he said.

"Think about your grandchildren, Whit," Patsy said. "You want to be around to see your granddaughters get married, don't you?"

"Not if I'm footing the tab," Whit said with a chuckle.

"Whit Delacourte, this is serious business," Patsy said. "We're talking about your life, here."

Whit assessed the situation and determined he was cornered. "Alright, alright," Whit said, waving her away. "Tell me what I gotta do, Trip."

Before they left the doctor's office that day, Whit was forced to swear on his mother's grave that he'd give up tobacco, whiskey, and anything deep-fried in Crisco, though he begged for a reprieve on Jack Daniel's at least until regular-season college football was over and longer if (by the grace of God and despite losing to second-ranked Alabama last year) the Georgia Bulldogs advanced to the SEC championship game, which in Whit's mind was a foregone conclusion since Mark Richt was head coach and Aaron Murray was throwing the ball.

Patsy snorted, folded her arms across her chest, and said, "You can watch football without your friend Jack. And I hate to break it to you, but Georgia ain't going to the big show anyway. You and I both know that."

Whit answered with a knowing nod, silently conceding both the fate of the Dawgs and his own declining health. "Maybe not this year or the next, but they'll get there."

Patsy rolled her eyes.

"Fine," Whit said finally. "No more liquor."

"You swear?" Patsy said.

"On my dear mama's grave," Whit replied, tossing his meaty palm in the air. "Are you happy now?"

Whit had no intention of keeping that promise. Besides, his mother had been dead for close to ten years, and he could see no harm coming to her just because he had a shot of whiskey every now and then, not to mention Emma Louise Delacourte died loving liquor and Georgia football (preferably in big doses and at the same time) almost as much as he did.

To everybody's surprise, including Whit's, he stayed dry for nearly three weeks before he gave in to the temptation of a round of shots at Chops.

One thing led to another, and before he knew it, he was spilled out all over the passenger seat of his Dodge Ram pickup truck, singing Travis Tritt's "Walkin' All Over My Heart." This time, like the last, Lucky Mitchell came to fetch him and drove him home.

Patsy shook her head as she watched him stumble up the redbrick walkway sometime after 2 A.M. She opened the screen door and stood to the side to let him by. Patsy mumbled something under her breath. She didn't know which one she was madder about: the drinking or the fact that he'd missed dinner with his daughter and son-in-law, who'd come all the way from D.C. with their granddaughters to see them. He shuffled up the winding stairwell, stripped down to his skivvies, and crawled into bed.

Whit figured Patsy was blazing through Saks Fifth Avenue by now, where she would try her able best to spend him into the poorhouse. She would rest her feet over chamomile tea and frosted petits fours at the St. Regis Hotel.

A book rested on the nightstand. He'd promised himself he would get around to it at some point. Whit had reluctantly sat for hours of interviews with Hampton Bridges.

"Might as well tell it," he started.

His brother, Virgil, was dead now, shot dead in a robbery gone bad as he left the Cathedral of Saint Philip on Peachtree. The assailants were never caught. They left his pockets turned inside out and a bullet in his chest.

Watching his granddaughters play in the yard below, Whit released the tinge of regret perched in the small of his back. It had been a year since Virgil died and six months since he and Rosetta sat down with Victoria. There had been a lump of tears, mostly from him.

"I'm sorry," he said. "We did what we thought was right."

Victoria reached over, hugged his neck, and said, "I'm sorry too."

"I want to make it up to you, if you'll let me," Whit said.

"You've given me all I will ever need," Victoria said wistfully.

The girls were still small enough to snuggle up in the bend of his arms. He figured it would be soon enough before they developed a taste for designer clothes and started treating their granddaddy like an all-night cash box. At that moment, Whit couldn't think of anything he wouldn't give them.

Maya and Mahalia headed back toward the house. Whit smiled. His eyes glistened as they skipped through the stand of magnolia trees that lined both sides of the redbrick drive. If there was anything he loved more than watching them, he couldn't think of it right then. They were as beautiful as the day itself, though the slightly damp wind and its earthy smell promised more rain.

Whit stepped out onto the long balcony, barefoot and shirtless, wearing only the pair of rumpled lounging pants he'd fished out of the hamper. He eased into the large wicker armchair and rested his feet on the padded footstool. There, underneath one of three Marble Queens suspended from the veranda roof, he closed his eyes and surrendered to the day. He decided going after cigarettes was a bad idea. After all, he was in no mood to drive, had no idea where his truck was, and knew those sweet little granddaughters of his would tattle on him as surely as day leads to night.

He took a deep breath, let his chest fill with air, and decided Patsy Jo wasn't so bad after all.

Miss Bea appeared before him with a serving tray. "I didn't mean to wake you, Mr. Delacourte," she said.

"I wasn't sleeping," he said with one eye open and one eye closed.

"I thought you might want to put a little something in your stomach," Miss Bea said, setting the tray down on a side table.

Whit opened the other eye, pulled himself up from a slump, planted his chubby feet on the deck boards, and let out a soft grunt, which Miss Bea took as a yes.

He reached over, unfurled the cloth covering the small basket of buttermilk biscuits, and let the warmth escape. "They do look good," he said. "Perfect as always."

"I hear Cole is moving to Florida."

"Week after next. With the divorce and all, the change of scenery might be good for him."

"You oughta take it easy, Mr. Delacourte," Miss Bea said, pouring the coffee. "You're a long way past twenty-five."

"Oh, I'm alright, Bea. A little bourbon ain't never hurt nobody. Hell, I've been drinking since I was—"

"—fifteen," she said, finishing the story she'd not only witnessed but had also heard a hundred times.

Miss Bea had caught young Whit and his brother, Virgil, sneaking nips of his father's whiskey. Big Whit had been angry, but Miss Emma Louise wrote it all off to the gene pool. The boys got off scot-free without so much as a swat to their backsides.

"How long have you been with us, Bea?"

"Longer than I ever thought I would be," she answered with a pearly smile.

"No, really, Bea. How long has it been?"

"Too dern long."

"Hell, you raised us up, Miss Bea," Whit said, laughing.

"And you ain't no better for it," she said.

"I should give you a raise."

"Mr. Delacourte, you gave me a pay raise three months ago and another one six months before that."

"Well, I'm the boss, and I say it's time for another one. You can retire anytime you want to, you know? We'll take care of things like we always have."

"You know I appreciate it. You won't ever hear of me turning away good money," Miss Bea said as she left the balcony.

"Is there any such thing as bad money?" Whit called after her.

He smeared the first biscuit with a dollop of apple butter, ate it, decided it tasted like heaven, and had a bite of a second. He could hear the girls singing again as he lifted the elegant porcelain cup to his lips. From the sound of things, they'd made their way into the house. That was a good thing, seeing as how the light drizzle had turned into a hard, insistent rain.

Victoria found him two hours later, sprawled out on his back across the cushioned deck chair, his mouth slightly open, snoring like a two-day-old kitten. She kissed his forehead and crawled in beside him.

ACKNOWLEDGMENTS

It is near on midnight, two days before Christmas, and my two grandchildren are snuggled together in my bed, their heads rustling with curiosities and dreams. Their mothers, my daughters, are two of the most amazingly beautiful women I have ever known. The eldest, Katherine, is here with me tonight and together we are struggling in the darkness to find enough space for the four of us—the children, her, and me. My baby girl, Haley, is now a woman in fullness, too, and is herself the mother of the wickedly smart four-year-old, whose warm brown toes are nestled against my tummy. She is, like her mother, the perfection of my reflection.

For me, tonight is a reminder of what yesterday looked like—struggling in the dark to find space, a snatch of quiet in a house bustling with my three stair-step children, all born fifteen months apart, stretching another paycheck that did not go quite far enough, and pausing just long enough to catch the glints of light, the promises of better, in my then-six-year-old son Joshua's eyes. But for them, I may never have embraced my life as a writer.

I am grateful to Joshua, my writing partner and creative soul mate, for pressing me forward. And also to Katherine, who was the first to read the compete draft and then phone me from her home on the West Coast with much-needed chapter-by-chapter critiques. Together, we walked through the characters, plot lines, scenes, and the all-too-familiar settings to be sure I was getting it right.

But, before I had a decent fifty pages, I bumped into my dear sister-friend Lisa Bloom in between segments at MSNBC. She introduced me to the woman who would quickly become my agent. The Universe, I believe, conspires to deliver goodness on our behalf. Laura Dail has been that goodness—gently poking and prodding me along. She was convinced of something I could not tell myself. Once I had a full manuscript, we set off to find the right publisher, and, again, The Universe delivered. I could not have asked for a better editor than Adam Bellow of All Points Books/St. Martin's Press and his assistant, Kevin Reilly.

I am thankful for the "Ladies Who Lunch"—Darlene Trigg, Esther Green, Necole Merritt, and Patrice Tilford—women who know exactly what to do with a bottle of vodka, triple sec, a couple of lemons, and a bit of superfine sugar! Our decades-long friendship has steadied the rolling seas and stilled the winds.

It is because of "believing mirrors" like Stephanie Frederic, Steve Smith, Marcia Allert, Denise Taylor, Natasha Smith, and Sarah Burris that I am able to rise each morning knowing the fullness of grace. They are my before, during, and after friends.

There are my fellow "Beasts" at The Daily Beast, where I am editor-at-large. Among them are John Avlon, Harry Seigel, Michael Daly, Katie Zavadski, Tim Teeman, Kevin Fallon, and Noah Shachtman. Thank you for making me better.

To my "angels in the outfield"—Ahmir "Questlove" Thompson, Tamron Hall, Joy Ann Reid, Joan Walsh, Jake Tapper, Greg Sargent, Jon Allen, Arti Freeman, Terry McMillan, Bobbi Gillette, Caesar Mitchell, Keith Parker, Josh Mankiewicz, Soledad O'Brien, Ryan Grim, Bill Marks, Bill Crane, Brenda Wood, Bomani Jones, Stephanie Beasley Russell, Maggie Savarino, Eric Jerome Dickey, Debra Johnson, Gordon Hutchinson, Darrell "Pete" Peterson, Will

McDade, Kasim Reed, and Andy Stanley—if I thanked you a thousand times each day for a thousand years, it would never be enough.

And, finally, as I lie here tonight, rapt with joy and gratitude, there is my sister Lizz Winstead, who opened her heart when mine was broken and gifted me with the time to heal.

ABOUT THE AUTHOR

GOLDIE TAYLOR is a veteran journalist and cable news political analyst. She is currently editor-at-large at The Daily Beast, where she writes about national elections and social issues. A prior service U.S. Marine and former campaign strategist, Taylor has also served as a contributor for NBC News and MSNBC, and frequently appeared on CNN and HLN. The mother of three grown children and grandmother of two, Taylor lives in Atlanta and is wholly convinced—in her words—that "God has a sense of humor."

www.goldietaylor.com